IN

As the car wound along the yesterday
Annie felt her pulse quickening with anticipation,
and then suddenly the hacienda was in front of
them, its pale stucco walls sparkling in the morning
sun. Would she get any answers here? What was
David Shields' game? What was an OB doing with
a cardiologist? Once again Annie felt as if she was
outside her body, watching herself. Who was this
woman who had left her family to travel with a couple she hardly knew? What kind of woman eavesdropped on friends and secretly expected to
discover some evil medical mystery hidden in all
these luxurious surroundings? Annie didn't recognize herself, and somehow that emboldened her. . . .

Listening In

Sorrell Ames

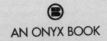
AN ONYX BOOK

ONYX
Published by the Penguin Group
Penguin Putnam Inc., 375 Hudson Street,
New York, New York 10014, U.S.A.
Penguin Books Ltd, 27 Wrights Lane,
London W8 5TZ, England
Penguin Books Australia Ltd,
Ringwood, Victoria, Australia
Penguin Books Canada Ltd, 10 Alcorn Avenue,
Toronto, Ontario, Canada M4V 3B2
Penguin Books (N.Z.) Ltd, 182–190 Wairau Road,
Auckland 10, New Zealand

Penguin Books Ltd, Registered Offices:
Harmondsworth, Middlesex, England

First published by Onyx, an imprint of Dutton NAL,
a member of Penguin Putnam Inc.

First Printing, June, 1998
10 9 8 7 6 5 4 3 2 1

PUBLISHER'S NOTE
This is a work of fiction. Names, characters, places, and incidents either are the
product of the author's imagination or are used fictitiously, and any resemblance to
actual persons, living or dead, events, or locales is entirely coincidental.

For my husband and children, who patiently made room in their lives for these characters, and who loved and believed in me when I needed it most, and for E.L.F. and his cohorts who whisper encouragement always.

And

For Roz, whose enthusiasm is undaunting and whose perseverance is the eighth wonder of the world.

ACKNOWLEDGMENTS

It is with heartfelt gratitude that I thank the following people: Shirley Brown and Everett Leonard for teaching me how to jump off cliffs; Tony Shore and Bill Fritzmeier for daily inspiration, childcare, endless xeroxing and Fed-Exing, midnight runs to Staples, uplifting pep talks, and mostly for always believing: Beecher and Bailey Leonard-Fritzmeier for their countless babysitting hours; Beecher, Bailey, Turner, Tilden, Isaac, Moses, Lucy and Abel for countless hours without their mom, and for waiting for Disney World: Sarah Leonard for researching books and providing them; Peter Brown for helping me calculate height and weight statistics; Mitchell Glickstein for sharing his extraordinary brain and the fount of wisdom that resides there; Don Kirk for relentlessly sending me "into the light"; Audrey LaFehr for her insight and guidance; Raj Mangat Rai for the care he took in sharing his slides, his memories, his time, and his knowledge; Mary and Sandy Moore for regularly sharing their home and computer; Jagdish Sachdev for his unfailing belief and supportive phone calls; Lindsay Shaw and Sally Gilliland for doing what few friends would or could—being an objective reader and offering immeasurably helpful suggestions; James Stevens for the miracles past, present, and future and the vanity plate; Robert Taylor for his years of tutelage, constructive criticism, friendship, and his assumption that I could write; Marge Thompson for taking time in the midst of an incredibly daunting schedule to send important articles to me.

These people also lent their friendship, support and wisdom: Nancy Allen, Liz Barksdale, Richard Fisher, Emily Freidman, Peggy Gilliland, Robin Greitzer, Kathy Healy, Susan Houser, Fran, Jay and Bernie Perlman, Anne Schuster, Consuelo and Chuck Sherba, Sonny and Miriam Shore, Lydia Sinclair, Sadie Solomon, Wilson Utter, June Vinhateiro, and Ben Vogel.

Thanks also to the Providence Athenaeum for writing and research space, and to the Providence Bookstore and Cafe and to CAV for letting me spend days writing and kindly interrupting me only when I looked like I really needed food.

Thanks to all of you who kept me and this project in your thoughts.

Prologue

He'd never minded being woken up for an emergency. Tonight was no different. He pushed open the double doors that led to the examination cubicles and strode confidently to the chart hanging outside a drawn curtain. An orderly scooted a cart around him, quickly, not wanting to waste a nanosecond of the Chief of Obstetrics' time. Two nurses whispered at the desk. He looked over his shoulder and gave them a wink. He read the chart quickly and entered the room. The patient, a young college student, was sleeping. He slipped the syringe out of his lab coat pocket and plunged it into the IV cable. The girl continued to sleep as he stepped out of the cubicle and pulled the curtain back into place.

"I've got a patient to check on in the high risk unit, since I'm here," he told the young blond nurse at the desk. Was her name Heather? He couldn't remember, but it seemed like a lot of them were named that.

"All right, Doctor." She smiled at him.

"You can page me if you need me. Otherwise, I'll check in before rounds in the morning."

"Very good." She smiled again, leaning toward the counter, he thought so that he could see her generous cleavage.

After all these years he still liked this part of the hospital best. The clinic was the proving ground. As residents they'd all been like sharks, circling around for a complicated case; something they could grab and glide with, show off their superior diagnostic or surgical skills. The clinic was a feeding frenzy for young arrogant doctors and he had been the acknowledged leader. It wasn't long before the difficult cases were practically being handed to him. He never minded getting called in the middle of the night. He actually enjoyed the thrill of working against time, stopping a bleed or delivering a breech vaginally.

He preferred the patients, too. They were deferential, still thought doctors were at the top of the evolutionary pecking order. No hotshot med-mal lawyers watching him like a hawk here. No one watching him. The clinic records were largely ignored. Whatever he wanted to do was fine as long as the hospital got their Medicaid reimbursements.

And so he'd kept his hand in, telling the administration the clinic was helpful for his high risk research. Keeping babies inside inhospitable wombs was his specialty. Preventing miscarriages. There was a lot to be learned from the clinic patients.

The nurses thought he was a saint, still coming in on routine clinic emergencies even now that he had a successful private practice. Plucking a few lucky patients now and then out of the clinic and into his private care. The patients were in awe; he wasn't a raw resident. He was the genuine article. Something big for nothing.

Stepping through the double glass doors, he caught sight of his own face reflected back at him. He had gained some weight since his residency days, but that only helped him, he thought. His face was better fuller—it fit his strong chin. His mother swore her descendants came over on the *Mayflower*, and for generations were British, but how did that explain his high, wide cheekbones and his slightly tanned complexion? Someone had dipped into the native waters somewhere along the line. He smiled to himself.

Like clockwork, just as he reached the high risk unit his beeper went off. He turned and headed back to the tunnel connecting the clinic to the main hospital. It was a narrow passage, and everyone he passed moved quickly out of his way. Wherever they were headed, they knew his work was more important.

They were apologetic at the nurses' station. "It's the primip," the head nurse told him. "We thought she was being a princess. She only came in for hyperemesis and the nausea subsided with the IV fluids—now suddenly she's screaming her head off."

"But," Heather-of-the-amazing-cleavage broke in, "she's definitely aborting. We thought you'd want to come, since she's one of yours."

He was already heading for her cubicle. Pulling the curtain back, he saw the girl was panting hard and her eyes were wide with fear. "I'm dying," she gasped.

"You're not dying," the nurse told her. "Your body's just trying to pass the tissue."

She shot the nurse a look of pure hatred.

He stopped by her bed to put on gloves. She grabbed his sleeve. "Please." She panted. "Please stop this. Give me something to make the pain go away."

"Yes," he told her. "It will stop." He pushed her knees up and apart, and reaching up to the cervix, gently removed the tissue coming down through the opening. The pain stopped instantly, as if someone had flicked a switch. The girl sobbed with relief.

He felt the girl's eyes on him as he carefully lifted one of the blue plastic-backed pads that she had been lying on. He angled it over a kidney dish and transferred the tissue into the dish. She turned away.

"I want to examine this myself," he told the nurse. "I'll be back. Check her vitals and arrange for an OR for the D & C. I'll be in my lab."

He turned back and took an eyeball inventory of the girl's blood loss. "Give her twenty units of Pitocin, just to play it safe," he said. And cradling the kidney dish in the crook of his arm as if it were a newborn, he pushed open the door and was gone.

The sooner he got the tissue onto dry ice, the better. This was a valuable specimen he was carrying around in a barf bowl—worth at least thirty thousand dollars each to him and Jaime. But he had also done this enough times to know exactly how much time he had, and he was not worried. As long as some idiot resident didn't get in his way, he'd have plenty of time to store it and call Mexico before anyone at the hospital had time to miss him.

He pushed through the doors marked EMERGENCY and took a quick left toward the room with the refrigerator. After listening to make sure no one was inside, he cautiously stepped through the door and quickly pulled it shut behind him. He crossed the room to the shelves of transport equipment and selected a cooler. Deftly packing the tissue in dry ice, he smiled at the thought that he used to carry sixes of St. Pauli Girl to the beaches in Newport in this same kind of cooler during college. When he was satisfied that the "donation" would keep until it reached La Cucharita, he affixed labels to the top and sides and pulled a red indelible marker from the pocket of his lab coat.

In capital letters, he wrote: "PROPERTY OF HIGH RISK OBSTETRICS UNIT. DO NOT TAMPER."

Fifteen minutes after leaving the girl in her cubicle, he was back in his office at the clinic, punching Mexico's international code into the telephone.

Jaime answered the phone himself.

Chapter One

"Finally," said Annie Morgan as her six-week-old daughter Rebecca's eyes fluttered shut at last. Annie eased her way out of the room and tiptoed down the stairs. She went into the living room and walked over to the desk. She had to be at her postpartum checkup in three hours, and had to get caught up on her work, but she couldn't get Sam Casey off her mind. When she'd been pregnant with her son, Alex, Sam Casey had seemed the ideal doctor: attentive to her concerns, never rushing through appointments. But by the time she was pregnant with Rebecca, his practice had grown and he had changed. She couldn't exactly put her finger on it, but he seemed somehow distracted. She would discuss something of importance, her birth plan for instance, at one appointment, and at the next he would not remember their previous discussion. That could all be chalked up to a busy schedule or sleep deprivation, she supposed. Or, she thought, to drugs. Substance abuse was a real problem with doctors. It had been on the *Today Show,* which she chastised herself now for watching too much lately.

Annie thought about her hospital stay, when she had told her hospital roommate that Sam was her doctor. The woman's face had registered surprise. Annie saw it for a split second before the woman recovered. "What?" Annie had said. "Why are you surprised that he's my doctor?"

"Oh, no reason, really. You know how you just hear things."

"What things?"

"I don't like to repeat them unless I know they're true."

"Please," said Annie, "I'd like to know."

"No. I'm sorry. You've got a beautiful baby. You're fine. He did all right by you. Forget it. Be happy."

And that's what you should do, she told herself. Forget it. Be happy. And get some work done.

Her desk was strewn with children's clothing samples for the upcoming season. Annie's job as a freelance copywriter for the popular Cotton Tales catalog hadn't allowed for much of a maternity leave. But she was the one who had pushed for another baby, convincing Jim it was for Alex's sake.

"Only children can't cope with life's hard knocks," she had said. "You need that push and pull of sibling struggle to get tough, to be prepared." She didn't like feeling that she was manipulating Jim, but she had honestly felt that it would be better for their six-year-old to have a sibling. And she couldn't think of one woman friend who didn't admit to at least a mild form of husband-manipulation every now and then. Besides, she had really wanted another baby.

So she had told Jim, trying just as much to convince herself, "It will be fine. We won't lose any money. I'll have to start the fall copy right around the birth but that'll work. Alex will be at school and I'll work while the baby naps. Remember, newborns sleep all the time."

"Huh!" she had said out loud. "*Some* newborns, maybe." How long could she go with so little sleep? she wondered, bending down to pick up a stray Ninja Turtle. Had she been crazy to make this pact with Jim?

Then she saw the moving van. The FOR SALE sign had gone down from the huge Victorian across the street over a month ago but she hadn't known when the new people would move in. The problem with this neighborhood was that people weren't very talkative. It was that famous New England reserve, she guessed. This wasn't, after all, suburbia, where she imagined people chatted over fences. The people on her block were mostly older movers and shakers, the corporate officers and deans at the university. They said hello in passing and admired the "little boy." But none of them had sent over gifts or casseroles or anything when the baby was born. Everyone else's children were grown or else they had never had any.

The sun streaming in was making her feel wonderfully relaxed, her limbs comfortably heavy. Jim had taken Alex and a carload of his fellow first-graders to the zoo—if she could only get herself to stop procrastinating she might have time to finish the copy before Rebecca woke up again. Thank God Jim wasn't one of those absentee, workaholic husbands. Devoted as he was to his work as a Legal Aid attorney, his first priority had always been his family, and it showed. It was hard to know who had been more excited about the zoo trip, her son or his father.

She moved to the couch beneath the window for a closer look at what was going on across the street. She'd been dying to see who the new neighbors were. She was hoping for something a little more interesting than what was in the neighborhood now. From her upstairs bathroom window she could see into several houses on the street. Sometimes at night she would shut off the light and stand looking out at her neighbors' lit living rooms. She never saw anything more exciting than someone having a cocktail with the evening paper. In college she once saw two women dancing cheek to cheek in a dorm room across from hers. They'd dipped each other and spun around the room.

Maybe she'd be able to tell something about the new arrivals from their furniture. "I'll just watch them unload the van for a while," she thought, "and I'll work on some copy in my head."

The four movers had unloaded a Victorian velvet couch, two brocade wing chairs, and a full-size grand piano before Annie remembered that she hadn't turned the baby monitor on. She hurried to the foot of the stairs and listened—nothing. Must still be sleeping. But she felt a touch of anxiety until she flicked the switch on the living room's receiver of the monitor and heard Rebecca's even breathing coming across as if she were right there in the room with Annie. It amazed her how well the monitor picked up every little sound. What had people done before they were invented? she wondered. Probably been a lot more relaxed and a lot less neurotic.

A black turbo Saab convertible pulled up behind the moving van. Annie could see a reclined infant car seat in the back, but she couldn't tell if a child was in it or not. A woman was in the driver's seat, and Annie felt herself getting ready to dismiss her as a possible friend simply because she drove such a yuppie car and had paid, according to the neighborhood gossip (money was the one thing they did whisper about to each other), $450,000 for her house. But then the woman opened the car door, and Annie saw that she had on old blue jeans with a hole across one knee and, in place of expensive running shoes, a pair of Converse canvas hightops, bright red. She also had on the same dungaree jacket with the corduroy cuffs and collar that Annie had bought two years ago on sale at Ann Taylor for forty-nine dollars. Maybe, Annie thought, she could get to know this woman. She found herself liking her even more when she saw her open the car's back door and pull out a cardboard carton full of coffees for the movers.

If she could only rouse herself out of this lethargy that had descended over her since Rebecca's birth, she could get up now and make brownies and take them over before the boys came home. But she couldn't take the time to visit, she remembered, because she had to fax the first batch of copy by Friday, and she had that damn appointment. She really needed to hire a sitter to watch Rebecca while she worked. That way she would have two or three afternoons while Alex was in school and she could be done in time to meet him at the bus stop. Plus, she could start running again. She really missed her time at the track and felt desperate now to get back in shape. Exercise and work, perfectly good justifications for the money spent on a sitter. She must have been insane to think she could get any work done with a newborn in the house.

The woman took a step toward the men and then turned back quickly. She placed the carton on the car roof and opened the back door. The woman backed out of the car with a baby in her arms. It looked to be about fifteen months, maybe one and a half. The woman shifted the baby to one hip, and balancing the coffee carton on her free arm, she carried it to the movers.

Annie wanted to hear what was going on. She pushed on the window above the couch. A winter's worth of being shut made it stick. She pushed harder, and with a loud scraping of wood against wood it finally shot up. The woman's head turned in the direction of the noise. Annie ducked so that her head was up against the couch, her heart pounding. Had she been caught staring? She edged her way up to the other end of the couch and stretched out on the cushions. How embarrassing if she had been seen.

What if the woman came over to introduce herself? Annie was in a T-shirt and a pair of Jim's sweatpants. She hadn't even brushed her hair yet. She glanced around the living room. A bowl with a thin coating of hardened chocolate ice cream was on the coffee table from last night, a basket of Legos lay dumped and scattered across the rug. "Please don't come over, please don't come over," Annie

willed the woman. She inched her head to the top of the
couch and then peeked around the curtain. The woman was
standing by the Saab's passenger door with her back to
Annie.

"Say bye-bye, Millie," the woman said to the baby, and
the little girl opened and closed her fist in the direction of
the movers. Then she yelled, "I'll be back in about an hour."

"Okay, Mrs. Shields, thanks for the coffee," one of the
movers called to her as they disappeared into the back of the
huge truck.

Feeling a little ridiculous, Annie reached for the notebook and pen on the coffee table and tried to focus on her
catalog copy.

Okay, she told herself, you've got two and a half hours
till you have to be at Dr. Casey's. Start with the clothes you
like; those neon twills. Picture them on a kid like Alex, but
with John Lennon glasses.

Annie had been waiting for forty-five minutes and had already read as much as she wanted of the only available issue
of *People*. Why was this office always so busy? And why
did they ask you to bring your baby to the postpartum
checkup? With her first, she had felt flattered, and believed
that the women in the office and her doctor had liked her so
much and had taken such an interest in her personally that
they just wanted to see her wonderful baby. But now, the
second time around, she knew they had everyone do it. Rebecca was sleeping now and had been for a while at home
before the appointment. She could feel herself beginning to
sweat in anticipation of being called to the examining room
in the middle of nursing or worse still, being flat on her back
on the examining table having her breasts checked just as
Rebecca let rip her first hungry cries. She glanced over anx-
iously at a three-year-old approaching Rebecca's infant seat.
Mercifully the child's mother dragged her back to look at a

book. There was nothing left to do but thumb through parenting magazines or surreptitiously examine the other waiting women. The girl across the room didn't look like she could be more than eighteen or nineteen years old—probably just here for birth control. The woman sitting next to her was huge. She must be past her due date and she looked tired. Just wait, Annie thought. You don't know the meaning of tired.

How could Rebecca sleep so well during the day and so poorly at night? She glanced at her watch: 1:30. Her appointment was for 12:45. This was really inexcusable. Sam had really gotten out of hand. He obviously had too many patients now. Maybe that was why he seemed so distracted lately. And what had that woman in her hospital room been referring to? *Something* questionable. What, though? An affair? Drugs?

She sighed. Alex would step off the bus at three, and she had wanted to go grocery shopping before meeting him. "Lots of luck," she told herself.

The mother of the three-year-old had already been called in. The three other women still waiting, one with her husband, were unremarkable. One was reading, one was scribbling quickly on a legal pad, and the teenager Annie had noticed earlier got up now and push-pinned a notice to the bulletin board. The fringe on the bottom of the paper made a name and phone number available for the taking. Annie raised her eyebrows—potential babysitter? She should maybe try and talk to the girl but Donna, the receptionist, was beating her to it.

"Jessica Kelleher?" The girl smiled and followed Donna down the hall. Annie went over and scanned the notice. As she had hoped, Responsible College Student with flexible hours and references offered babysitting services. Hmmm— maybe her guardian angel hadn't completely deserted her. She tore off a piece of fringe and stuck it in her wallet. If

Jessica didn't return before Annie was called in, she'd phone
her later.

Sitting back down next to the sleeping Rebecca, Annie's
eyes wandered to the inner office. Donna was talking on the
phone. "I can't give you those results, only the doctor can,
and he's with a patient now . . . at five-fifteen. He'll make
all his calls then. You're already on the list . . ." There was
another woman in white, standing at the Xerox machine.
Annie recognized her as the nurse who did the weighing in
and took your blood pressure before you went to the examining room. She had a Barbie-doll body and an absolutely
beautiful face. And gorgeous red hair. What was her name?
Annie tried to remember. Pam? Just then, this Pam looked
over her shoulder and smiled at someone. There must be
someone standing at the back door. Annie knew there were
two doors into the office because at her first visit when she
was pregnant with Alex she had gone to the wrong one. Beyond it was the crossover to the hospital and it opened directly into the clerical office area. Still standing at the
copier, Pam looked over her shoulder and smiled again.
There was something suggestive about that smile, Annie
thought. She felt certain it wasn't a *woman* from another office waiting for the forms that the nurse was copying. Annie
got up to put her magazine back on the rack and casually
glanced into the office on her way across the waiting room.
She smiled to herself. It was definitely a man. A bank of filing cabinets blocked her view of his face. It looked like it
might be Sam. The man was obviously tall, like Sam. He
was wearing impeccably pressed khakis. She looked at the
feet and saw expensive tasseled loafers. Nothing unique
about those, she thought. Pam turned back to the Xerox machine, but the man didn't leave immediately. He stood a
minute and Annie imagined him appraising Pam's backside.
Annie did the same thing. Pam had great legs and a quite

lovely rear end. Annie wasn't surprised the guy was having a hard time tearing himself away.

She looked down at her baggy maternity pants and could imagine with dread what her own backside looked like. It had taken six months for her to get back in shape after Alex's birth, but everyone said that the second time was harder. She wandered back to her seat. What if she stayed like this forever? Suppose her stomach always looked like jello that hadn't quite set?

"Annie?" She looked up to see the smiling face of Donna, who was holding up her chart and waving her in. Rebecca chose that moment to wake up, so Annie didn't see the nurse walk back to the staff door and begin talking in low tones to the terrifically handsome man who waited there.

Annie lay back on the examining table waiting for Sam. Rebecca was in her infant seat on the floor, a thoughtfully placed mobile keeping her entertained. Annie glanced up at the diploma from Yale University hanging on the wall. The door opened and from where Annie was lying all she could see were two long legs. Feet in tasseled loafers walked toward her.

"Well, Annie," said Sam in his deep, confident voice, "how are you?"

"Exhausted," said Annie.

Sam began to rifle through her file. Had it been Sam with the nurse? The nurse had definitely been flirting with whoever was at the door. Is that what her roommate had been alluding to—rumors of Sam philandering?

"Annie," Sam interrupted her thoughts. "Your hemoglobin's thirteen. You can't be *that* exhausted, there's no anemia . . ."

"I just can't remember feeling this tired after Alex."

"You don't remember pain, either," Sam laughed. "Or you wouldn't have had a second child."

Annie studied Sam's face. He *was* very attractive.

The phone on the wall buzzed. Sam ignored it. It buzzed again. "Damn," he said, and grabbed the receiver. "I'm with a patient," he said with undisguised irritation. "All right, no, you were right to put him through . . . hello? Hello? *Shit.* Hello?"

Annie felt very uncomfortable and didn't know where to look. Sam was clearly angry. He was punching the intercom button on the phone. She began to feel irritated herself. This was her appointment time. She was paying for this and here he was taking calls.

"Donna," Sam was saying, "there was no one there. I need to speak to him today. Call the international operator. See what she can do."

He turned back to her. "Sorry, Annie, I'm going to have to take this call when it comes through again." He paused for a minute while he slid the speculum in and did a hasty manual exam. "The baby's fine? You're tired? It'll get better." He slid his fingers out and began unscrewing the speculum. "Had sex yet?"

"Yes," said Annie.

"And?"

Annie looked surprised.

"I don't need to know all the juicy details." He smiled. "Any pain?"

"No," said Annie, feeling that his tone was somehow inappropriate. She didn't like a doctor being lewd, even in a joking manner. She was trying to think of a way to confront him and explain her discomfort when the phone rang again.

"Any questions, Annie, talk to Donna or call me tomorrow." He glanced down at Rebecca. "Cute kid," he said. But it was robotic. He used to care about his patients, Annie thought. Now he was going through the motions.

He grabbed the phone. "Donna. Good. I'll get it in my office." And then he simply turned and left the room.

Chapter Two

Annie congratulated herself. She had read Alex his two stories, tucked him in, and left him listening to his favorite Bill Harley tape and it was only eight-thirty. That had to be a record. With Rebecca down as well, Annie knew she should go to sleep now, too, but to have some "grown-up" time felt so luscious. Her arms felt the way they did at the end of that childhood game where you flattened the backs of your hands hard against each side of a doorway, counted to thirty, and then stepped out. Your arms would float of their own accord up toward the ceiling. It was a heady feeling of release. She practically skipped down the stairs, but then in the hall she could see the door of her study and she knew she should work on the dreaded copy. She looked longingly at the living room couch and the TV set. Jim came through the front door.

"Garbage is all set," he announced.

Ah, Monday night, thought Annie. There were two domestic chores that Jim seemed to actually enjoy: putting the trash out every Monday and doing the laundry. That is, putting it in the washer and the dryer and then dumping huge loads onto their bed or Alex's bed. Somehow the folding didn't appeal to him as much. She often felt left out of other wives' conversations when the talk turned to complaints about husbands not knowing how to operate the washer, and one wife always got a laugh when she said her husband wouldn't know where to find it.

"You should see the cars in the driveway across the street," Jim said to her. "There's a Jaguar, a turbo Saab, and a Land Rover. I thought you said they only had one kid. How many cars do two adults living in a city with public transportation need?"

"I only saw one kid—they may have others," said Annie. "Besides, they probably have a place in Maine or the Vineyard or somewhere where they think the Land Rover is appropriate." She shrugged. "The woman looked nice. She was wearing jeans and high tops . . ."

"Don't judge a book by its cover, Annie. Look at the house."

"Oh, come on, Jim, you've always loved that house. If you had the money, you'd buy it and play at being the Addams family. We already have Pugsley and little Wednesday is, I think, a demon baby . . . You know, our new neighbor brought coffee to her movers."

"Well, maybe she's not all bad . . . I've got to work on a brief, but I think I'll do it in bed. You coming up? Want me to get you some Chocolate Fudge Brownie?"

"Oh, sweetie, bed sounds great . . ."

"For sleeping, right?" Jim winked. "Sorry, couldn't resist." He knew she wasn't especially interested in sex so soon after giving birth, but he did tease her.

"Right. And no, no ice cream yet, but will you lock the doors before you go up? I've got to spread some samples out and get inspired. Oh, and will you bring the monitor in here? It's in the living room."

She listened to Jim go up the stairs and, sitting down at her desk, wished she could go with him. Now that there were two kids, they hardly ever had a minute as a couple. Besides, she hated being the last one up at night, hated putting out the lights and climbing the stairs with nothing above or below but darkness.

Annie leaned over and switched on the monitor. It took less than a second for panic to take hold. She jumped out of her chair. Someone was in Rebecca's room! She couldn't hear Rebecca's breathing, but a woman's voice came clearly over the monitor. *"Okay, little girl, I've got you now."* Instantly Annie was out of the study and up the stairs.

"Jim!" she croaked. Terror had made her lose her voice. Rebecca's door was open a crack, just the way she'd left it. She flung it open all the way. There was Rebecca, her cheek squished against the mattress, little round bum up in the air, and the receiving blanket rising and falling with her even breathing. Her merry-go-round night light cast huge shadows on the wall: first a horse, then a goose, now a camel.

Jim appeared at her side.

"What is it? You sounded frantic. What are you doing?" She had just finished looking in the closet, and now she was down on her knees lifting the crib's dust ruffle and looking underneath it.

"I—I don't know. It sounded like a woman was talking to Rebecca." He looked at her with his brow knit, obviously not knowing how to respond.

"Come here," she said as she took his hand and led him downstairs to the study. "Listen." She held up the monitor, and loud and clear they heard a man say, *"Are you going to that baby class tomorrow?"* And the woman answered, *"Gym 'n Swim? Yup. Every Tuesday and Thursday. I wouldn't miss it."*

Jim and Annie stared at each other. "What is it? Who are they?" she said, and in spite of herself she knew her voice sounded frightened. She had just been in the baby's room. She knew there was no one there. But where were these people? They didn't sound threatening; they sounded nice. But didn't they *have* to be in her house? The other end of the monitor was on in Rebecca's room, not out in the backyard or somewhere where it might pick up other people.

"Nee nee nee nee, nee nee nee nee," Jim started humming the theme from *The Twilight Zone*.

"Cut it out. It's really spooky," she said.

The conversation on the monitor was blocked out by the sound of water running. Then they heard, *"You know, I think she's the star of the class, aren't you, Millicent Magnifi-*

cent?" The female voice singsonged, *"Millie the Magnificent."* Then they heard a baby giggle and a loud wet smooching sound.

Millie?

"Jim, that's the new people across the street. It's got to be. I heard her call the baby 'Millie' when she was talking to the movers today." Then, over the monitor they heard a toilet flush.

"Oh, Millie, what a great big beautiful poopie that one was. The diaper service is going to love this diaper. Maybe they'll frame it. You do the most beautiful poops in the world."

"Kinky," said Jim.

"Can you come with us?" the woman asked. *"You've never seen her swim, Dave. Jackie says that she'll be able to start taking flotation out of her suit soon. She hasn't said that to any of the other moms."* Annie thought the woman sounded defeated, like she knew ahead of time the answer would be no. And it was.

"Uh-uh. Can't, babe. You go at ten, right?"

"That's when the class starts; we have to leave by twenty of."

"I've got grand rounds. I'm presenting."

"Well, class is over at eleven, but we have to shower and dry our hair and play with our friends, right, Mill? So we never get out until twelve. Then we're going to the club for lunch with Timmy and his mom—why don't you join us there? You could finally meet her."

Jim nudged Annie, and with a triumphant wink, whispered, "The club?"

"Well, I'd love to, but I've got to get right back to the office. I told Sheila to start appointments at twelve since I'd be at the hospital for the morning. It'll be a log jam, no lunch for me. But I'll tell you what, since I don't have morning office hours, let's go out for breakfast together. I won't have to

leave till eight-thirty to get my rounds done before Grands start."

When Jim picked up the monitor and switched it off, Annie was startled. She had wanted to hear what would happen next. Would they fight? Despite being unnerved by having strangers broadcasting over her monitor, she definitely wanted to hear what they would say next.

"Does this thing have different channels?" Jim asked her.

"It has two," said Annie. "The directions said to experiment and see which one gives you better reception. It works best on A. The button's on the side. You know, this afternoon, Alex—"

"Look," said Jim. "It's on B." He turned it back on. They heard Peter Jennings say something about "a strange twist in world affairs." He flicked the switch to the A channel. The room filled with the sound of Rebecca's amplified breathing.

Jim smiled. Mystery solved.

"What about Alex?"

"Oh, this afternoon when I was making supper he came out to the kitchen all excited because he thought the monitor was like a police 'walkie-stalkie.' I told him it only picked up Rebecca's noises, and he said no and showed me and said TV was coming out of it. I just assumed that we were picking up somebody's TV signals. Alex must have switched the channel and I didn't realize it." Annie opened the study curtains, put her head against the window, and looked across the street. The house was mostly dark, but she could see the blue glare of a TV coming from a second-floor window.

"It *is* sort of creepy," said Jim. "I wonder if they can hear us. I'm glad the monitor's not in our bedroom. We could give them an earful." He walked across the room and hugged her. "Come up to bed," he whispered. "We can snuggle."

"Oh, I can't. I've got to do some copy. I'm sorry I panicked. I really thought someone was in Rebecca's room." She noticed she had goose bumps, and the hair on her arms was standing straight up.

"Those are your hardworking maternal hormones," said Jim. "I only have your typical, run-of-the-mill horny ones."

"Yes, I know," said Annie, laughing. "But, Jim," she said, looking across the street, "it *is* sort of creepy. I mean, they weren't saying anything we shouldn't have heard, but it's still weird that they didn't know anyone was listening. They could have been saying private things."

"They could have been plotting a murder," said Jim, laughing diabolically and rubbing his hands together.

"Yeah, right," said Annie.

"The Baby Monitor Murder," said Jim. "A modern day *Rear Window.* Night, Anna-Banana." He blew her a kiss and closed the door.

Back downstairs again, she sat at her desk. She had forgotten to close the curtains. She couldn't work with them open. A few years ago in the suburbs some high school kids had gone around shooting randomly into windows. For a couple of weeks no one got hurt, and then one Saturday they hit an old man and killed him. When the teenagers were caught and asked why they picked the old man, they said they hadn't; they just drove around until they found a window with curtains open.

Tonight she felt especially vulnerable. She got up to close them, changed her mind, and first shut off the overhead light and her desk lamp. The room was pitch black now except for the eerie orange cast of the streetlight outside. She made her way through the dark and stood looking out. Nothing unusual, just a big, elegant Victorian. Someone had put two enormous clay pots full of geraniums on either side of the tall front door. They were huge. Everything about the house suggested things done on a grand scale. The TV glow was still coming from the second floor. Were they silently watching TV together? Were they thrashing around on the floor making passionate love with the glow of the TV lighting their glistening bodies?

"If you're going to write trash, go write your copy," she told herself. But just as she was about to turn away she heard the scrape of metal on concrete. She strained to make out a figure with a large garbage can coming around the corner of his driveway out to the front curb. This man obviously didn't share Jim's enthusiasm for trash night. Jim always hoisted the can up onto his shoulder, "the way the professionals do it," he once told her. This guy was dragging it awkwardly, banging it into the side of his leg and, from the angry shake of his head, probably swearing. Annie couldn't hear his voice, but the dragging can was loud enough to hear all the way down the street. The man roughly deposited the can at the curb and the streetlight caught his face before he turned away. It was a handsome, prep school kind of a face with longish, but neat, dark brown hair. The kind of face Annie had found irresistibly handsome in high school and now appreciated as a work of art but also found boring. She was glad it wasn't what she woke up to every morning. She watched him walk back up the driveway until the dark swallowed him and then she closed the curtains.

She shuddered, then forced herself to walk across the dark room to her desk. She switched on the small desk lamp. The polka dot capri leggings were taunting her. "Okay, okay," she told them. "Back to the grindstone . . . if you get the copy written by ten," she told herself, "you can have some ice cream."

Chapter Three

The following morning spring was finally making a belated arrival, and Annie felt almost back to normal as she watched Alex and his friends playing Power Rangers at the playground. She didn't have the heart to rush him out, so it was almost dark by the time they made the turn onto their block. Driving up to the house, she saw her new neighbor pushing a stroller on their side of the street. The woman stopped at Annie's driveway and motioned for her to turn. Annie pulled into the driveway, stopping when she was abreast of her new neighbor, and rolled down her window. Here goes, she thought, and blushed as she remembered how she had listened in on them the night before.

"Hi." She extended her hand. "I'm Annie Morgan. And"—she turned toward the back seat—"this is my son, Alex . . ." Alex smiled shyly and waved. "And this is Rebecca."

"I'm so glad to meet you," the woman said, also smiling. "I'm Lesley Shields, and this is Millicent." The woman beamed down at her baby. "We call her Millie. You're the first people I've seen. To talk to, I mean. This neighborhood is very reserved, isn't it?"

"Yes, it is," said Annie. "I'm still adjusting myself, and we've been here six years."

"I've been wanting to come introduce myself, but it's

been so crazy with the unpacking and everything," said Lesley.

"Oh, please don't apologize," said Annie. "I should have welcomed *you*. I didn't know when you were moving in, and I've had this work deadline . . ." She let her voice trail off. Why was she making excuses? Guilty conscience.

"We've just been walking around, getting a feel for the neighborhood," said Lesley. "I'm so glad to see your kids—we haven't seen a tricycle or a toy on the sidewalk. I was beginning to wonder whether they allowed children."

Annie laughed. "Alex and Rebecca are the only kids on this block—and now there's Millie," she said kindly. She liked this woman. She was open and funny, and Annie had that rare sensation of knowing ahead of time that they would be friends.

"Maybe we could all go to the park sometime?" said Lesley.

"Sure," said Annie, "the weather's getting warmer every day. That'd be great."

"Well, I'll see you soon," said Lesley, and she backed up her stroller so that Annie could pull all the way into the driveway.

"Bye, Lesley," said Annie. "Bye, Millie."

Once inside the house, she discovered she already had the ingredients for quiche and found a couple of hot dogs for Alex. She would have to get to the market tomorrow. She hoped Jessica worked out—she longed to do the marketing without two children in the cart. When Annie had called the number she had torn off in her doctor's office, Jessica had sounded great; she was coming over next week for an interview. She put the infant seat on the counter in front of her, and Rebecca sat happily while Annie chopped onions.

The woman, Lesley, had certainly seemed very friendly just now. It made it hard for Annie's jealousy to really take hold, but a twinge still managed to creep in. Their house was

so much bigger than hers, and two cars would make life a lot
easier, not to mention the beautiful furniture, as opposed to
Annie and Jim's mishmash of hand-me-down semi antiques
and IKEA specials.

She knew Jim was happy in his job and that meant a lot,
but there were moments when she wished he had used his
law degree differently. Legal Aid attorneys weren't exactly
in a position to take their wives on Caribbean vacations.
Jim's law school buddies, now working in corporate offices
or at big firms, were making lots of money, and they were
already acquiring second homes and expensive cars. She
wondered if Lesley and her husband had a summer place.
No doubt. Or maybe a condo somewhere warm.

But when Annie really thought about her life, she knew
that she and Jim had the important things—good health,
wonderful children, and they were still crazy about each
other. Lots of people couldn't say that. Jim felt good about
the people he helped at Legal Aid. He had gone to law
school to help people, and now he was providing represen-
tation to people who couldn't afford it otherwise. They had
a Volvo station wagon. It was seven years old, but it was still
reliable and they had a wonderful house in a beautiful neighborhood.

That had been a stoke of luck. The neighborhood around
the university was generally very expensive. A few profes-
sors were still hanging on to houses that they had owned for
twenty years, since before the real estate market took off,
but mostly the neighborhood was full of doctors, investment
bankers and people who seemed to have money with no ap-
parent means of earning it. They had heard about their house
through their insurance agent, who was also a real estate
broker. He was at their apartment upgrading their life insurance. She was six months pregnant with Alex, and they were
trying hard to finish growing up before the baby came. They
had decided that getting more life insurance and making out

a will were adult acts worthy of the parents they would soon become.

"You people need a house," Mr. Ashburn, the agent, had said, looking pointedly at her belly and gesturing at the small living room and tiny galley kitchen. "There's a beauty in my neighborhood. Hasn't even been listed yet. I was talking with them tonight. If you move quickly, you could save yourselves a bundle. You two are lucky to be living in one of the last affordable cities in southern New England. Take advantage of it." She and Jim glanced at each other. "Tell you what. Drop by my office tomorrow. I'm showing it to someone else, but you can tag along, too. She won't mind— she's a professional looker. This time she's trying to find a place for her daughter. *You* need to buy. Come by around eleven." And so, having no intention of actually going, and thinking they would call in the morning and cancel the appointment, they shook his hand and said good night. In bed they had talked about it, while she squirmed and tried to arrange pillows between her legs and under her abdomen so that she could minimize the kicking from the baby and sleep some.

"How can a house in that neighborhood be on the market for that price?" she said.

"It's still a lot of money," said Jim, "but not for there."

Annie said, "It's probably really ugly."

"Or it needs to be totally rehabbed."

But in the morning she found herself driving by number 25 just to see. And she hadn't believed what she saw: a run-down but totally charming gingerbread cottage sandwiched in among brick federal colonials and huge Victorian arks.

"It's wonderful," she had said, tossing Jim the paper. "We have to see the inside." The inside was overwhelming: damp and musty-smelling—she was sure the wallpaper was mildewed. Huge sheets of plastic hung from doorways in an attempt to keep drafts contained in the long center hallway.

But there was a window seat at the top of the stairs and another long one in the living room bay. She could picture herself sitting with a pudgy toddler, reading as the sun streamed in. The other woman looking had gone through the entire house while Annie was still marveling at all the closets on the first floor, and Jim was still in the basement.

"It's impossible," the other woman said to the agent. "You'd have to put a hundred thousand dollars in just to bring it up to snuff, and we've just broken ground on the house in Maine. I've got too much to do there. Show me something less absorbing."

The current owners were sitting at their kitchen table. Annie winced at the thought that they might have overheard this brash dismissal of their home. She poked her head around the kitchen door, looking for Jim.

The wife looked up at Annie and said apologetically, "We haven't kept up with the house the way we should. But he's getting too old." She gestured toward her husband.

"We raised a family here, all four of them," her husband said. "None of them want this place, they've got their lives in other parts now. One's in California, the baby can't make up her mind. She's in New York now, and the other two are in Pittsburgh. Which is probably where we'll go."

"They take turns helping us out," said his wife.

The old man looked at Annie's pregnant belly and said, "This house needs a family."

That night Mr. Ashburn had called them.

"They wouldn't go for ten less," he said. "But they'll accept six less, and I'll throw in two from my commission. Can you do eight?" And although they really couldn't, they had somehow, and they had been happy. Until now.

Now the house seemed small to her. How had those people ever raised four children in this house? There were only three bedrooms. Why had she ever thought there was a lot of closet space? What she needed was a mudroom. What she

needed was a place for roller skates and basketballs and bi-
cycle helmets. What she needed was a new life.

She sighed. Wouldn't it be nice to be Lesley? To be back
in that time when you have just one baby to concentrate on?
And enough money to really enjoy it? She had to get inside
that house. It must have at least five bedrooms.

She pulled Rebecca, who was now fussing, out of the infant seat and walked into the living room. She stopped at
the window and gazed at her new neighbor's house. They
had had the outside newly painted, and the hedge along the
driveway was trimmed perfectly. Come on, don't be jealous, she told herself. It would be so nice to have a friend
right across the street.

Chapter Four

Jaime Ruiz hung up the phone, a satisfied grin on his face, and made a notation in his Filofax. He was pleased about the referrals they were getting, this one from a British doctor posted in Riyadh, Saudi Arabia. The British tended to be among the most conservative, shunning experimental research until there was indisputable, empirical proof. As Jaime had suspected, the Arabian patient confirmed that his doctor had given him the usual spiel: "Research is always being conducted, but it is still in the testing stages. As it happens, I've heard of a neurologist, worked in the States, at Yale University, on a project involving fetal brain cells and Parkinson's. They actually did a few procedures. People got very excited at the time. But the whole thing was too controversial. Eventually, President Reagan imposed a ban on fetal cell transplants. But it isn't as if a cure was suddenly removed from the market. They had only done a handful of procedures. They were optimistic, but it was much too soon to know anything definitive. There's a clinic in Mexico, but it is by no means a sure thing." The patient had insisted, and in the end the doctor made the referral.

Jaime looked up the doctor's name in the registry, checking the graduation date. Just as he had suspected—a young man, smart and ambitious, Jaime thought. Practicing in Riyadh—the British national health plan pay obviously wasn't enough for him. Jaime noted the doctor's name for future reference. Hungry young men were almost always useful.

Something bothered him about this patient, though. As he was only in the initial stages of the disease, the results of the fetal tissue transplant would be less dramatic. Still, a video of the extreme tremor in the right arm and then that side doing some fine motor skills, shot before the inevitable relapse . . . It could work, and as his partner had suggested, it would be another number to add to their file—not to mention the fee.

He walked to the door of his office and stood surveying his lab. It was like no other lab in the world, he thought. He and his American partner both had impeccable credentials, but of all of the facility's employees, only he and his American partner possessed any formal medical training. The rest of the staff of his lab and its adjoining clinic were all trained solely by himself. Each one knew only their specific task, no general medical knowledge. Some could use the electron microscope, some could fill syringes and administer injections, others, take blood pressures, or draw blood.

Jaime prided himself on running the lab that way. He didn't want his staff to know what was being done there. Didn't want them returning to their superstition-laden villages and talking about the lab. He didn't want anybody finding out about their work until it was perfected; until he could publish exact and successful findings. He didn't want the world to know about his work until he stood at the dias in Stockholm accepting the Nobel Prize, showing all those cold New England bastards. Each and every one of those sons of bitches who had looked down their noses at him— that a Mexican could win the prize! One day—one day soon—he would show them all.

Chapter Five

"Where were you?" Annie met Jim at the door.

"I had a beer with Chris after we moved his fridge." Jim looked guilty. "I'm sorry. You're tired. I'll take the kids to the park in the morning. We'll see how Rebecca does with a bottle."

"That'll be great but that's not why I'm angry. We have to be at the Shields' in half an hour. I asked you to come right home." Annie could hear the hysterical pitch in her voice. She was exhausted, she thought. Going to the neighbors should be fun, not a chore. But this felt like a bigger deal. These neighbors seemed out of her league and now, thanks to Jim, they would be late.

"Shit, Annie, I'm sorry. I completely forgot."

"Freudian slip." Annie smiled, but her teeth were gritted. "You don't want to get to know them cause they're rich."

"Okay, okay, guilty as charged. I won't judge them until after we've had an incredibly sumptuous meal and they've showed us all their possessions. I promise it'll take me two minutes to shower."

"Great, but Rebecca was up the entire time you were gone, and fussy, and so *I* still need to shower."

"Okay, I'll shower first because I'm faster. She's asleep now, isn't she?"

"Yeah, so we'll have to wake her up, and then she'll be fussy there."

"You worry too much." Jim kissed her on the forehead. "Go lie down while I shower."

Annie lay down on the bed. It felt so wonderful to stretch out, but she didn't dare close her eyes. Sleeping during the day was deadly when she was so exhausted. The groggy feeling lasted for hours after she woke up.

She could hear Rebecca's noisy baby breathing over the monitor on the bedside table. She wondered what the neighbors were doing. Lesley probably had everything made in advance. She and her husband were probably relaxing with drinks, reading the Sunday paper, Millie sitting happily at their feet, all of them just waiting for the Morgans to arrive.

She looked over at the monitor again. She could find out exactly what they were doing. Just flick the switch, she told herself and she reached out and held the monitor. She could hear the shower running—just listen until the shower stops, she thought. No one will know. But it felt wrong. Eavesdropping? On the other hand, they couldn't possibly know she was doing it. Her heart was beating fast. She flicked the channel selector. She knew the Shields couldn't catch her eavesdropping but Jim could. The sneaking, the danger, were exciting.

"You know how I feel." He sounded annoyed.

"I know," said Lesley.

"That's why we didn't buy in the suburbs," he continued. *"I don't want to entertain the neighborhood."*

"We aren't," said Lesley. *"It's just one couple. You'll like them, Davey."* Lesley's voice had a whiny edge.

"That's not the point, Lesley. I don't want to get something started. We invite them. They invite us. Pretty soon he's suggesting we buy a mower together and go out every Saturday."

Annie could feel herself blushing. Who did he think he
was? Who did he think they were?

"Davey"—Lesley sounded cajoling now—*"you're making too big a deal out of this. They aren't like that. I bet they
feel the same way. They aren't 'neighborly' types. He's a
lawyer and she's a copywriter. They're interesting."*

"Artsy," Annie said out loud. "Cute little collectible
neighbors." She felt angry now.

*"And why did you invite them, anyway? They should be
inviting us. We're the newcomers."*

"David"—Lesley sounded annoyed—*"now, really. You
sound like my mother. Will you just relax? It's only one
evening."*

David sighed loudly. There was the sound of kissing.

Annie lunged for the monitor and just managed to switch
the channel selector back as Jim walked into Rebecca's
room.

"Honey," he said soothingly, coming up behind her and
putting a hand on her shoulder, "what's wrong? Did I startle
you?"

"Oh." She managed to laugh. "Yeah. You scared me. I—
I just didn't hear you coming . . ."

Jim cocked his head to one side and his eyes narrowed.
"I'm worried about you, Annie. You've been very jumpy
lately. Do you need some time off? You really didn't have
much of a maternity leave. I could try to expand my lunch
hour for a while, come home and spell you for a bit."

"No, honey, really, I'm okay. Just startled." She handed
him a pile of clothes. "Here, you do Alex, I'll do Rebecca."

"Change their clothes? They look fine. This isn't an au-
dience with the Pope, you know."

"I know," said Annie. "I just want them to look nice. It's
the first time we're going to the Shields', and I just don't
want us looking like slobs." She glanced at his frayed collar.
When Jim and his brother, Hal, were kids they used to have

a contest for "shirt of the year." They each chose a favorite and had a ceremony on New Year's Eve for the best of the past year. They took it very seriously, and Jim would still occasionally remark, on opening a present from his mother, "Hey, this could be a contender." He was now wearing one from God-knew-what year, and it was worn through in several places. "And could you put on a clean shirt? Please?"

As Jim went off to find Alex, Annie heaved a sigh of relief. Stupid! What was her problem? She'd been so captivated by David and Lesley, she'd almost been caught! God, she would die if Jim knew she was listening in on them. Dammit, why had she done it? She and her family were expected at the Shields' for a barbecue in less than half an hour. How was she supposed to look them in the eye and eat their food now? Especially knowing that David didn't really want them to be there.

God, she was *eavesdropping*. The very word made her cringe. When she was very little, and they still lived in an apartment, her mother used to complain about a neighbor, Mrs. Tull, a disgusting woman in her greasy housecoat with her ham slab upper arms that practically flapped in the breeze. In their apartment if she became angry and began a tantrum or if her father began to speak in a loud voice about bills, her mother would shush them, urgently hissing, "Mrs. Tull," and she would jerk her head in the direction of the apartment above. "She listens to everyone. She *eavesdrops.*" The word was spit out at them.

It was funny how memory worked. She hadn't thought of Mrs. Tull since the day they moved away from there. Had she sunk to the level of a Mrs. Tull?

She wanted Lesley to like her. Now Lesley'd invited Annie and her family over (when it really *should* have been the other way around, like David said) and Annie already felt like a bad neighbor. If they were going to be friends, Annie would have to stop spying on her.

*   *   *

David Shields threw his head back under the stream of hot water and relaxed. This bathroom was state of the art, he thought with a satisfied smile. All ridiculously expensive Dornbracht fixtures, of course. The shower head was adjusted to a relentless stream of tiny spears, zapping the tension out of his taut neck and shoulder muscles. Deep breaths, he told himself. He had to relax this afternoon and put on the charm.

He toweled himself roughly, pulled on a pair of khaki shorts and the blue polo that Lesley always said was terrific with his eyes and jogged down the back stairs, whistling.

Lesley was leaning over into the refrigerator.

"Looking good," he said and pulled her hips back against him. She straightened up, turned around, and kissed him lightly. He felt her breasts flatten against his chest. He had worried about how she would react to the news that she couldn't have children of her own. But Millie was a great kid. And besides there were compensations for Lesley never bearing children. These beautiful breasts, for one.

"Mmmm," she said. "I love you in that shirt." He held on to her, twisting her hips back and forth against him.

"What time are they due?" he asked.

"At four," she said. They both looked at the clock: 3:50. David raised his eyebrows. Lesley laughed.

"David, we can't. What if they come early?"

"Then we could come together," he said and gave her his most seductive smile. But she was all business, not biting.

She pushed him gently away. "Be a good boy and start the grill." He was about to try one more time but Millie began crying loud and clear over the kitchen monitor. Lesley threw him a kiss as she hurried up the stairs.

Lesley was just coming down with Millie when the front bell rang, nearly drowned out by the enormous mahogany grandfather clock in the hall grandly tolling the hour. David got to the door first.

"Hello," he boomed in his deep, rich voice. Lesley was so proud of him. How handsome and self-assured. She squeezed Millie. This was adult life. It was full of a handsome man with a deep voice and charming ways just as she had imagined when she was little. She hurried down to greet her guests.

She and Annie tripped over each other in introducing their husbands. Annie's finally broke the jam. "I'm Jim." He reached out a hand, first to Lesley and then to David. He was shorter than Lesley thought he would be—only a couple of inches taller than Annie, maybe five ten—but then, most men looked short next to David.

"Good to meet you. And, Annie"—David flashed a welcoming smile—"Lesley tells me you're a copywriter. I always wondered how people come up with that stuff. Tell me about your process." He seemed genuinely interested in her, in spite of the argument she'd overheard. If he was being insincere, he did a terrific job of hiding it.

While Annie talked, David led them down the long, expansive hallway to the kitchen. Lesley brought up the rear, where she could watch Jim and Annie. Annie stared straight ahead at David or watched Alex, making sure he kept walking. But Jim's head turned back and forth, looking first at the living room, then the study and the dining room. She could tell by his body language that he was impressed. The Aubusson carpeting. The carved Victorian dining chairs, more like thrones than seats. The oversized vases full of fresh flowers.

"How about a drink? Gin and tonic? Beer? Glass of wine?" David opened the Subzero.

"I'd love a gin and tonic," said Annie.

"And I'll have a beer, please," said Jim.

"Great," said David to Jim. "What'll you have?" He opened the door wider to display a shelf full of various imported beers. Jim chose a Harp while David squeezed a half lime into the bottom of a Baccarat tumbler for Annie.

"Let me know if that's too strong," he said as he handed Annie the glass. "Lesley says I tend to have a heavy hand." And he watched as she tasted it.

"Delicious." David gave her another smile and then turned his attention to his wife.

"How about you, honey?" He reached up and lifted Lesley's hair, casually rubbing her neck.

So they're one of *those* couples, Annie thought. The ones who touch each other publicly the way they all did when they were newly in love. She felt a little bubble of jealousy.

"Seltzer and lime," said Lesley, brushing her cheek against David's shoulder and then walking to the patio door.

"Oh, you've discovered the seltzer delivery man," said Jim.

"Well, actually," said Lesley, "we had him at our old house."

"Oh, that's right, sorry," said Jim. "I forgot you aren't new to the city, just to this venerable neighborhood."

David looked up. He didn't like the scoffing tone in Jim's voice. What was so terrible about being able to afford a great house in the right neighborhood? And being proud of it? He followed the others out to the brick terrace.

"This grape arbor is wonderful, Lesley. It feels like Nantucket," said Annie.

"You could make jelly in the fall," added Jim.

David raised an eyebrow at this, then said to Annie, "You're right about Nantucket. It's one of the reasons Lesley liked this place. She spent her summers between overnight camp on the island and her parents' place in Tuscany." Lesley blushed, Annie supposed, because she was embarrassed at the show David had made of her wealthy upbringing. But the bubble of jealousy grew a little bigger.

While David grilled the shrimp they relaxed and had their

drinks. Alex got down on his hands and knees and chased a giggling Millie, who grabbed her father's leg. David reached down and stroked her head, then gently turned her in the direction of the sandbox. Rebecca slept. Lesley and Annie talked incessantly.

"Oh, Millie's at my favorite age," said Annie.

"Yeah, she's really fun now. She understands so much," said Lesley.

"I remember thinking Alex was like my contemporary, a real friend, when he was eighteen months old."

"I feel that, exactly," said Lesley. "Are you going to join a pool club this year, or do you go away?" Annie glanced toward Jim. He was by the grill with David.

"I'm not sure. We used to rent a house every July with friends, but they live in London now and we haven't found anyone else that we felt we could live with."

"We just joined the Agawam." Lesley rolled her eyes and crinkled her nose as if something smelled bad.

Annie didn't respond. The Agawam Hunt Club was so snobby, but she didn't know Lesley well enough to offer her opinion.

Lesley went on. "I know it's full of some real idiots, but a couple of doctors' wives that I actually like belong . . ." She seemed to need some encouragement, so Annie put in, "Why not, then? You'll be glad when summer hits. Millie loves the water so much."

Lesley looked at her, a puzzled expression on her face. Annie could feel herself blush. How did she know Millie loved swimming?

"I mean . ." she stammered, "babies her age always love pools and splashing."

"Yes," said Lesley, "she takes a Gym 'n Swim class and she does love it. She goes under more than the others. Oh, God, I'm bragging. Sorry."

"Don't be silly. If you can't brag to a friend, who can you

brag to?" There, she had said it, called her a friend. Would this wealthy woman-who-has-everything recoil in horror?

"Thanks," said Lesley, and her smile was full of warmth. "Will you be my guest at the Agawam—a lot?"

"Thanks. I think they have a limit on guest appearances. But we'd love to come and see how the other half summers." She laughed so that Lesley would know she meant no offense.

Over at the grill, David and Jim were feeling each other out.

"So you're an attorney." David wasn't really making it a question.

"Yes. And you're an OB?" said Jim.

"That's right. Do you do any med mal? Should I watch what I say?" David laughed and looked down at Jim.

"No med mal," said Jim. "Civil rights. Illegal search and seizure. Employee drug testing. Minor's right to abortion. That kind of thing."

"Ah," said David. "Got your law degree so you could save the world, eh?"

"Look," said Jim, who felt particularly short and immature next to this behemoth in easily a week's salary of Ralph Lauren, expertly flipping shrimp as big as his fingers, "give me a break. I'm just trying to do something I believe in. I'm charging a fair price for a worthwhile service."

"Easy, man," said David. "I meant no insult. We were the same way in med school."

Lesley arrived then with a serving platter filled with steaming wild rice. "Put those right here on the rice, Davey."

By seven o'clock the Morgans were back home.

"You better hurry, honey," said Annie. "Don't you meet at the gym at seven-thirty?" She was in Rebecca's room changing her, hoping to do it without waking her. She had felt uncomfortable when she nursed tonight at the Shields'.

Knowing that David was an obstetrician, she'd assumed he wouldn't pay any attention to her nursing. But twice she had caught him peeking—and it had unnerved her. Her hand knocked the monitor over as she reached for a clean diaper. Righting it, she thought with a rush of excitement that she could listen to them tonight. Jim was going to play his weekly game of basketball. Alex was spending the night at his friend, Jeremy's. There was no school tomorrow, due to some teachers' conference—Alex had been ecstatic. Rebecca was sleeping. She would be able to listen to them talking about her and Jim. She put Rebecca down, kissed her silky head, and turned on the night light.

She rushed down the stairs. Jim was lying on the couch.

"Jim! You startled me! I thought you'd left already. Aren't you playing tonight? You haven't even changed."

"I know. Come here. I'm not going. I called Al." She went to the couch. "How often do we get a night alone like this? I couldn't pass it up." He pulled her down on top of him and began to kiss her. Annie's mind raced. What were they saying across the street? She wanted to turn the monitor on. She wanted Jim to go play basketball. She wanted to be alone to listen in. But then she felt his hands, his fingers unbuttoning her blouse and reaching inside her bra. She felt his breath against her neck. Oh, yes. She remembered this now. This is what couples who didn't have children got to do whenever they felt like it. It was all right that he stayed home. She forgot the monitor. Eavesdropping was a disgusting habit, anyway. She felt good.

Later, in their room, Annie and Jim sat on the bed, a pint of New York Super Fudge Chunk between them. She loved this part, too—their talking afterward.

"I like Lesley," she said.

"Yeah, she seemed very nice. She sure loves that baby, cute kid. What a prick he is, though."

"Gee, he didn't seem so bad. Charming in his own way."

She couldn't let Jim know what she'd overheard. "He's awfully good-looking."

"He's a son of a bitch, Annie. He pegged me for a bleeding heart liberal and then tried to tell me *he'd* outgrown all that. Condescending bastard."

"Sweetie, I'm sorry. You got stuck with him more than I did. I wanted to like him, 'cause I like her so much, and it would be so nice if we could like them both. But he did give me the creeps when I was nursing."

"What do you mean? What'd he do?" Jim's voice had a territorial edge. Men really were like dogs, Annie thought and almost laughed, but thought better of it.

"Well, when I was nursing, I felt really uncomfortable. I don't think I'd want him for a doctor."

"The sight of your breasts was probably more than he could bear," said Jim, leaning to kiss her left breast. They were, no doubt, the most beautiful pair he'd ever seen. "Lesley's are nothing compared to yours."

"Oh, I see," said Annie. "You were doing some scoping of your own."

"Well, weren't you? You're the one who commented on his looks first."

"I meant he had a nice face. I didn't go on about his ass or the bulge in his shorts."

"But you noticed them, admit it. That's what these grown-up cookouts are all about, checking out the other people's setup and comparing them to your own, right?"

"I see," said Annie with a smile. "And how do we compare to them?"

"Well, they've definitely got us beat on house, cars, furniture, all the worldly goods. But the things of the flesh? I bet you our sex is miles above theirs."

"We could listen and see," said Annie. She made her voice sound light and teasing, but maybe, just maybe, he was feeling playful enough. And she was so curious.

"No way." He was emphatic. "Besides"—he threw the empty ice cream container into the wastebasket and pulled her close—"I know they couldn't come close to what we've got."

Chapter Six

It was the first really warm day they'd had. The smell of spring—damp earth and green buds—enveloped them on the way to the car. As Annie parked the car in the zoo lot she was thinking how much the weather affected her moods.

"There they are, Mom. There they are, hurry." Alex was unbuckling his seat belt and scrambling for the door.

Annie could see MacCarthy James and her son, Sam, heading toward the elaborate wrought-iron entrance gate.

"Okay, Alex, relax, we'll catch them." But she rolled down her window and yelled, "Mac!" as loud as she could. Mac kept walking.

"Aw, Mom." Alex laughed good-naturedly. "Your voice is pathetic. I mean, I don't want to hurt your feelings, but you're just not a screamer. Your voice gets all funny."

" 'Funny,' Alex?"

"Yeah, you know: 'Mac, Mac' " Alex raised his voice as high as it would go and then almost whispered. "It just kind of disappears when you try to make it loud."

Annie leaned over and kissed Alex on the top of his head. "Undo your sister's seat belt for me, will you please, sweetie?" They caught up with Mac and Sam at the admissions booth.

"I forgot my card again," said Mac. "They're looking us up." Annie smiled and hugged her friend.

"Hi, Sammy," she said. The boys raced ahead to climb on the bronze sculpture of a larger-than-life Labrador, a zoo ritual. Annie, with Rebecca in the stroller, trailed behind them slowly, waiting for Mac to catch up. Annie and Mac had met at college and had been roommates their last two years. Mac had moved to town four years ago, and their friendship had continued as strong as ever. It was wonderful; Mac felt like a sister. They could talk about anything, and Annie never tired of Mac's Louisville accent.

"So, Anniekins"—Mac linked her arm through Annie's—"What's the new neighbor like? How was the BBQ?"

"She's really nice. I think you'd like her a lot. We'll go out to dinner with her some night, okay? He's pretty typical doctor fare. He and Jim did not get along."

"Surprise, surprise. Jim usually loves rich jerks." Mac beamed at Annie.

"Okay, I know, but I like her, so I had hoped that Jim would at least like him a little."

"So did you have a huge blowout when you got home?"

"No." Annie couldn't help smiling.

"Oh, I see," said Mac. "Say no more. I'm sure the pictures in my head are much more exciting than the real thing!"

"Don't be so sure," said Annie, blushing in spite of herself.

"That's good. No wonder you're all smiles this morning. Listen, I have a great story for you."

Alex and Sam came running up. "Ice cream," Alex said, gasping. Sam clutched at his throat.

"It's so hot, we need ice cream," he said.

"Guys," said Mac, "we just got here."

"Yeah," said Annie, "let's see a few more animals first. How about the polar bear? I bet he's swimming today."

The boys stood on the wooden edge of the huge picture window and the large white polar bear lunged under the water at them, his mouth open, his great paw striking the glass as he banked for the turn. They laughed and shrieked. Annie gave an involuntary shudder.

"So," said Mac, "I went to that church on Hope Street. You know, 'cause somebody told me that the minister there was finding jobs for a group of Nicaraguan women who had come here to work for six months and then take the money home to their families."

"God," said Annie, "imagine having to leave your kids for that long."

"Well," said Mac, "there are times when I think it might be nice to take a sabbatical from Nick and Sam, but I admit it wouldn't be to clean other people's houses! Anyway," Mac went on, "I told him I needed someone to clean once a week, and he sent a really sweet woman. Pilar was her name, and she was probably about twenty-five. She had no English, not even yes or no, and you will well remember, no doubt, that I flunked Spanish." Mac took a deep breath. Annie loved her stories.

"I motioned with my hands, running my finger along the mantel, showing her the dust. Showed her the vacuum cleaner. She had never seen one. At first she was scared of the noise, covered her ears and started to run toward the door. But then I did the old vacuum cleaner salesperson routine. I went and got some oatmeal, uncooked"—Mac smiled—"and poured it on the living room rug, then, holding her wrist so that she couldn't run away, I showed her how the vacuum sucked up that oatmeal. She was amazed, and she grabbed it from me and took off. The house looked great—Nick was thrilled, *I* even liked it, and Sam started talking about bringing friends home again." Mac loved to exaggerate. She continued. "Well, last weekend Jack came for a visit." Mac rolled her eyes.

"Oh, how is he?" Annie had dated Jack once in college. He was Mac's brother-in-law.

"Just the same—funny and cute and totally immature. He and Sam had a great time all weekend, which brings me to the climax of my story. Jack knows how Sam lives and breathes Indiana Jones, so having recently returned from the rain forest and other less politically correct corners of Brazil, he brought Sam his own personal bullwhip."

"Oh, my God," said Annie, "what did you do? Is your house completely trashed?" She looked quickly at Sam. "He didn't hurt himself?"

"No, fortunately Jack showed it to us at night when Sam was in bed. Even Jack realized it might not be the safest toy. We couldn't decide exactly what to do about it, so we tossed it under our bed and forgot about it.

"So Monday morning I go to the church and pick up Pilar. She's all smiles, eager to use the vacuum again. First I show her the bathroom, and she has it sparkling in half an hour. She is amazing. I feel like I've won the lottery. I have this nice woman who cleans my house till it shines and I can feel that I am doing a good deed by employing her. So I get the vacuum cleaner out and go to do some errands. When I come back, I call to her—no one answers. The arrangement with the minister is that I will pick her up and drop her off at the church. With no English the minister doesn't think it's safe for her to travel alone. She's nowhere in the house but the vacuum cleaner is in our bedroom—and it's still on. Now I'm really feeling frantic. Has someone broken in and killed her? There's no blood. Is it all a scam? Have I been robbed? All Nick's grandmother's silver is still in the dining room. The camcorder's still in the closet. So I get in the car and drive to the church, looking down all the side streets on the way.

"The minister is in his study, but he's not all smiles when I burst in. 'Is Pilar here?' I say, all out of breath.

" 'Yes, she's here, but quite upset, Mrs. James, and I must tell you that I am as well.'

"'But why, what happened?'"

"'Pilar walked here alone. She was hysterical when she arrived, and it took us quite some time to calm her.' He went on and on and then finally cut to the chase. 'Pilar won't be continuing in your service, Mrs. James.' Now listen careful, Annie darlin', because the following was said with a completely straight face by a grown man." Mac paused. "Maybe that's wrong, are they ever grown?"

"Come on, Mac, go on."

"All right. 'Mrs. James,' he says, 'Pilar says you are the devil and that your house is evil. She's afraid you've fixed her with the evil eye, and she is so upset she may return to Nicaragua immediately.'

"'Oh,' I said, feeling enormous relief, because I've realized what's happened by now, and figure I can explain. 'I can explain this,' I say. 'It must be the whip under our bed.' Well, Annie, I could tell by his face that relief was not the appropriate emotion."

Annie laughed so hard she had to wipe tears away.

"You should've seen his face. There was no way I could explain myself, so I just left. But now I have no cleaning lady and my house is a mess again. It's all Jack's fault. Nick is mad as hell."

They left the polar bears and cruised by the monkeys. Rebecca woke up and stared with a dreamy smile on her face at the mother gibbon with her infant.

"Species memory," said Mac. Annie smiled and kissed Rebecca. It was spring, and spring babies were grand. She and Alex were reading *Charlotte's Web* and he had started calling Rebecca their spring pig. Life was quite wonderful, Annie decided.

"How's Jane?" Mac asked about a mutual friend.

"Oh, she's great. She's pregnant!"

"She must be ecstatic. What happened?"

"Well, it's funny, actually. She went through all kinds of

tortuous tests; you know that one, laparoscopy or something—where they blow the air through your tubes?"

"Yeah. Why do they always test the woman first? It seems much simpler to test the man."

"I know. It costs more to test the women probably. And no doctor wants to hint that a man might be lacking in such a masculine area."

"Oh, Jesus," said Mac.

"So finally Walt decided to get tested and . . . surprise, he has a low sperm count. We were having dinner with them and Walt was telling us this and I had just read this article on infertility, so I said, 'You know, the doctor has probably already told you this, but there are some incredibly simple causes of low sperm count. What kind of underwear do you wear?' "

"You asked him that?"

"Yes, why?"

"Well, he always seems like such a tight ass, I can't imagine talking about his underwear with him."

"Well, I did, I mean, he was really baring his soul, and the timing just seemed right. So, he said, 'Jockey briefs.' So, I said, 'Well, this article said that sometimes Jockey briefs heat up the testicles too much and kill sperm and that switching to boxer shorts can lower the heat and increase the sperm count.'

"He said he always hated boxer shorts, and just then Jane came in and heard us talking about underwear and said Walt was incredibly fussy about his undies, that they had to be Brooks Brothers briefs."

Mac broke in, "It goes without saying, I suppose, that they have to be white. I can't believe you actually had this conversation with him."

"Well, you know, I'd had a glass of wine."

"Oh, right, loose lips sink ships. So did you get him to switch?"

"Well, I could tell he was intrigued, but you know Walt. Mr. Lab Research. Mr. 'Show me some empirical data.' So here I gave fate a nudge. I embellished a bit."

"Um-hmmm."

"I told him some doctors at Harvard Med School had done a study, and 75 percent of the guys who switched raised their count and the doctors thought that was conservative because they thought some of the guys cheated and sometimes wore their briefs still. I told him I read the article in the *Journal of OB and GYN.*"

"And where in fact was the article?"

"I don't know. I read it in a magazine in the doctor's office. I don't remember."

"But he bought it and she's pregnant. You're a hero."

"Well, he actually did call and thank me and gave me the news himself."

"Annie, Annie."

Chapter Seven

Days like this were Pam Fowler's favorite kind. She got so immersed in her paperwork that she wasn't concerned with what would come next. Then she'd feel her neck getting a crick from bending over so long and she'd straighten up and survey the waiting room and there would be a young girl (a friend of hers said to call them "women," but she thought of anyone younger than herself, twenty-five, as a girl), sitting by herself with no gold band, not even a diamond on her left hand. Then she felt as though she'd been given a surprise gift. Maybe this one would need help. Maybe she could actually save this one's life. That's how she thought of it. If she—and Dr. S., of course—could get them back to their original lives—college classes, jobs, whatever—with as little fuss as possible, then, she thought, maybe they weren't altered forever. They certainly wouldn't have to go on welfare to support a child that they must, on some level, resent. All those plans down the drain. And what about the poor baby? It didn't ask to be born, certainly wouldn't have chosen so young a mother and no father at all. And in one of those magazines in the waiting room, *McCall's,* maybe, or *Reader's Digest,* there'd been that article on child abuse. One quarter of all American girls are molested by a man living in their house, it said. She felt efficient and helpful, a shining savior. She'd question this one carefully. When the girl looked up from picking at her cuticle, Pam gave her an extra warm smile which she hoped transmitted caring and an overall feeling of comfort.

After seeing two expectant mothers in their thirties who had questions about the glucose tolerance test and false positives in the AFP, Pam felt she would scream if she had to repeat what now sounded like a pretaped message on the risks and benefits of prenatal testing. And then in walked the young girl from the waiting room. Maybe this one would make up for the Kelleher girl's miscarriage. He had been after her to find another donor for that couple—he really seemed to share their sense of loss at the added delay. It struck her for the millionth time what a sensitive man he was.

"Hi," the girl offered hesitantly. "I was in last week for a pregnancy test. They said I should come to your office today after three . . ."

Pam was pleased that the girl thought she was important enough to have her own office. In actual fact, she floated, using the office of whatever doctor wasn't in that day.

"Yes," she said in what she hoped was a confidential, big sister tone. "Come on in. Have a seat."

Pam stayed behind the desk. Later, when she felt the time was right, she would ceremoniously come around and sit next to the girl for a feeling of closeness and "we're in this together now." But for the moment she felt she needed to maintain the air of authority that the patients expected.

"I just need to ask you a few questions," she explained. "When was the date of your last period?"

"Uh, I think it started around the middle of January."

"And this office has confirmed your pregnancy?"

"Yes. Actually, I had a test at my school clinic, and then my mother made me have another one at the lab here."

"How did you find out about this practice? Did someone refer you?"

"Dr. Casey is my aunt's doctor. My mother was too embarrassed to have me go to her doctor, but she wanted me to go to a good Catholic practice. I guess she didn't want me going someplace where they'd discuss my 'options' with me."

"Options?" Pam repeated. This answer could be important. If she had decided on an abortion, there wasn't much Pam could do. On the other hand, she could have had that done by now.

"Yeah," said the girl, nervously, "you know." Then she paused. "You must not be Catholic . . ."

"Lapsed," said Pam.

"Well, 'options'—you know, it's a euphemism for abortion."

"Euphemism"—this was a bright college kid. What a shame. She mustn't let this girl's life go down the tubes. Not when there were so many people waiting, hoping for a baby to be their own.

"Do you *want* someone to discuss 'options' with you?" ventured Pam. She didn't want to say the word "abortion." She didn't want to discuss abortion with this girl or anyone else. She did believe that if someone was raped, especially by, say, their stepfather, or in cases of incest, they ought to be able to have an abortion. But she didn't honestly know what she would do if something that awful happened to her and she got pregnant. Abortion was something you lived with for a long time, thought Pam, but so was keeping a baby. That's why adoption made so much sense. . . .

"Not exactly," the girl answered slowly, "at least, I mean, I know that I don't want an abortion. I am Catholic, and although I'm not so sure I believe everything I once did . . . I mean I guess I wouldn't be pregnant if I believed everything they tell you. But, still, I do believe that people need a spiritual leader. I mean, they need someone to point out the moral way to them. You know what I mean?" She didn't wait for an answer, but Pam nodded anyway. "And it's just that if you are going to be a Catholic, then the Pope is that guy for you. I mean, he tells you what's right and what's wrong and, at least on the really big issues, you can't question him. I mean, if you say you're a Catholic, if you buy into that idea, if you agree to the spiritual pact, then you have to accept his guidelines. I talked to my adviser at the university, and he seemed to think that this was a valid theory."

"So, you know you want to keep this baby?" said Pam with a hint of hesitation in her voice, opening the door, she hoped, for the girl to express some doubt.

"Well, not exactly. See my mother has said, more or less, that I made my bed and now I have to lie in it, except she's willing to help, she says. But I'm not so sure I want her kind of help. She has it all worked out. She wants me to take a leave of absence from school—she thinks that she can get one of the doctors here to write a note saying I have really bad mono. Then I'll have the baby before Thanksgiving, and I can go back to school in January like nothing ever happened."

"What will you do with the baby?" asked Pam.

"Well, that's the part that I'm not so sure about. See, she wants to keep the baby. She wants me to go on and get my degree and get a job and get married and have babies and pretend that this baby is my sister or brother. She'll tell the baby that she's its mother." The girl looked like she was going to cry.

"How do you feel about that plan?" asked Pam as she slid a box of Kleenex across the desk to her.

"I hate it. I think it's creepy. I don't want to lie to this baby." The tears were starting. "But I don't want to be its mother, either." She was sobbing now.

It was time. He was going to be so pleased. This one would make forty-eight. Forty-eight girls whose lives they'd put back on track—and all those happy, adoptive couples! Pam stood up, walked around the desk, squeezed the girl's shoulder.

"Don't worry," she murmured, handing the girl another tissue. "You've come to the right place."

Chapter Eight

Tuesday morning dawned cold and wet. Jim got up at seven announcing he had to do some last minute research before being in court at nine, so he'd just grab coffee and go. Alex woke up in a bad mood, spilled his orange juice, and took advantage of her having to nurse Rebecca by quietly putting on the TV and becoming obsessively immersed in *Power Rangers*. When she got Rebecca down, she followed a trail of Cheerios to the study TV and found Alex with only his pants and socks on, still in his pajama top and not even aware of her presence or the smoke that she was sure was pouring from her ears. She felt the rage build inside her. It was eight-thirty. The bus would stop in two minutes. Alex would definitely miss it. Her anger threatened to burst the dam that she was scrambling to build in front of it. Lately, her temper seemed to have developed a life and will of its own, rearing unexpectedly and blinding her with its force. She abruptly turned and left the room. He's going to miss the bus anyway, she told herself and then went to the laundry room and hurled the brittle plastic measuring cup onto the cement floor several times until the cup finally broke and she felt better.

When she got upstairs, she was greeted by Alex's sheepish smile. "I'm sorry, Mommy, I couldn't resist. I'll finish dressing now and be ready in a jippy." They got to school at nine-ten, too late to walk in with his class, but not late enough to require a tardy slip. When she saw Mac hurrying Sammy along the wet sidewalk, and Alex, probably still trying to make amends, agreed to walk in with them so that she didn't have to unbuckle Rebecca and drag her out into the rain again, she thought that maybe today wouldn't be all bad. "Bye, sweetie, have a good day." She hugged Alex and sent him out into a huge gust of wet wind.

"Can you wait a minute?" Mac called.

"Sure," Annie yelled back, and sat waiting, keeping the motor running so the stop wouldn't wake Rebecca.

"Annie"—Mac jumped in the passenger side and closed the door behind her—"I need you to pick up Sam this afternoon. I'll be able to pick him up by four at the latest. I totally forgot about this stupid doctor's appointment, and I'm just afraid I won't make it back in time. Can you do it?"

"Of course." Annie smiled. "No problem."

"Ah, honey, you're the best. Now tell me, how are your new neighbors doing? Are they nosy or normal?"

Annie blushed. "Nosy" was an interesting word choice. She couldn't help herself. Mac would think it was funny, not disgusting.

"Oh, Mac, I'm so embarrassed. I've got to tell you something. Oh God . . ."

"Sugar, what is it? True confessions? I love it. Did you fall in love with the husband already? Are you going to abandon your children and break Jim's heart? Come on, tell!"

"No, no, don't get excited. It's nothing that good. See, before we ever went over there for the cookout, actually, before I even met Lesley, this weird thing happened with our monitor. I was starting to do some work after the kids were in bed, and suddenly I heard this woman in the baby's room."

Mac looked puzzled.

"Her voice was coming over the monitor. I thought, naturally, that it was coming from Rebecca's room. I even ran upstairs and ransacked her room looking for the intruder." Mac was laughing now. "It's not funny. I was terrified." But then Annie began laughing, too. "You should have seen Jim's face. He didn't know what the hell I was doing. I was like a raving lunatic."

Mac shook her head. "No, I know what you're talking about. We used to get our neighbors over our cordless phone sometimes. But it was only once in a while, and you never knew when it was going to happen. Like, you couldn't *count* on it. But then Nick called the company and they sent us a new phone that was set to a different channel or something, and it stopped happening."

"Well, this is a little different," Annie said slowly. "All I have to do is flick the channel selector switch, and if they're home . . ."

"You hear them?" Mac asked, her eyes bright.

"Loud and clear." Annie had to laugh at the look on Mac's face. She was chomping at the bit. "Not that it was especially thrilling."

"Aw, you mean you didn't catch them doing the nasty?" Mac giggled.

"Sorry to disappoint you. The most I got out of it was the knowledge that while David's at grand rounds on Tuesdays and Thursdays, Lesley takes Millie to one of those Gym 'n Swim classes."

Mac snorted. "I took Sammy to those when he was a baby. What a joke. He screamed every time he got near the water and spent the entire winter on amoxicillin due to a steady stream of ear infections. I think I sent the entire staff of College Hill Pediatrics to the Bahamas that year."

"Well, apparently, Miss Millicent *loves* the water—"

"Of course."

Annie stopped for a minute. She didn't like the way she

sounded. This sometimes happened when she was with
Mac. She got into this catty thing that she really didn't like.

"Anyway, I feel terrible now because right before the
cookout I listened in again and they were fighting and now
I know all this stuff I shouldn't know and I really like Les-
ley and I just feel like a big jerk, so I had to tell someone.
Now that I've confessed, you can give me a couple of Hail,
Marys and I'll be able to kick the habit."

"Now, Annie, you always feel guilty about everything.
You didn't hurt anyone. And nothing bad's going to come of
it. As long as you promise to tell me every detail next time
you do it!"

They laughed so hard, Rebecca woke up screaming.

The jarring music of the commercial snapped Annie out
of her reverie. She had been picturing them all at the beach
this summer. The baby sleeping peacefully under their
bright umbrella, Alex and Jim building a drip castle in the
wet sand down by the water's edge, and herself stretched out
with a trashy suspense thriller. Nursing always relaxed her.
She would start out worrying about everything she needed
to do, and five minutes into the nursing a calm drowsiness
would descend. It reminded her of a feeling she sometimes
had as a child when her best friend would brush her hair. It
was a feeling of absolute relaxation, as if her whole body
had let go of every muscle it was tensing. The stress left her,
and she sat in a pleasantly drowsy stupor until the commercial's music woke her from her daydreaming and she was
confronted afresh with the reality that was her life: a sleeping infant at her breast, a cereal bowl with a shallow pool of
leftover milk coating its bottom, and three bloated Cheerios
beginning to stick to the side, a half empty mug of coffee,
and a trail of crumbs leading to the burnt, crescent remains
of an English muffin, with a drop of sticky orange-colored
jam smeared next to the muffin . . . and in the study, the

ever-present pile of clothes and a new batch of copy to be
written. Moving was the last thing she wanted to do, but
with every ounce of willpower she had she hauled herself
off the couch and carried Rebecca up the stairs to her room.
She edged the door open with her foot, shifting her weight
carefully, so as not to wake Rebecca. The room was tiny.
She had to smile, remembering a babysitter who had
watched Alex while she and Jim painted this room. The sitter had referred to it as "the nursery." That seemed a grand
term for this shoebox, Annie thought. An adult standing at
the changing table could keep one hand on the baby and still
reach a receiving blanket hanging over the side of the crib;
the room was that narrow.

She laid Rebecca down and covered her with the blanket
she had lovingly crocheted in those pregnant months that
now seemed another lifetime ago. How had she ever had
time to crochet? Would she ever have time like that again?
She leaned into the crib and kissed Rebecca on her silky
head. Turning to leave the room, she noticed the monitor on
the bureau, and felt a now familiar twinge of curiosity. She
knew listening in was wrong but it *was* exciting. Glimpsing
somebody else's real life had made her want to hear more.
She glanced at her watch—ten o'clock. And it was Tuesday.
She put temptation aside. No one would be home across the
street this morning—weren't Lesley and Millie at Gym 'n
Swim? And David at grand rounds? She quietly closed Rebecca's door and went to the study desk. She flicked on the
monitor, and to the rhythm of Rebecca's even breathing,
began to write the copy for the pants lying in front of her.

"We wish these came in grown-up sizes, they look so
comfortable: a covered elasticized waist and a nice full
cut with slightly tapered legs that can be rolled up or not
to suit the wearer's fancy . . ."

The sudden whoosh of car wheels on the soaked street broke her concentration. She looked up when she heard the crunch of gravel from the Shields' driveway. There was the black Jaguar with David at the wheel. No one in the passenger seat, she noted with disappointment, and immediately was disturbed to realize how excited she had been at the thought of hearing another conversation between Lesley and David.

She picked up the pants and tried to concentrate. Her eyes wandered to the window. He hadn't turned on any lights across the street, even though the rain made it a dark day.

Oh well, she told herself, he's probably at the back of the house; maybe he's working in that incredible study of his. Maybe he forgot some papers or something.

She looked back at the pants. Pants, pants, but what made these special? She called up one in a series of imagined children that she used for models in her head. She had the blond curly-headed girl stand blowing the fuzz off a dandelion— the pants looked unremarkable. She switched to a boy sticking a frog in a pocket, an overused image, she thought, but it made her focus on the pockets. They were nice and big; you actually could get a frog in them. Do kids really do that? she wondered. Being a city kid, Alex didn't see any frogs. They should move. She felt a pang of urgency about leaving the city.

Don't start, she told herself. You'll get nothing done if you begin obsessing about how small the house is, how tiny the yard is, how bad the city is for kids. Pockets, she reminded herself, and wrote:

"Two large, front patch pockets, angled for expansion, can hold just about anything. A terrific pant for boys and girls."

She looked out the window again: rain and a dark house across the street. She looked at her watch. It was 10:25. He would have had time to grab a forgotten paper, she thought. She glanced at the monitor. Just for company, she said to herself as she fingered the channel selector switch. All I'll hear is David moving around his house. I probably won't even hear that. He's probably nowhere near the baby's room, she thought, unless they move it around like I do, depending on where I put the baby down. Her finger pushed the switch to channel B. Nothing. Just a quiet, steady background hum. She was relieved. She couldn't be a demented person who eavesdropped on neighbors if all she was hearing was a hum. She left it on channel B and picked up the shorts again.

Annie was startled once or twice when she heard a rustle or some change, something moving above the hum on the monitor, but then she settled down and focused on her work. She had spread the different-colored tank tops across her desk and was contemplating how to describe the terrific tones when she heard a sigh over the monitor. She turned up the volume. It sounded like steps on thick carpeting: climbing stairs, she thought, because the breathing sounded labored. Mr. Jag's out of shape, she said to herself, if walking upstairs makes him breathe like that. Too much steak, she thought, and smiled to herself. At least I won't die young— I don't have the income to eat myself into an early grave.

There was another sigh and a thud, and she had a mental image of herself carrying the laundry basket upstairs and dropping it on the landing to be dealt with later. Why was this guy carrying laundry upstairs when he was late for grand rounds?

Wet, smacking noises, like kissing, she thought, and her eyes widened.

"You're heavy," she heard him say in a teasing voice.

And Annie felt the hair stand up straight on the base of her neck. He wasn't alone.

I shouldn't be hearing this, she thought, and then, in spite of herself, she listened, transfixed, not wanting to miss a sound. Somebody was running down a hall, a woman's giggle, heavier footsteps down the hall. Bedsprings, as if someone had thrown themselves down on the bed.

"Mmm . . . bring that over here," she heard David say.

"Again," a woman said. *"Already?"* And then the breathing intensified and moaning began, very quiet at first, and then higher and quicker. Annie shut off the monitor. She put her hand to her forehead. She was breathing quickly, and she felt sick to her stomach. She had never heard anybody making love except in the movies. She knew what she and Jim sounded like, and she knew their noises were necessarily stifled now that the children's rooms were so close to theirs. But hearing somebody else—they sounded like animals.

She shook her head, trying to banish the sounds that were replaying in her head. Now she'd really heard something she shouldn't have, like some kind of depraved Peeping Tom. Could it possibly have been Lesley there with David? She almost didn't know which was worse—finding out that Lesley's husband was cheating on her or knowing exactly what her neighbors sounded like having sex. She really felt sick. Don't vomit, she told herself, and sat very still wondering what exactly made her feel so nauseated—their noises or the fact that she had listened in on them?

Chapter Nine

"Oh, damn." Annie pulled a black stocking with a huge run off her leg and flung it into the bedroom wastebasket.

"You're getting pretty dressed up," Jim said. "Don't you and Mac usually go for fish and chips or Indian?"

"Uh-huh, but Lesley's coming tonight and—"

"Say no more," interrupted Jim. "I don't think a fish fry is the Shields' idea of eating out. I'd like to be a fly on the wall for dinner with Mac and Lesley."

"Ow, oh, my God." Annie collapsed on the bed, rubbing the ball of her foot which now bore the deep imprint of a Lego block. "Boys," Annie said, her jaw set and her eyes narrowed, "can't you play somewhere else while I'm dressing?" She turned toward Alex, her voice softening. "Sweetie, get Daddy to take his toys into your room."

"But, Mom, everything's all set up."

"No, come on, Alex," said Jim. "Let's get out of Mommy's hair."

Annie watched them in the mirror while she combed her hair and debated which earrings to wear, simple silver hoops in deference to Lesley's understated taste or the funky wire nudes that she knew Mac would appreciate.

She heard the doorbell ring and Alex's trademark two-stairs-at-a-time sprint. Then Mac's low voice singsonging to

Alex. She decided on the nudes. She stood up and kissed Jim
good-bye.

"Have fun, beautiful. You look great. Call me if you're
going to be later than eleven. Otherwise I call the cops."

Annie and Mac walked across the street to Lesley's.

"You look like you're going on a blind date, Annie.
Loosen up."

"I feel nervous. I want you to like each other. Go easy on
her, Mac, okay? I mean, keep the shock quotient to a mini-
mum."

"You're worried about me? Think I might say something
inappropriate? Is she that much of a princess? Are we going
to have any fun?"

"It'll be fun. She's not a princess. I've just never heard
her swear, for instance, and she doesn't talk about sex."

"Sex," said Mac in mock horror and hip-checked Annie,
who shoved her back, so they were giggling like adolescents
when David answered the door.

It turned out that Lesley was eager to try Phoebe's. She
had heard a lot about it, but David never wanted to go. And
Annie knew from long experience that it was one of Mac's
favorite restaurants. So why did she feel like she had to be
the host of the evening?

Sarah, the waitress, who had served Annie weekly
through her last pregnancy, greeted her with a hug.
"Where's the baby tonight? At home with Daddy? Bring her
next time. I'll hold her while you guys eat."

"A waitress with a heart of gold," said Mac, winking at
Lesley. "Sarah has seen Annie and me through morning
sickness and many mental health evenings." Lesley smiled.

They drank a bottle of zinfandel and ate a loaf of the oatmeal bread. Mac made Lesley laugh with stories about
Annie as an undergrad.

"Is your father-in-law Bart James?" Lesley asked.

"Yes," Mac said, rolling her eyes. "The dear old over-powering bear is ours."

"David has a lot of respect for him. He was a real micro-surgery pioneer, Dave says."

"Mm-hmmm," said Mac, her eyes glazing slightly. "Everyone, including Bart, thinks he's a god. It made my husband's childhood pretty unbearable . . . but then I rescued him!"

"He's always charming to me," said Annie.

"Oh, sure he is, he's on when you see him. And you're young and pretty. He makes life hell for Betty. He expects her to be at his beck and call, and she is. He treats the kids the same way. To this day, Nick can't make love in his parents' house."

"Oh, I think that's pretty common," said Annie.

"How would you know? You've got Jim, who would do it anywhere, anytime."

Annie glanced at Lesley. She was smiling.

"I know what you mean," Lesley began. "My father is very forceful. David never wants to make love when we visit my parents."

"Mm-hmmm," said Mac. "Annie cannot add to the conversation because what I said about Jim is true." She stuck her tongue out at Annie.

"Bart was very sweet to me the other night," Lesley said. "David invited them to sit at our table at the Agawam, and Bart asked me all about where I came from and about Millie."

"Oh, sure. He is charming and he loves to welcome young couples into the Gagawam."

Lesley laughed. "Is that what you call the Agawam? There *are* some pretty disgusting people there."

"Tell me about it," Mac continued. "Bart is always offering to buy us a membership, but thank God, Nick stands firm. I'm just not the type. With my mouth, I'd be strung up the flagpole. And with all those waitresses in those ridiculous black-and-white uniforms looking like maids from central casting, offering you food poolside . . . My little monster would have us bankrupt the first summer!"

Maybe it was the wine, but Annie felt herself relax. Mac was funny and Lesley wasn't as naive as Annie thought. They seemed to like each other.

"Have you met Missy Phillips?" asked Mac.

"I think she's the one who gave us a tour of the facilities," said Lesley.

"Right. She would. She's Miss Gagawam, although you'd think they would have drummed her out of the corps long ago."

Annie smiled. Mac used phrases from a generation ago and they seemed fresh coming from her.

Lesley's eyes widened. "Gossip? Great."

Gossip. Annie suddenly felt sober. Gossip, eavesdropping. She was such a hypocrite, inviting Lesley out to meet Mac, and listening to her and her husband behind her back. What a jerk.

"Oh, yeah," Mac was saying. "She was screwing this young French tennis pro they brought in to teach the kiddies."

"You're kidding."

"No. They were always popping into her cabana. Talk about indiscreet."

"What about her husband?" Annie asked.

"He was always on the golf course. It was her kids that made it so sad. I mean, everyone was talking about it. They must have picked up something. The oldest boy was probably twelve then."

"What finally happened?"

"Well, a bunch of the venerable fathers of the club, Bart included, shipped Andre back to France and then gave Missy some sort of talk and that was that. But every once in a while some member goes haywire, and you get a summer soap opera."

"Did her husband ever find out?" asked Lesley.

"That was a mystery," said Mac. "If he knew, he never let on. Although who knows what he did at home. He's pretty much of a bastard. He could have done anything."

"So, if he knew he forgave her?" said Lesley.

"Oh, I doubt it," Mac snorted. "I imagine he found little ways to make her pay. I don't think men ever forgive screwing around. The night before Nick and I got married, he said 'If I ever find out you've cheated on me, I'll kill you.'"

"Nick said that?" Annie asked, incredulous.

"Does that surprise you? That I could provoke jealousy?"

"No, Mac, I think you're capable of provoking every instinct known to modern man. Nick just seems so laid-back . . ."

"What about you, Mac?" Lesley asked. "What would you do if you found out Nick was cheating on you?"

"Well, little darlin', it would never happen. Nick knows I'm the best around. Did y'all ever hear that story about Paul Newman? Some interviewer asked him why it was he was never in the tabloids, how he and Joanne Woodward managed to stay married in Hollywood. He said, 'It's simple. Why go out for hamburger when you can have steak at home?'"

"Another nice woman-as-meat analogy," said Annie.

Mac winked at Lesley. "I think it's romantic."

"Do you think some men just cheat no matter who they have at home?" asked Lesley.

Annie glanced at Mac, who had no way of knowing how important this might be.

"Yes," said Mac. "I think for some men it is something they are driven to do. They've never really grown up, I guess. They still think with their peckers, like a fourteen-year-old."

Lesley looked at Annie. "What do you think?"

Annie chose her words carefully. She wished she knew if David was cheating or if it had been Lesley with him that morning.

"Well, I used to think that I could never stay married to Jim if I knew he'd had an affair. It seemed the cruelest betrayal . . ." Annie paused. Lesley didn't seem particularly pained. She doesn't know, thought Annie. Or maybe it was Lesley with David the other morning, she thought hopefully. Yeah, right. "But now—"

"Now that you're older and wiser," Mac interjected.

"Right," Annie smiled. "Now I think marriages are extraordinarily complex. There are no general rules. All sorts of pressures and circumstances can cause actions that once would seem unacceptable to be something that you find yourself able to work around. I'm not so quick to judge anymore."

"Annie?" Mac said, "Queen of the moral high road mellowing?"

Lesley laughed.

"Oh, come off it, Mac. I was always *your* friend, wasn't I?"

Mac reached over and patted her hand. "Yes, you were, darlin', even though I was such a slut."

Annie looked at Lesley. She seemed to be enjoying herself. "You were no sluttier than any of the other Southerners."

"Well, thank you, Anniekins. But let us not forget that the slut of the dorm was a Yankee."

Annie laughed uproariously and managed to gasp, "Amherst."

Mac wiped her eyes with her napkin. "Let's tell Lesley about the girls we went to school with."

"You," Annie got out before she was laughing again.

"Well," began Mac, "we had these two girls on our floor.

They were seniors when we were sophomores, and they were infamous. They had roomed together since freshman year and they kept a running tally—"

"—competing with each other," Annie interrupted.

"—of all the guys they slept with. They started freshman year, and by the time we knew them they had a couple of hundred—"

"More like three," said Annie.

"—between them," said Mac. "And they had developed an intricate grading system. They had this large sketch pad propped up in the corner of their room, and they added each new name."

"They had a key," said Annie, "you know, like on a map, a symbol key."

"Right, and they would grade each guy on things like kissing, foreplay, pillow talk . . ."

"And they also had categories, stuff like, nice person/lousy lay, great lay/yucky person, or Liked Him Better Before having sex or Liked Him Better After having sex, whether or not they would stay the night with them . . ."

"Oh, yeah. It was very thorough, and they had some interesting symbols thought up . . ."

"That's right," said Annie, "penile size was color-coded. I remember that one. Hot pink was for the largest and black was the smallest, and there were gradations in between."

"And they used a clock for the Duration of Actual Act."

"And they shared guys."

"Shared them?" said Lesley.

"Not what you're thinking," said Annie. "They were promiscuous, but they weren't kinky. They had set limits on what they would or would not do. The Amherst story proves that. No, they traded names . . ."

"You know," said Mac, "if someone got a really high rating and a hot pink code, the other would try to check him out."

"They used to see if they agreed . . ." suggested Lesley.

"If hot pink for one was hot pink for the other." Mac laughed.

"Tell me the Amherst story," said Lesley.

Annie held out her hand, palm up, indicating that Mac should tell it.

"Well, one Sunday night Sally and Hope came back from a weekend at Amherst and went right in to fill in their sketchpad."

"We knocked on their door to see how the weekend had gone," said Annie.

"Hope was filling in a record on a guy named Brad. He was getting pitiful marks. We said, 'Pretty bad weekend, huh?' Hope said, 'Tell me about it. I spent the whole weekend trying to get this guy, Brad. The first night he passed out. Saturday I finally nailed him, and he kept pushing my head down in his lap. So I thought, okay, I'll give him a warm-up thrill. So I start doing it, and practically at once he came in my mouth!"

Lesley was looking green.

"Wait until you hear the punch line," said Annie.

"So Hope told us she couldn't get to the bathroom because she was naked and it was down the hall, so she just spit it out on his desk and he was pissed 'cause he had an open baggy of dope on the desk and she drenched it."

"So Sally said to her, 'Why didn't you just swallow it, Hope?' "

"And Hope, who had slept with, let's not forget, over a hundred guys, said in a genuinely shocked voice, 'I didn't know him *that* well.'"

Lesley was laughing so hard she couldn't speak. She reached for the bill, and when she'd finally caught her breath, said, "That story was worth the price of dinner. It's my treat."

The others protested, but they'd all had enough wine to

make the figures seem muddled, and in the end they gave in
and thanked her. They drove home in comfortable, sleepy silence. Lesley got out first. Mac turned to Annie.

"You're looking pretty pleased with yourself."

"Well, I had fun, didn't you? It went well. She's more fun
than I thought."

"Yup. I didn't seem to horrify her. I think she's got potential."

"Mac, what did you think about the infidelity question?
Do you think she's worried about David?"

"Huh? Oh, I thought she was just making conversation."

Mac looked closely at Annie. "Do you know something,
Annie?"

"I don't know. I listened on Tuesday morning."

"Tsk, tsk," said Mac.

"And I heard David with some woman—maybe Lesley—couldn't tell."

"You've been holding out on me! Couldn't you recognize
her voice?"

"There wasn't a lot of conversation." Annie smirked. "Do
you think she could tell I was nervous?"

"Oh, no, you were very cool. If it was an oral you would
have aced it."

"It didn't sound like she suspected anything, did it?"

"It sure didn't seem that way. You know it's possible it
was a conjugal visit. Have you heard anything else?"

"No, I haven't listened. Jim's been around and I've been
trying not to. It's too creepy. She's a friend, and I listen to
her husband doing God-knows-what with God-knows-
who?"

"Whom," corrected Mac.

"It's so sordid. Aren't you disgusted with me?"

"Are you serious? Annie, I'd be hooked so fast, I'd be listening every minute I could. You know how I always eavesdrop in restaurants. I can't get enough of other peoples'

lives. I even like looking at photo albums full of people I don't know."

"I know. It's just that I feel so dishonest around her now, and I like her."

"Well, that's your moral high road again. You're not hurting her. In fact, if she comes to you for advice, you are in a better position to help her."

"Oh, Mac, you're the queen of rationalization."

Mac laughed. "Hey, Anniekins, did you hear the one about Cleopatra? Why didn't she ever go into therapy?"

Annie sighed. "I don't know, Mac, why didn't she?"

"She was Da Queen of De-Nile."

Annie rolled her eyes while Mac laughed at her own joke.

"Right," said Annie. "I love you, Mac. Talk to you tomorrow."

"Okay, kiddo, sleep well."

Annie turned to wave after she unlocked the front door and after watching Mac drive away, she entered the dark house.

She headed for the stairs but then turned instead toward the living room. She sat on the couch, propped a pillow up against the arm and, leaning back, stared across to the Shields' house. The bedroom light was on, and at the back of the room she could see shadowy movement. She'd love to be listening now to their conversation. She wanted to hear how Lesley would describe the evening; what she'd share with David. What would she say to him about me? Annie wondered. And how would she describe Mac?

Annie pulled her legs up and rested her cheek against her knees. She watched the Shields' window but nobody appeared. Lesley had really opened up tonight. Annie was surprised at how much Lesley had seemed to like Mac. She'd thought Lesley was more of a prude, more reserved. It was a nice surprise to discover that maybe eventually she and

Lesley could be really close friends, confidantes. The shadows at the back of the Shields' bedroom reappeared, and
moving closer to the window began to take shape. It was
Lesley. She was wearing a white terry robe and had a white
towel wrapped around her hair. She reached up to draw the
curtains closed. They were sheer, and for a minute Annie
could still make out Lesley's outline behind them and then
she was gone, out of Annie's view. To bed? Annie wondered.
She was all showered. Annie had a mental image of David
waiting on the bed, Lesley letting her robe drop to the thick,
creamy carpet. "Umm, bring that over here," David would
say. Had it been Lesley last Tuesday on the monitor with
David? Were those Lesley's noises? Annie didn't like to
think about the noises. It made her feel doubly creepy about
listening in, made her seem like a deranged pervert, a Peeping Tom. Still, they had sounded so hot for each other. Annie
loved making love with Jim, but it hadn't been like that
since college, when they were first discovering sex and each
other, and still somewhat taking their cues from the movies,
making sounds they'd heard there. Could David and Lesley
still have that incredible first falling-in-love animal attrac-
tion? Annie felt genuinely jealous if that were the case. She
thought that she and Jim had a good marriage, maybe even
a great one, but that incredible white hot passion wasn't really part of it, she thought sadly. Could it really have been
Lesley with David? She thought about it. What was the difference between what she had heard and her own experience
with married sex? She decided it was the element of wonder
and surprise present only with someone new. You discover
something that they love and that drives you wild and your
excitement makes them crazy with desire and on and on.
Once you know someone as well as she knew Jim there
weren't many surprises left—and that had its own wonderful side—but it was different. The question was, did the
Shields know something she didn't about keeping the ro-

mance alive? Coming home to make love at ten-thirty in the morning was certainly a start. Was Lesley a closet wild woman? She couldn't make the image stick, not even with the more relaxed Lesley she'd seen tonight. She was pretty sure David was up to no good with someone else. Poor Lesley, she thought. But as she climbed the stairs, her thoughts turned to Jim and the idea of some regular, old, married sex seemed great to her.

Jim whispered "Hello" as she tiptoed to the bathroom. And while she was preparing for bed her mind kept wondering about Lesley and David. Was Lesley the woman she had heard with David? And if she wasn't, did she know that there was another woman? She had asked that question— "Do you think some men cheat, no matter who they have at home?" Did she know? Was she trying to decide whether to live with it or not? Or was there anything for her to know? The thoughts went round and round, chasing each other in her head. She shut off the light and a new thought appeared. The only way she would find out the answers was to keep listening in. She pulled back the covers and reached through the darkness for Jim.

Jaime calculated the time difference. He would have to call him at home, maybe even wake him up, but waiting until morning and calling the hospital was impossible. He might reach David, he might not. It was too time-consuming and uncertain.

On the second ring Lesley answered, sounding sleepy.

"Lesley, my dear, this is Jaime Ruiz."

"Hello, Jaime."

"I am sorry to have disturbed you at this hour."

"You haven't disturbed me. I was reading."

"Is it possible for me to speak with your charming husband?"

"Of course." Jaime could hear muffled movements and then David's deep voice.

"Jaime, hello. What is it?"

"I have had a call again from our Mr. Aziz. He is most anxious to begin. He will be arriving sometime next week."

"I understand. When, exactly?"

"I am waiting for his travel plans to be confirmed. You will be the first to know. But I wanted to give you time to obtain all the necessary materials."

"I see. I appreciate that. I don't anticipate any problems—good night, Jaime." David hung up.

Jaime was furious. David had just dismissed him. "I don't anticipate any problems. Good night, Jaime." How dare he? Jaime had placed the call. It was *he* who should decide when to terminate the conversation. Shields was no different from any of the others from the States. It had been clear to him, even in his residency days, that as a Mexican he would never rise in the hospital ranks. He would always be a wetback, no matter how superior his surgical skills. They made all their snide comments about incompetent docs, their degrees in Mexico or Mexican correspondence schools, with him standing there. One of the kinder ones might say, "No offense, Ruiz." What did they think? How could it not be offensive?

And David was no different, with his superior attitude. Jaime knew that from David's point of view the partnership was all about money. David could never afford to outfit a clinic personally. Not without asking Lesley—and risking exposure. He needed Jaime's capital. Well, that was a two-way street. Jaime needed David's supply of samples. In his own Catholic country, he never could have obtained the necessary steady stream of tissue without arousing suspicion. But David also had no idea about Jaime's plans. When the time came to publish, and Jaime went public there would be only one name on the findings—Jaime Ruiz, MD. And David would cause no fuss because it was illegal in his country. He would never admit his role. Jaime would leapfrog over all of them and show them he was no ignorant Mexican but the genuine article; a medical genius, a humanitarian hero—an Einstein, a Schweitzer.

Chapter Ten

This was the part Pam hated. Entering the parking garage furtively, like some criminal. She darted by Tommy's booth while he had his back to her but she was always afraid he'd turn around. She could imagine his thick, nasal voice. Poor Tommy, still a child at age—what was he, forty? Forty-five? "Hey, Pammy," he'd say, "where ya goin'? Today is"—a pause and obvious mental strain, then a relieved, proud smile—"Tuesday. This isn't one of your mornings."

Why are you so nervous? she chided herself. She could just say she was picking up some paperwork. Tommy would accept that. He knew nothing of locked files or confidentiality; that patients' files were never removed from the office except, of course, for the cover sheet that went to the hospital two weeks before each patient's due date. Still, although it seemed silly, every week her heart pounded until she was around the corner and out of Tommy's sight. Then, of course, she had to deal with a more serious anxiety attack. Tommy was easy—he'd believe anything she said. But what if a doctor came through, or a girl from another office? She still hadn't worked out a believable response if they asked. She was at David's car now. She stood and listened. The elevator was just around the corner from Tommy's booth. She could hear the door open if someone came down, and she'd be able to hear footsteps. Chances were it would just be a

patient from another office who wouldn't recognize her.
And she knew she could count on Tommy to shout out a
greeting. Thanks to the small staff cafeteria very few people
needed to leave the building for coffee. Many offices didn't
even open until 9:30 so it was still too early at 9:45 for many
patients to be finished and on their way out. She gave herself this same pep talk every Tuesday.

She fumbled with the key, and in spite of herself, her
hands shook. The key had been David's idea. Once she had
managed to work her schedule around his free time, so that
Tuesday was her late day (she didn't have to be at work until
one), he had suggested that she take the key to his car. "That
way there's no risk of anyone seeing us together," he had explained. This was a small, intimate New England city. And,
as David often told her, it was so ingrown that there was always someone who knew someone who knew you, so to risk
going to a hotel was impossible. There was no time to drive
out to the country, so they always went to his house with its
private back entry.

"You can come into the garage and slip into the back, get
down on the floor, cover yourself up with that cashmere
throw back there, and nobody, not even me, will know what
a sexy surprise package is hiding in my car. After we're out
of the garage and driving along you can surprise me." And
he had smiled his sleepy, longing smile at her. She felt something flip over inside her belly and a wet warmth spread between her legs. No one had ever made her feel this way. His
very gaze could make her feel more sexually excited than
she had felt during the actual lovemaking with other men.
And in bed . . . she couldn't even think about that without
quivering. She sometimes felt that she was losing her mind.
The sexual pull she felt toward David was so overpowering.
She didn't feel in control of herself, especially once he
started touching her, spreading her open with his wonderful,
long fingers, teasing her nipples with his tongue. He seemed

to read her mind, or more accurately, her body. He antici-
pated her every desire. Just when his fingers felt too rough,
there was his tongue with its light, flicking licks. Before
David, she had always been silent in bed, believing that sex
was much overrated and that moans and yelps were a Hollywood invention, but with him she was always glad they
were in his empty house and not some thin-walled hotel
room. The sounds that escaped from her were so animalistic; deep moans, shrill screeches. She heard them in the
background as if they were coming from someone else and
now, opening the lock, pausing to listen for the elevator and
to look over her shoulder before stooping quickly to the
backseat floor, she blushed, remembering the sounds he
drew out of her.

She glanced at her watch, a gold Rolex with diamond
chips surrounding the crystal, a one-year anniversary gift
from David, with the inscription on the back that read: "For
P.P. Love, D." "P.P." stood for Pamela Perfect, a name David
had made up for her. He never called her Pam, always Ms.
P. or P.P. No one had ever given her a pet name before and
she felt it meant a lot.

It was 9:50. He should be coming off the elevator any
minute. She reached up and relocked the back door. David
didn't like any telltale signs that she was in the car. He liked
to be totally surprised by her presence. "Every week I tell
myself that you haven't been able to meet me. Then it's all
the more exciting when I feel that incredible hand of yours."
This week she would give him an extra surprise, she decided, and pulling the blanket over her head she began taking off her clothes. The wonderful smell of the Jaguar's
leather interior and the incredible feel of the soft cashmere
against her bare skin were intoxicating. By the time she took
off her underpants, she was shocked at how damp they were.
She strained to hear the elevator doors or his footsteps but
the car was so well made that no outside sounds penetrated

her hiding place. She felt her whole body start at the sudden opening of the driver's door. She felt the gentle rocking of the car as David, all six three and two hundred pounds of him, settled himself in the driver's seat. She heard the engine purr and felt the car smoothly turn toward Tommy's booth. She heard the electric buzz of David's window being lowered. "Bye, Tommy. I'm off to the hospital. See you at noon."

"Bye, Dr. Shields." Tommy sounded thrilled. She could picture him waving energetically until the car was out of sight.

Then the electric buzz again and then silence. The car stopped at the first traffic light. Anytime after they passed this light she could make her move. Usually she tried to hold out, tried to keep him in suspense. Was she in the back or not? Once, she actually waited until he had pulled into his driveway and later, after they had made love twice, he confessed that he had felt crushed thinking that she hadn't kept their date. His eyes had actually looked moist as he told her this and she considered that absolute proof of his love for her.

Today was different. She couldn't wait to touch him. She wanted to fondle and tease him. She wanted to make him feel as desperate a pull toward her as she felt toward him. As soon as the car accelerated she slipped her hand out from under the throw and slid her arm up over his thigh. Unzipping his pants, she reached inside. Her fingers closed around his already incredibly stiff erection, and she began stroking quickly up to the tip and then slowly back down to the base. She could hear her own breath coming quicker. David let out a quiet, deep moan. The car turned into the driveway, swung into the curve at the back of the house, and pulled up by the back door. It was pouring rain. She pulled the blanket loosely around her body and up over her head. As soon as the kitchen door closed behind them she dropped the blanket. She saw the look of utter pleasure as David looked at her naked body. "Oh, baby," he groaned and reached for her. They sunk to their knees and he pushed her back on the soft cashmere, and there, without even going upstairs, they made love.

Annie woke up feeling terrific. Help was on its way. She held on to the prospect of the upcoming interview with Jessica Kelleher as if it were a lifeline. Soon she might actually be able to get some work done. Just thinking of it, she felt the pressure lessening already. She was patient with Alex and he still made the bus. When she was able to relax he was charming, pointing out the flowers on the way to the bus stop, flooring her with all he knew about them. He remembered everything anyone ever said to him. At times like this she felt awed by the near perfection of her children.

Rebecca was now asleep at her breast. Knowing that she would probably nap for a while, Annie ticked off her options. She could bake bread. She could get a jump on dinner. She could read—no, too indulgent. She probably ought to just try to get some copy written. She looked at her watch: ten-fifteen. She glanced at the monitor. She thought of last Tuesday—had it been Lesley with David? Lesley went to Gym 'n Swim on Tuesday mornings. But an affair? In his own house? In Lesley's bed? She made a face. He'd probably get a thrill out of the riskiness involved. She lay Rebecca down on the couch and walked to the monitor. No, she wouldn't do it. Those sounds last week . . . she didn't want to hear them again. But she *did* want to know. She almost felt she *should* know, for Lesley's sake. Not that she could tell her if she did hear anything—it was hardly her place. Or was it? Wouldn't I want her to tell me if it were Jim having an affair? She looked over at the house. Was he home? No clue. The house looked empty, and the driveway curved around in back, so that you couldn't necessarily tell if a car was there. She had seen Lesley leave with Millie earlier, so if she heard David with a woman it couldn't be her. Then she'd know for sure. No, she told herself, mind your own business. But then she flicked the switch from A to B.

David's deep voice. *"God, I love those legs."*

A woman's voice. *"I love those legs."*

"Give me a break," thought Annie. The woman's voice didn't sound like Lesley's, but she couldn't be sure yet. Had Lesley come home? Sure. Two weeks in a row she skips Gym 'n Swim, ditches Millie somewhere, and sneaks back home to make passionate love to her husband. Uh-huh. Annie sat down, inclining her head toward the monitor.

"You're a beauty," David's voice continued. *"A fresh-from-the-farm beauty, peaches and cream. I'd like to see you in all your freckled splendor lying on a pile of hay."*

"It's going to be hard to find hay here in the city, Big D."

"Ooh, look what happens when you call me that."

"It looks mighty inviting, sir, but we don't have time. I said I'd go in early today for a nurses' meeting."

"Oh, Pam."

Annie felt the wind knocked out of her. Pammy. That shit, David. Sam Casey's Pam? It could be, and it could have been David at the back door of Casey's office. Or, she reminded herself, it could be some other "Pammy" completely.

"You know, David, if you were to fly home with me and meet my parents, I could show you lots of hay."

"Oh, I bet you could, babe, but I can't do that just yet."

"Have you said anything to Lesley?"

"Not yet. She's been so thrilled with the baby and all that I can't pull the rug out from under her yet."

"Bastard," Annie said. "Right in your own house. God-damn bastard, Lesley is crazy about you." She was yelling at the monitor.

"Oh, shit," said David. *"Look what all this talk about her has done to me."*

"We don't have time anyway. I told you that . . . David, no!"

Annie shut off the monitor. "Well," she told herself, "now you know. Satisfied?"

The answer, of course, was no.

Chapter Eleven

"What are you going to wear tonight?" Annie asked as Jim came into the room, still wet from the shower. She loved the way he looked with his curls damp and falling down his forehead.

"What am I *allowed* to wear?" he asked with that same smirk that she had seen countless times on Alex's face.

"Very funny." Annie smiled. "How about your dark suit but with that funky tie?"

"See what I mean?" said Jim. "I was thinking about my khakis—the ones with no holes—and this shirt." He held up what she thought of as his Ernest Hemingway shirt. Forever formulating catalogue copy, she'd describe it as a butter-soft Egyptian cotton, a sage green color with two button pockets cut full. It hung soft and loose and made her think for some reason of Hemingway lounging in the afternoon at 27 rue de Fleurus with Gertrude Stein. It was a great shirt, wonderful for raking leaves or cuddling on the couch, or even an informal day at the office, but not for David and Lesley's party.

She shook her head gently. "Sorry, James. Not tonight. Tonight we dress up. Please?"

Jim reached in and pulled a suit from the closet.

"Quite right, madame. Just as you say," and he kissed her on the cheek. "Mmm, you smell good." He held her away

from him. His eyes wandered slowly down her body. She
had on nothing but a black bra and matching panties.
"Mmmm. You *look* good. Doing anything after the party?"

She stepped toward him, lifting her face and kissing him,
one long kiss. "More of that, I hope."

They dressed back-to-back and Annie listened happily to
all the small, pleasant domestic sounds: the hairbrush in her
hair, Jim's change jar clinking as his top drawer opened, the
smooth swoosh of his socks going on, her lips' soft smack
against the Kleenex, Jim swearing softly to himself over his
tie. Maybe she'd swallow her pride and tell Jim about the
listening in tonight. She didn't want to have a secret inner
life that Jim knew nothing about. Now she really had a secret—a big one—and she had no one to blame but herself.
Maybe he could guilt her into stopping—she *did* want to
stop, especially if they were going to go on seeing the
Shields socially.

She smiled to herself remembering the opening of *Peter
Pan,* which she was currently reading to Alex. Mr. Darling
brings his tie to Mrs. Darling for her help, telling her that it
won't cooperate with him. Around the bedpost, it was fine,
but around his neck it begged to be excused. The thought of
the ritual of grown-ups, married people, getting ready to go
out on the town was exciting to her even now that she was
part of it. Her parents' room had always seemed magically
transformed into a bustling, exciting whirl of activity when
they were preparing to go out. During the week, it was a
place of comfort, a safe haven from a nightmare or a sunny
expanse of soft pillowy warmth to lie in and read a book.
But occasionally, on Saturday nights, it filled with wonderful smells; her mother's special perfume, her father's after-
shave. Bright silk colors would slide over her mother's head,
layer after layer, lace slips would be pulled and adjusted,
earrings put in, necklaces on, and bright red lipstick, leaving
a perfect kiss on the Kleenex. She would sometimes retrieve

it from her mother's wastebasket and smell it in her mother's bed after the babysitter had shut out the light. That was the special deal, that when her parents went out, she was allowed to sleep in their bed until they came home.

And now here she was at the other end of the mystery, the tired, disheveled mom who goes up to shower and dress to go out and emerges from her room, miraculously glamorous in a black mini sheath with shiny black high heels, pink lip-sticked lips, and sparkly jewelry.

"Wow, Mom, you look beautiful. You really do." Alex was beaming. "You, too, Dad, totally handsome."

Annie knelt down to hug Alex. He looked dazzled by her perfume, her jewelry, her transformation. I know, she thought, it is magical, and tomorrow morning I'll be just plain mom again.

"I love you, sweetie. Take good care of your sister and have fun with Mrs. Franz." Alex made a face, and started to say something.

"I know," Annie whispered, "but it's only for tonight. I'm going to try to have someone more fun for you here next time. Daddy got you *Hook* at the video store. Why don't you go down and get it? You can watch it on my bed until you fall asleep."

She laughed as he ran down the stairs, whooping, to get the movie. Then she dropped her lipstick into her little black purse with the tissues and her emergency twenty and, snapping it shut, followed Alex downstairs to give the sitter her final instructions.

"David sure knows how to do things right," said Jim as they pulled into the Agawam's parking lot and could see a valet with white gloves motioning them to stop by the front door. Annie reached down—a MacDonald's bag and a plastic cup top lay at her feet. She threw them onto the floor behind her seat.

Inside, the club's smaller ballroom was crowded with people they didn't know. Everyone was drinking cocktails and talking in small groups. Annie recognized Mac's father-in-law, Bart James, across the room and waved. He gave her a courtly bow and resumed talking to a handsome, silver-haired gentleman. "Is that the governor with Bart?" Annie asked Jim.

"Yup," said Jim, "and that's Bob Dylan serving the cocktails. Annie, you need to get that glasses prescription filled. Actually, I believe that's the new head of the university. I recognize him from his picture in the paper."

"Oh sure. You're probably right. Mac said Bart wants to become head of the med school."

"Annie"—Lesley hugged her—"you look fantastic."

"Hi, Lesley." Jim bent and kissed her cheek. "You look pretty fabulous yourself."

"Thanks, Jim, so do you. I love the tie."

Jim winked at Annie.

Lesley did look radiant, Annie thought. David was approaching their group. It felt to Annie like a dark cloud about to descend. Why couldn't he see how lovely Lesley was, how kind, how in love—and stick with her alone? David made Annie feel suddenly cold.

"Good evening, neighbors." David put his arm on Lesley's shoulder. He took Jim's hand and kissed Annie's cheek. "We're glad you could come celebrate with us." He pulled Lesley close to him. "Annie, you look marvelous; Cinderella is put to shame tonight." He chuckled. Annie felt deflated and angry at the same time. What kind of a back-handed compliment was that? David was the type who could probably sound charming even as he was telling you you had a terminal illness. He seemed perfect—but she knew better now. She shivered. Jim, noticing the goose bumps on her arms, rubbed her shoulders. David had already turned to Lesley.

"Darling, I want to introduce you to Morris Bigler, the new chief. Excuse us. The band's out on the terrace if you feel like dancing," David called to them over his shoulder as he led Lesley away.

Annie and Jim headed toward the terrace. These must be mostly hospital people, Annie thought, and she began scanning the crowd for Pam. It would be just like David to get some doc to bring her along. His mistress at his wife's anniversary party. But Pam wasn't in the crowd. Maybe it was over. Maybe David was finally making a commitment to Lesley. Maybe he wasn't a complete sleazebag. Jim handed her a canapé that he had grabbed from a passing tray.

"Mmmm," she said, "crabmeat and guacamole." It was delicious.

"I might be able to get used to this," Jim whispered in her ear. "Especially if you're always dressed the way you are tonight. Do you think anyone would notice if we went upstairs for a while?"

"I don't know." Annie smiled. "Mac told me the pool cabanas have been put to good use on occasion." They crossed through the open French doors onto a terrace that had been transformed into a fairyland. Every bush and tree had garlands of tiny white lights, and luminaria with tiny star cutouts lined the paths to the pools and cabanas. Annie began swaying back and forth. It was a jazz band and Annie closed her eyes and let the saxophone solo wind around her and then pull away.

"Oh, let's dance," she said to Jim.

He took her in his arms and danced her out to the freshly laid floor. "That's Scott Hamilton," he said.

"Right," Annie said. "I think I remember Lesley telling me that David went to school with Scott."

"And that's Warren Vache," said Jim. "I think he and Scott play together a lot."

"They're on that album we have," said Annie.

"Jesus," said Jim, "the band alone must be costing David thousands."

"Quiet," ordered Annie gently. "Dance. You're so romantic."

Annie was in heaven. She loved to dance with Jim. Holding each other close, his leg lightly pressing in between hers. She nuzzled his neck. He smelled so good. And she loved twenties and thirties jazz. "I was born too late," she whispered and then began singing along with the band's tune.

Everyone clapped at the end of the set and David took the microphone. "Good evening and thank you all, dear friends, for sharing this special evening with Lesley"—he held out his arm and, blushing, Lesley joined him—"and myself. For ten years now I have had the exquisite pleasure of waking up to this beautiful face every morning." Lesley blushed even deeper. "This woman has put up with my crazy schedule and my personal foibles without a complaint. She's my foundation and my fantasy and I love her." David, beaming, reached for Lesley and kissed her, a discreetly passionate kiss, amid applause from the crowd. A you-may-kiss-the-bride-now kiss, Annie thought.

"Pretty words," Jim mumbled next to Annie.

"I just hope he means them," Annie said. Jim looked a little puzzled but Annie whispered, "You're the one who's not so fond of him."

The band played Cole Porter's "Your Fabulous Face" and everyone watched David and Lesley dance.

When they swung into "They Can't Take That Away from Me," Annie pulled Jim out to join David and Lesley.

Sam Casey and his wife, Susan, danced over to Annie and Jim. "Hi," said Susan. "I've missed you at Montessori." Their son, Sean, had been in Alex's nursery and kindergarten classes.

"Oh, I've missed you, too, but we wanted to start him off in public school early because he'd have to end up there once Rebecca started school. There's no way we could afford two in private school."

"How is Rebecca?" asked Susan. "I've meant to come over and bring you something for her . . ."

"Oh, just come over," said Annie. "Don't bring anything." She liked Susan and wished she didn't have doubts about Sam.

"Look at you, Annie," said Sam, "three months postpartum and dancing like a teenager."

Annie felt uncomfortable. As her doctor, Sam shouldn't be making flirtatious comments. Or was he just being friendly, trying to be nice in a clumsy, chauvinistic way. Am I too sensitive? Annie thought. Did Susan know there were rumors about Sam?

The four of them walked over to the bar. "What are you two drinking?" Sam asked.

"Oh, yes," said Susan. "Let's toast to the new baby."

Annie had just taken a sip of her Absolut and grapefruit juice when David appeared.

"May I borrow your wife?" he said to Jim. Then, smiling down at Annie, "May I have this dance?"

In spite of herself, Annie felt her cheeks turning red. She felt people were staring at David singling her out. Of course, that's ridiculous, she told herself. It's just the host being charming to his guests. But still as he held her elbow and guided her through the crowded room to the terrace a nursery rhyme chased itself around her head: "Come into my parlor, said the spider to the fly."

David held her close but not intimately so. He seemed perfectly comfortable and confident in his dancing ability. Annie concentrated on following his lead. She danced slightly on tiptoe. He was much taller this close. She worried that her hand felt sweaty in his. It reminded her of nothing more than the anxious afternoons at her preadolescent ballroom dancing lessons. And she began to feel angry. She resented him for making her nervous.

He gently pushed her away from him a bit so he could speak to her. "Your friendship means a lot to Lesley," he began. "I'm always so busy. It's wonderful for Lesley to have your company."

"I have a lot of fun with her. You're a lucky man, David," Annie said pointedly.

David smiled. "Yes, I am," he said. He was surprised by the edge to her voice. He wasn't thrilled about Lesley's choosing this woman as a companion—all indications pointed to her being a real pain in the ass, the type that could convince your perfectly happy wife that she was being oppressed by her husband. He decided to change the subject.

"So, Annie, how's the writing going? Should I be looking for the Great American Novel at Barnes & Noble anytime soon?"

"Well, you know, it's really just *copy*writing for now," said Annie. "Maybe when the kids are older—"

David jumped in. "Fascinating work, writing. You have to have a great imagination. Doctors do, too, you know."

Great, thought Annie, this was probably his favorite subject: himself.

"They have to be able to imagine what could be happening on a cellular level. They have to dream up an entire kingdom of evil and good and plan defensive battles. Not enough of us have great imaginations."

"But you do?" asked Annie.

"Of course," said David and smiled warmly. "I like the way you think, Annie."

His hand gave hers a squeeze. And was it her imagination, or did he pull her just slightly closer?

Jim watched Lesley, who was watching David and Annie dancing. He walked in her direction, thinking he would suggest that they dance, too, but just as he reached her he felt a strong hand on his arm as a voice said, "Jim!"

He turned around and saw Jack Bates, an acquaintance from his law school days, standing beside him. He and Jack spoke briefly and then approached Lesley together.

Lesley had been thinking how nice it was of David to dance with Annie. She wanted David and Annie to like each other. She felt very close to Annie already; she was so warm and open. Most of Lesley's adult friends had come to her through David. Doctors' wives, mostly, and she never felt close to them. The relationships always seemed superficial. No one talked in anything but general terms; complaining about the odd hours, the unpredictable schedule. They all did community volunteer work, Junior League committees, but never, it seemed, because they really cared about the disadvantaged; more because it was the done thing. It was so different from Annie and Mac, whom she also liked, although she was a little intimidated by her, and maybe even a little jealous. Mac had known Annie so long and they were so close. Lesley wanted to have a history with Annie, to have a long-standing friendship. But she knew that would require opening up more. Annie and Mac talked about everything together. Which fathers at PTA they thought were sexy, what their sex lives were like, what their husbands wanted. . . . She wished she knew what David wanted. Lately he seemed so distant, his advances insincere, a caricature of himself. It was as if he was trying to *act* interested but really wasn't. Sometimes she tormented herself, wondering, was it her? Was it because she couldn't bear him children?

She looked around at all the smiling guests, the sparkling chandeliers. He had done all of this for her. And that toast he had made, about her being his fantasy—she blushed thinking about it. Of course he loved her. How many women had a husband this thoughtful and this generous? She scolded herself for creating things to worry about.

She caught sight of David and Annie again, amid the twirling couples. She wondered what they were talking about. Annie had her back to Lesley. She could tell when Annie spoke, though, because her head moved. Annie always became animated when she spoke. She couldn't use her hands because she was holding onto David, so she used her head. David had begun the conversation with a smile and Lesley thought he must be telling Annie a joke because it looked like he chuckled at the end of one of his comments and she thought Annie's shoulders shook slightly. But now they seemed to have finished speaking and David was just looking out over Annie's head and Lesley could see a worried wrinkle across his forehead. He looked thoughtful. What could Annie have said to him?

"Lesley?"

She snapped her head away from David and Annie and saw Jim and a man she didn't know standing next to him. She smiled uncertainly.

"Lesley, this is Jack Bates. He's a friend from law school and he knows David, but he's never had the pleasure of meeting you."

"I find myself in an awkward position," said Jack. "David sends his patients to me when they need legal advice regarding adoption. We've done quite a bit of work together over the years but it's always been work. I'm enjoying sharing a social event with him, but feel sorry that I have never met the beautiful bride being honored tonight." Lesley smiled while he spoke but she kept looking distractedly over his shoulder toward David and Annie.

"I'm so glad you could come," she said.

"Well, the pleasure's all mine, Lesley. I just regret that my association with David didn't bring me into your orbit earlier."

Oh, Jesus, thought Jim. Now he remembered why he hadn't kept in contact with this guy. Endless talk, circular, often pointless or inappropriate—and a compulsive womanizer. David referred people to this guy? Jim wanted another drink. He wanted to get away from Jack but he couldn't stick Lesley with him.

The music stopped and David and Annie made their way through the crowd to Lesley and Jim and some man, Annie noticed, in a very bad suit. Just as they reached the others David reached down and took Annie's hand between his two.

"Thanks for the dance," he said. "It was a pleasure." He turned to Jim. "Your wife is a fine dancer and an enlightened conversationalist."

"Thank you," said Annie, but she didn't smile. What did he mean by that? Was David coming on to her? Had he held her too tightly? Or was he just automatically like that with women—so sure of his looks and charm. Assuming they all wanted to be dazzled . . .

"Honey." It was Jim. She whipped her head around in his direction.

"What?" she said, too loudly.

"I was going to ask you if you want another drink but you look a little spacy. Are you tired? Do you want to go home?"

"Oh, sorry. No, I mean I am pretty tired—I don't think I'll have another drink. But we don't have to go yet. I want to dance some more."

"All right. Is everything okay? Did David do something to upset you?" He put on his macho voice. "Hey, did he come on to you?"

"No. I don't know. I don't think so. Maybe . . ."

"Annie, what do you mean? What'd he do?"

"Nothing, really. It's no big deal." Annie looked over her shoulder to see where David was. She took Jim's arm and pulled him out to the dance floor.

"Annie, tell me," said Jim.

"It was innocuous, you know, just a certain look in his eye and a kind of too intimate squeeze. It happens to women all the time—it could be just trying to flatter you or it could be a come-on—and usually you can't be certain."

"I'm certain," said Jim. "I used to do it, remember?"

But Annie was obviously distracted. Jim followed her gaze. It was on Lesley, who was watching David talking to a stunning young woman with an older man. David was holding the woman's elbow as he spoke to them.

"See," said Annie, noticing that Jim was watching, too. "He just acts like he's God's gift to women. He's going to go around and touch all of us before the night's over. Spread his charm. Poor Lesley. Why can't he pay more attention to her?"

"I'd say this party's pretty attentive."

"Yeah, it is, but anyone with money can throw a great party. We're all supposed to think what a great guy he is 'cause he did this for his wife."

"I don't know, Annie, maybe *you're* being a little hard on the guy now. He has an ego, but he seems genuinely fond of Lesley."

And to Jim's surprise, Annie blurted out in an angry tone, "Well, he's not. He's cheating on her."

Jim turned to look directly in Annie's eyes and saw a look of shock on her face. She froze with her mouth open like a deer in headlights.

"Oh, my God," she said and thought to herself, the vodka, too much vodka.

It was the guilty look on her face that made Jim uneasy.

"How do you know, Annie?" He had the distinct impression that Annie knew something Lesley did not. For one sickening moment he thought Annie might be about to confess that she knew because it was her—that she and David—his gut wrenched and his mouth went dry.

"I—" Annie began, "Remember when we heard them over the monitor?"

Jim nodded, feeling his breath returning.

"I listened another time after that. I was bored, home alone with Rebecca." Annie's words tumbled out quickly. "I didn't expect to hear anything, but I did and then I had to find out—I had to know if it was Lesley or not."

She wasn't making any sense to him. But the idea, the fact that she had used a device to listen in on their neighbors, came through clearly to him.

"So I listened again until I knew. But it wasn't Lesley. It's a nurse. One of Sam's nurses. He's cheating on her in their own house, in her bed." Annie had tears in her eyes.

"You did *what?*" Jim hissed. He was furious. The anger seemed a by-product of his initial fear, some perverse reaction to the threat he had felt. Even as he unleashed the anger, he knew it was out of proportion to the crime being confessed, certainly a far lesser crime than the one he had imagined, but he was powerless before it and couldn't shake the idea that his wife was a criminal.

He took hold of her upper arm and guided her off the dance floor to a secluded spot on the patio.

"I knew you'd hate it," Annie began.

"You *listened* to our neighbors? You snuck around like some CIA creep, invading their privacy?" Jim's eyes were wide.

"Jim, I'm sorry. It didn't seem real. It was like a soap opera. It didn't hurt anyone, except maybe me, because now I know something that I wish I didn't."

"It is real, Annie. It's illegal. It's unconstitutional. It's a gross invasion—"

"I know, I know, it was wrong. Please, Jim, don't spoil the evening."

"I should throw the fucking monitor away, Annie, if you're going to abuse it like that."

Now Annie was angry. "I'm not your child, Jim. I'm your wife. You have no business threatening to take things away from me. You go off to your job and go out to lunch with friends and save the world and get paid and I'm in the house all day with an infant. Entire days go by and I don't hear another adult voice so if I go a little zooey and eavesdrop on my neighbors—well, it's not the worst thing in the world. I'm not beating the children or drinking all day or cheating on you." She sniffed. "Sometimes you are so goddamn unfair and so fucking pompous." She was crying in earnest now. Her pride was wounded and one of her breasts was starting to hurt. Rebecca had only nursed on one side before they left the house.

Her crying was like cold water on his anger. Maybe he was an ass, he thought. One of those lawyers in love with the law. But a flame of anger still flickered; what she'd done was wrong. He reached out tentatively and drew her head to his shoulder. She let her weight go against him like a tired child. He stroked her hair.

"I'm sorry," they both said at once. Annie laughed softly. She lifted her head from his shoulder and they kissed.

"I want to dance with you," said Jim, and then he began to sing a Fred Astaire tune. And standing up, he did a soft shoe routine in front of her.

He was goofy, Annie thought. He didn't care who saw him being corny. She stood up. Jim danced her around and dipped her. "Let's take tap dance lessons."

"Right," said Annie. "How much have you had to drink?"

"Don't know," he said. "But you be the designated driver, okay?" And both of them laughing, he kissed her loudly.

Chapter Twelve

Annie sat smiling at the young woman sitting across from her. She hated interviewing for babysitters. It didn't feel that long ago that she had been a nervous teenager looking for work. Although she'd been a mother for six years, she still felt a little bit like an imposter when she was the one doing the hiring. She tried to take a businesslike tone.

"I'm looking for someone who has a flexible schedule. I'm a copywriter—freelance—and my work comes in fits and starts. During high pressure weeks I'd need someone for half a day every day. Other weeks I'd need probably two mornings. If I wasn't working I could get errands done . . ."

"That sounds great. My classes are over by one-thirty on Monday, Wednesday, and Friday and on Tuesday and Thursday I have evening classes so those days are totally free."

So far so good, thought Annie. Now for the hard part.

"How do you feel about cooking and cleaning? I'm also looking for someone who wouldn't mind fixing a dinner once a week and would help out with laundry or straightening up. Of course I would pay extra for that."

"I'm not incredibly experienced at cooking but I know how to do some basics and with help, you know, if you give me a recipe or something, I can do it. I like to cook. When my mother went back to school each of us kids had a night when we were responsible for dinner. It was sort of like trial by fire."

"How many brothers and sisters do you have?"

"Three, two sisters and a brother; he's spoiled rotten." She paused. "I actually really like vacuuming," she said and blushed. "My roommate always makes fun of me."

Annie laughed. "Jessie, you are too good to be true. When can you start?"

"Um, today's Monday—how about tomorrow? Whatever time's good for you."

"Okay, how about one o'clock? I can show you around and you and Rebecca can get to know each other. Maybe you can vacuum some while she naps. Alex will be home at three and you could take them to the park. Is that good?"

"Great. I'll see you then."

"Oh, Jessie, you know, I just thought of something. If you need the hours on the slow weeks, I've got a friend across the street who might need you now and then. They've just moved in, actually, but I think she'd be nice to work for. Their name is Shields and they have one kid, a little girl named Millie. If you're interested, I'll give your number to Lesley. He's a doctor and I think the childcare is pretty much completely up to her . . ." Annie stopped talking. Jessie suddenly looked awful. "Jessica? Are you okay?"

Jessica nodded. She seemed to be trying not to burst into tears.

"Dr. Shields. The obstetrician?" asked Jessica.

"Yes, why? Do you know him?"

Tears were spilling from Jessie's eyes. "I'm sorry, I can't believe I'm doing this. I guess it's just still so fresh. I really apologize, I—"

"Jessie, it's okay, here take my hankie. But what's wrong?"

"Three weeks ago I had a miscarriage." She cried harder. "Dr. Shields was going to help me put the baby up for adoption. It's just all been so awful and the miscarriage was so painful. I can't believe how upset I am to have lost the baby. I was going to give it away anyway, but now I find I was getting attached to it . . ." She was crying too much to go on. Annie went and knelt beside her chair and put her arms around the girl.

"It's okay, Jessie, just go ahead and cry. Those feelings are all very natural. And don't forget, you're still dealing with hormones here. You'll feel much more like yourself when they calm down."

"Oh, Annie, you're so nice. I'm so embarrassed. I understand if you don't want me to work for you now. You must think I'm a basket case, or at least some kind of awful person—"

"Of course I don't. Look, I really understand and I still want you to work for me. I promise, you are going to feel better, soon. Those hormones can really do a number on you."

Jessie nodded and blew her nose. She started to get up and then stopped and pointed at the ceiling.

"I think I hear Rebecca."

Annie looked up, surprised.

"You're right. Well, you've certainly got the ears for the job. I didn't realize I'd forgotten to turn on the monitor. I guess I've been relying on it too much—my ears are out of practice." She smiled. "Want to come up and meet her?"

"I'd love to," said Jessica and she followed Annie up the stairs.

David was using his speaker phone. Annie felt her heart pound with excitement. She'd hear the entire conversation, both sides. Maybe he was calling Pam.

"Sanders and Lowe," an efficient-sounding woman answered.

"This is David Shields. Give me Bernie Sanders."

"Oh, yes. Let me see if he's available, Dr. Shields." For a

minute Annie and David listened to a Muzak version of "Eleanor Rigby."

"Dave." A hearty, deep voice. *"Thanks for getting back to me. What's the good word?"*

"I'm not sure, Bernie. We're having a bit of a dry spell. Maybe the AIDS scare is hitting the campus. I don't know. We've got one prospect, but she's got terrible hyperemesis."

"Hold on, what's that? I'm a lawyer, remember?"

"Right, sorry. It's extreme nausea—vomiting. Can't keep anything down. It's a fairly rare complication. Usually resolves itself, but sometimes it requires hospitalization and what amounts to intravenous force feeding. Sometimes the woman miscarries because the fetus is so severely compromised."

"Okay, so what you're saying is you don't have a definite."

"Right, I don't."

"So I can't tell the Carters anything yet. They're important as hell, Davey. They want it now, yesterday if possible. We might lose them. Some friends of theirs saw that damn 20/20 on the Gypsies in Romania. They're getting antsy enough to hop a plane and do it over there. You've got to do better."

"What do you want me to do, Bernie, jump some college girl?" It's a tough job, thought Annie, but somebody's gotta do it. Right, Davey? *"Hey, guy, I'm beating the bushes. I've got all contacts working on this. Impress upon them how careful we're being. Give them a good scare about the Romanian health issues. It'll all be true. The kids coming out through improper channels are turning up with AIDS. I just talked to a doctor in London. They didn't do the testing our guys do, and now a whole load of folks who were desperate are having to go through hell. Tell them we're trying to save them more grief. Tell them we're the good guys. Buy me some time, Bernie."*

"I'll do my best. You just keep your ass in high gear, 'cause letting these people down would be bad for business. Talk to you the end of the week."

"*Good-bye, Bernie.*"

Annie heard a muttered "Jesus Christ," and then she heard him ask the operator for the international dialing code for Mexico. She could hear him punch in the phone tones, lots of them.

"*Ruiz Clinic.* Como puedo aiuda?" A heavy Spanish voice.

"Necessito hablar con Dr. Ruiz, por favor." Annie's mind raced. She'd had only first-year Spanish in college. Hablar was the verb "to speak." He wants to talk to a Dr. Ruiz. Damn, was the whole conversation going to be in Spanish? David was whistling. She had listened in enough times to know he did that when he was tense or nervous. Strange to know these intimate habits and not really know him at all. She and Jim should repay that barbecue. Have them both over. Maybe next month. But knowing what she now knew about David and "Pammy," how could she keep up the charade?

"Buenos días, soy Dr. Ruiz."

"Ola, Jaime, *it's David. How are you? And the family?*" English! Thank God, thought Annie, and she began picking up the baby toys that Alex had dumped all over the floor "for Rebecca" that morning.

"*Very well, thank you. And your lovely Lesley, and the baby?*"

"*Great, great. Has our Saudi friend arrived yet?*"

"*No, David, but he's standing by. Do you have a donor?*"

Donor? thought Annie. Another adoption?

"*I think I do. It's not 100 percent. I've got to ascertain exact age and run a few other tests. But certainly by the end of the week I will know. I wanted to alert you.*"

"*Very good. Excellent news. I will talk to you on Friday then and confirm. Why don't you deliver it yourself? Mexico is beautiful this time of year. We would love to see you. Bring the family. The girls can sit by our pool while I give you a tour of the facilities. We have made some improvements since you were here last. Oh, and, David, another client has contacted me. Very young, very tragic. We can discuss this case when you come."*

"Thank you. I'll think about that. Speak to you Friday." Click.

Annie waited for the phone tones. There was nothing. Then a toilet flushed. Was that why he was using the speaker phone? Annie stuck out her tongue in disgust. So, what did all that mean, anyway? A lawyer. Romania. An anxious couple. Did David help somehow with private adoptions? She heard the gravel driveway churning across the street. Walking to the window, she saw David in his usual busy doctor mode, spraying gravel into the street as he sped out his driveway. Mexico? Annie thought. A donor. David dealt with high risk obstetrics. Maybe he had an especially sick baby. Maybe he was hoping to console his grief-stricken couple with the idea of their baby's kidney or heart or liver helping some poor Mexican child live. But why Mexico? There must be kids here who needed transplants. Probably even in David's hospital. Could you send body parts across state lines? Of course you could, it was always in the newspaper. Across international lines? And why would he deliver it himself?

Oh, Annie, she told herself, forget it. It's his life. You shouldn't have heard any of this. And once again she was struck by how powerless she was to stop listening. She was driven to hear more. It was like a book you were dying to read the end of, only there was no end, there was always something new to pursue. She was like the stereotypical housewife/slob, munching on chocolates and watching the soaps. God, she had been so smug about avoiding the soap opera trap when she was on maternity leave with Alex. But now she was hooked on the real thing. She had to know what would happen next. She was repulsed and fascinated and the combination was too much for her. At least the people who watched it on television weren't committing a crime. Suddenly she had a mental image of David and Lesley listening to her and Jim, and she flushed with embarrassment.

She reached for a legal pad and replayed the conversation in her head, scribbling down what she could remember. Maybe David was involved in private adoptions. In Mexico? Maybe *donor* is baby. Or baby's mother? But why not say *baby*? Why speak in code? Private adoptions are legal, unless, of course, Annie's heart raced, you do it for money. She could feel her eyes widening. What was it Sanders had said? "Letting these people down would be bad for business?" Had he meant that *literally*? The Shields did have tons of money ... "The man's a high-risk OB, Annie, of course they're loaded." She could almost hear Jim's mocking tone. Forget it, she couldn't tell Jim. After their fight at the party, how could she? Jim, who held the Constitution and the Bill of Rights dearer than life itself. Jim, who fought against FBI phone tapping and illegal search-and-seizure. Admit to him that she was still eavesdropping? Jim would never forgive that.

She just had to stop listening in, that was all. She shut off the monitor and flipped to a fresh page on the legal pad. She should really get back to work.

But instead she picked up the phone and dialed Mac's number.

"Mac? Hi, it's Annie. Listen, do you have a minute?"

"Sure thing, sugar, I'm just marinating the steak. I have become a truly domesticated animal. In a minute I was going to run upstairs and put on my Saran Wrap, but that can wait. Nick's not due home for a couple of hours."

Annie giggled. "Will you just listen? I heard something."

Mac gasped. "You did? Oh, Annie, you evil thing! What? Tell."

"Well, I don't know, it's just kind of weird. I mean, maybe it's nothing, but I wouldn't put anything past David . . ."

"Annie, you are driving me crazy. What did you hear?"

"Okay, okay. David was using his speaker phone—"

"Ooh, how considerate."

"Yes. Well, he called this lawyer and they were obviously talking about an adoption they were arranging for this couple—"

"Yeah, so? Maybe this David character has a good side after all."

"No, Mac, if you could've heard them, it wasn't like this nice thing they were doing. The lawyer kept bugging David to hurry up and said the couple were so anxious they were talking about going to Romania to get a baby."

"So, he doesn't want to let them down, right?"

"I don't think that's it, Mac. At the end of the conversation, he was practically yelling at David, telling him to get his ass in gear, and he actually said, 'Letting these people down would be bad for business' in this really creepy voice."

"So, what do you think? They're making some kind of outrageous profit on these people?"

"Exactly. The only thing is, I can't understand how Mexico figures into all of this."

"Mexico?"

"Yeah. After he talked to the lawyer, he called this guy at a clinic in Mexico. Anyway, this conversation was even more creepy, in a way. The other doctor had this really sinister voice and he referred to Lesley as 'your lovely Lesley'—"

"So?"

Annie groaned. "You know, Mac, it was that awful, totally insincere Latin crap they do about women."

"Hmm, racism rears its ugly head. And this is my Annie talkin'?"

"Listen, Mac, the guy just sounded evil to me, okay? It's not just a Latin thing—it was a universal kind of thing, all right? But the point is, he was talking about a donation, but not money, like an organ, or something, and he talked about 'our Saudi friend.'"

"Annie, darlin', I think the guilt has gotten the better of you. You've got to see something evil in this because he's got to be a worse person than you are for listening in on him."

"Mac, I know he's a worse person than me."

"Oh, yeah? How's that?"

Annie paused. This would be adding to Lesley's betrayal, telling Mac. But she had to tell someone.

"The other day, I heard him with a woman again—and I know now it's not Lesley."

"Ow, shit, Annie, now I've got honey and vinegar all over my kitchen floor. Another woman? *Finally* we've got something juicy! Why the hell didn't you tell me this before?"

"I didn't want to betray Lesley. It's bad enough that her husband's cheating on her, without me spreading it all over town."

"Don't worry, sugar, mum's the word. But what's this got to do with the lawyer and Mexico and all that?"

"I don't know yet, I just think, if a man's a sleaze in bed, he can be a sleaze in business, or ethically, or whatever. I think he's doing something awful, I just don't know what yet."

"Well, we can worry about that later. What about this other woman? Come on, Anniekins, are you going to make me beg?"

Chapter Thirteen

He had only minutes ago summoned Ricardo to his office and yet when the massive Indian suddenly appeared at his side, he was startled. It always amazed him how a man of Ricardo's size could move so silently and stealthily. The Indian looked down at him, grinning, obviously deriving a brutish pleasure in disarming his benefactor. Or was Jaime only imagining that? He could never be sure with Ricardo.

Ricardo had lived at the hacienda most of his life. He was the cook's son. When he was a child, Jaime hardly noticed him, but during adolescence he had grown to such a striking size that Jaime began to train him for clinic work, first as a security guard. Then, as time went on, his role expanded to that of a spy of sorts. He kept track of the hacienda servants and clinic staff and kept Jaime abreast of any possible problems.

Jaime said, "We will have a guest soon, from Saudi Arabia."

Ricardo raised his eyebrows.

"Yes, and I want his daughter, who will accompany him, to have the lovely big corner room. She is to have fresh flowers daily. We want them to return to their country full of nothing but praise for our clinic. This could open up an enormously wealthy market."

The Indian nodded.

"Please let Humberto know that I will need him to go to the airport and wait for a patient arriving from Riyadh via Kennedy airport. He should be ready to go at a moment's notice." Jaime started back into his office, then stopped and looked back over his shoulder.

Jaime had expected Ricardo to walk away. Their conversation was over. But he didn't. He stayed.

"Yes?" asked Jaime.

"The little kitchen worker—" Ricardo began.

"Immaculata?" Jaime asked. He prided himself on knowing all their names. It increased loyalty, he believed. "What about her?"

"She is with child."

Jaime snorted. Few Indians spoke English but when they did, it always sounded strangely archaic, pieced together as it was from listening to the Catholic liturgy.

"Keep your eye on her," Jaime said, and dismissed him with a wave of the hand. The massive Indian moved soundlessly down the hallway and disappeared around the corner. Looking after him, Jaime mulled over this latest piece of news. How many did this make? Four? In just under two years. He should probably put a stop to Ricardo's little "indiscretions," but it was tempting to let it go on. For one thing, it kept the Indian happy. And then, of course, it would be a cheap, low-profile way to obtain the necessary tissue, in case his colleague from the U.S. got cold feet.

There was one other reason he did not wish to cross the Indian. A Mexican, a Catholic, with so little regard for his own flesh and blood was rare, and not a man to be trifled with. Jaime was not eager to interfere with Ricardo's private life.

Jaime went back into his office. The Saudi would arrive soon, and then so would his American guests. And according to the call he'd just received, they'd be bringing along a "donation" of their own.

Chapter Fourteen

The two women entered the Atrium prepared to shop. It was Annie's first time at the new upscale mall, but Lesley seemed to know the place well.

"What shall we do first?" Lesley asked. "Outside or inside?" Annie looked puzzled. "You know, jackets, coats or underwear? Don't you do it that way?"

Annie laughed. "You've got a system for everything, Lesley. I'm much less organized. I wander aimlessly until something catches my eye, then try to justify spending money on it."

"Ah," said Lesley. "An impulse buyer. I'm sure that's much more fun, but my mother trained that out of me. Whenever I wanted something, I had to show clear need. But let's do it your way today." She linked her arm through Annie's and they headed off. "Let's go in here," she said, pointing to Shreve, Crump and Low. "I need something for David's birthday. I try to get him some little silver trinket each year, but I think I've just about gone through their inventory."

Oh, brother, thought Annie. Shopping for the asshole—great.

They paused at the sterling case. Lesley pointed at the items. "He has the money clip, the toothpaste key, the key ring, the hairbrush—"

"Does he play golf?" she asked brightly.

"No, thank God. My father did and we never saw him. We were at school all week, and he played golf all weekend."

"Forget the golf tee, then," said Annie. "Oh, Les, I've got it. Look, a sterling toothpick."

"Believe it or not, I got him one already!"

Annie laughed. "Somehow I can't picture David sitting around picking his teeth."

"Well, you know, everyone has to do it sometimes, and I thought he'd appreciate an elegant tool. You're right, though. David doesn't like to make a display of body hygiene. He likes to spring spotlessly clean into public view."

Was Lesley complaining? Annie wondered. She'd never heard her say anything less than worshipful about David.

"How did you meet him?" Annie turned to Lesley.

"At home in Canada," Lesley said. "He was a med student and I was an undergraduate. He knew my cousin, who brought him to my grandfather's one weekend when I was there, too. I thought he was unbelievably beautiful. I still do," Lesley confessed and blushed.

"He is very attractive," Annie said, and thought, and he knows it, too. "Did you fall in love that weekend?"

"Well, *I* did, but it was awkward, because I had another boy there, someone I'd gone out with on and off for years. You know the type, a family friend. You're pushed together from the beginning. Club dances, house parties. A lot of my friends married that way. And a lot of them are now divorced."

"So what happened?"

"Well, all the way back to school I kept scheming, plotting a way to see David again. A way to make our paths cross. He was so hard to read. He seemed very quiet and serious and I couldn't make up my mind if he had seemed interested or if he hadn't noticed me at all. I had this friend who had just discovered she was pregnant, so I wrote a note to David asking him if I could speak to him about a medical matter."

"And?" Annie was enjoying picturing Lesley as a timid, insecure student. She seemed so self-assured and worldly now. And yet not when she was with David.

"He met me at a small campus restaurant. We talked about my friend's problem and the options available, and then he asked me to the movies for the next night."

"What did you see?" asked Annie.

"*Elvira Madigan*," said Lesley.

"Oh." Annie sighed, remembering the tragic love story depicted in the film. "Pretty romantic evening."

"I'll say," said Lesley. "We've been together ever since and played the title theme music at our wedding—it's Mozart, you know. Pretty corny, huh?"

"No," said Annie, "I love that piece. And I'm a sucker for anything romantic." She suddenly felt depressed, remembering how casually David regarded his bond with Lesley. With some difficulty, she turned her attention back to the case of silver extravagances.

"So," said Lesley, looking at the display. "There's nothing here he doesn't already have."

Annie pointed silently to a belt buckle.

"Got one," said Lesley. "So let's go to Victoria's Secret and get some romantic things."

This was really fun, thought Annie, standing in a dressing room next to Lesley's. She hadn't shopped with another woman since college. She either went alone or with Jim and they always argued. She would hear him sighing outside a dressing room, his boredom audible. And he would grill her—did she really need that skirt? Did she have things that went with it? Where would she wear it? She'd accuse him of taking all the joy out of it, and she'd start to feel guilty about the money. They would drive home silently, sulking. But this was money with no guilt. Her mother-in-law had sent a modest check for a "postpartum pick-me-up," and she was supposed to spend it on herself. She tried on a French lace bra with tiny violets on the white batiste and enough lace to be very seductive. "Schoolgirl in the bordello," she called to Lesley.

Lesley laughed. "Is that the one with violets? I just tried one of those. I just don't have enough to pull it off. I bet you look terrific in it. Nursing really improves a figure, doesn't it?"

"Well," said Annie, "it does while you're nursing, but when you finish . . ." She laughed. "When I weaned Alex and before I got pregnant with Bec, I was smaller than I'd ever been."

"Yeah, but I have a feeling you had enough to start with."

"Well, I guess I did, but forget it. When I'm through nursing they'll just shrivel up again. They remind me of balloons that someone let the air out of."

Lesley was laughing so hard she had a coughing fit. Another dressing room door closed and someone rattled hangers. Lesley and Annie were quiet.

"If I could just avoid seeing my stomach in the mirror," said Annie, really just thinking out loud. This time even the woman in the other dressing room laughed.

"I'll meet you at the cash register," said Lesley. "Don't hurry."

When Annie emerged with the violet bra and a garter belt to match Lesley was just sticking her Visa card back in her wallet.

"Do you like those?" said Lesley, pointing to the garter belt. "I haven't worn one since junior high. I remember it being really uncomfortable."

"I love them," said Annie. "I hate panty hose, but I really love stockings. They make me feel really dressed up."

"Maybe I'll try one. I know David likes them." She rolled

her eyes. "Sometimes I look at catalogs in bed, and it's as if he has some kind of antenna. He'll be reading his book and I'll turn to a page of garter belt models and he'll roll right over to check it out." Lesley wandered to a revolving rack hung with pastel garter belts. She chose a pink one with delicately embroidered lace inlays.

Going out of the store a few minutes later, Lesley became serious. "Do you buy this underwear because you like it, or do you buy it to make sure you keep Jim interested and happy at home?"

Annie was taken aback. She didn't think about keeping Jim interested. She took for granted that he was. Their sex life had always been good, and she never doubted Jim's fidelity. But here was Lesley, obviously feeling shaky, and Annie knew she had reason to be. But she couldn't share that with Lesley. And for at least the hundredth time since she had known Lesley, she wished that she hadn't listened in. She didn't want to know more about Lesley's marriage than Lesley did.

"Well"—she paused—"I buy it because I like to feel sexy. But if there wasn't a man in my life, I'd probably still buy it. It makes me feel more confident. Whenever I have a meeting with the president of Cotton Tales, I always wear my sexiest underwear."

Lesley looked questioningly at her.

"No," said Annie, "don't get the wrong idea. I'm not about to jeopardize the life I have with Jim. It's just that I feel more confident that way. I like lace bras and garter belts. What about you?" she ventured hesitantly.

When Lesley didn't answer, Annie just kept on talking. "And I kind of like the look of surprise on Jim's face when I pull off my sweatshirt and jeans and I have this incredible underwear on underneath." God, why didn't she just get off the subject?

"That's nice, isn't it?" said Lesley, but it sounded as if she was thinking about something else.

Two grueling shopping hours later they sank gratefully into a booth at Legal Seafood. "My feet are killing me," said Annie. "We must have walked miles."

"You're just out of shape." Lesley laughed. "This was just a warm-up for a professional shopper like me. You should see me when I shop in Mexico."

"I've never been, but everybody says the bargains are great, especially the silver."

"It's true, but it involves a lot of walking to hunt up the best buys."

"Do you go often?"

"If David had his way we'd go all the time. As it is he goes five or six times a year and I go two or three."

"Why does he go so much?" Annie tried not to sound too curious.

"Well, he has a very good friend who runs his own private clinic in La Cucharita, a small village about an hour south of Mexico City. Jaime is a cardiologist, and apparently he has pioneered some microsurgery techniques. David is very interested in microsurgery and he loves learning from Jaime. Also, David has become a pretty devoted collector of Aztec art, so he combines business with pleasure."

Jaime. Annie thought back to the conversation she'd overheard. "Dr. Ruiz," "our Saudi friend," a "donor." The doctor on the other end of the phone had suggested that David bring Lesley on this trip. Annie had a strange feeling of déjà vu, as she realized that she had known, before Lesley, that David planned to bring his wife along.

"Is it very beautiful there?"

"Oh, in La Cucharita it is gorgeous. Lush and beautiful, full of exotic flowers. But I miss Millie too much. Lola,

Jaime's wife, says her nerves won't tolerate children. Obviously, we don't have much in common."

"Oh, but just to get away to some place sunny . . ." Annie and Jim hadn't had a real winter vacation for three years now.

"Well," allowed Lesley, "that is nice. David wants me to go with him on this next trip. He talked to Jaime the other day and he's going to be trying some new procedure." Lesley paused. "Annie, I would love it if you would come with me." At Annie's surprised look, she rushed on. "We could go shopping and lounge by the pool. They have this incredible hacienda . . . it's right out of *Lifestyles of the Rich and Famous*."

"Oh gee, Lesley. It's a great invitation . . ."

"Oh, it would be wonderful. David would be thrilled because I wouldn't be bugging him to leave Jaime and go to the pyramids—which you have to see, they are absolutely breathtaking—or to go shopping. You and I could do those things. You said yourself you need a break. It's just for a long weekend. I bet Jessica could help Jim with the kids."

The kids. Annie had actually gotten caught up in Lesley's fantasy but now she plunged back down to earth. The kids, her babies, how would they get along without her? And how could she bear to leave Rebecca so soon?

"Or could Jim take some time off—does he have any vacation days coming to him?"

"He has," said Annie, "about a year's worth of time not taken. Convincing him to take it is the issue, and I don't know if I could leave Rebecca. She's still so new . . ." But Annie couldn't help thinking that this trip could be the perfect opportunity to see what David was really up to.

"On the other hand," said Lesley, "you're tempted. Think of all the sleep you'd get, Annie. And it's only a few days— you could pump and Jim could give Rebecca bottles. Come on—it'll give them a chance to *bond*." She giggled. "Please say you'll at least talk to Jim about it."

"Yes, okay, I'll talk to him tonight." And despite her anxieties she found she had caught Lesley's excitement for the plan and could feel a bubble of anticipation rising within her. She *would* talk to Jim tonight, she told herself. She felt her pulse quicken as she imagined herself sleuthing around the clinic at the hacienda. She could have a little vacation for herself and at the same time find out what kind of "donation" David was bringing to Mexico. Watch out, David, she thought to herself, 'cause here I come.

Chapter Fifteen

The black Mercedes limousine took the deeply rutted, mud-soaked road as smoothly as possible, but still the driver heard the young woman's gasps each time the wheels skidded and the car jerked forward again. He didn't understand their language, but he could hear concern and worry in the woman's voice as she comforted the man. He was her father, the driver thought, although he was still young-looking himself. But something was wrong. The man had had to be lifted into the car. And his hand shook so much his daughter had taken the money from him and handled the tipping herself. The tip had been more than generous. If she would reward him in the same manner when they reached La Cucharita he would feed his family for a month on that alone. This job was the answer to his prayers.

At the hacienda he got out and retrieved the wheelchair from the trunk. A large Indian came from the house and without saying a word to anyone opened the car door and lifted the shaking man as if he were an infant, placing him gently in the chair. The daughter was out of the car in an instant and, speaking to the Indian in high-pitched bird chirps, she chopped the air above his arms in short, violent motions with her hand. The Indian backed off, looking puzzled. The young woman turned to the driver, handed him some money, nodded her head ceremoniously to him, and, followed by the

Indian, pushed her father's chair through the open front door.

Inside the Mercedes the driver counted the money—even more than he had hoped. He knew others had left this job. There were many rumors about the place. "Casa Diablo," black magic, curses. He did not believe in those. He was not a poor Indian. He was a citizen of Mexico City. He had even managed to take two courses at the university. Let the others think what they would. He knew a good job when it came along. He was planted firmly in the twentieth century.

Ricardo wheeled the chair into Jaime's office and stood behind it. Jaime stood up quickly and came around his desk to shake hands with Mr. Aziz. "Welcome to the Ruiz Clinic. We hope you will be comfortable here and we will endeavor to meet your every need."

Hammed nodded.

"We have some paperwork to complete. It should take only a few moments." Jaime noticed that Ricardo was standing against the wall.

"Ricardo, please take Miss Aziz to Consuela." Jaime turned toward Hammed's daughter. "Consuela will show you to your room." The daughter registered alarm at being separated from her father. "Your room, Miss Aziz, is in the clinic wing, immediately next to your father's. He will be up shortly." The girl's father nodded at her and spoke to her shortly in Arabic. The girl obediently followed Ricardo.

Jaime didn't like the way Ricardo lingered, having to be given a reason to leave. Jaime didn't want him to learn anything of the clinic's finances. Having dismissed him, he turned his mind to the matter at hand.

"The clinic's operating expenses as you can imagine are astronomical and all energies and resources are devoted to one patient at a time. That is why as our literature explained

we must ask for the full payment in advance. I trust you
have brought the bank check as requested?"

With great difficulty, Hammed extracted the paper from
his briefcase and with a shaking hand held it—and all of his
hopes—out to Jaime.

Chapter Sixteen

Jim was kissing the back of her neck.

"Mmm."

She stopped packing long enough to turn around and return the kiss. With feeling.

"Wow," said Jim. "What was that for?"

"Are you kidding? You're only the most incredible husband a woman could wish for—"

"Perfect in every way," Jim agreed, smiling.

"No, I mean it." Annie laughed. "Are you sure it's okay? Am I a terrible mother to leave Rebecca already? And how will you cope?"

"Whoa. How can I be perfect in every way if you don't even trust me alone with my own children for a few days? That is exactly what I needed. I couldn't be here much right after she was born because of the McNulty thing, and I've been wanting to spend more time with Alex . . . and you, my dear"—he held her at arm's length and looked her in the eye—"you will be a better mother for having taken a few days for yourself. You've been pretty hyper lately. I really think you need this trip. Besides"—he stroked her hair—"it'll give us time to bond." She looked up to see a mischievous gleam in his eye and burst out laughing.

"That's exactly what Lesley said!"

Annie snuggled against his shoulder and sighed, thinking

nervously of her ulterior motive for going on this trip. If she got into trouble snooping around down there, Jim would have no idea. Her imagination was running away with her again. Trouble? What trouble? She was going to Mexico with a girlfriend for a long weekend. Get real, Annie, she thought. But the knot in her stomach didn't go away.

Annie had never flown first class. It had always seemed a silly additional expense to her except, now that she was doing it, she could see how people could get used to it. The flight attendant did seem friendlier—certainly more attentive—and having her glass continually refilled with free champagne did a lot to ease her anxiety level.

She had originally booked her ticket in economy class. Lesley had told her they usually flew first class and then, seeming embarrassed the way she often was when the discrepancy in their economic status came up, she had backpedaled, downplaying as she always did the amenities their wealth allowed them to take for granted.

"David likes the extra leg room, you know."

"Of course. That's fine," said Annie. "I like to read on planes anyway, so you and David sit up front and we'll meet in the airport."

"Oh, no," said Lesley. "We're traveling together. I'll book us economy tickets, too."

"That's nice, Lesley, but don't feel you have to. Talk it over with David. Either way is all right with me."

That night when she tuned in, she heard them fighting about it over the monitor.

"No, Lesley, I can't stand flying back there. Those seats are so tight. I can't move, my knees are up under my chin, and some jerk always sits next to me and finds out I'm a doctor and then I have to listen to his history of hemorrhoids."

"David, you can sit in between Annie and me. We'll be your buffers against the outside world."

Ugh, thought Annie. What an adult baby the guy was.

"No, look, I think it's great your friend can come. I know you get bored with me working so much there. And I know Lola isn't great company, but it's just not worth traveling in coach."

"David, Lola is brain-dead. She can make an entire day's project out of painting her nails. She doesn't get up until eleven, and at two she takes her siesta until four. Then she dresses for dinner until six. I can't take another visit with just her. I need Annie. Don't make her sit back there by herself like some third wheel." There was a pause. *"You can have the aisle seat."*

Oh, God. Why'd I say I'd go? thought Annie. I'm going to be like a ball and chain. He'll be complaining about me the whole time. He'll snap his fingers, Lesley will run, and I'll get stuck with Lola and her nail polish.

"I won't sit back there, Lesley. Just bump her up to first class. Call the agent, put it on our card."

Now, sipping her champagne, Annie wondered if she had seemed surprised enough when they boarded the plane. She felt like a poor relation having to lean over strangers to thank David. Oh, well, what was a little humility against four days in the sun with no children to watch out for? The problem was she missed them already. When they were boarding the plane, an infant had begun crying, and Annie had felt a physical ache for Rebecca. She would have to use the damn breast pump before they even got to Mexico.

For the last hour of the flight Annie slept. Her head felt thick and foggy as they went to claim baggage and find the car Jaime Ruiz had sent for them. For once she was glad of David's take-charge ways. He had skycaps fighting each other to do his bidding. The drive through Mexico City seemed like a dreamscape. It was so different from anything she had experienced, from anywhere she had been before. The poverty was on a different plane from any she had witnessed at home. Bare-bottomed children, some with the rotted teeth of the elderly, played in filthy gutter water. Houses made of cardboard cartons filled a block and then out of the rubble sprang a pristine high-rise, all glass and mosaic with chrome art deco doors and doormen from Oz. At every intersection the scene changed, a living kaleidoscope of despair and disorder.

Annie reached for a window crank suddenly, wanting to stick her head out and breathe in the Mexican air. The sights were so unreal, she needed to ground them in a reality. She needed her other senses, maybe this was a dream. She wanted to smell the vendors' food, to hear the children's voices. But there was no crank, just a row of automatic buttons. She and the others were all sealed up tight, insulated in the air-conditioning. Annie pushed on the first button, and her window slid down with a mechanical buzz. David whipped his head around and, hanging over Lesley, punched the button so that the window shot back up.

"Are you crazy?" He glared at her.

"David," said Lesley between clenched teeth.

"I'm sorry I snapped at you, Annie. But you must never put your window down when we're stopped in traffic like this. They'd be on us in a second, like a swarm of bees. You wouldn't be able to get the kids' hands out of the window."

"Are you serious?" Annie was incredulous.

Lesley came to his rescue. "It sounds awful, Annie, but the kids are trained to beg and they will lean right into the car. I've seen them do it. It's too heartbreaking. You just want to scoop them up and bring them home with you."

David let out a long sigh. Looking at Annie, he said, "It's too upsetting for Lesley. She wants to make everything better for any kid she sees. We'd be here all day. Let's just get to the Ruizes', have a bath, some breakfast. We'll all feel better." He patted Lesley's knee, gave Annie a dazzling smile, and turned around.

Lesley shrugged her shoulders. Annie managed a half smile. She looked forward to the luxurious hacienda. Lesley had described it to her, but she also wanted a chance to explore the countryside. Was this a mistake, she wondered. David was so controlling. Would she and Lesley be able to explore the city or would they tour it in a hermetically sealed car? Lesley had said David would get caught up in working with Jaime. And Lesley would want to shop. They'd get back to the city. Take it easy, she told herself and leaned back into the soft leather seat, breathing in the wonderful smell. If this was a dream, she wasn't ready to wake up.

As the car wound its way along the lush drive Annie felt her pulse quickening with anticipation and then suddenly the hacienda was in front of them, its pale stucco walls sparkling in the morning sun. Would she get any answers here? What was David Shields' game? What was an OB doing with a cardiologist? Once again Annie felt as though she were outside her body, watching herself. Who was this woman who had left her family to travel with a couple she hardly knew? What kind of woman eavesdropped on friends and secretly expected to discover some evil medical mystery hidden in all these luxurious surroundings? Annie didn't recognize herself, and somehow that emboldened her.

Chapter Seventeen

Annie lay on the bed in just a long white T-shirt, enjoying the breeze blowing across her bare legs. It was heavenly. What a great night it would be for skinny-dipping. David's friends Jaime and Lola were so uptight. She and Jim would have such fun living here. Lola acted bored all the time. She was so lacquered and made up. It was all so weirdly formal, wearing dresses to sit by the pool . . . and Jaime and David had spent all day sequestered in the clinic wing. The three women ate dinner alone. Annie now knew why Lesley had been so anxious for her company.

She should be tired. They had basically been up all night on the plane. But doing nothing all day at the hacienda had made her restless. She was anxious to explore her surroundings, do some sightseeing, but she was a guest. She had the all too familiar sense of being the entertaining but poor relative around Lesley, as if she had stepped out of the pages of a nineteenth-century novel. She felt obliged to let the day take shape around Lesley's desires. And Lesley seemed to bow to Lola's boring concept of fun. But tomorrow they were planning to go to the pyramids, so at least she'd see something of Mexico.

She rolled onto her stomach and resting her chin on her clenched fist, gazed longingly at the empty Perugina foil that lay crumpled on her bedside table. Lola really knew how to make her guests comfortable. The chocolate had been waiting on her pillow, just like in a five-star hotel. She was hungry.

She thought back to that afternoon. Lola had gone off to her siesta and Annie and Lesley had the pool to themselves. They had lounged in their suits eating chocolates and drinking ice water with wedges of lemon. It had really begun to feel like a vacation—until David showed up, demanding a massage from Lesley and acting annoyed that Annie was there.

He'd nuzzled Lesley's neck and said, "You're looking a little cooked, Annie. Don't want to overdo, the sun's rays are stronger here."

"I'm fine, thanks." She'd smiled, but then closed her eyes, giving them the illusion of privacy.

"Your neck is a knot, Davey," Lesley said. "Why are you so tense?"

"Oh, I'm concerned about a patient Ruiz has. I came down to watch a specific microsurgery procedure and we've hit a snag. Why Ruiz insists on working here I'll never know. He could have a real lab in the States instead of this Mickey Mouse bullshit."

"But I thought you said he has much more freedom here. Not so much bureaucratic red tape, testing periods, all that."

"Right, right. I don't know, everything about this place is so ass-backward, it's as frustrating as hell."

"I'll agree with you that it's hellish," Lesley said. "Lola's done nothing but complain about her help since we got here. And who's that spooky woman running around covered in black from head to toe? Is she a patient?"

Annie pricked up her ears. What was this?

" 'Woman in black'? What are you talking about, Lesley? I think you've had too much sun, my dear."

"No, David, I saw her when we first arrived this morning and then again after lunch in the back garden. I even tried to talk to her, but she ran away when she saw me. She's Arabian, or something."

"'Arabian'? Honey, that's crazy, she's probably some kind of maid who has old-fashioned ideas about speaking to guests. Black is hardly an uncommon color for women in this country to wear."

Why was David acting like an Arabian was a crazy notion? A snip of the overheard conversation between Jaime and David replayed in her head. "Has our Saudi friend arrived yet?"

Lesley pressed on, uncharacteristically, Annie thought. "No, David, I'm sure she wasn't Mexican. Everything but her eyes was completely covered up—"

"Look," David interrupted her, "there are no Arabs here, and that's final. You can sit here and imagine people from every nation on the globe if you want to, but I am going to have a swim."

It wasn't like Lesley to argue with David. She must have been sure about what she'd seen, and if that was the case, why was David denying it?

The memory of the chocolate and ice water strengthened her resolve. The combination had been so wonderful this afternoon by the pool. There must be a whole supply of it in the kitchen. Why not? she asked herself, then tiptoed to her door, slid the bolt back, and opened it. The hall was empty, all doors closed. She walked to the railing and looked down to the floor below. All was absolutely still. She walked back into her room and got her robe from the bathroom hook. She had bought the robe especially for this trip. It had seemed a perfect choice for poolside or as a cover-up. Terry inside and white cotton with a wild rose print on the outside. It would be hot now, but she couldn't possibly leave the room in just a T-shirt. She tied the sash around her and tiptoed out, closing her door quietly behind her. She was barefoot—but that

was quietest, she reasoned, and she didn't really expect anyone else to be up. What time was it anyway? Late. They had
talked until midnight. Under the hall sconce, she checked
her watch: one forty-five. She realized with a shiver that this
would be a perfect time to look around for the clinic. David
was up to something, and she wanted to know what.

By keeping close to the wall Annie was in almost total
darkness. The hall was carpeted with a thick, locally woven
runner that silenced her footsteps. The stairs at the end of the
hall were bare but so highly polished that by holding on to
the banister she could slide from one stair to the next
silently. At the foot of the stairs the hall to the kitchen was
terra cotta tiles, so cold that Annie felt a chill run up her
back when her feet first touched them. A dog barked outside
and Annie jumped. Her heart pounded. She leaned against
the wall to catch her breath. Looking down, she saw that her
bathrobe had opened and one bare thigh was exposed. She
rewrapped the robe and tightened the sash. Why hadn't she
slipped on underpants? She suddenly felt vulnerable and
foolish, walking around in only a T-shirt and robe. She
looked longingly over her shoulder, up the stairs toward her
room.

Don't be a ninny, she told herself. You need more than
chocolate—you need to find the clinic and see about this
mysterious "woman in black." Where had ninny come
from? Annie didn't normally use that word herself. She
smiled—but her mother had—when she egged her on to
climb higher in a tree, swim farther than the raft, race
against the boys—"Don't be a ninny, Annie," she'd say.
"You can do it. I know you can."

She walked cautiously forward. If a light was shining
under the kitchen door, she wouldn't go in. That would be
foolish, dressed as she was. She had an eerily pleasant sensation, like a rush, as if she were starring in a Nancy Drew

story; the beautiful, poised girl-detective, about to solve another case.

She turned the corner and could see the dark swinging door, no chinks of light around its edges. She pushed against it gently. Not even a squeak; thank God for Lola's obsessive nature. She hurried to the back of the room, where she easily found the chocolate on a pantry shelf. Having filled her robe pocket, she quickly eased the refrigerator door open and was momentarily blinded by its light. She closed it to just a crack until her eyes were adjusted and then retrieved a small Evian. It went in her other pocket.

Coming out of the pantry, she was momentarily disoriented and turned in the wrong direction. She came to a large stove that she hadn't seen on the way in. Where was she? She took a few steps forward and stopped just short of walking straight into a door. Should she go back or continue through the door?

She felt a hand on her arm. Before she knew it, she had screamed. The hand withdrew hastily and a light was switched on. Annie stood blinking, staring at the young Indian woman who had brought her coffee that morning. Annie fumbled in her robe for the Evian bottle and held it up apologetically. The girl smiled and brought a finger to her lips, then turned and looked nervously over her shoulder. When Annie smiled back, she reached out tentatively and putting her hand on Annie's shoulder, turned her firmly away from the door.

"No, señora," she said earnestly. She had stopped smiling and was pointing at the door. "No go there." Her eyes pleaded with Annie. She gestured to the kitchen, sweeping her arm to encompass the large room. "*Sí*." She nodded. "Good." then she turned and pointed to the door again. "No." Her eyes darted about. She looked over her shoulder again, then looked back at Annie and shook her head repeatedly. "No go there." She put her finger to her lips again and motioned agitatedly for Annie to go back the way she'd come.

"*Gracias*," Annie managed. "*Buenos noches*." She hurried back through the kitchen to the stairs. Her heart pounded as she ran up the stairs, not caring whether they creaked or not now.

The door to her room was swollen and didn't open when she turned the knob. She felt panicky as she pushed against it, willing it to open. She almost fell when it finally gave way and as soon as she was inside she locked it behind her.

"Annie," she told herself, "get a grip. So there's a room the maid doesn't want you to go into. That's okay." But she knew it wasn't. Not the way the maid had acted. It wasn't a simple, "FYI, this room's off limits." The maid was nervous, scared even, and obviously concerned that someone would see or hear her. What was all that looking over her shoulder? Who was she afraid of?

Annie had that odd sensation again, of being apart from her body, a spectator of her own life. It was as if she had entered a piece of fiction, but not Nancy Drew this time. Bluebeard, maybe. The woman is shown a secret room. Even given a key. But told never, under any circumstances, to look in the room. But of course eventually she does. Annie shuddered because she could see herself in her mind's eye being drawn inexorably, like so many of Bluebeard's wives, down a well-worn path to a room she had no business entering.

Chapter Eighteen

The cook's son had decided to choose his time carefully. Just as he had waited the night before in the shadows of the kitchen, so he waited now for the right moment to present itself. And when it came, he made his move. David was alone on the terrace with an early morning cup of coffee. Ricardo approached him, careful to make enough noise so as not to startle the doctor, who appeared to be deep in thought.

"Sir, excuse me, there is something I feel you would want to know."

David looked up, irritated.

"What is it?"

The man did not immediately answer. David understood. He reached for his wallet and handed the man several bills.

"*Gracias*. It is about your guest, the dark-haired Americana. She was in the kitchen last night, very late."

"She must have been hungry," said David, angry with himself for paying for a discourse on Annie's nocturnal habits.

"I do not think so. I was alerted when she screamed. It seems one of the maids surprised her near the entrance to the laboratory and the medical wing." He paused, and David felt his heart skip. "She showed Immaculata a bottle of water but she was not coming from where the water is kept."

Keep it cool, David said to himself. Calm and cool. What does this peasant know? What does he think he knows?

"She probably lost her way," said David.

"Perhaps you are right, sir. That would account for the panic in her eyes."

David stood up and cleared his throat.

"Thank you for telling me," he said. "She will be traveling to the pyramids with my wife today. That should tire her. I do not think there will be any more nighttime rambling." He nodded his head to indicate that their discussion was over.

Ricardo knew his first loyalty was to Dr. Ruiz and whether the American doctor was concerned or not, his lovely guest looked like trouble. The pyramids? He wasn't needed at the hacienda today—it would be a fine day for a history lesson. And if he should learn anything, it would mean more cash in his pocket.

David watched as the Indian disappeared into the bougainvillea. Troublesome. Just then Annie, dressed for the day's expedition, arrived at the other end of the courtyard and joined Lesley and Lola, who were sitting at the breakfast table under an umbrella. He moved in their direction, keeping the wall of greenery between them. He wanted to be close enough to overhear their conversation, but not close enough to be obliged to share a meal with his hostess.

"I am so sorry, Lola." Annie smiled nervously. "I didn't mean to sleep so late. I thought the sun would wake me."

"It is I who must apologize, Annie," said Lola, but she sounded angry. "The maid is ill. These country girls, they do whatever strikes their fancy—whatever their witch advises or whatever they see in the weather. Omens, oracles. Please sit down. Maria will bring you some breakfast." She turned to ring the bell at the end of the table. Lesley raised an eyebrow and smiled at Annie.

Maria brought Annie a plate of fresh breakfast rolls, her

gold tooth flashing as she proudly set down the beautifully garnished dish. Then she cleared away Lesley and Lola's empty plates.

"Now"—Lola was at her side, patting her arm—"all set? Very nice. I must leave you now. All this domestic turmoil. I am exhausted and my head, aii, jumping beans. Jaime will make me a tincture. I will see you ladies later. Please have Maria bring you anything else you might need."

When they could no longer hear the click of her heels, Annie innocently asked, "What happened? What 'domestic turmoil'?"

"I'll tell you in the car," Lesley answered.

Now that Lola was gone David came and joined them. The Indian had probably just been trying to squeeze more cash out of him.

Lesley held up her backpack and said, "Lucia's made us a wonderful lunch; are you sure you won't come?" David shook his head.

"I'm sorry you have to work, David," Annie said sweetly. "Lesley tells me you collect early Indian art. You must know an enormous amount about the pyramids."

"I'm sorry, too. I would love to accompany you two beautiful explorers." He was smiling when he said it, but he was mentally regretting having let Lesley talk him into bringing Annie along.

As he left them, Annie saw the smile turn off abruptly, as if an unseen hand had flipped a switch.

The road to the highway felt familiar now, the way places do, thought Annie, when you are traveling. When everything seems so different from home that your second or third glance of a thing gives it an artificial familiarity. They passed quickly along the lush, winding road with wrought-iron gates leading to long driveways whose curves hid opulent houses—similar, no doubt, to the one they had come from, Annie thought. Occasionally there was a shrine, always to the virgin, at the end of the driveway, just inside the gate.

"Our Lady of Guadalupe?" Annie asked Lesley.

Lesley nodded.

"Okay," Annie said. "I'm dying of curiosity. What's the 'domestic turmoil'?"

Lesley laughed. "I only know what Lola told me. According to Lola, Immaculata, the maid who helps out in the kitchen, is pregnant. Apparently this has been a somewhat chronic problem with their maids. Lola is furious because she just heard a rumor. The other servants say the cook's son rapes all the new maids. She's afraid he'll jinx their house, that maids will stop coming to them, and Jaime is refusing to fire him."

Annie could feel her anger rising. This woman had a servant that she knew was a rapist and she was upset about it because it might impact on servant supply? She had no feelings for the young woman involved? And why was Jaime refusing to fire him?

Lesley continued, "Lola doesn't want to lose this girl, Immaculata. She says she's the best maid she's had in a long time. Lola's hoping she'll go to the cook for help."

"The cook?" asked Annie.

"According to Lola, the cook is a witch or actually I think a kind of witch doctor. Apparently some of the other maids got some potion from her that made them miscarry."

"So is Immaculata doing that? Is that why she's sick today?"

"Lola doesn't think so. Lola said Immaculata is scared."

Is that what was going on last night? Annie wondered. Was that Immaculata, looking for the cook? Was she looking over her shoulder because she was afraid of running into the cook's son? And why was she trying to keep Annie away from that door? What was back there? The clinic? The son's room? Or maybe it was the place where the cook kept her potions.

"Scared?" asked Annie. "Of what?"

"Miscarriages are very painful," said Lesley, and she brushed away a tear. Annie realized with surprise that this was a personal issue for her friend.

"Did you have a miscarriage, Les?"

"Yes. Before we adopted Millie." She wiped her eyes with a tissue from her purse. "It was awful."

"I'm so sorry. How far along were you?"

"Oh, it was early—eleven or twelve weeks. I wasn't showing yet. But I was already in love with that baby."

Annie leaned in closer to Lesley and held her hand. "It must have been awfully hard. We don't have to talk about it if you don't want to."

"No, sometimes I like to talk about it. It makes the baby seem more real. She would have been a girl."

"But you weren't far enough along to tell, were you?"

"David had them do a chromosome study. He wanted to figure out what went wrong."

"Was he able to?"

"Yes." Lesley covered her face and wept in earnest, great, gasping sobs.

Annie got a damask napkin from the sideboard and handed it to Lesley. "It's okay," she said softly, stroking Lesley's hair. "Go ahead and cry." She heard the soft singsong voice that she used when the children were upset and felt a stab of longing so sharp for them that she knelt down again. What was she doing thousands of miles away from her babies and husband? How had she gotten caught up in these other peoples' lives? She wished none of it had ever happened.

Lesley wiped her tears away. She now patted Annie's head. "You're a good friend, Annie. I bet you miss the kids. I miss Millie."

Annie nodded.

"I was going to name the first baby Millicent if she was a girl. I had a Raggedy Ann book when I was little, and Raggedy's owner was named Millicent. I loved the sound of it. My own name sounded heavy and boring to me, but Millicent was beautiful and romantic. When David put Millie in my arms, all I could think was, 'You're finally here.'"

Annie raised her eyebrows slightly. Without noticing, Lesley went on.

"I know this will sound silly, but I have never felt Millie was adopted. I mean, I've never felt any distance, the way you think you would, any sense that this is another woman's baby. I've always felt that Millie was mine, that she was ours, that she was"—Lesley paused—"the other baby, the one I miscarried, finally getting through. When David handed her to me I felt it, and when I was all alone with her I whispered to her, 'You finally made it—you're here.' And she looked at me, really stared at me and she looked wise and amused. It was as if she thought it was all funny, as if she wanted to say, 'Well, of course I did.' A kind of O, ye of little faith sort of thing." Lesley looked at Annie. "Do you think I'm crazy?"

"Of course not," said Annie, and reached for Lesley's hand. "I think there are all sorts of strange knowings, déjà vus, things of that sort, in life. There are just too many of them to dismiss as coincidence."

"I think," said Lesley very hesitantly, "the more open you allow yourself to be to these sorts of experiences, the more frequently you have them."

Annie smiled. She wasn't sure how she felt about that, but she was enjoying Lesley opening up to her. She felt them relaxing with each other, a real friendship building.

"That's what I love about Mexico," Lesley went on, "about the pyramids. You feel centuries of people. You feel a presence. But it is spooky there. Parts of it are places of great torment. You feel the terror." Annie shivered. "But you feel their joy, too. You see that life has a pattern. People are born and live and feel and think many of the things that you feel and think, and then they believed the soul lives on, and I believe it, too." She hesitated. "David hates it when I talk like this."

"Oh, well, he's a doctor. Science is all powerful," said Annie.

"I don't know, I think it's sort of dangerous to not humble yourself before these natural forces. Sometimes it makes me very uncomfortable, the work that David does."

Annie held her breath. Would Lesley confide something?

"The babies that he saves," continued Lesley, "they're getting younger and younger. He had one recently that was twenty-three weeks! The baby didn't live, but he thought it might. But if it had lived, it wouldn't have been whole. It would have had something wrong neurologically, probably several somethings. I just think David needs to stand back more."

"I think it should probably be up to the parents, how far the doctors go," said Annie. "They're the ones who will care for the child."

"Sometimes they don't even ask the parents. They just reflexively start trying to keep it alive. David's very proud of the fact that he holds the record for days keeping a twenty-three-weeker alive."

"What do you think he should do?"

"I think he should focus on finding ways to keep the babies in the mothers longer. They should focus all their energy on that. The rest just seems like cowboy medicine to me."

Annie was amazed. Lesley had never said anything remotely negative about David. Annie had been imagining sinister transactions in the clinic, illegal doings—testing, or manufacturing—and now here Lesley was attacking David's medical practices.

Lesley was still talking, Annie realized.

"I can't have children myself. It turns out that I'm one of those women whose bodies are inhospitable to their own babies. It's as if my uterus is allergic to the baby. It won't let it burrow in and stay. It just pushed the baby out. I was so depressed after the miscarriage that David wouldn't even let me try again. Once he knew what the problem was, he begged me to get my tubes tied. He said my depression scared him, and he couldn't bear the thought of losing me or another child."

Losing your money is more like it, thought Annie. Lesley stopped and stared at their hands clasped in her lap.

"Did you, Lesley?"

Lesley nodded.

Annie said nothing. There was nothing to say. The sadness hung over them. It was very still in the car, only the gentle hum of the Mercedes' engine around them.

Annie looked out the window. The houses weren't on top of each other anymore. Small, dusty dirt yards separated them, and often there'd be a few chickens scratching at the ground or a mangy dog tied with clothesline to a stake. There were lots of children. Some waved enthusiastically, others just stared vacantly. They were often strikingly beautiful—wide faces with large brown eyes and beautiful deep brown straight hair. They were dirty, the dust sticking to their small bodies in sweaty streaks.

The houses eventually ended and they went through a stretch of dry land with occasional goats and a lone goatherd, with nothing growing except cacti and scrub grass.

Finally they came to the lush valley that housed the pyramids to the moon and the sun. It was beautiful. As far as they could see, everything was green—green grass, green trees, and, in the distance, rising into the clouds, mountains, green and blue with vegetation.

"If you go high enough the mountains are covered with pine trees," said Lesley.

Annie nodded and tried to imagine what it must have been like five hundred years ago.

The car stopped and the driver helped them out. "I will be here whenever you are ready to return."

"Thank you," said Lesley.

"Be careful, ladies." The driver looked Annie in the eyes. "The pyramids are steep. The steps can be treacherous."

"Yes," said Lesley.

"Thank you," said Annie, then to Lesley as they were walking away, "Was that a warning or a threat?"

Lesley laughed and linked her arm with Annie's. "Come on," she said. "Mystical Mexico is getting to you."

They joined a group with a guide under the shade of a tree at the foot of the Pyramid to the Sun. Looking down the broad central avenue to the Pyramid to the Moon, Annie was shocked by the enormity of the pyramids. The trees were dwarfed by them. People were insignificant. Living all day in the shadow of these man-made wonders must have made individuals seem inconsequential. That must have made it possible to accept the barbarism. She tuned into the guide.

"Under Moctezuma I, adobe was replaced by stone and the gardens were planted. An aqueduct was built to pipe fresh spring water to the city.

"Huitzilopochtli, the Aztec God of War and the Sun, required a steady stream of human hearts. Most of these hearts were obtained from captive prisoners of war. The Aztecs were not a peaceful people, and because of the constant need for sacrifice victims, they amassed a huge empire. Under Moctezuma I's son, Ahiutzol, the Aztecs took control of one hundred thousand square miles, about the size of modern Italy.

"When Ahuitzol became emperor in 1468, he ordered the sun god's temple rebuilt. Upon completion he dedicated the temple by sacrificing twenty thousand captives. He marched them to the top of the pyramid. A priest there cut their rib cages and pulled the still-beating hearts out. The sacrifice lasted four days from dusk to sunup. Can any of us imagine waiting through one of those nights, knowing what was coming? As you are climbing the pyramid today, keep those four days of sacrifice in mind. The blood ran down those steps like a river."

A tiny groan escaped from Lesley. Annie felt herself shiver. She wished they could move out of the shade.

"If you will follow me into this building"—the guide pointed to a low stone house—"you will be able to see Aztec relics and read some of Moctezuma II's own words. Then you may go on your own to climb our mighty pyramids."

The house was a small Aztec museum, designed like a primitive stone chamber, constructed of the same types of materials as the pyramids. The tourists mostly crowded around the glass display cases housing sculptures of the sun god and bowls and other vessels from the period.

Annie moved down the aisle of relic cases to a display mounted on the wall. The corridor was darker down at this end, and quite narrow. Annie felt a small wave of claustrophobia, and looked back at the clutch of tourists, still mostly taking in the first few exhibits nearest the door. Someone had asked the guide a question and she saw that Lesley stood, her back to Annie, listening to the answer.

Annie turned back to the wall display. It was a slick public relations ad for restoration work being done on a new discovery. A magnificent mural, intact, had been found at Cacaxtla. There was a poster-sized photograph. It was at the same time beautiful and horrifying. Annie could only imagine how intense the colors must be in real life. They were strikingly vivid in the photo. The depicted scene was of a mass sacrifice. A man with Medusa-like hair wearing a jaguar skin was stabbing a warrior in the heart. The blood appeared as bright globules in his dark chest. The victim's face was contorted in agony and terror.

Annie stopped reading. She felt warm, too warm. She needed to get some air. She felt the hair on the back of her neck rise and felt instinctively that she was being watched. She turned around and gasped as she found herself face-to-face with a very tall, muscular Indian. As Annie's eyes struggled to make the adjustment from the brightly lit exhibit case to the shadowy hallway, he came a step closer and looked down at her, a knowing grin on his face. For a long moment they stared at each other, and then, he suddenly made a small bow and swept his arm out toward the exit as if to say "After you."

Annie nodded at him and hurried out past the cases, very much aware of the strange man's presence behind her. As she was about to reach the door she felt a hand on her shoulder. She spun around.

"Sorry," Lesley said. "I didn't mean to scare you."

"Oh, Lesley!" She laughed shakily. "It's okay. I was just letting my imagination run away with me." She looked over Lesley's shoulder but the Indian was nowhere to be seen. "This place is so evocative. It's so easy to imagine the horrors that happened here."

"What about the twenty thousand captives? How'd you like to have been one of them?"

Annie shuddered. "Can you imagine?"

"Are you ready to climb?"

"As ready as I'm ever going to be. I'm not wild about heights."

The two women strolled over to the base of the pyramid and started up. The climb was more difficult than Annie had imagined. The steps were less than a foot wide and tall. There was no railing, only a wide side piece that was flush with the steps—nothing to grab on to. Nothing to stop you from falling. The higher they climbed, the steeper the steps seemed. Annie bent over as far as she could without being on her hands and knees.

"Do you want a hand?" asked Lesley, who didn't seem distressed.

"No thanks. Being touched would make me more nervous."

"Are you okay? Don't look down."

"Right," said Annie. "I can't look up, either. How much farther to that first plateau?"

"Looks like about ten more steps," said Lesley. "You can do it."

They sat on the plateau and looked out on the valley. It was so green. It must have seemed like paradise to the Spaniards with the flowers and the lake and the gold.

"Can you make it up one other level?" asked Lesley.

"I think," said Annie. She wanted to go as high as she could, to see what the captives saw last.

After a while she asked Lesley how many more steps.

"Five, maybe."

Annie made herself look up. She scanned the plateau. At the top of it, to the left, standing and looking down at them, was a tall Indian. Annie's foot slipped, and her sunglasses fell off, clattering endlessly down the stones. She caught herself with her knee. The impact hurt. Could it be the man from the museum? If so, he had moved quickly. She squinted into the sun's glare. The man was gone.

When they reached the plateau, they sat again. Annie rubbed her sore knee and looked around. There was no sign of him on the plateau. She looked up at the people climbing to the next level. She didn't think he was among them but it was hard to tell—everyone was bent over, and the glare from the sun was terrific. He could be climbing down, but there was no way Annie would look. It must have been someone who just looked like him. Jim was always teasing her about mistaking people.

They climbed the remaining steps and looked out over the valley. This was what the captives had seen last. A beautiful valley that then would have been full of life. How sweet it must have seemed, how hard not to be able to be part of it. Did they think of their families then? Did the people walking below, tiny as they looked, remind them of their wives, their children? Did they wish they could sprout wings and fly back to their village, back to the ones they loved?

Climbing down was terrifying. Standing up was out of the question. Annie and Lesley sat down and inched their way off each step to the next. It was a long, slow process.

Lesley stood up and ran down the last few steps. Annie gingerly walked them.

"We did it!" Lesley said. Annie smiled.

"You look so pale," said Lesley.

"I knew I didn't like heights," said Annie, "but I had no idea how deep the fear was."

"What you need," said Lesley, "is some shopping. That will get the blood flowing again."

Annie marveled at Lesley's energy as they headed to the small gift shop. Outside the door to the shop was an Indian woman with a canary in a cage. The cage was wooden, obviously handmade and painted with abstract decorations. The woman motioned to Lesley and Annie. When they were close enough she held a small tray full of inscribed cards out to the bird. The bird stuck out its head and picked out a card. The woman handed it to Annie.

Annie held it up for Lesley to read.

"You are more powerful than you think."

"Thank you," said Annie. Lesley reached in her pocket and handed the woman some pesos.

"*Gracias, señora.*"

"That was great," said Annie. "A fortune-telling bird."

"Feel better?" asked Lesley.

"Much."

The gift shop had the usual street vendor wares; baskets and silver, bark paintings—but there was also a kit with supposedly authentic adobe clay and instructions for reproducing an Aztec sacrificial bowl.

"The kind that held the hearts?" Lesley asked when she saw Annie examining it.

"I think I'll get it for Alex," said Annie. "I may leave out its original use."

"Oh," said Lesley, "look at the masks." A stand with amazing feather masks stood at the other end of the store. Lesley headed in their direction. "Help me choose one of these," she called. "I want to take one back to Alex."

They chose a replica of a mask worn by a high priest. It had azure blue plumage and a hammered gold piece across the forehead. It was magnificent.

They went to the silver case and each chose a five-dollar bracelet to remind them of their climb.

Annie paid for her purchases first and then took a final look around the shop to see if there was anything she had missed while Lesley paid for hers.

There was a man trying on masks at the stand where they had gotten Alex's. His back was to her, but she could see his head bobbing up and down as he tried new ones on. He was tall, with dark hair, and even from this distance, she could tell—it was him. He put on an intricate jaguar mask and turned toward Annie. Slowly, he pulled the mask off and stood smiling at her. She gasped. He was wearing her sunglasses. With several long strides he covered the distance between them, took off the glasses and, sneering down at her, held them out. Annie took the glasses, and without a word the Indian turned and walked out of the store. Annie unfolded the glasses and felt the still-warm slippery wetness of the man's sweat. She looked around for a trash can and finding none, shoved the glasses in her bag. She wished she could wash her hands. Lesley turned away from the cash register.

"All set?" she asked brightly.

Annie nodded and they left. Outside, Annie looked over her shoulder. The Indian was nowhere in sight. What was he doing with her? And why was she frightened of him? It's the place, she told herself. The sun was eclipsed by gray clouds now and the pyramids looked dark and foreboding. It no longer resembled paradise. The rain would begin any minute.

Lesley hurried them in the direction of the car. Before she ducked into the backseat, Annie looked back and saw the pyramids now as places of horrifying pain and death. Heading across the parking area to a large, old American sedan was the Indian. He saw Annie and gave her a desultory wave. Heart pounding, she stepped into the black Mercedes.

The drive back to the hacienda was long and hot, in spite of the limousine's air-conditioning unit. Bumping along the rutted road, Lesley dozed off and Annie was left to her thoughts. That man had really given her the creeps, the way he kept popping up wherever she was, almost as though he had been following them. And that sneer—like he knew all about her.

Yeah, sure, Annie, she chided herself. Everything's all about you, right? What was she doing getting herself all worked up about some guy who had basically just found her sunglasses and then returned them to her? There was probably more evil going on for real back at the hacienda. That was it, she realized—she was just trying to talk herself out of what she knew she had to do. Here she'd been out sightseeing, shopping, relaxing by the pool—and finding out nothing. Hadn't she come down here, at least in part, to get some answers? Tonight was the night. She was running out of time.

Chapter Nineteen

She thought the evening would never end. David and Jaime were noticeably absent from dinner again. Lola, claiming exhaustion, went to her room at ten but Lesley wanted company while she packed. Finally, at midnight, the house was quiet.

It was impossible to know what servants were still about, but if she used that excuse she'd be waiting all night. She pulled on her robe and remembering how vulnerable she'd felt the night before, pulled on a pair of underpants.

The hall outside her room was dark except for the wall sconces and there were no lights under the other doors. She pulled her door shut but not tightly, remembering her panic when it had stuck. Keeping to the edge of the hall, she made her way silently to the stairs. She went over her plan in her mind, trying to calm herself as she inched her way down the steps. She would go to the kitchen first. Knowing the way made her feel more confident. She'd get a bottle of water. She could always use that as an excuse if she bumped into someone. After the water she'd go to the door. If caught, act dumb, she told herself. Speak some broken Spanish. That wouldn't be hard, she thought, since that was all she knew. And if the door led to the clinic? Same thing, she told herself, act dumb. "Looking for water, wrong turn, ha ha." Try to be cute. She wasn't sure which would be worse: running into David or the cook's rapist son.

She was at the bottom of the stairs now and had to tra-
verse the long expanse of open hallway to the kitchen. She
looked over her shoulder, fearing somebody would be
there—a servant? Jaime? David? In this strange darkness,
this alien country, this unknown house, the men all seemed
dangerous. How badly do you want your questions answered? she asked herself.

And then she surprised herself. Badly, she thought. I
want answers badly. I'm becoming good friends with Lesley. If David is doing something illegal or immoral or un-
ethical or whatever, I need to know. She walked quickly,
hugging the wall the rest of the way to the kitchen and cautiously pushed open the heavy wooden swinging door and
stepped into the darkness beyond.

It took several moments for her eyes to adjust and she
headed carefully for the end of the kitchen that housed the
refrigerators. She got a bottle of Evian and slipped it into her
pocket. She had to stop and rearrange her robe so that there
was enough fabric in front to make her feel securely covered. She wished that she had her street clothes on but if she
were discovered it would seem bizarre for her to be fully
dressed at this hour. What if the cook's son really was a
rapist though?

Calm down, Annie, she told herself. It's a servants' rumor
and even if it is true, he rapes the maids. He's not going to
rape one of the boss's guests. She wanted to believe that, but
her legs felt weak as she began walking toward the opposite
wall, where she'd seen the door the night before. Halfway
across the room she heard a sound that raised the hair on her
arms. She froze, holding her breath, straining to hear it
again. It came almost immediately, a moan like an animal
starting from deep inside the house, low and rising, not quite
a howl. She couldn't tell what it was; distance muffled it.
Could it be a cat? It was too forceful, too wild. Were there
tigers in Mexico? Oh, Annie, get a grip, she told herself.

Tigers? And she almost laughed out loud, but then it came again. And this time it was distinctly human. She was really scared now. She wanted to run back up to her room as fast as she could, lock the door, and throw herself under the covers, but instead she felt herself moving toward the sound until she came to another door.

Her eyes were completely accustomed to the dark now and she could see well enough when she pushed open the door to see that this must be the food preparation section of the kitchen. It was long, and steel counters lined both walls. She stopped to get control of her breathing. She had been straining so hard to hear and her heart was pounding so loudly she could hear nothing but the rush of her own blood. She leaned against the counter and immediately lurched forward. She had been expecting to place her hand on a solid counter and almost called out when she fell instead into thin air. Her hands met the cold metal several inches lower than she had expected. When she had gotten her balance, she proceeded to slide her hands gingerly along the solid edge of the counter, down a slope, and into what appeared to be a trough of some kind, which then sloped back up to the main counter. Ugh—like an autopsy table. It was too dark to see any of this very well. Damn, she thought. If only I had a match, a flashlight, something. Then the moaning echoed through the dark house again. Annie went more quickly now. There was something familiar about this sound but she still wasn't sure what it was. She turned the doorknob slowly and eased the door open a few inches. The hall was dark and when the sound came again it was clear and recognizable. Annie had given birth herself recently enough to identify the sounds of a woman in the middle of a painful labor. Her whole body gave in to the sound and she wanted only to help. She forgot where she was and what she was wearing. Her only thought was to find the woman and comfort her. A flight of stairs was to her right, and to the left an-

other hallway. The sound seemed to be coming from overhead. She took the stairs. A heavy fire door was at the top.
This no longer seemed like a home. She must be in the clinic
wing. For a brief second she let her mind register that what
she mistook for a food preparation area of the kitchen must
be a lab of some sort. She peeked through the glass panel in
the fire door. The linoleum-tiled hall was dimly lit and lined
on both sides by doors, some open, others not. She opened
the door a couple of inches, and the moaning hit her loud,
clear, and insistent. The moans were coming closer together
now. Annie thought suddenly of how she was dressed. She
straightened the robe around her and walked into the hall.
She had better take control of herself now. She should get
the hell out of here, it was lunacy to think that she could
help. She had no medical training and anyway, the woman
was in a sort of hospital, wasn't she? All right, so it wasn't
a maternity ward, but Jaime and David *were* physicians. Besides, she was a guest of Jaime's. She shouldn't be prowling
around his house. David would be furious if he caught her.
Lesley would think she was crazy. But she had been there
too recently herself to ignore this woman's anguish. She
held the robe tightly clenched at her throat, feeling vulnerable now. Hugging the wall, she inched her way down the
corridor to the first open door. Through the crack between
the hinges she could see a woman dressed in the black robes
and veil of the Arabs. Lesley's woman in black! The woman
was kneeling on a small oriental rug, fingering beads and
murmuring, then chanting in a quiet but high-pitched, atonal
wail. Annie shuddered. Why had David lied? A strong sense
of foreboding filled her. The woman all in black, her desperate tone, the animal-like moans. Annie felt faint. *Don't*,
she told herself. The image of her being discovered uncon-
scious with her robe splayed open, her T-shirt having ridden
up to expose her body to who-knew-what eyes was terrifying enough to keep her from giving in to her fear. She took

one large silent leap past the Arab woman's door and came
to another. In this room a man lay sleeping in bed. How
could he sleep through the noise, Annie wondered. He must
be the cardiac patient Lesley had told her about. He's probably under sedation. Annie was going to go past his room
when something made her look in again. Strange. On TV
and in all the hospitals she'd ever visited, cardiac patients
were hooked up to all sorts of monitors; wires, tubes, beep-
ing noises were everywhere. But this room was peaceful,
quiet, and perfectly empty—except for the man and his bed.
The man had dark skin and what she thought of as Middle
Eastern features. Was he with the woman in the veil? Probably. Even in the dim light Annie could see he was handsome and his face looked peaceful, at ease. He must be
medicated. Suddenly he shifted in his sleep and Annie saw
a shaved patch on the man's head. Annie's mind was racing
but she didn't dare stop to think. Any minute someone might
open a door and find her. She looked down the hall—the
next door was closed and the one after that, but across the
hall the last door was ajar and she thought the moaning came
from there. She held her ear against the first closed door.
Male voices. She strained to make them out. She recognized
Jaime's and then David's. David's voice moved closer to the
door. "I'll see what's happening with her." Annie raced back
to the Arab's room, which was the first open door and just
made it inside as she heard the next door open. She looked
about frantically for a place to hide. The room was so bare.
How odd. The hospital bed was so high and open underneath, there was no hiding place there. There was a door to
her right. She opened it—the bathroom, complete with tub
and shower curtain, thank God. She stepped in and pulled
the curtain closed around her. Her lungs needed oxygen. She
gasped and the sound was deafening. Suddenly she heard
bed springs and the rustling of sheets. Oh my God, no, don't
let him have to pee. She stepped out of the shower and

peeked through the crack in the door. The man was reaching
for a glass of water on the table next to the bed. As he raised
it to his mouth, she could see that his hand was shaking uncontrollably, and the water was sloshing over the side onto
the bed linen. After drinking, he slowly returned the glass to
the table and closed his eyes. Almost immediately, his chin
drooped down to his chest, his mouth fell open, and he
began to snore softly. She breathed easier. She could hear
footsteps out in the hall, but they stopped short of the room
she was in. She heard the door of the next room open, and
then David's voice—"Almost, Jaime." Then the door closed
and she could hear nothing.

She waited, listening, but there were only the moans now.
She stepped from the shower and tiptoed across the Arab's
room. She glanced over her shoulder to look once more at
the sleeping man. His chest rose and fell evenly. His breathing was so smooth. He certainly didn't seem to be sick, but
what was the shaking?

She tiptoed across the hall and stood again peering between the hinges of a door but this time she saw a young
woman, a girl really, lying on her back, her knees drawn up
against what must be terrible pain. Her head was turned
away from Annie. Suddenly a piercing shrill cry rose out of
her and she turned her face toward Annie. Her eyes pleaded
for help. But she can't see me, Annie thought. She turned
and ran down the hall and back through the fire door, then
sat on the top step and wept silently. The girl's eyes would
always haunt her. She should have gone in to her. Suddenly
she focused on the memory of the girl's face, not just her
eyes. It was the maid who had given her the warning in the
kitchen the night before. She didn't look like she could be
any more than sixteen, maybe even younger. She hadn't
looked pregnant. She must be the one—Immaculata. The
poor thing, she was a baby herself. That last shriek—Annie
had heard that echoing off the walls at the maternity hospi-

tal where she had birthed Alex and Rebecca. By Rebecca's birth she and Jim had managed to ease their anxiety by saying knowingly to each other, when that desperate shriek came through the walls of their birthing room, "Pushing!"

But couldn't David and Jaime have helped her more? They stayed in that closed room, leaving her all alone. Annie wiped her nose with the sleeve of her robe. Her hand shook as she reached for the banister and eased herself down the stairs.

She hurried through the lab and into the kitchen, past the stove and around the corner, and almost tripped on an outstretched foot. Annie gasped—the man from the pyramids—here! He laughed derisively and made a kissing sound with his lips.

"*Buenos noches, señora.*" He nodded his head and smiled widely, the end of a cigarette stuck to his lower lip.

Annie fumbled in her robe for the Evian bottle. "*Agua,*" she whispered. Her voice failed her. She skirted his other foot and ran from the room. He did not follow her. The sound of his laughter did. Upstairs she fell on her bed and lay there shaking. It was all too much. The Arabs, the maid, the man in the kitchen. She tried to sleep, but couldn't. What did it all mean?

She got up and went to the desk by the window. She looked out at the driveway and the small fishpond. The moon was full and bright. She wished she could talk to Mac about all of this. She would make a joke out of it and make Annie laugh. No such luck, kiddo, she said to herself. This time you're on your own. She took her journal out of the desk drawer and began to make a list of what she had seen.

1. Some sort of lab—metal counters, a trough? Like on autopsy tables? Autopsy tables, she asked herself. How do I know what those look like? Old *Quincy* reruns? She would like to see that room in daylight.

2. The Arab woman praying. Related to heart patient?

3. The man in bed. If a heart patient, where are the monitors, the resuscitation equipment? Lesley said this was very high-tech experimental medicine. Seems awfully low-tech to me.

4. Immaculata. Definitely in labor. Alone.

Annie opened the Evian and took a sip. It was still wonderfully cold. She checked her watch. She had only been out of the room for half an hour. It seemed much longer—it seemed like a dream. She lay her head down on her notebook and closed her eyes—to think.

She awoke with a start. The Evian had spilled and was soaking through her robe. The light had changed outside her window. The sun would be up soon. Her eyes felt gritty and swollen. Her notebook lay open and drenched.

"Damn." She went into the bathroom, grabbed a towel, and after blotting her journal's soaked pages, left it open on the counter to dry. Straightening up, some movement outside the window caught her eye. She leaned toward the glass. A figure, a woman with a brightly colored shawl pulled up over her head and shoulders, running awkwardly down the driveway, keeping to the dark, shadowed edge. Now and then, when the woman moved out of the shadows into the bright moonlight, Annie could see that she was bent over, as if the running caused her pain. Annie looked up, expecting to see a full moon, and instead saw an incredibly bright star. It must be Venus, she thought. Her grandmother had taught her to recognize it during their summers together. When she looked back, the figure had disappeared around a bend in the drive.

"Immaculata," Annie whispered. But what about the baby? She wanted to run through the sleeping house, out the door, and catch the girl. Offer to help, giver her money, see her safely home to her family. But she was a guest in this house, the affairs of which were not her province. They would all think she was acting like a fool. David especially would be embarrassed and, Annie thought bitterly, he would take it out on Lesley. She hung her wet robe over the chair and got into bed. The cool cotton sheet felt delicious against her legs and it was a relief to give in to sleep.

The bird sounds and bright sun woke Annie and for a minute she felt excited about going home and happy with that as her only thought. Then, as she came completely awake the horror of the night before broke through her consciousness. Immaculata's pain and anguished cries, the Arab woman wailing prayers, and the "heart patient," dribbling water down his chin. Annie was sure now that David was involved in something that he didn't want discovered. She was also sure David and Jaime hadn't detected her presence, but what about that Indian in the kitchen? Was it a coincidence that he had also been at the pyramids? Would he tell David what he'd seen? What did he see? He saw me leaving the kitchen with a bottle of water. And then a new fear gripped her. He was obviously at home in that kitchen. Was he the cook's son? Had she been alone with *him*? She couldn't leave here soon enough. She tossed the covers back and reached for the traveling clothes she had laid out the night before. While she dressed she eyed the room to make sure she hadn't forgotten to pack anything. Nothing of hers remained on the bedside table, the desk, or the bed. She looked closely at the carved bedposts. The squatting men with hair like dreadlocks and mouths gaping in terror. She closed her eyes and shook her head before frightening images could form. She opened her eyes to the bright sunshine coming in the window. A light breeze blew the gauze curtain in against her arm. Pushing the curtain aside, she looked down at the gravel turnaround and the long driveway beyond. The front of the hacienda was quiet. There was no

sign of the hulking Indian, Annie noted with relief. Her eyes
followed the edge of the drive where Immaculata had run
away. At the curve in the drive the sun hit the bright chrome
of the Mercedes' bumper and momentarily blinded Annie.
Then the entire car, shiny as new patent leather, pulled into
the turnaround and stopped. Annie watched the driver open
the back door, just as he did for her. A middle-aged couple
got out. The man, tall with a trim, gray beard and a tweed
coat stood facing the house, taking it all in. Annie stood off
to the side of the window, hoping she couldn't be seen. His
wife was leaning into the car, as if reluctant to leave someone or something behind. Now Annie could see the Indian
making his way across the lawn, coming from the clinic
probably, because he was pushing a wheelchair. He got to
the car and the woman stepped aside. The Indian effortlessly
lifted a young man from the backseat. In the Indian's arms
he looked child-sized, but Annie could tell he was in his late
teens or early twenties. Dark brown hair fell across his eyes,
one arm hung immobile at the Indian's side. The boy
reached up with his good arm to brush his hair aside, and
even from this distance Annie could see how his hand
shook. The Indian placed him gently in the wheelchair and
pushed him in the direction of the clinic. The older couple
followed, the man with his hand at the small of the woman's
back, as if guiding her. Annie watched the sad procession
until they disappeared behind the bougainvillea. Then she
turned away. It had to be incredibly difficult pushing a
loaded wheelchair across the lawn. The Indian did it seem-
ingly without effort. Annie shuddered to think of his
strength. She had been alone with him in the kitchen last
night and if the servants' rumor was true . . . Stop it, she told
herself. Just get ready to go. She slipped on her sandals and
walked toward the bathroom. She could see that the window
was wide open. Funny, she thought, I know I closed that
when I took my bath last night. A sudden chill went through

her. At the threshold to the room she stopped and covered her mouth to stifle a scream. On the center of the floor was a beautiful black cat so still it was obviously dead. Tucked under its chin was a small sheet of cardboard with something written on it. Annie stepped gingerly toward the cat and poked the toe of her sandal against its chin. The nudge made its head flop grotesquely back at a bizarre angle. The cat's neck had obviously been broken. She leaned in closer to read the writing on the cardboard. In crude block letters the message was scrawled in charcoal: "CURIOSITY KILLED THE CAT."

Chapter Twenty

Annie stood looking down at Alex. "What a sweet boy," she whispered to herself. She bent down and kissed his cheek. He rolled over and without opening his eyes, threw one arm around her neck.

"I'm home, sweetest boy in the whole world. I love you," she whispered. "See you in the morning." Then she gently removed his arm and crept across the hall to Rebecca's room. She ached to nurse her as soon as she saw her lying there with her knees tucked under her, her small butt sticking up in the air. Jim tiptoed in and put his arm around her.

"I want to wake her up," Annie said.

"I know," said Jim, "but don't. I've got her sleeping through the night. Besides, I missed you, too, you know." Annie hugged him.

"Oh, God, I missed you, too. More than you'll ever know."

Jim led her into their room.

"Are you tired?" he asked.

"Not too tired," she said with a grin, "but let me soak in my very own bathtub first. I'm filthy from traveling."

Jim came and kissed her. "Okay. I've got a witness I need to call tonight. I'll meet you in half an hour?"

"Great."

Jim sat on the edge of the bed and slipped off his moccasins. He reached in his back pocket for his appointment book.

"Aren't you going to call in your study?" Annie asked, feeling a twinge of disappointment. She had been hoping for a few minutes alone with the monitor. She felt like some kind of junkie. After several days without it, she badly needed a fix. She was dying to hear them talk about the trip—and her. She pulled her old robe from its hook in the closet.

"No. It's going to be a long one. It'll be more comfortable here."

Damn, thought Annie, and pulled the twelve-inch portable TV off a shelf in the closet. It was an old black-and-white clunker that she'd had since college. Jim hated it because she took it into the bathroom with her. Whenever he caught her lugging it out he chastised her. Watching it while she was in the tub involved a complicated series of jerry-rigged extension cords. There were no outlets in the bathroom and the nearest one was inconveniently located behind their bed. "You'll forget to unplug it sometime, Annie, and someone will get really hurt!" Jim's words replayed in her mind as she set the TV down on the bedroom chair. Jim's back was to her. She rummaged behind her shoes for the coil of extension wires. Was this worth it? Yes, she told herself, if she couldn't have the monitor, she could have a dose of good old American TV. She still felt tense, a state she had developed being around David, and TV would help her un-wind. Then, clean and sweet-smelling at last, she would completely relax in bed with Jim. Her stomach did a flip at the thought of sex with him—after eight years she still felt eager.

She picked up the cords and tucking the TV under her arm, headed for the bath. Jim was already involved in his call when she passed the bed, but he shot her a disapproving glare when he saw the TV. She stuck her tongue out at him.

Settling the TV on the shelf above the tub, she plugged it into the first extension cord, plugged that one into the second cord, and squirmed on her stomach under their bed to reach the outlet. She straightened up and Jim, not missing a beat in his legal conversation, lunged to swat her behind as she stepped back into the bathroom. She sashayed through the doorway, wiggled her butt at him, and swung the door closed against the extension cord. She dropped her robe onto the floor and sunk into the thick bubbles and hot water. Then she closed her eyes and listened as Barbara Walters, in her nasal singsong, reduced Goldie Hawn to tears with a question about her father.

"Is there anything better than New York Super Fudge Chunk?" Annie asked an hour later in bed.

Jim nodded and winked at her.

"Just one thing I can think of, but I don't think it's marketed by Ben and Jerry."

Annie laughed. "I missed you, too, honey."

Jim moved closer.

"Oh, Annie, I really did miss you." Jim took the ice cream carton out of her hand and putting it on the windowsill behind the bed, took her in his arms and buried his face in her hair.

"Don't ever go away again."

"Okay." Annie traced a pattern on his shoulder with a fingernail. "I promise." Suddenly she sat up and reached for the phone. "I've got to call Mac and tell her I'm home."

Jim sat up, too, and pulled her back down under the covers.

"She knows, Annie. God, she's only called three times to confirm your travel plans with me. I almost think she missed you more than we did, which reminds me, Annie, you've got to call Jane in the morning. She left about eighty messages on the machine."

"Jane?" Immediately she thought of the baby Jane was expecting. "Is she okay?" She hated to think, after all Jane and Walt had been through trying to conceive, that something might've gone wrong.

"Yes, calm down, she's okay. I finally called her to tell her you were out of town. She's fine, the baby's fine. I think she just needed a sympathetic ear. Sounds like she's got morning sickness to rival yours with Alex."

Annie groaned. "Poor thing." She remembered how cruel the term "morning" sickness had seemed to her when she was feeling nauseous around the clock for the entire first trimester. She looked at her watch.

"I guess it's too late to call anyone now."

"Mmm." Jim grunted and rolled over. Annie watched him until his breathing became deep and even. She pulled the covers up around his shoulders and kissed him on the ear. She turned off the light and stared up at the glow-in-the-dark stars Alex and Jim had put on the ceiling for her birthday the year before. Her body ached with exhaustion but she was still hyped up from traveling. Maybe there was something on television. She reached for the remote control, then stopped and turned to look out the window at the house across the street. All was dark except for the blue glow of the TV set in David and Lesley's room. She looked up and down the block. It was windy, and beyond the window the trees across the street thrashed their branches silently against the moonlit sky.

When she turned around, it took a minute for her eyes to get used to the dark again. At first she couldn't see a thing, but slowly shapes began to take form. Without a sound she slipped out of bed and walked over to her dresser. She picked up the monitor and stepped out into the pitch black of the hallway.

She flipped the switch, at the same time turning the vol-

ume knob down, and held the monitor to her ear. She was in
luck. It sounded like David was on the phone again.

*"Did the Slater kid's procedure go? Good, good. Look,
I'm sorry I couldn't stick around for that one—who'd you
have assisting? Dammit, can he be trusted? Okay, okay, if
you say so, but I don't like it. I want to talk to you about—"*
Then Annie heard Lesley's voice. *"Davey, come to bed."*
She could just barely make out David's next words. *"Uh,
I'll call you back from the office tomorrow . . . Yes. Good-
bye."* She heard him hang up the phone and mutter, *"Jesus
Christ."* And then nothing, and she was alone in the dark
hall, holding a silent baby monitor to her ear.

Annie waved at the back of the bus and quickly turned
the stroller in the direction of home before the cloud of black
exhaust could surround Rebecca. Bumping backward up the
steps of the back porch, she put the brakes in the locked position and left the baby to finish her nap outside. What a gorgeous day. Maybe she'd indulge in a little nap in the
hammock next to Beccs. It really almost felt like summer.
But first things first. She really ought to call Jane and see
what was up.

Positioning herself so that she had an unobstructed view
of the stroller through the window, she dialed the number.
As she waited for Jane to pick up, her mind wandered.
Should she plant portulaca again this year? Alex loved the
"trofical" colors (as he called them), but she was getting
bored with it. She was really in the mood for something
more formal. Probably David's influence. Every time she
looked out her window, she saw his stuffy rose garden. Forget it. Portulaca it would be. Or maybe petunias and impa-
tiens—they were a nice combination.

Realizing that the phone must have rung fifteen or twenty
times by now, she was about to hang up when she heard
Jane's feeble "Hello?"

"Jane? Are you okay? It's Annie."

For several seconds there was only sobbing on the other end of the phone. Then, "I can't take it anymore, Annie, I can't take it."

"Oh, poor baby," Annie crooned sympathetically. "Is it morning sickness?"

"This isn't morning sickness," sniffled Jane, "this is slow death by torture. The reason it took me so long to answer the phone is I—" She broke into sobs again. Annie waited.

"I had to *crawl* to the phone, Annie. I haven't kept anything down in days, I just keep having dry heaves. I'm too exhausted to move. When you called"—another sob—"I was just lying on the kitchen floor."

Jesus, thought Annie, where the hell was Walt?

"Jane, honey, where's Walt? Why hasn't he gotten you to the doctor?"

"He went to Chicago on business a couple of days ago. He'll be home tonight."

How could he have left her like that? Annie was furious.

Jane read her thoughts. "I wasn't this bad when he left. And I had just been to the doctor. *He* said it was just morning sickness and not to eat anything that upset my stomach." She managed a weak laugh, which turned into a moan.

She went on. "Annie, I really think I need to go to the hospital. Maybe Dr. Bates will take this seriously if they call him from the ER. Could you—"

Annie was one step ahead of her. "Rebecca and I will be there as fast as the old Volvo can carry us. You just hang on, okay? We'll be there."

Annie parked by the emergency room entrance and ran in for a wheelchair. It had been hard enough getting Jane out to the car, her back was already throbbing.

Once they had given the triage nurse all the pertinent information, they had to wait to be seen. Jane lay across a chair with her head in Annie's lap and Annie nervously rocked Rebecca's infant seat in the chair next to them.

Annie was just about to go in search of a nurse when Jane was summoned. They were taken to an examining room and a thermometer was stuck in Jane's mouth. "Dr. Bates is on vacation, Mrs. Barrows," said the nurse, "but Dr. Shields is covering for him." Jane looked questioningly at Annie. The nurse noticed and added, "Dr. Shields is the chief of obstetrics, as well as a high risk specialist. You're in excellent hands."

Annie smiled quickly at Jane. She hoped to look confident. She didn't want Jane to worry, but inside Annie was troubled about David handling Jane's case. The Mexican clinic was fresh in Annie's mind. David was involved in something illegitimate, Annie felt quite certain, but she couldn't share that with Jane, not now anyway. Annie played with a spot of cradle cap on Rebecca's head.

There was also that business of David being so inattentive to Immaculata's pain. Annie didn't want Jane treated like that. But surely David couldn't act that way here; patients would complain. And he *was* the best at what he did, wasn't he? Whatever went on in Mexico had to be unrelated to his practice here. She squeezed Jane's hand. "It'll be fine. David will take good care of you." She nodded at the nurse to confirm it, and as she did, she suddenly felt a new responsibility settle on her shoulders. She had to find out what David's extracurricular activity was.

She shuddered, remembering the dead cat at the hacienda. Had it been a sick prank or a serious threat? It seemed completely unreal now that she was back home, and she told herself it was the cook's son who had scared her, not David. Of course Jane would be safe in David's care—he was head of high risk. She had gotten Jane the best. Right?

Chapter Twenty-one

Tuesday morning Annie took Rebecca in for her well-baby visit and, still feeling guilty about having gone away, she was thrilled to have Rebecca pronounced fat and hearty.

"The ninetieth percentile in height and weight, her head's a great size; she's thriving. You're a good mother, Annie." The pediatrician's praise couldn't have come at a better time.

They were back in the house by eleven. Annie managed to transfer sleeping Rebecca up the stairs to her room. When she lay her in the crib Rebecca stirred and began a soft cry but stopped in the middle and remained asleep.

Downstairs, Annie paused in the living room. The monitor was on the coffee table. Her plan was to go to her desk and catch up on the work she didn't do in Mexico. She had thought she'd at least work on the plane, but of course she hadn't.

She looked across the street. It was Tuesday—were Pam and David up in Lesley's room? She really didn't want to hear them. Not those noises again. Annie glanced at her watch; they'd probably been in the house for half an hour, and those two worked fast. Maybe she'd hear something more interesting instead. She turned on the monitor.

"God, I missed you," Pam was saying. *"I hate it when you go away with her."* Her voice sounded pouty, Annie thought.

"You know I'd rather go with you." Kissing noises. *"But it was mostly work, anyway."*

"Why can't we go away? You keep saying you want to but we never do." She definitely was whining now.

"It's not that easy, Pammy. You know I want to."

Poor guy, thought Annie sarcastically. You really have it tough.

"We'll just have to pretend that we're away when we come here."

"I don't think so," said Pam. *"Not with all her stuff in here."* Was that a sniffle? Annie wondered. Was Pam crying?

"Oh, Pammy," said David. *"Don't be sad. I need you to be my brave, strong girl, my partner, my helper. Think of all the good work we do together."*

Good work? Annie's interest was piqued.

"I—I know," said Pam. *"And I'm sorry about the Kelleher girl. We'll find another one."*

"Of course we will," cooed David. *"I have such confidence in you. I know you'll find a replacement. I count on you, Pam, more than you'll ever know."* More kissing noises.

"We'd better go." David's voice. Then the sound of rustling sheets being moved around. Do they make the bed? Annie wondered. Does he leave it for the housekeeper? The shower began running and Annie could hear their voices but not the words. She switched the monitor's channel back to Rebecca's room.

So, thought Annie, they were going to arrange the adoption of Jessie's baby. You better not be making money from that, David, thought Annie. Selling babies is illegal. Annie looked across at the Shields' huge, beautiful house. It's also very lucrative, she thought. Lesley would die, Annie thought next. Whoa, Annie, she told herself. You don't know anything for sure. She thought back to another overheard conversation. It certainly sounded as though he and Pam and that lawyer were placing babies but, she told herself, you don't know that they're getting paid. What was it that lawyer had said? "We can't afford to lose these people." Once more she wondered, was he speaking figuratively or did he really mean afford, as in money?

And was it somehow connected with Jaime's clinic, and Immaculata, and David lying about the veiled woman in black?

Annie closed her eyes. This wasn't just eavesdropping on your neighbors. This wasn't just discussing your neighbor's having an affair. This was something much bigger—and whatever it was, she wanted to know.

Wednesday night was Jim's late night staff meeting. Annie nursed Rebecca while she let Alex finish *Swiss Family Robinson*. He had fallen asleep watching it with Jim Saturday night. Once Rebecca was down Annie got Alex settled in the tub and went across the hall to her room. Both doors were open so she could hear Alex chattering to himself and splashing. In a moment of unutterably stupid weakness, she and Jim had agreed to a puppy, and Alex had broken him in with a romp through the muddiest part of the yard, so she figured he needed the time to soak. Usually she sat with him and tried to control the water damage but tonight she sat on the bed and reached for the monitor. Somebody was rushing up the Shields' back stairs, their feet hitting against the bare wood hard. Probably David, Annie thought. It sounds too heavy to be Lesley.

Lesley's bright voice. *"She's asleep. What a little love."* Les sounded so glad to see him.

"Like her mother," David said, and there was a light kissing sound. Annie imagined that David had grabbed Lesley around the waist as she came out of Millie's room. They must be right outside in the hall for the monitor to pick them up so clearly, Annie thought.

"How about an omelet? Cheese?" There was a pause and the sound of a door opening. *"Tomato?"*

"No, I don't think so. Come here, beautiful." Another kiss.

"Let's just order in, ummm." More kissing. David continued. *"You're tired. I'll call for—what do you feel like?"* Before Lesley could answer, David said, *"Indian. I'll call."*

The chair groaned slightly. A moment of heavy breathing and more kissing.

"That'd be great," said Lesley. *"Thanks."*

"It's the least I can do," said David, *"for my beautiful wife."*

"Mmm," said Lesley. Her voice was faint. They were going out of range.

Annie snorted disgustedly and snapped off the monitor. What a bastard! Letting Lesley think he adores her and sneaking another woman into their bedroom. He was too sleazy for words. She put the monitor down and went across to the bathroom.

"Oh, Alex!" She couldn't help but yell; the bathmat was soaked through and water was pooling under the sink.

"Sorry, Mommy, I was in my submarine but a great squid came and—smoosh!—I had to surface quickly." Alex threw his arms up, splashing Annie in the process. "Oops." He smiled sheepishly.

She couldn't be angry with him, just herself. It was her own stupid fault. Listening in on the damn monitor, instead of overseeing bath time.

"C'mon, guy, hop out now." And while she toweled her son, she idly wondered if mothers being so easily charmed by their small sons was the reason grown men expected their wives to find their adult foibles charming.

Chapter Twenty-two

Jessica straightened the coffee table's contents, approximating as best she could the studied casual display of magazines. *The New Yorker, Vanity Fair, Architectural Digest*. She sighed as she bent to pick up the polished colored stones that Millie had dropped one by one onto the rug. What a week this had been. She really liked Mrs. Morgan—*Annie*, she was supposed to call her Annie—and so she'd given her some extra hours this week. Annie had been away for the long weekend with Mrs. Shields and now she was panicked about her work deadline. Annie had introduced her to Lesley Shields and Mrs. Shields (she hadn't said to call her Lesley) had asked if she could do a few hours a week for her, too. Thank God, this morning it was only while she worked out. Jessica'd been babysitting all week plus trying to study, and she felt she was still recovering from the procedure. She called it that, the way the nurses had; that way she didn't let the pain in. If she called it by its real name she'd cry, and she didn't have time for that. The baby was heading for the table again, intent on destroying the straightened magazines. Jessica grabbed her.

"Upsy-Daisy, Mill," she said and kissed the top of her head. Her hair smelled so good. "Let's get you a cracker." She headed for the kitchen but then saw that the door to Dr. Shields' study was open.

It was strange to be in someone else's home when they weren't there. It felt like trespassing as she stepped over the threshold and glanced around the room. Dark wood paneling and bookshelves lined the walls. A deep red, expensive-looking Oriental practically wall-to-walled the floor. The heavy drapes were closed against the sun. A few rays of light pierced through the cracks and fell across the top of an ornately carved desk. It looked like a museum piece, easily six feet across, each carved leg bigger than one of Jessie's thighs.

She felt a tingle of adrenaline as she approached this massive piece of furniture. These were his personal things. She knew she was getting a crush on Dr. Shields. The nurse, Pam, had promised that he would take care of her, and he had. At first she had been embarrassed by her behavior at the hospital, but he had pooh-poohed her, made little jokes, insisted that he would have been screaming even louder if it had been him. He had assured her she'd have no trouble getting pregnant when the right time came, in spite of the miscarriage. And he'd even been wonderful before, when she was planning on putting the baby up for adoption—asking her so many personal questions. Not your usual medical history. Stuff about her sisters. Which was her favorite? Had she told Shelley about the baby? Or the adoption? She couldn't believe he remembered what all his patients told him from one visit to the next, but seemed to, with her. It made her feel special, like maybe he felt certain things for her, too. Thought she was attractive . . . *He* was gorgeous. But old. Close to thirty-five, if not that. And married. Now that she had met Mrs. Shields and was actually working for them, she had relegated her feelings to their proper category—fantasy. A little mind game she used to cheer herself up.

She sat down in the masculine swivel chair behind the desk. *His* chair. She giggled at herself, and inhaled the old-leather smell. She closed her eyes and imagined that she was on his lap and he was kissing her.

The phone on the desk rang, and she flew out of the chair as if it were on fire. Heart racing, she ran past Millie and went for the kitchen phone. She couldn't pick up the one on his desk. She would die if Lesley came home and found her there.

"Hello, Shields residence." She was out of breath, damn it.

"Jess?" Mark's was the last voice she expected to hear. She had hoped for this phone call for the first month, and then when it didn't come, something in her had hardened and closed up. Now this call was just too late, in more ways than one.

"Mark? How did you get this number?" She had control of her breathing now.

"Jen gave it to me. I called your apartment, and when you didn't answer I called her to see if she knew where you were, and she said you were babysitting. Look, I have to see you. I know. I know everything. I went home last weekend. I was at a party. I was with Sue Lyon. Your brother Pete came in. He was totally trashed, and he said to Sue, 'So, when are you going to make him a father? His last girlfriend's going to.' I went to your house in the morning when he had sobered up, and I made him tell me the truth."

"I—"

But he wasn't through. "He said he didn't know what you were doing. You—you haven't already done something, have you?"

"Mark, will you let me speak. It's too late to have this conversation—"

"What? You had an *abortion*?"

"God! No, Mark. I was planning to put the baby up for adoption, but then I had a miscarriage. My morning sickness was so terrible the doctor admitted me to the hospital, and it happened while I was there. Thank God."

"Jess, I'm sorry."

"And relieved?"

"That's a rotten thing to say. As a matter of fact, I was calling to do the right thing."

"The 'right thing,' Mark? What's that? Get married? You didn't call me once after I caught you with that slut."

"Come on, Jess. I didn't know then that you were pregnant. It makes everything different. I really am sorry about the miscarriage. Is there anything I can do?"

Jessie swallowed hard, trying not to cry. "Yeah, Mark, there's something you can do. Leave me alone." She hung up. The tears were coming, even though she knew she was doing the right thing. He didn't love her, never had. A sliding noise, like magazines falling off a table, reminded her where she was. "Oh, my God. The baby!" She flew back to the study. Millie had pulled open the bottom drawer of the desk and spilled its contents onto the floor.

"Oh, Jesus." Her voice startled the baby, who began to cry. She leaned over and hugged her. Millie sniffed and said, "Millie goo' girl."

Jessie held her at arm's length. "What did you say? You're smart, Mills." Millie giggled. Kids didn't usually speak in sentences at her age, did they? It would be wonderful to have a baby and watch her change. Not now, though. Not now, Jess.

She began gathering the papers and tamping them into a neat pile. Now, with his work strewn all over the floor, she felt certain that Lesley would come home any second and find her there. In a rush she dropped a small black notebook facedown on the rug. Hastily she shoved the medical reprints and manila folders into the open drawer and reached for the notebook. Several pages had bent back on themselves. Shit, she thought. He's going to know someone's been messing with his things. Maybe I'll tell Lesley that Millie got in here. Right. And I didn't know because I was taking a personal call that was more important than watching the baby I was being paid to watch. Calm down, she told herself. The conversation with Mark had upset her more than she realized but it was silly to feel so jumpy. Lesley wasn't due back for a half hour at least. She turned the notebook over and began straightening pages. She folded the bent group back and held them in place. The top page had a list of names, followed by columns of information, dates and figures. The names all seemed to be female. She thought a lot about names now, even though she knew there was no reason for it. Here was an interesting name for a girl—Fleur. *Fleur Graves.* A couple of months ago the resident assistant in her dorm was talking about the importance of talking out problems and she had talked about a girl who had gotten pregnant, given the baby up for adoption, seemed okay with it, but then committed suicide. Her name was Fleur Graves. Jessie looked down at the list again. What was that name doing there? Had she been one of Dr. Shields' patients, too? Strangely, there was no city or amount filled in after Fleur's name, just an asterisk.

Her eyes ran down the rest of the list—names, dates, figures, cities. One place, "Cucharita," showed up most. She gasped. There at the bottom was another name she recognized . . . *Jessica Kelleher.* Next to it, the date that she'd miscarried and again, Cucharita. In parentheses, a figure was penciled in. $50,000.

She felt goose bumps coming up on her arms. Money? Why money? She felt light-headed and sat back down in the desk chair. And why Cucharita? God, Annie had just gone to Mexico with the Shields. She had told Jessica that David went down there for "working" vacations. What kind of work was he doing down there, Jessie wondered now. She looked at the list again. After every name except Fleur's there was a date and a place. And then a sum, all in the neighborhood of $35,000–$50,000. She turned back to the previous page. More names, earlier dates, more money.

She was scared now. The important thing to do was put everything back, as if no one had ever touched it. But where should she put it? She had no idea what order all this stuff had been in. Would he be able to tell someone had been in here? She tamped down all the folders neatly and laid them carefully in the drawer. She slid the notebook underneath it all. There. That looked tidy, at least. Now she'd call Annie. She'd know what to do.

Chapter Twenty-three

Annie put Rebecca in her infant seat on the kitchen counter. She bent down and kissed her tummy, rubbing the top of her head against the baby's chin.

And she heard, faintly but distinctly, a giggle. Annie pulled her head up and saw Rebecca staring solemnly at her.

"Was that you, Rebecca?" She smiled at her daughter, who smiled back. "It was you, wasn't it? You know how to giggle!" And, in answer, Rebecca obliged by issuing forth another delicate peal of baby laughter. Annie kissed her on the cheeks, the hands, the feet. It was true, what all the books said; little things, like an infant's first laugh, instantly make all the sleepless nights, the endless caring and rocking and singing all worth it. None of it seems arduous in the face of this laughter.

Annie brought the cordless phone over to Rebecca's perch and dialed Jim's office. When he picked up, his voice was warm and concerned.

"Hi, honey, is everything okay?"

"Yes, fine, sweetie, I just had to call you. Rebecca just giggled, really laughed—out loud. Listen."

Annie held the phone out by Rebecca's head and walked her fingers up and down her terry cloth-rompered belly, opening her mouth and shutting it quickly, making a low, smacking sound with her lips. Alex used to laugh at that every time. But Rebecca was not amused. She wrinkled her nose and began whimpering.

"Sorry, Jim, I guess not." Rebecca was really crying now.

"Listen, I was going to call you, anyway. I've got some big news," said Jim.

"What?" Annie reached out for Rebecca to comfort her.

"Well, we got a call today from the State Society for Parkinson's Disease Victims. Their national office wants to sue the federal government."

"How come?" Annie bounced Rebecca lightly up and down and walked around the first floor while Jim talked. She could barely hear him over Rebecca's crying.

"Well, the federal government—Ronald Reagan, initially, but Bush upheld it—banned research on doing fetal tissue transplants."

"So, how does that affect the Parkinson's people?"

"It seems that right before the ban took effect some researchers—in Sweden, maybe, and here, too—had begun looking into transplanting fetal tissue into the brains of people with Parkinson's and apparently they saw some encouraging results. So the Parkinson's people are up in arms. They feel the government is withholding a possible cure from them. They've tried to get the legislation overturned by lobbying for an amendment to the ban, but no go. So now they want to sue."

"But why is the federal government opposed to the research? No, wait." Annie stopped herself. "I think I get it— the Right-to-Lifers?"

"Exactly. They're afraid it would encourage abortions. Women would sell their fetuses to research groups."

"Right," said Annie. "It seems to me that the ban would just encourage a black market mentality."

"I would think so, too," said Jim. "But anyway, the Parkinson's people want to start this case locally and get press coverage and then move it nationally. And—drumroll please—they specifically requested that I handle it for them."

"Oh, Jim, that's great."

"Yeah, it's pretty terrific. It's the kind of case that gets written up in law journals."

Being walked around had finally put Rebecca to sleep. Annie started gathering sweaters with her free arm. "Congratulations, honey," she told Jim. "I'm going to have to run now," she said, "or we'll be late for Alex's dentist."

As she maneuvered Rebecca into her bunting she thought about Jim's news. Maybe he would see that it was possible to do good work, good cases outside of legal aid. Maybe a good old civil libertarian firm would hire him. He said the case would be high profile. Maybe he'd be noticed and pursued. Maybe he'd make more money. As she headed upstairs to find Alex she felt herself slipping off into a pleasant fantasy of more money, a bigger house, travel.

Then the phone rang again. Always, when she was trying to get out the door. She thought about not answering it, but she never could ignore a ringing phone; probably a neurosis left over from high school, when any call could be *the* call from the current boy of her dreams.

"Annie?"

"Yes?"

"Hi, it's Jessie. I hope this isn't a bad time, I—" Annie heard her tension.

"Jessie, what is it?"

"I don't know, I found something."

"What?"

"Like a list of some kind. It belongs to Dr. Shields, I mean, I think he made it. Oh, Annie, I'm scared."

"Where was this list?"

"In a notebook, this little black notebook, I didn't know, I didn't mean to . . ."

"No, I mean, where did you find it?"

"Oh, right. In his drawer, in his desk drawer—in the study. Millie got into his things when I went to answer the phone. It's bad, Annie. I *want* to think that it's nothing but I think it's something."

"What do you mean, Jessie?"

"I don't know, I think I did something bad, or Dr. Shields did something bad. Something evil." She began to cry. "I don't know, maybe I'm just going crazy."

"Jess, listen, you're not going crazy. Where are you now?"

"At my place. I'm trying to study for finals."

"Okay, look, I'm on my way out the door now to take Alex to the dentist, but I'll be back in an hour and a half. Can I call you back then and we'll figure out what's going on?"

"Okay, Annie, yes. Thank you so much."

"No problem."

"And, Annie? Are you sure it's okay about tonight? About my not being able to sit for you and Jim? I really want to ace this final."

"Jess, I told you, it's all taken care of. You're allowed to have a life, you know. Jim and I will keep our fingers crossed for you, okay?"

"Okay."

Annie hung up the phone, got Rebecca out of her infant seat, and started for the door. "Come on, Alex, we'll be late."

She opened the front door. She couldn't stop thinking about Jessie's call—"Oh, Annie, I'm scared." What was that all about? Jessie usually seemed so levelheaded, so in control. But on the phone she had sounded really shaken. She really hadn't known Jessica very long. Maybe she wasn't as together as Annie thought she was. Jim was always telling her she gave people too much credit. No, she reasoned, the girl's just gone through a major trauma. She's allowed to fall apart a little—as long as she doesn't do it when she's with my kids! She would have to reevaluate things this afternoon when she talked to her about the mysterious notebook.

"Mo-om," shouted Alex. "Why do we have to go to the dentist?"

"Because it's time for your checkup. Come on, Alex, you like Dr. Strauss. You'll get a balloon. Hurry, please." Alex appeared on the landing at the top of the stairs.

"I don't want to go. Balloons are dumb. Rebecca doesn't have to go."

"She doesn't have any teeth, Alex. You can play Pac-Man in the waiting room." Alex folded his arms across his chest in a display of stubborn intention to stay put.

"If it will make you happier, I'll put her in the chair first and Dr. Strauss can examine her gums." She walked out the front door, leaving it open.

Behind her she heard him bounding down the stairs, laughing. The front door slammed and he was by her side.

"Will you really? You promised." How had that popped out of her mouth? Would Dr. Strauss examine an infant?

"Hold Rebecca for a minute, honey." She leaned over to unlock the car.

She drove on automatic pilot to the dentist's, thinking about Jessie all the way. What could she have found that upset her so? She said a "list." A list of what? Something "evil." What did she mean? Jessie had said her family was very Catholic, but Jessie hadn't had an abortion. She'd had a miscarriage—*like Immaculata*. It certainly was strange that both David and Jaime had been attending to Immaculata. She remembered David's words. "Almost, Jaime." Why would they both be up in the middle of the night to wait out a maid's miscarriage? It wasn't as if they were actually staying in the room, caring for her. No, they had definitely been waiting—for something. Could there be any connection between Jessie's miscarriage and Immaculata's?

Or was it just a coincidence that the same "evil" doctor had been involved?

She was still thinking about it when she arrived at the receptionist's desk. Alex gave his name to the young woman. At the sound of her son's voice, Annie snapped out of her reverie.

"I need to speak with Dr. Strauss," said Annie. She squeezed Alex's hand. "We have a rather unusual request."

Chapter Twenty-four

When she hung up the phone, her tea water was boiling and, pouring it, Jessie saw that her hand was shaking.

She blew into the mug and took several quick sips. Closing her eyes, she tried breathing deeply. But instead of calming her, it only reminded her of that idiot nurse yelling, "Deep breath, deep breath!" during the miscarriage. She made herself remember that now. Dr. Shields had seemed like a savior, talking quietly and making the pain stop. But then he left so abruptly, and she was stuck with that nurse cleaning her up, rolling up paper bedding with the blood on it, tucking new paper under her. But Dr. Shields was the one who'd taken the fetus. Oh, she despised that word. The baby? No, she corrected herself, it wasn't a baby, not yet. It was just cells and probably something was wrong and that's why she miscarried. He'd poured it into that little dish. She saw him holding it gently in the crook of his arm, backing out the door. A "blighted ovum," that's what he said at the clinic later. An egg that just thought it was fertilized or got fertilized by a stale sperm or something. She only half listened. It all hurt. She wanted to have dreamt it. From now on she was going to pretend she had, except of course, now that was hard because of the list. Did doctors always take the specimens out of the room? To the lab, or wherever they went? Maybe they did or maybe it was extra busy that night.

How would she know? She wasn't exactly experienced. Maybe you had to get these things under a microscope right away or you couldn't tell what had happened. Maybe he went right to the lab to check it himself. He seemed like that kind of guy. Like he really cared. He wouldn't want some lab tech checking his specimens. He'd want to know for sure himself to tell her. Anyway, that's how he seemed.

But now this list—it changed all of it. Maybe nothing was how it seemed. Maybe he wasn't nice. Maybe he wasn't being conscientious. Maybe he was doing something with the stuff in the dish. Maybe . . . her head hurt. She looked at the clock: 11:15. Only fifteen minutes since she had talked to Annie. She was supposed to wait another hour and a half? Next to the clock were her prenatal vitamins. Were they really vitamins? She picked up the bottle. It was a clinic prescription bottle. She'd had it filled there at her first appointment. It must be legit. He couldn't have an entire clinic in on his . . . his what? Calm down, she told herself. This is making you crazy. What do you think, that Dr. Shields somehow got some sort of miscarrying drug into this bottle, made the pharmacist and you think it was vitamins, and caused you to miscarry? She had to collect her thoughts. She needed Annie to believe her. She needed an ally. Don't jump to conclusions. Stick to the list. But of course, she didn't have the list, and now she couldn't remember everything on it, just the shock and terror of finding it. Fleur Graves was there. And money—a lot of money. Fleur gave *her* baby up for adoption—that's how Jessie found Dr. Shields. The resident assistant had given her his name; she had known Fleur.

There were a lot of names. Why hadn't she counted? Twenty, twenty-five? She got a piece of notebook paper and counted the spaces. Twenty-five—and there had been almost two full sheets of names, all with money and cities . . . A bunch had a Spanish name. La Cuca-something. And that silly song played in her head. "La cucaracha, La cucaracha, da da da, da da da daaa." Then a bunch of small children were dancing and laughing in her head. One of them was her baby, the one she'd never had, the one she'd never know, the one Dr. Shields took away, and she was crying hard. Moaning and yelling, calling for the baby, for her mother, for Annie. Calling for anybody who could help her now. She was scared, of what she did not know and that scared her more. Things were not as they seemed, not as she had thought they were. Dr. Shields must not be the kind and caring man she had assumed he was. And her life was not the smoothly unwinding surprise ball she had always thought it would be. She could have been a mother; she could have spent the rest of her life wondering what kind of life her child had. As long as she had been pregnant she had felt disconnected from the baby. She would go to school, have the baby during break, give the baby up to some happy home and go back to school and her life. Even during the miscarriage her one overriding thought had been relief—it would be over, no fuss, no muss, no getting big and fat. Since the miscarriage, though, she realized that it would not have been like that. It would have been wrenching. Maybe she wouldn't have given the baby up at all, and then what would her life have become?

Was it just guilt, good old Catholic guilt? She had been a bad girl, she had sinned and then she had been spared, rescued, miscarried—really just a bump on her life plan. So of course she should punish herself, feel miserable. But it wasn't that simple.

The baby had been a part of her and now it was gone, forever. And no matter what happened in her life, she'd never have that child with her again. Would it have felt like this to give it up, even knowing that it would have a good life? That other girl, Fleur, had given her baby up. What had happened to Fleur? Did she feel the way Jessie felt now, completely unhinged, out of control, crying constantly, never knowing when? Did she feel she was a horrible person to give her child away? Right now Jessie hated herself. The thought terrified her. Suicide and madness were intertwined for her: Sylvia Plath, Anne Sexton, genius driven to an extreme. Everyone said Fleur had been brilliant. There: that was a thread to cling to—Jessie was not brilliant. She had gotten into her prestigious university by being an overachiever, studying long hours. It had been difficult and it was still hard now, but she did it. She had goals.

She sniffed, blew her nose, wiped her tears. She needed to find out what was going on, what the list was about. She needed to put this all behind her. She couldn't go on like this, she'd flunk out. There was still an hour before Annie would be home and probably more time—Annie was always late. She stood up and paced the small living room. She couldn't stand waiting. She began putting things in her pocketbook. Car keys, a notebook, a pen, and her micro tape recorder. She wouldn't wait for Annie. What could Annie do really, anyway? She'd go to Dr. Shields and ask him outright.

Her hand shook unlocking her car, and by the time she pulled into the parking lot her heart was thumping against her rib cage with such insistence she was afraid she might black out. As she walked through the lobby, people's voices sounded muted. The blood rushing in her ears was as loud as a freight train. She had imagined a wait in the crowded clinic but as she turned the corner she was surprised to see him standing behind the check-in counter, laughing with a couple of nurses. His back was toward her. At the counter she willed her voice to be even.

"Dr. Shields?"

He spun around, but then didn't seem surprised, probably thought she had an appointment.

"Hello, Jessie."

"I need to talk to you."

He raised his eyebrows. "All right."

"I don't have an appointment." She felt she owed the nurse who was staring at her some explanation. Another nurse was already glancing at the list of scheduled names. "But it is important. It won't take long."

"All right. If it's quick. You can see how busy it is." He gestured vaguely to the women and young children in the waiting area. "Have Maggie do the vitals and keep the ones that I need to check. Drag out that video on interpreters or something appropriate if you need it. Come through here, Jessie." He lifted the end of the counter, and she followed him through a door and down a corridor to a private office away from the clinic. It was furnished beautifully, Jessie thought. An oriental rug on the floor, two velvet wing chairs in front of the large desk, and a couch under the window, which had a view of the river and the skyscrapers beyond it. For a moment Jessie wished that she could just float out the window and fly weightless and free of worry out over the river, circling the tall buildings, relieved of all the pain and anguish the people hurrying along the sidewalks were feeling.

"Jessie?" Dr. Shields' voice brought her back to her unpleasant reality. She needed to confront him now. "Here, sit down please. You look upset. Is everything all right? Have you stopped bleeding yet?"

Jessie sat in the chair across from the one he was standing near. As soon as she was seated he sat, too.

"Dr. Shields, I babysat this morning at your house. I really wasn't snooping, but I had gone into your study for a minute. It's such an incredible room, I just wanted to look at it. Then the phone rang, and I ran down to the kitchen to answer it. I—I didn't want to disturb anything of yours, so I didn't use your phone. While I was on the phone Millie got into the bottom drawer of your desk, and when I came back she had strewn papers all over the floor. I wasn't looking at them, really, just straightening them and putting them back in the drawer. There was a notebook. It was open, and when I went to close it some pages had gotten bent back. I was smoothing them out. I couldn't help but see my name . . ." Dr. Shields was frowning and had opened his mouth as if to interrupt. Jessie hurried on. "And there were other names, too. Fleur Graves was one I know, but there were lots of them and names of cities—"

David stopped her, holding up his hand. "Jessie, please." He had to choose his tack carefully. "I understand that you weren't prying into my personal affairs. I realize it was an accident. Probably you shouldn't have left my daughter alone. Accidents, as you have now discovered, take only a matter of moments, but I think you've learned that lesson and nobody was hurt.

"You stumbled upon my adoption list," he continued, "the list of young women who come to me, wanting me to help them place their babies for private adoption. I am upset only because that list is, of course, confidential. But I trust you will do your best to forget any names you may have read and will certainly not repeat them to anyone."

Jessie was stunned. *She* was the angry one. She had discovered a list with criminal implications, and now he was lecturing her on responsible behavior? This new burst of outrage gave her the courage she needed.

"Dr. Shields, the names and cities also had money, large amounts of money, attached to them. I really feel, since my name was on the list, that I deserve an explanation."

"You what?" The timbre of his voice was frightening, and Jessie felt herself pressing against the back of her chair, trying to put as much distance as possible between the two of them.

"You rifled through my personal papers." He seemed to notice her fear, and lowered his voice, but his tone remained menacing. "You read a list that was confidential, and now you say *you* deserve an explanation? You college girls are all the same." He spat the phrase out with genuine contempt. "Spoiled and pampered. Think the world owes you something. You get in trouble and you come running to me to make it better."

Jessie was feeling nervous. This wasn't what she had imagined. She thought he would have some logical explanation and that she would either be able to accept what he said or know that it was an obvious cover-up. Either way she thought he would be his usual calm, charming self. She hadn't expected this kind of raging anger. He looked at her with real hatred.

"I—" she began, but his angry gaze stopped her.

"Listen," he hissed. "You want me to fix it all for you. Put your life back exactly the way it was before. You don't care how I do it. You just want it done."

"No," Jessie said, "that's not true. I do care. That's why I came here today. I need to know. I need to know why my name has a town with a Spanish name next to it. And fifty thousand dollars." She was crying. "Don't you see I can't put this behind me unless I know the whole story?"

Tears were streaming down her cheeks. He was staring at her with a look that was more puzzled than angry. He turned his back and walked to a cabinet behind his desk. She sat sobbing, unable to stop, her face buried in her hands. She felt his hand on her shoulder, and she jumped, startled. But now he was smiling, the kind doctor again. "Here, Jessie, drink this. It will help you. Your nerves are shot to hell." He gave a short sympathetic laugh.

"What is it? I don't drink."

"It's just a little brandy, for medicinal purposes."

She made a face and shook her head. Her shoulders were still shaking, and her breathing was ragged and labored from the sobbing.

"Just a sip, Jessie. Do you a world of good."

It burned her throat terribly, but then it felt wonderful, something warm shooting down her arms and out her fingertips. He held the shot glass for her, and she took another sip. This time the warmth filled her chest. He handed her the glass. "Go ahead, finish it up." She took another sip. This time she didn't even notice the burning in her throat, just a wonderful warmth coursing through her blood and winding around her thighs.

"I had no idea you were so upset by all this, Jessie. I thought the miscarriage was a bit of a blessing for you. You really should have called the office. We could have made a referral. I know some excellent therapists on staff right here."

She knew this should be making her angrier. He was twisting things again, somehow putting it on her, when it was him, *he* was the problem. But somehow she couldn't make the anger come. It was as if she could vaguely remember what being angry felt like, but she couldn't summon it completely. There seemed to be a mist enveloping her brain. And it felt like too much effort to slog through it, so she abandoned the attempt and listened.

"'And then this business of the list. Well, of course, unexplained it doesn't look good." He clicked his tongue against his teeth. "Not good at all, I suppose, but I think you'll feel very differently when you hear the explanation." He came over to her chair and squatted down beside it. "I am in the business of helping people, Jessie." He took her wrist in his hand, and holding up a finger for her to be quiet, he concentrated on the face of his watch.

Taking my pulse, she thought, and then the idea of whether this should alarm her or please her flitted back into the mist and was lost to her.

He put her wrist back on the arm of the chair and patted her hand.

"We need to monitor people who are having their first brandy. Very good." He smiled at her. "You're doing fine, just as expected.

"Now, where was I? Oh, yes, I am in the business of helping people. I save lives, Jessie. I save the lives of teeny tiny newborns that no one else will touch. And I save the lives of young women like you. I arrange adoptions, make sure your unwanted babies get lovely homes." Something he was saying was causing Jessie pain but as soon as she tried to focus on it the sadness dissipated and the memory of it vanished. She came back to him in the middle of a sentence.

" . . . can get on with your lives, knowing that your babies are safe and happy. But there is one more group that I help, one more group of lives I save and this is what you are waiting to hear, Jessie, so pay attention. Jessie, Jessie, you're beginning to droop. Not yet, dear." He came over and lifted her under the arms so that she was sitting straighter in her chair. He patted her cheeks.

"Come on, Jessie, stay with me here." She concentrated hard on focusing on his face.

"I'm all right," she managed. "It's stuffy in here."

"Yes, you're right. You can get some air in a minute. But first listen carefully. This is what you came here for. This is your explanation. There are terrible diseases in this world. Ghastly, grotesque diseases that rob people of themselves, take away their ability to walk, to talk, to think. Jessie—I save those people. I give them back their abilities, and people like you help me. You must be very proud, Jessie. You did a wonderful thing."

Jessie smiled. She didn't know what she had done, but Dr. Shields was happy, so she took the last sip of her brandy and tried with all her might to part her brain's curtain of mist so she could reach in and see what she was supposed to be happy and proud about. She lowered her glass and saw too late the white granules coating the bottom. The danger signal got through the mist; the curtain parted enough to let a good measure of terror out. She stared at Dr. Shields. She was breathing hard with panic.

"What is it?" she demanded. "Seconal?"

He smiled at her. "Relax, Jessie, go home and sleep. You're not used to drinking. Don't make a scene. Remember, as far as the staff here are concerned, this is *my* hospital. And you're nothing but a drunk college student." He held his hand palm up and shrugged his shoulders.

Jessie spit in his face and ran from the office. Her body seemed to remember without help from her confused brain where the bank of elevators was. She pushed the button and mercifully the doors opened immediately. Alone in the elevator, her panic threatened to overtake her. Her breathing was so fast she began to see black in her peripheral vision. She sat down with her head between her knees and, covering her nose and mouth with her hands, took some deep breaths. The tingling around her mouth diminished. She stood up as the doors slid open onto the lobby. She ran to her car. She gripped the steering wheel and made it out of the parking lot. She headed for the highway on-ramp. She needed help, she knew that. Driving was difficult. Her reflexes felt slow and her eyes incredibly heavy. She wanted to go to the emergency room right there at Maternity but she didn't think they would treat her—some crazy drunk college student rambling about being purposefully overdosed by a doctor. She'd go to General and demand to have her stomach pumped, tell them she tried suicide, anything, just get them to do it, straighten it out later. She raced up the on-ramp and headed into the left lane. She pressed on the gas.

Get there fast, don't fall asleep. Go, go. She bit her tongue to keep awake. Turn on the radio, she thought—loud, louder. Oh, she wanted to sleep. "No!" she yelled. She pinched her cheeks. She could taste blood on her tongue, she was biting so hard, and even so she just wanted to sleep.

"Let me close my eyes, just for a minute," she said to whoever was trying to keep her awake. "Then we'll go, I promise. Just for a minute . . ."

Chapter Twenty-five

Jesus, that little surprise visit had put him behind schedule.
It was the kind of thing that could make a man paranoid.
Mentally, he went through a checklist of precautions he took
to avoid exposure. If, for instance, someone from the hospital began to check into his spontaneous abortion stats? He
was sure there was nothing suspicious there; high risk OBs
were expected to have higher rates and, anyway, he was
good, so good that he could add some in because he didn't
lose as many as Joe Shmo someplace else. He needed to suc-
ceed with some of the trickier cases, so he saved his "inter-
ference" for the low-risk pregnancies—ones that wouldn't
figure into his high-risk stats. That way he could write up his
plentiful triumphs and get the fame and glory he deserved.
Could somebody be noticing his *low risk* stats and wondering? It didn't seem likely, he was careful with his timing.
Well, actually, he had gotten sloppy lately, with Jaime placing pressure on him—he was so fucking greedy. Things
were getting too close, too dangerous. He'd make Jaime
back off. He'd provide only what he'd already promised
Jaime and then he'd keep a low profile and do what he did
best for a while, save at-risk fetuses. So what if someone at
the hospital came forward with some questions about recent
cases. He didn't think they were about to, but . . . What
could they prove? Nothing, not without the notebook. And

the only person who knew that the notebook even existed? History.

David jumped up and started to clear away the "debris" from his little interruption. Morris Bigler, his chief of staff, was expecting him in his office ten minutes ago. He was the type who frowned on things like tardiness—a real stickler for the straight and narrow. He'd have him over to the house some night soon and Millie could do her cute kid routine. She was a cute kid, smart, eighteen months now and she knew some letters. She got all excited at the playground last weekend because some climbing toys shaped like animals had large letters on them. She went nuts for the turtle; "T, T," she kept saying. The other mother there was obviously impressed when she asked David Millie's age. Her kid was a sandbox blob, still eating dirt and making animal grunts. Maybe Millie'd go to med school. He could use a good researcher close to him. They could publish together, lecture together. He wasn't a chauvinist pig, like some docs he worked with. Some of his female colleagues were the most brilliant. Who wanted to work with men all day, anyway? Millie's mother had been great to work with. She always took work a step further than asked. She had a natural curiosity about medicine and she made logical connections, not just emotional ones. She was fascinated by medical problems and arguing ethics with her was completely satisfying.

Fleur had been so refreshing. She was pragmatic. She could make judgments quickly and accurately. She avoided sentimental attachment to the women or their babies. A twenty-three-weeker wasn't a baby to her, it was a laboratory, an incredible research tool. Each one she worked on brought her closer to an understanding of keeping them viable. And, in the end, she had been pragmatic about the two of them, as well.

God, he hadn't thought about Fleur for a long time. He

didn't like to think about her. He had been completely out of
control with her. Never would he let that happen again. That
first day she walked into the clinic his life had changed. "Dr.
Shields? I'm Fleur Graves. Your student intern." She
reached out and firmly shook his hand and an electrical current shot up his arm and down through his gut to his groin.
And for the rest of the summer it was as if there were a force
field surrounding her that, if he came within its range, just
sucked him in. He had never been remotely interested in the
students before. They usually weren't all that attractive and
it seemed a dangerous quagmire. You couldn't count on
them emotionally and they were incapable of being discreet.
It just seemed like professional suicide. With Fleur, he never
had a choice. He was driven. At lunch they would go straight
to her apartment. They only had fifteen minutes there. He
kept his own time and answered basically to no one but she
was monitored closely. They were on each other the minute
the apartment door closed. She was always ready. Their
foreplay always came as afterplay. The fucking was first and
that was what it was—fucking. Hard and fast—no kissing,
no tentative touches—just at each other—on the floor, at the
kitchen counter. She would go to get dressed and he would
grab her and pull her down for more or just as often the other
way around. He couldn't foresee how it would end. He
thought they might just fuck each other to death. But then
September came.

   She left the clinic and went back to classes. She said
good-bye to him, like everybody else, with that firm hand-
shake. She wouldn't return his calls. Desperate, he finally
went to her apartment and waited for her. An incredibly stupid move, he now thought. She agreed to let him in and they
made love. He thought of it that way, because it was slower,
gentler; but afterward he felt foolish and had the uneasy
feeling that she had done it as a favor.

   "David, I had a wonderful time this summer. But it's not

summer anymore. I need to concentrate on my work now. I crave experience. I told you that. You were my middle-aged married man and you were my mentor and that's an overused cliché—young girl having an affair with her professor—but why does it happen so often? Power and knowledge are incredible aphrodisiacs. Now go back to your wife. This is a silly conversation. We have no future together, we both knew that. It would just be silly and risky to drag it out. Good-bye, David." This all said from her bed, where his daughter had in all probability just been conceived.

She came to him six weeks later saying she was pregnant and didn't want an abortion. There was no talk of him leaving Lesley. Fleur didn't want him. She made it clear she just liked sex, liked men, but didn't want one man in her life now. She wanted him to help her find a good home for the baby.

Lesley was in the thick of a terrible depression brought on by her miscarriage and the subsequent news that she was incapable of carrying a child to term. She was desperate to adopt but David was originally pained by the idea. Here was a ready-made solution. His own child, from a mother with a terrific gene pool. He didn't share the plan with Fleur, just agreed to help. To Lesley, he said he'd decided she was right about adoption and that he might be able to obtain a healthy, white infant faster than the agencies. Now Lesley was thrilled when people remarked that Millie resembled David. "I had heard that adopted babies came to look like their adoptive parents, but she looks so much like you, David. Everyone says so. It just seems right, like she was meant to be with us."

Once he got over the longing for Fleur, life went back to its predictable rhythm. Lesley, happily obsessed with the baby, left him alone to work long hours and he was able to make several short trips to Mexico with no complaints from her. Jaime was getting lots of requests—word was out that there was a clinic that cost a fortune but had few qualifying requirements and a short waiting period. Everything was going smoothly. And then Fleur changed her mind.

That day when she came to his office he was struck by how pale she was, with deep circles under her eyes, and how nervous.

"David, I know you care for me and I know I didn't treat you well. I was a terribly selfish person but I need your help now."

David had a pit in his stomach. He *had* cared for her. He had, for the first time in his life, been swept off his feet. He had humiliated himself, he had begged, he had all but groveled at this girl's feet and now, strangely, he felt almost nothing—except dread that she was going to ask him for something he couldn't do. Had she changed her mind about him? Did she want him to leave Lesley?

"I made a terrible mistake. I want my baby back." She began to cry quietly. "She's all I think about. I can't get any work done. Please, David. You know where she is, please get her for me."

"Fleur—I don't know what to say. You were so sure . . . I . . ."

"I didn't know, David. I didn't know how I would fall in love with her. That morning that I held her she looked right in my eyes, really deeply, as if she knew me, as if she knew everything. I should have kept her then. I should have told you no then. But I kept thinking I was being selfish, that she'd be better off with two parents, with money and secure jobs and a nice house with a yard." Fleur cried harder. "I was wrong."

"No, no, Fleur, you were right. You're a student. You can't be a mother. Later, after you have your degrees and you're married, you'll be a wonderful mother then. Don't forget I always told you you'll be a wonderful doctor. You can't throw that away."

"David, lots of people would be great doctors. I can't throw my daughter away. I know kids at school who were adopted. Here they are, practically adults, and they still wonder all the time about their biological parents. Why did they give them away, why didn't they want them, how can they find them? One girl I know is panicked because her adoptive parents just sold the house she's always lived in. She's terrified that her birth mother will come looking for her and she'll miss her because the house has been sold. I won't do that to my daughter. David, please, please help me. I'll do anything. We can start our relationship again." She looked him in the eye. "Please."

This was disgusting. What did she think, that he was so pathetic, so desperate, he would barter for sex?

"Fleur, please stop. The family who adopted your baby love her, too. They've taken care of her through these difficult early months. She's theirs."

"What difficult months?" her voice was panicked. "Was she sick?"

"No, no, any early infancy is difficult. Infants require endless care. They don't sleep through the night . . ."

"Please, David, talk to them?"

"Fleur, I . . ."

"Please. The counselor at school told me I have a legal right still. I have six months to change my mind."

David realized he had to play hardball.

"Look, these are wealthy people who adopted your baby. I don't think you want to take them on in court. You simply can't compete with the resources they have available to them. It'll only mean more heartache for you. Forget this baby. She's happy, she's well cared for. You've made a childless couple very happy. This is your hormones talking, not you, not Fleur, who will find medicine so rewarding and who will marry someone someday and have as many babies as she wants. Let me give you a prescription to try to get those hormones on track again."

"No, David, no, this isn't hormones, this is me finally doing the right thing. If you refuse to help me I'll go to legal aid. With or without you, I'll get my baby."

He thought about it for three days. What could he do? He could tell Lesley the birth parents had contacted him, but Lesley was so attached—that baby was hers. She would not let her go, he knew that. He couldn't let Fleur go to legal aid, he'd be subpoenaed, and he'd have to reveal the baby's adoptive parents. His practice would be ruined. God knew what else would come out—there could easily be criminal charges.

He was left with no choice. He paid a visit to Fleur and as soon as she started talking, he knew what he had to do.

Christ. David rubbed his eyes now and started down the hall toward the elevators. He hated remembering all that. He could feel a powerful surge of his original anger at Fleur. He had been right, he had done the only thing he could. Survival of the fittest. Fleur would have understood that.

Chapter Twenty-six

Alex crawled and slid in and out of the McDonald's outdoor tunnels. It had been so beautiful and sunny when they left the dentist's that on an impulse Annie had okayed Alex's request for lunch at McDonald's and once there, sitting on a bench on this glorious spring day, she decided against taking him back to school.

Rebecca lay on her back in her stroller, watching the leaves move above her head, a small smile forming from time to time as if she saw something amusing among the tree's limbs. Annie sipped the last of her Coke.

"Hey, Alex," she called, "how about going over to the playground?" The sun felt luscious. She didn't want to go back to the house yet.

"Which one, Mom?"

"Which one do you want?"

"The one with the twisty slide?"

That one was farther away but who cared? It was so nice out. They could walk from here and Rebecca could nap in the stroller.

"Okay, sweetie. Sure, let's go."

Halfway to the park the art school students had booths set up outside the museum. "Hang on, Alex," Annie said. "I want to take a quick look." She walked slowly among the booths. A grad student was selling her silver jewelry. Annie stopped to look at the earrings. There were a pair of silver hoops with lapis lazuli running through the silver. They were hammered to an incredible thinness. The hoops looked lovely and delicate, and the blue made them seem rich. The student was asking twenty dollars for them. Annie knew Lesley would love them. She had admired several pieces of silver with lapis in Mexico, and they would go nicely with the bracelet Lesley had chosen at the pyramids. Alex was getting restless, pulling at her shorts leg. "Come on, Mom, we're going to the park, remember?"

Annie hesitated for a minute. She had bought Lesley and David a big Italian pottery bowl for their anniversary already, and she had spent more than she probably should have. Still, she knew Lesley would love these. They looked so much like her. Annie had been wanting to buy her something to thank her for Mexico. She felt Alex tug her shorts again. "I'd like these," she said to the student and handed her the twenty dollars. The young woman wrapped them in purpley pink tie-dye motif tissue paper and Annie put the package in her shorts pocket.

The park was full of people enjoying the day. Annie saw several mothers and a dad she knew and felt comfortable leaving Rebecca asleep in the shade of a nearby tree.

"Play monster like Jessie does, Mom," Alex called. Annie chased Alex and a growing number of children in and out and around the climbing structure, growling menacingly when she got close enough. The game broke up when the frozen lemonade truck appeared, ringing its bell. Alex came back from the truck with a watermelon lemonade for himself and a plain lemonade for Annie. The two of them sat leaning against each other under Rebecca's tree. Annie thought about the earrings and how pleased Lesley would be with them. She wanted to give Lesley something just for herself. Knowing what she did, it was hard for her to think of David and Lesley as a couple at all. But Lesley seemed to have no idea. All the more reason to give her something special. What was it with David? Annie wondered. How could he lead such a duplicitous life? Be so hot for Pam and do such a romantic thing as that party for Lesley? But was it really romantic or was it just self-serving; a chance for him to showcase himself as the wealthy, successful doctor and loving, romantic husband? And what about all the other nagging doubts she had about David's professional ethics? Those phone calls to the lawyer? The incident in Mexico? Immaculata's miscarriage? And now a list? Jessie had found a list. *Jessie!* "Oh, my God," Annie said out loud.

"What, Mom?" asked Alex, alarmed.

"Oh, nothing, sweetie. It's just that I told Jessie I'd call her as soon as we got back from the dentist. It was so beautiful out here I forgot all about it. She needed Mommy's help with something. Honey, I'm sorry but I think I better call her. It's getting late anyway. Come on, we can finish our lemonade while we walk."

Shit, Annie thought, what a ditz. Jessie had been upset—Annie'd promised to call. There was a phone booth on the way out of the park. Annie headed for it.

Alex shifted his weight from foot to foot impatiently. "Call her at home, Mom."

"Just a second, Al. I'll just tell her I'll call her back when we get home. It'll only take a minute. Hang on—it's ringing."

Annie let it ring and ring. Damn, she thought. She hung up. "She's not there," she told Alex. "Come on, I'll try again when we get home."

But when she got to the house there was still no answer.

She fed Alex and nursed Rebecca. Jim had left a message that he would be staying late at work, so she would just fix herself a sandwich later. While she was drawing Alex's bath she tried Jessie again. Still no answer. Annie wanted to apologize. She felt flattered that Jessie had confided in her. It made her feel needed. Now she'd really let her down. But, she told herself, maybe it was a good sign. Maybe Jessie had decided that the list, whatever it was, wasn't so upsetting after all. She was in the middle of exams. No answer probably meant she was at the library studying and that must mean she'd calmed down.

Annie sighed. Maybe Jim was right, maybe she was too involved in other people's lives. And he didn't even know how involved she was in the Shields'. Thinking of the Shields, she reached for the monitor, which she'd brought with her to listen for Rebecca. She flipped the channel switch. Just static. They must not be using theirs. Disappointed, she switched it back to Rebecca's breathing. Jim was probably right about Jessie, she was pretty emotional. Annie would call in the morning and apologize.

She went to the top of the stairs.

"Alex," she called softly so as not to wake Rebecca, "bath time."

While Alex splashed she painted her toenails and, on the cordless phone, tried Jessie one last time. No answer. She wanted to believe that there was nothing to worry about but Jessie had used the word "evil." Annie couldn't dismiss the possibility that Jessie had stumbled onto something sinister. She knew too much about David to casually assume the best. She didn't know what Jessie had found but she knew for sure it wouldn't be good. And whatever it was, Annie wanted to find out, too.

Chapter Twenty-seven

"Who're you calling?" Jim put his arm around her and kissed her cheek.

"Jessie." Annie punched the last button. "Do you think it's too late?"

"Twelve-thirty? For a college kid during exams? Are you kidding? Did you ever go to bed then?"

"Okay, okay, I guess you're right. Anyway, she's not home."

"Or, she's home and not answering the phone," said Jim, raising his eyebrows. "Those were the days, huh?" Annie rolled her eyes.

"I feel awful," she said.

"How come?" Jim stopped teasing and looked serious.

"Jessie called me this morning. I was in a rush, on the way to the dentist. Alex was giving me a hard time about going and she wanted to come over. She sounded really upset, frantic almost. I wish I had canceled the appointment and just let her come."

"Come on, Annie. She's young, she's had a hard time lately. She's gotten kind of dependent on you. You did the right thing. You can't be everybody's nursemaid."

"I know, but still I had a really uneasy feeling about it. She really sounded like she was in bad shape. I told her I'd be back in an hour and a half and I'd call her and she could come over."

"So, that sounds good."

"Yeah, but I forgot to call. All the way to the dentist's I was worried about her. She mentioned seeing a list at the Shields' and it upset her somehow."

"A list? What kind of list? What could be so upsetting about a list?"

"I don't know. I didn't take the time to ask her, I was so concerned about being late for Dr. Strauss. And then I got all caught up in the dentist visit and I had gotten myself into this ridiculous situation . . ."

"What situation?"

"Well, to get Alex to come I promised Rebecca would get her teeth checked, too."

"Rebecca doesn't have any teeth. I hope the dentist noticed that."

"Very funny. I don't want to go into it. I'm just rationalizing, I got busy and involved. We left the dentist and Alex asked very sweetly, not whining at all, if we could go to McDonald's. And it was a beautiful spring afternoon and I forgot all about Jessie and went to McDonald's and the playground and relaxed with my kids and it felt great." Annie took a deep breath. "And now I feel awful. She really needed me and I forgot about her and now she's not home."

"Or she's busy," reminded Jim.

"Jim, I'm really worried."

"I'm sorry, honey. I just don't want you to take it so seriously, that's all. If it was really important she would have called you back."

That was probably true, Annie thought. There weren't any messages on the tape. "Come on, she could have called you tonight—you've been home. She probably confided in her roommate instead and now she's out partying and it's all forgotten. Besides, what kind of list could the Shields have that would be so upsetting?"

For the hundredth time, Annie wished that she could tell Jim that there were plenty of things about David Shields that were upsetting, wished she could confide this creeping anxiety she felt, this increasing sixth sense that something was very wrong, that David Shields was somehow dangerous. She had never used that word before. She had thought of him as conceited and sleazy, and perhaps immoral, but dangerous?

"Annie?" Jim was staring at her. "Don't worry. Everything seems like a crisis when you're eighteen or when it's the middle of the night. Come to bed. You'll talk to Jessie in the morning and you'll feel better."

He put his arm around her and steered her up the stairs. And she wanted to believe him, so she pushed the memory of Jessie's panicked voice out of her mind and told herself that everything was all right.

In her dream she came straight home from the dentist's office. She wanted to get home to see Jessie. She could hear the phone ring as she unlocked the front door. It rang again as she struggled with Rebecca's stroller seat belt. She told Alex to run and answer it for her but he tripped over the bat-mobile and fell against the sharp corner of the hall table. His forehead was bleeding a lot. The phone rang again. She was panicked. Grabbing Rebecca, she pulled her out of the stroller at last and ran to Alex. She put her hand against his forehead and it immediately filled with blood. The phone rang. Whoever it was could call 911 for her. She lunged to grab the phone, still supporting Alex. "Help!" she yelled into the phone.

"Annie?" It was Mac's voice.

"Mac? Alex . . ." Annie suddenly realized that she was lying down. Alex was gone. She was in her bed.

"Annie?" Mac's voice again. Her heart was still pound-

ing and her throat was dry. She sat up. A dream. She pulled
the receiver away from her ear, staring at it and shook her
head to clear it. She stared at the digital numbers on the bedside clock: 7:15 A.M. She heard funny, tinny sounds coming
from the receiver.

"Mac?" she said and put the receiver back to her ear. Already the dream was receding, crumbling into disconnected
fragments.

"Annie, it's me. I woke you, darlin'. I'm so sorry."

"Oh, Mac, it's okay. I think the phone ringing sent me
into one of those real quick intense dreams. Alex was hurt."
Annie realized that was all she could remember now, just the
sensation of horror and panic.

"I'm sorry, but I wanted to get you before you got the
paper."

"The paper?" Annie didn't like this. Mac's tone, something was very wrong.

"What?" Annie gasped. "Are you okay?" Nick, the kids,
who?

"Honey, now calm down. I'm sorry. There was an accident."

"Oh, my God." Annie's stomach lurched. Someone was
hurt. Her parents? A friend? A child? Annie had one second
to will Mac not to say something terrible.

She closed her eyes and braced herself.

"A car accident. Honey, Jessie's dead."

"Ohhh." The loud moan woke Jim. Annie felt bile leap-
ing into her throat. "No," she said. "No, no," and began sobbing.

Jim took the phone.

Annie felt his arm rubbing her back. She heard his voice
talking to Mac, but through her anguished sobs it sounded
far away.

"Oh my God," he said.

"How?" he said. Then, "Annie said she was very upset

yesterday." And, "All right, yes that'd be good. Thanks, Mac."

The phone hit its cradle with a loud plastic thud. Jim put his arms around Annie and rocked her. "There, there," he said. "It's okay, baby. It's okay. Mac's coming over. She'll be here soon. It was an accident, Annie. They happen."

"No," Annie said. "She was upset. I didn't call." Sobs overtook her.

"Accidents aren't anybody's fault, Annie. They happen. Please don't blame yourself."

She just sobbed harder.

Jim rocked her until she broke away and headed down the hall.

In a daze, Annie navigated the stairs, opened the front door, and stooped to pick up the paper from the mat outside. She slid down the open doorway and right there on the floor began looking through the paper. There it was. She skimmed the report, anxious for solid information that could begin to explain why.

> . . . police suspect the driver had either been drinking or had fallen asleep at the wheel but are withholding any further information until the lab results are in . . . the driver was pronounced DOA at the emergency room of the Crawford Maternity Hospital. Funeral arrangements will be . . .

Someone was wrapping their arms around Annie. Mac. Annie burrowed her face into Mac's shoulder and cried. *Crawford Maternity*. Suddenly she stopped crying and held Mac's shoulders out at arm's length.

"Mac—why would they take a victim of a car accident to a maternity hospital?"

Mac returned Annie's gaze. "Honey, didn't you see where the accident took place? The paper says it was right near exit 6—that's less than a half mile from Crawford. It would've taken at least half an hour to get her to any of the other hospitals." She squeezed her friend's shoulder gently. "They did the best they could, sugar."

Annie nodded silently and wiped her eyes with Jim's hankie. Jessie had gone to see David, Annie felt certain of it. Had she confronted him about this mysterious list? Whatever they said to each other must have upset Jessie terribly to make her so distracted that she drove off the road. Could that have happened? The idea that Jessie had been drinking was crazy—it just wasn't like her. Annie had a sense of being in the middle of something out of control. Horrible things were raging around her. She was in the eye of the storm, safe while all around her tragedy struck. She needed to know what had upset Jessie so much that it cost her her life. What was David doing? And what had he done to Jessie? Annie looked back at Mac. She opened her mouth to speak and then closed it again. She couldn't bring herself to put into words what she was really thinking. And anyway, she only knew one thing for sure. She had to get that list.

Chapter Twenty-eight

Lesley sat on the edge of her bed with the pearl earring in her hand. The post was bent from her bare foot hitting it hard. She had walked across the carpet from the shower, and the pain had stopped her cold. Bending down, she had spotted a tiny gold glint among the sea of cream wool. Now she sat in a daze. She didn't own any pearl earrings. David didn't like them, said they were either for matrons or for checkout girls who were trying to look like Somebody. She wanted to believe it was just Jessie's but she hadn't been here since the cleaning lady had last vacuumed and Rosana always wore the same earrings—miniature gold-filled crucifixes.

She took a deep breath. Okay, she thought. A logical explanation, there must be one. Review the facts. I'm here in my bedroom, in our bedroom, in my favorite Turkish towel. . . .

Millie, she thought suddenly, and turned up the monitor just to make sure. No, still sleeping. Okay, let's see, I'm showered, I'm ready to get dressed and start the day, and there's an earring that doesn't belong to me on the floor on my side of the bed. . . .

And that was the end of the calm. She didn't know which emotion was stronger—the anger or the sadness, but they broke over her at once and seemed to be waging a war for her very soul.

"Goddamn you, David," she screamed and hurled herself, sobbing, onto the bed. Then, jumping up as if she had been lying in filth, she ran to her chaise and sat down sobbing. She cried as if she were in mourning, and she was. It almost felt as if David had died, and with him, their loving times together, their most intimate moments. She now felt those memories had been stolen and trampled on, and she was struck by a wave of intense longing for David that, in turn, rekindled her fury. Remembering the way he would look at her when he wanted to make love, how she would go to him feeling warm and soft and feminine and desirable. And he was laughing at her the whole time.

God damn bastard. In my own house, in my own bed. She felt sick. Going into the bathroom, she vomited bile, and shaking and gasping for breath went back to her chaise.

She looked at the rumpled bed where just last night they had made love. How could he be so loving to her and have someone else as well? She closed her eyes and curled up in the fetal position, sobbing. Finally she slept.

She was dreaming that she and David were on their honeymoon, again. He was loving and attentive, and she knew without remembering what the explanation had been that the earring mess was all cleared up, that she had been ridiculously wrong in suspecting David. In her dream they were in bed and she could hear the surf. She turned to David and leaned to kiss him. His open mouth was about to meet hers, but then he was licking her instead of kissing her and it was awful, slobbery and wet and animalistic. She opened her eyes to see what was wrong with him and was horrified to discover that he had turned into a dog! She rubbed her eyes and, sitting up, saw that she was in her own room in her chaise and realized that a real dog, the Morgans' puppy, was jumping on and off the chaise and tearing around her room.

It wasn't the first time he'd snuck into their house through the old cat door put in by the previous owners.

It took her several seconds to remember why she was wrapped in a damp towel and why she had fallen asleep in the middle of the morning and then the awful sadness descended again, and she felt incredibly tired. She could see the pearl earring on her bedside table. She went and picked it up and put it in her jewelry box for now. She wasn't sure yet what she would do with it.

The puppy was now under her bed. She knelt down and, coaxing it out, grabbed its collar and led it to her bathroom. As soon as she closed the door, it began scratching wildly.

"Sit," she called sternly. Don't destroy the paint, she prayed quietly. Quickly she threw on jeans and a big T-shirt. She pushed the speed dial button for Annie's number on her bedside phone. "Damn," she said as she listened to the Morgans' message in Alex's sweet voice. "Annie," she began saying to the machine, and then she heard someone pick up.

The phone was ringing as Annie unlocked the front door. Alex ran for it, while she struggled with the buckle on Rebecca's stroller.

"It's for you." Alex's voice sounded irritated. He was always disappointed unless it was one of his friends.

"Hello?"

"Annie, it's Lesley. I have your puppy. He's pretty excited. I'd bring him over, but Millie's still sleeping."

"Oh, sorry, Les. I'll come right over." Annie hung up, blew her bangs out of her eyes, and turned to Alex. "Indy got loose. He must have dug under the fence. He's over at the Shields'. God, I hope he didn't destroy anything of theirs . . ."

Alex looked worried.

"It's okay, sweetie. We'll take care of it. There's not a lot he could do outside." She smiled at Alex, but her mind was filling with images of the expensively landscaped flower gardens all dug up and the wicker chaise chewed to smithereens, its down cushions ripped open and the yard strewn with feathers. "Come on, sport, let's go retrieve the wild beast."

Lesley was waiting in the yard for them. She opened the gate just wide enough for Alex to squeeze through. Indy sprang at him, almost knocking Alex over. Alex grabbed his collar and pushed him down. "Sit, sit," he said firmly, and miraculously, Annie thought, the puppy sat.

"See, Mommy, he really obeys me. If we take him to obedience school, he'll be great."

Lesley smiled at Alex. She badly wanted to seem as if nothing was wrong. She was afraid if she looked kind, sympathetic Annie in the eye, she would know, and then Lesley would start to cry and she didn't want to do that. Instead she turned and said, "That's a wonderful idea, Alex. When I was just about your age I got my first dog. My mom raised Airedale terriers. It was a passion of hers. She helped me train mine and I showed him. It was lots of fun. I'd be happy to help you train Indy, if you like."

"Can she, Mommy, please?"

"Sure," said Annie. "That'd be great." Then she noticed Lesley was staring at her with a stricken look on her face.

"Do you know one of your earrings is missing?" Lesley's voice sounded less than casual, almost like she was angry.

Annie gave a little gasp and reached up to feel her ears. Her right lobe was bare, but she could tell by feel that she had one of her pearls in the left one. Then she remembered.

"For a second there, you had me panicked, Les. It's not lost, though. See, this morning when I was getting dressed, Rebecca woke up and I ran in to get her and I just forgot to go back for the other earring. Pretty spacey, huh?" Annie suddenly felt embarrassed, Lesley was always so perfectly put together. She avoided meeting Lesley's gaze.

Yeah, right, thought Lesley. She can't even look at me. It did sound like something Annie would do, though. Suddenly what Lesley had thought of as Annie's casual approach to life—her mode of dress, her method of housekeeping (or lack thereof)—what Lesley had considered charming when she thought Annie was her friend now seemed absolutely disgusting. She probably had no idea it was missing, thought Lesley. She probably hasn't looked in the mirror for days. Could David really care for a slob like Annie? Lesley felt she would weep any moment so she managed a curt reply.

"Millie will be waking up any second. I've got to get lunch going." Annie looked up at her then, but Lesley was already walking to the back door.

"Okay, bye, Les," she called. "Sorry about Indy." No response.

"Thank you for taking care of him, Mrs. Shields," called Alex. Lesley didn't even turn around, just held up a hand and waved it behind her.

Alex didn't notice. He was undoing the gate and leading Indy out. But Annie noticed, and was worried. Maybe Indy had done something and Lesley's too polite to mention it, but she's really angry. Lesley had looked as though she was about to cry, though. Maybe David was especially cruel before he left for the hospital that morning, the bastard.

I can't deal with this, she told herself. I have my own family. I have to use my energy for them. I can't worry about things I shouldn't have even heard in the first place. But you're the one who chose to listen, she reminded herself. You *voluntarily* involved yourself. Well, I won't listen anymore. I'm through. I don't want to know. But she knew that was a lie.

Chapter Twenty-nine

David's body shuddered and collapsed on Pam. His shoulders stung where her nails had scratched them. She had taken to leaving telltale marks on his body—that was a problem. Still, he really had never had it quite as good as this. He had known a lot of women but there was something about this one. Maybe if he'd met her back in school. Jesus, he stopped himself, what a load of crap. Thinking with your prick again, like a fucking teenager. Terrific sex was not enough to threaten all his plans and work. And that was what was happening. Wasn't it? He was taking stupid chances. Bringing her to the house—mistake number one. He should never have done that. And then meeting her at night as well. Telling Lesley he had an emergency. Suppose she called the hospital? And the trips he made to Sam Casey's office, the weak excuse of picking up files—most doctors sent their girls for that. Certainly someone in his position didn't fetch his own files. Yet there he was, like a lovesick adolescent, panting at the back door, unable to stay away. And then with nothing else to do with his throbbing erection and his heated desire, riding the elevator to the doctors' gym on the top floor. Furiously pedaling an exercise bike, dizzy with looking down the fifteen flights to the river, driven to rid himself of desire for her. A quick shower and back to patients spreading their legs all day in his office and him feeling nothing but the appropriate clinical response. No matter how lovely their breasts, he was only interested in detecting lumps, so tied was he to this one woman's body with the slightest hint of dampness on her belly smelling always, faintly, of new mown hay and springtime, as if somehow the farmland she came from was rising from her pores. How desperately he wanted to bury his head against that belly, licking that faint farm perspiration, and then to bury his head between her legs. . . .

Across the street, Annie slid her arms out from under the sleeping Rebecca and propped pillows around her so she could nap on the living room couch while Annie worked. She sat down at her desk and, seeing the monitor, could not resist the impulse to turn it on. As soon as she flicked the switch, her pulse quickened.

David could feel sleep stretching its arms out to pull him down, trying to claim him. Pam shifted under him.

"David," she repeated sharply. "Are you listening to me?"

"Mmm-hmm. Uh, who are you talking about?" David had that distant look that he got a lot lately. If they weren't actually making love, he didn't seem focused on her.

"Jessie. Jessica Kelleher? The girl who died in the car crash last week? One of our donors? She miscarried? Ring any bells?" How could he not know who she was talking about?

"I know who you mean. Terrible tragedy. She seemed like a kid with a future when I examined her at the clinic." He remembered that first exam well. She had the greatest tits. Like round, ripe apples. And she was tight— he'd had to use a tiny speculum. . . .

"She was so young and her life is already over. It makes you think."

Jesus, what was she going on about now, thought David.

"I'm tired of waiting, David." Her voice sounded whiny. "I want you to talk to her."

She was being demanding again. What was this? In the beginning she had always been sweet and compliant.

"David?"

"What?"

"Did you hear me? I want you to talk to Lesley."

"I know you do, babe, but it's got to be done carefully. There's a lot at stake . . ."

"I don't care about the money or this house or whatever. I just want you." She rubbed those great breasts against him, and in spite of his annoyance he felt a tightening in his groin. God, that body of hers was a powerful draw. But if she kept up these whiny demands, he would have to stop her. End this. Get away.

"I know it's hard for you." She was kissing his ear. "You feel a responsibility to her." She was kissing his neck. "So I decided to help you." David pulled his head away, sensing danger—a trap—that she would tell him something he did not want to hear. "She needs to know, David." He held his breath, feeling his gut turn over. "I left my earring here last week."

"You what?" He was furious. He could strangle her. He threw the covers back and leapt out of bed, pulling on his boxers. He leaned over her, his fists on either side of her naked body.

"Where?" His jaw was set. She glared back at him. She wasn't scared! It made him even more angry.

"I dropped it on the carpet. Over there."

She patted the sheet next to her. "Lie down, Davey. Let me talk to you." She ran her fingernail down his belly. He pushed her hand away roughly. He pulled on his pants and then began to move his bare foot back and forth across the carpet where she had pointed.

Pam began to dress, too, but started talking to him. "I was putting my earring back in last week, and one of them fell on the rug. I was going to pick it up, and then I thought, 'No, leave it. Maybe Lesley will find it, and then finally things will be out in the open and we can start our life.' You won't have to tell her. It will just be done."

"It's not here."

"I know," she answered simply, and infuriatingly. "I checked when you were in the bathroom." David turned to her angrily.

"What made you think . . ." he began, and he felt his anger rising out of control. He wanted to hit her, wanted to send her flying across the room, out of his life. Goddamn stupid bastard, he was telling himself and then something out the window caught his eye. He walked closer to the window.

"Jesus Christ," he muttered. What the hell? This was all he needed. The Morgans' dog was digging furiously at the base of a ridiculously expensive new rosebush. Why couldn't they keep it in their yard?

"Get dressed, fast." There was nothing tender in his tone, just pure anger. Jesus, he shook his head. "This isn't fucking public domain," he said, gesturing toward the window. He grabbed his shirt and, glaring angrily at Pam, raced out of the room.

Annie stared at the monitor. She could hear David moving down the stairs fast and then only the rustle of Pam—getting dressed? She shut off the monitor and reset the channel switch. She moved to the window in time to see David jogging down his driveway. He was crossing the street, heading for her door. His face was set in anger. Should she hide, not answer the door? Why was he coming here? "This isn't fucking public domain?" Did he know that she'd been listening? How could he know? Panic was pushing against her chest, making it difficult for her to breathe. Was there some way they could pick her up at the same time—? He was banging on the door. Startled, she opened it.

"David, I'm sorry, I—"

"Keep your goddamned dog out of our yard!"

Then Annie saw Indy running recklessly across the street, following David. He rushed between David's legs and jumped, resting his muddy paws on Annie's chest.

"Oh. *Oh.*" Annie felt faint with relief, and her blood began to move again, rushing to her face. She wiped her forehead with her hand. "I'm so sorry." She took in the muddy paw prints smeared on David's neatly pressed khakis. "Oh, David, I'll never let it happen again. Really, I can't apologize enough . . ."

David hadn't expected her to be so contrite. He had hoped for some argument from her, he realized, some way to dissipate some of this rage toward Pam and his own stupidity.

"He must have dug out. Jim's been talking about installing invisible fence." She babbled on. "I'm just so sorry. Did he do any damage?"

David was still angry enough to tell the truth. "He destroyed Lesley's new rosebush."

"Oh, please, I'll buy her a new one. I'll talk to her about where she got it."

Right, David thought, as if the Morgans could afford to shop at City Arbors. She seemed too flustered, he thought, and what? Nervous?

"I'll come over with you right now, and see what I can fix . . ."

Oh, Jesus, David thought. "No," he said, "I'm in a hurry. I've got to get back. You and Lesley can work it out. She'll be home later."

"Right, right, whatever you say. Sorry. So sorry."

What was with her? David looked over her shoulder, into the living room. Did she have some guy stashed in the house? She was jumpy as hell.

"I've got to go. Just keep the dog on your side of the street."

"Right. Sorry, bye." She closed the door and slid down it until she was sitting on the floor. She didn't know whether to laugh or cry. She was relieved and terrified by what seemed like a close call, and annoyed with herself for getting into a situation where she could be afraid of her neighbor because she was spying on him. The puppy jumped at her, nipping her ankles. She laughed and pushed at him, but he was relentless in his pursuit of a playmate. She covered her face with her hands to keep him from licking her, and after a minute she was surprised to discover that her laughter had turned to tears. And with frightening clarity it suddenly occurred to her that just as seamlessly as a car skidding slowly on black ice, her life was sliding out of her control.

David slapped the muddy paw prints off the thigh of his pants and went in his kitchen door. Jesus, Annie had acted weird, but he'd think about it later. Now there was Pam to deal with.

She was brushing her hair at Lesley's vanity and, he saw with horror, using Lesley's monogrammed sterling brush. He wanted to rip it from her hand. He wanted to bludgeon her with it. Who did she think she was, trying to blackmail him?

"Put it down," he said, trying to disguise his anger. She watched him in the mirror. Her hand with the brush paused in midair. "Put it down, Pammy." He forced himself to smile. "Come over here." He held out his arms.

She put the brush down and turned toward him. She sat in her slip, the tops of her breasts spilling out of the lace.

"You scared me, Davey, swearing and running out of here like a madman. What did you see out that window?"

"The goddamn neighbor's dog. It's a crazy puppy, dug up our yard last week and it was out there again getting at the new rosebushes. Come here." He tried not to sound menacing.

She came and straddled his lap. "Okay, Daddy, here I am. You're not going to spank me, are you?"

"Cut it out. Listen to me. I know what you want. I want it, too."

"It sure didn't sound that way a few minutes ago."

"It's just that I don't want it to happen that way. I owe her more than that. She's the mother of my child."

"Of your adopted child, Davey."

Jesus, he really had been careless. She knew way too much about his personal life. Careful, he told himself, make her angry and she can't be trusted. Ease her back.

He kissed her and reached inside her slip. She moaned softly and pressed herself against his lap.

"Oh, Pammy," he said, "I really need you. Please be patient just a little longer. I need to do this my way. I'm not angry, really. I know you thought you were helping. The maid probably vacuumed your earring. I'll buy you a new pair."

Pammy smiled. Oh, you charmer, he told himself. Back in form. Natural order preserved.

"No more surprises for Lesley, okay?"

She did not answer.

"Be my good girl and promise you'll let me take care of this."

"How do you know it's not already taken care of?" She was still smiling. She was enjoying herself. Fuck her.

He felt cold. Had she done something else? He braced himself. Stay calm. "What do you mean?"

"Just that she might have found the earring and you might not know."

"She's my wife, Pam, I'd know."

"Don't be so sure, Davey. There are many layers to a woman."

Was she angry with him? It had never occurred to him that she might be. Actually, it had never occurred to him that she *had* feelings, other than wanting him. He couldn't have her angry. Too much unpredictability. Defuse her.

"There are many layers to *you,* Pammy. Do I know them all?" He stared into her eyes. She stared back.

"Yes, David," she answered solemnly, "you know them all." Then she kissed him, and it felt like all her other kisses, but he was nervous now. He wasn't sure he knew her at all. What he did know was that she was no longer to be trusted.

Chapter Thirty

The morning of Jessie's memorial service was gray and blustery. It felt more like March than May. It seemed appropriate that it should be a miserable day. Annie had arranged to ride to the service with Lesley and David. Jim took the car to work early. They'd meet at the service and go on to the reception following it together. The Shields' housekeeper was going to look after Rebecca and Millie.

Annie and Jim had talked about Alex going to the service. He had grown close to Jessie in a short time—they all had, Annie thought sadly. But finally they decided it would probably be a very emotional morning. This service for the university community was to be a memorial in the school's Quaker tradition. Anyone who wanted to could share their thoughts. Alex was so impressionable. Jim was afraid it might be too intense for him, and in the end Annie agreed.

Driving to the service, Annie felt like a child again, two parents in front, and her alone in the back seat of David's Jaguar. She reached out and rubbed the cashmere throw folded next to her. Lesley was dabbing at her eyes with a Kleenex and sniffing softly. David was cursing under his breath at the driver in front of him, stabbing dashboard buttons and fiddling with the speed of the windshield wipers. It was raining in earnest now, and even though Annie knew it was corny she couldn't help but think that the sky was weeping at the death of someone so young.

Annie swallowed hard. She hated to cry in public. She concentrated on the back of David's head. How would she ever find out about the list now? Had Jessie called anybody else about it? What had she seen? She had really sounded scared. Maybe she could talk to some of Jessie's friends at the service. But how would she know which friend was a confidante?

David was aware of Lesley's sidelong glances in his direction. He could tell she was annoyed. He punched the defrost button. "C'mon, c'mon," he said as he watched the vapor slowly melt. So what if Lesley was embarrassed by his behavior? She wanted him to be subdued and funereal to impress her friend, Annie. Well, tough shit. He didn't have to please anybody, least of all Annie, who seemed to have a real hold on Lesley. He'd known it the night of the party— she was the type who just couldn't leave well enough alone. Lesley had never found fault with him before she met Annie, and now suddenly she seemed to have this simmering anger going on.

Just last night she'd gotten pissed because he was sitting on the kitchen couch while she did the dishes. He'd thought he was being sensitive and keeping her company. Christ, there was a journal he was itching to flip through, but no, he tried to converse with his wife instead and suddenly— bam—she's pissed because he isn't doing the dishes. The dishes, for Christ's sake! He needed his hands for surgery. He couldn't mess around with dishes. Just because Jim across the street was a wimp. Annie says "jump" and that sucker says "how high?"

David rubbed his temple. He was getting a headache. Not enough sleep, he thought. He'd had to do that woman last night. He'd had to hang out until the shift change so they'd all be yakking at the desk and he could get in and out unde-

tected. Then he'd had to go hide out in the residents' lounge
and try to sleep, unsuccessfully, of course, and then just happen to make his presence known in time to handle the procedure and get the sample. He couldn't risk a resident
routing it to the incinerator or the path lab. Jaime had that
American waiting, and he wouldn't use the native talent so
soon again, David knew that. What a country, still ruled by
magic and witchcraft.

"Jesus." He banged the steering wheel. Lesley flinched.
His life was just full of demands: Jaime, Lesley, Pam, Morris Bigler. God damn them all. He could have slept last night
in his own bed. The last thing he wanted to do was a collection. But that patient was so sick, it was just too perfect, so
now he had Jaime off his back but he had this frigging
headache and this goddamned service to go to—plus Lesley
whining at him about going, and then, to top it all off, they
had to drive Annie. Whoever heard of only one car? Jesus.

The car swung sharply to the curb and stopped. The valet
opened Annie's door for her. Of course, thought Annie,
David would belong to the Faculty Club, all the big deal
doctors did. She idly wondered how long Jim had had to cir-
cle, searching for a legal parking space. David held an oversized black umbrella for Lesley. Annie opened her
own—covered with parrots in tropical colors, a birthday gift
from Alex three years ago—and once again had the unnerv-
ing feeling of being a child as she hurried across the parking
lot behind the Shields, dodging puddles, and passed under
the marble arch entry to the campus quad. The walk leading
to the chapel was full of students. David steered a path
through them.

"Hurry up," he said over his shoulder. "I don't want to
have to stand through this thing." Annie could feel the wet
soaking through the thin soles of her black heels. She looked
up at the chapel and saw a familiar figure holding an umbrella and pacing at the foot of the steps. Why was Jim wait-

ing outside in this weather? They had agreed to meet in the foyer. Annie felt an anxiety that was becoming all too familiar lately. Bad news, bad news, her brain flashed. The discomfort only increased when she saw that Jim had spotted them and was not smiling a greeting to her. Her heart pounded and she felt the umbrella slip against her sweaty palm. She saw Jim reach out and kiss Lesley on the cheek and then he motioned to Annie to stay by him.

"I need to talk to Annie for a minute," he said, by way of dismissing the Shields.

"Go on in," said Jim. "We'll be right along."

Jim turned to Annie. Over his shoulder she could see the Shields going through the chapel door. She badly wanted to follow them. She never ever wanted to hear another bad thing and she knew from Jim's eyes that she was about to.

"Annie," he said, and his voice sounded tired, as if he didn't want to say what he had to. He put his umbrella down and leaned under hers, holding tight to both her arms.

"Walt called me at the office. He tried to get you at home but I guess you'd already left. Honey." Jim paused and sighed. "Jesus. Jane lost the baby—early this morning."

Annie groaned as if someone had struck her. She collapsed against Jim's shoulder. Students passing them stared briefly, probably assuming they were grieving relatives.

"No, no, no." Annie beat her fist against Jim's shoulder. She wanted him to take it back, to rewind his words, to rewind the deed, to make Jane's baby live, and while he was at it, bring Jessie back, too.

"What's happening?" she said. "Oh, Jim, what's happening?"

He pushed her gently off his shoulder and looked in her eyes.

"Annie, you've got to go to her. She needs you. Walt says she's really falling apart. He wants you to go to the hospital."

Annie reached for the package of tissues she had brought for the service. She wiped her eyes and blew her nose. Her hands shook. She was wet and freezing but deep inside she felt nothing. She vaguely wondered if she was in shock. She was still so sad about Jessie that the pain was raw, something she felt she held in her center but avoided touching. In another day or two she had thought she would begin gingerly exploring it the way the tongue cautiously explores a sore tooth, but now with this fresh sadness added it felt too vast to avoid. She felt the sadness would slip out of her, ooze out her pores, spill from her lips. She glanced up to the top of the steps to the door that David Shields had entered. She felt an irrational anger toward him. It seemed to her suddenly that he was causing this pain. An idea that must have been forming for days was now firm and presenting itself clearly: the list and Jessie's death were connected, and they were somehow also connected to Jane's miscarriage. She was surprised by the thought but there it was, demanding her attention. Refusing to be denied.

She looked up at Jim again. He was pale and looking at her intently. "Do you want me to drive you?" he said.

"No," Annie said. She felt strangely calm now, as if the anger that had presented itself had control of her grief. "I want you to go to this service. Meet Jessie's parents. Tell them how much we loved her. I'll call you from the hospital." She kissed Jim and hugged him hard. He was so sweet, so good and kind. He had no idea what she was involved with. It wasn't even clear to her but she sensed now that it was much more than she was aware of and that it was no longer only vaguely ominous.

Walking away from Jim to their car, Annie felt a wave of fear catch her, and on its crest she made it through traffic to the hospital parking lot, and on into the lobby, and up the elevator, and down the corridor to Jane's room.

*   *   *

Annie peeked through the door's glass square. Jane lay on her side in the bed. Walt sat on the edge of the bed, looking at Jane. He seemed badly shaken. Annie pushed open the door, and Walt looked up, his face full of relief.

"Annie's here," he said to Jane, who was sobbing into her pillow. Jane did not look up. Annie stood in the middle of the room, not sure what to do. Walt had called her, but she felt like an intruder on Jane's grief. Did Jane want her there? Walt came and took her arm. He kissed her on the cheek.

"Thanks so much for coming. Jane began asking for you almost immediately. Her heart is broken—" His voice cracked. He looked out the window and then turned back to Annie.

"Coffee?" He tried to smile. Annie nodded.

"I'll go get some." He seemed anxious to leave the room. Annie went and sat on the edge of the bed where Walt had been. She gently pulled Jane's hair off her neck and smoothed it against the sheet. She began rubbing Jane's back in a circular motion. It was what she did for Alex when he woke up sobbing with a growing pain. Jane reached out and squeezed Annie's other hand that lay on the blanket.

"Thank you," she managed to say.

"Oh, Jane," Annie said, "I'm so, so sorry." She leaned down and kissed Jane's cheek. It was wet and salty.

"I know," Jane said. "I'm just so sad. It all seems so hopeless." She sobbed. "This baby took so long to get here and now it's gone." She was crying hard again. Annie rubbed her back. It had taken them forever to conceive this baby. Oh, it wasn't fair. Jane wiped her eyes, trailing her IV tube across Annie's back.

"I couldn't even hold it. I mean, I guess it was way too tiny to hold but, look at? I didn't even get to do that. Dr. Shields was gone with it before I even got to ask."

"David got here to help you?" Annie asked.

"Yes, I guess he was already in the hospital for something

else because he had checked on me earlier." But Jane sobbed again. "I really wanted to see it. All the books I read—" She caught her breath. "They all said to ask to see whatever you miscarry or a stillbirth or anything like that. It helps you, they said."

"Did you ask a nurse to get Dr. Shields to bring . . ." Annie wasn't sure what to say here—"it" sounded so cold but "the baby" didn't seem like a good idea either. Jane rescued her by interrupting.

"Walt told them we would like to talk to Dr. Shields about it. The nurse told us she paged him and he said he was sorry but pathology was already running tests. He said he was anxious to find out as much as he could for us."

"Oh, Jane, I'm sorry. But I guess David is probably right. They can probably find things out if they get on it right away."

Jane blew her nose. "I hope so, but, Annie—" Jane's face was crumpling again. "What if I never get pregnant again?" She fell back on the pillow and wept.

"There, there." Annie patted her back gently. "Try not to think of that now. I know that's easy for me to say. Try to wait and see what David has to tell you."

Jane just kept on sobbing. Annie tried to think of something encouraging to say.

"Jane, you *will* have a baby. I just know it. You will be such a wonderful mother. Remember before you got pregnant you were talking to adoption agencies?" Jane nodded shakily. "I know you want to be pregnant and I really think you will be, but even if the very worst thing happened and you couldn't, you can still have a baby. Somehow, somewhere, there is a baby out there waiting for you and Walt."

Jane's sobs subsided a bit. "Oh, Annie. I wanted this baby so badly. I never should have come to the hospital. I should have been stronger. I'm not a good mother. I didn't protect the baby."

"What? What do you mean? You took wonderful care of yourself, Jane. You *had* to come here. You were too sick. You had to come here for the baby's protection."

"No, no, if I had stayed home the baby would still be with me."

Is this what they called "magical thought"? Annie wondered. Was she supposed to argue or listen?

"What do you mean, Jane?" Annie tried to make her voice gentle, but she felt panicked. Jane seemed to be losing it, getting irrational. Where was Walt? How long did it take to get coffee?

"I—I was weak. I couldn't take the vomiting anymore. I just wanted them to make me better. I should have stuck it out."

"But, Dr. Shields admitted you. You didn't beg him to do it. He told you you had to do it. The baby needed the nourishment. Please don't blame yourself. You didn't have a choice."

"But the baby was all right before I came here. I was sick but I should have stuck it out. I should have made myself eat."

"You couldn't, Jane."

"No, Annie, I came here and they gave me the IV and I started feeling better. I should have left as soon as I started feeling better."

"But they wanted to keep building you up."

"But I think that's what did it. I think that's what killed the baby." Jane was sobbing again.

Annie was completely puzzled. She rubbed Jane's back and waited for her to begin again.

A nurse came in.

"Mrs. Barrows," she said to Jane, "let me give you something to calm you down."

"No!" Jane managed.

"This isn't good for you. You'll get yourself worked up and start bleeding too much."

Annie looked up at the nurse. Did this woman know Jane's history? What did they think, that she'd cry for half an hour and then be a model patient?

"I don't think she can talk to you about this now," Annie said.

The nurse glared at Annie. "Are you a relative?" she said.

"No," Annie said, "Mrs. Barrows called me and asked me to come over."

The nurse appeared to be thinking this over. "You'll have to leave soon. Mrs. Barrows is too upset." Before Annie could decide whether to argue or not the nurse was gone.

"Annie." Jane was sitting up and not crying. She looked desperate. "Listen. I think they'll make you leave soon. They don't want me talking to anyone. I think they're afraid of a lawsuit."

Annie felt sick. This was getting very weird. Jane was making less and less sense. *Was* she losing too much blood? Where was Walt?

Jane went on. "Last night in the middle of the night, I woke up. Dr. Shields was in my room." Jane said this as if it were a major revelation.

"He was probably checking on you. He probably came over for another patient and decided . . ."

"Annie, he didn't turn on any lights. I'm used to the nurses coming in to take my blood pressure and stuff. They always turn on the lights."

"Maybe he was just being sensitive." But as Annie said it she knew it couldn't be true. Sensitivity to patients didn't seem David's strong suit.

Jane ignored the comment. "He had that little pen light that doctors have. He had his back to me but he was shining the light on my IV bag and then he got something out of his pocket. And then he fiddled with the bag some more." Jane looked like she was going to break down again but she went on. "I pretended I was sleeping."

"What are you saying, Jane?"

"I'm saying that I should have stayed home. I never should have let them give me medication. Once, in the waiting room at Dr. Bates', I heard this woman talking. She used to go to Dr. Shields. She was complaining about how fast Dr. Shields was, how he never had time to answer her questions. She said he was really arrogant, and that he cares more about research and getting published than his patients."

What was Jane trying to say? Annie couldn't figure out if she was accusing David of something.

"Annie, I should have listened to her."

Annie must have looked puzzled.

"Don't you see?" Jane said. "I felt fine, then Dr. Shields came in, and then I woke up in terrible pain and lost the baby." Jane's face crumpled. She bit her lip. "Annie, I think he put different medication in my IV. I think he was trying something that probably wasn't tested enough. Maybe even something he developed. But it didn't work." She was crying again.

Annie tried to take this all in. Jane thought David used her as a guinea pig to test some new drug?

Jane caught her breath. "He specializes in hyperemesis. He's probably trying to be the first with a cure."

"And you think the nurses are in on this?" Annie was trying to figure out exactly what Jane was thinking.

"Well, I think they're covering for him. I told Walt about Dr. Shields and he went right out to the nurses station. He told them he wanted to know what Dr. Shields had done when he checked me in the night. It was different nurses on duty so they said they'd check my chart." Jane paused. "They said Dr. Shields hadn't been in my room last night. There was no notation on my chart. They told Walt I must be confused from all the pain of the miscarriage. They said I probably had a dream."

"What did Walt say?"

"Not much. I think he probably believes them. But, Annie, it wasn't a dream, he was in my room. Now do you see why I should have stayed home?"

Annie's answer to Jane was to hug her.

Walt pushed his way through the door then. "Sorry, Annie," he said too heartily. "They were brewing the coffee and it wasn't quite ready. Do you want some, honey?" He smiled sadly at Jane, who shook her head.

"I'm going to have to go," said Annie. "I'll call you later." She hugged Jane again and whispered in her ear, "I'll find out what happened. I promise." Jane hugged her back, hard.

"Thank you, Annie," she said.

Annie felt the nurse from Jane's room watching her while she waited for the elevator. She was relieved when the doors opened and no one else was in it. Thoughts were piling up on top of each other in her head. Jane was upset with David. Jessie had been upset with David. Images of the Mexican clinic flashed through her mind. Immaculata writhing on the bed. Was there an IV pole in her room? Annie tried to remember. She could picture one next to the bed but she didn't know if it was a true memory or something she was adding now. The dark-skinned man banging his water glass against his teeth with the odd shaved spot on his head. Why shave a heart patient's head? Jane and Jessie both sobbing. She had stood by at the emergency room when they told Jane Dr. Shields would take care of her. She remembered the questioning look in Jane's eyes. It was Annie who'd answered the nurse in the end. Should she have said no, demanded another doctor? Could she have? *Was* David in Jane's room last night? She had to believe he was—Jane was levelheaded. She said she saw him before the pain started. Annie couldn't believe she was confused. She remembered Jessie's voice on the phone. "I have to talk to you . . . I found a list in Dr. Shields' study . . . I'm scared. It's evil . . ."

Annie knew she had to find the list. She had to see it. She could no longer ignore her gut feeling. David was doing something bad. If he *was* in Jane's room last night Annie didn't think Jane had it right. She didn't think he had been trying out a new hyperemesis drug. A deeply disturbing thought was taking shape in Annie's mind. And she was pretty sure that saving babies was not at all David's top priority.

Chapter Thirty-one

Annie had thought that she would join Jim at the reception after the service but she didn't feel equipped for that when she left Jane. She felt on the verge of hysteria—grief for Jessie and rage for Jane. She didn't know what had happened in Jane's room last night. But she felt certain Jane hadn't dreamt an appearance by David. So why wasn't it noted on her chart? She felt somehow that Jessie's list would answer some questions.

She drove directly home and walked across the street to pick up Rebecca. She knew David would have been anxious to get back to work, or to Pam—it was Tuesday, after all—so Lesley would probably be back. She began rehearsing a dialogue in her mind while she waited for Lesley to answer the door. Casual, low-key, she coached herself. She saw Lesley's face through the glass turn from an uncharacteristic look of hostility to one of absolute joy. Weird, thought Annie.

Lesley hugged her and pulled her inside. She could barely contain herself—it wasn't Annie! This morning at the service she'd been too upset to notice, but coming to the door just now she'd seen them—one small pearl earring—in each of Annie's ears! In spite of everything else going on today, she felt like dancing. She tried to reel herself in for Annie's sake.

"I'm so sorry," Lesley told Annie. "Jim told me about Jane. David of course knew about it already, but he had no idea Jane was a friend of yours."

Annie felt she would scream. She sensed that she had a limited time before she really would break apart and weep. She wanted to be alone when that happened.

"You poor lamb," Lesley went on. "What a week. David says—" Lesley paused and her eyes filled with tears. "He says Jane will be able to carry another child. I mean, there's nothing to indicate she can't complete a successful pregnancy. That should comfort her, I hope."

Now Annie reached out to stroke Lesley's arm. "Thanks, Les. In her case there was such an infertility problem I think that's what's scaring her. But, look," Annie said. "Life has to go on. If I stop and think about all this it will swamp me and I can't be overwhelmed now. I have that damn catalog deadline."

Lesley smiled. "I can't believe you have to deal with velvet in this weather."

"I know, it's pretty hard to whip up holiday excitement, snow and mistletoe when you get out the shorts and T-shirts, finally."

Lesley nodded sympathetically.

"I don't know how I'm going to get it done," Annie continued. "I just can't face finding someone to take Jessie's place right now. If *I* can't deal with it, I think it would be even harder for Alex."

"He really loved her, didn't he?"

"Yeah. He did." Annie had to get out her tissues.

"It was a really beautiful service," said Lesley. "I'm sorry you had to miss it."

Don't, Annie told herself. Not yet. Hang on. She wiped her eyes.

"Do you want some tea? Rebecca's still sleeping."

Tea. Yes. Tea would help. She could sit on Lesley's chintz

kitchen couch and let the hot vapor caress her face. Lesley wouldn't jabber at her. They could sit quietly and sip their tea while the babies slept.

"Thanks, I'd love some."

Lesley turned the burner on under her kettle, the same one that Annie had fallen in love with at the Museum of Modern Art last summer, she noted with a twinge of jealousy.

"So what do you need?" asked Lesley. "Do you want me to watch the kids?"

Lesley was really quite wonderful. It wasn't like Mac and Jane, where she could absolutely be herself. There was some posturing with Lesley, some holding back, even beyond what Annie had to hide because she'd heard it over the monitor. But Lesley was a terrific friend. She really wanted to help. She wanted a solid friendship.

"I do need to ask you to watch Rebecca, I'm afraid, sometime later this week or early next. I don't have the exact time with me, and I have to go to a layout meeting. But"—she paused so Lesley would know this was really important to her—"I won't be comfortable asking you unless you let me take care of Millie."

Lesley started to object. "But I've got—"

"I know you've got Rosaria, but she isn't here all the time. You used to use Jessie on Wednesdays. Please."

"Look, Annie, I know how you feel, but nobody's keeping score. You're working now and I'm not. I can easily help. I'll ask when I need you, I promise."

"Come on, Les. I'm probably being silly but I'd just feel better if we were swapping. If it'll make you feel better you can go out while Millie's napping and I'll bring some work over to do here. I know tomorrow's Rosaria's day off. I'll come by in the morning, around ten? And you can go work out or go to Border's for coffee and a good browse."

Lesley laughed. "Okay, okay. You drive a hard bargain—

Border's is too good to pass up. I need a couple of birthday presents. That's great, Annie. Thanks."

They sat and sipped their tea. Annie closed her eyes and reveled in the gentle steam. Just until tomorrow, she told herself. You'll see the list tomorrow. She didn't stop to worry about if she would actually be able to find the list, or what it might contain. For now she could only manage fixing on a goal. She ached all over. Sorrow, she felt, was not an intangible—it had weight and mass. It was a solid one picked up and carried. She was exhausted. Tomorrow she'd find the list and then she'd deal with it.

Mac brought Alex home. He and Sam came spilling into the living room.

"Hi, Mom." Alex gave her a quick hug and then remembered where she'd been. "Are you okay?" Nothing was sweeter, Annie thought, than filial concern.

"Yeah, I am, sweetie. Thanks."

"Mom, can I show Sam Wolverine?" Annie looked at Mac to see if she was in a hurry. Mac was settled in the striped butterfly chair. She nodded at Annie.

"Sure, sweetie. I think he's down in the playroom."

The two boys ran out of the room. Annie could hear their excited voices in the hall. "Which Wolverine?" Sam was asking.

"Wolverine II—the blue and yellow dude. You can pull his claws back in." The cellar door closed.

Mac held out her arms to Annie, who went and sat in her lap.

"Oh, Anniekins," said Mac. "Are you really okay?"

Annie shook her head. "Did you hear about Jane?"

Mac nodded. "Walt called Nick. Nick said he sounds awful."

"He does," said Annie. "He looks like hell. He looks like someone has conked him on the head and I don't think he has a clue how to deal with Jane. I was there today. He called here, but I was on my way to Jessie's service, so he called Jim at the office. Jim thought he was so desperate that I didn't go to the service, I went right to the hospital."

"How is she?" asked Mac.

"I see why Walt's so freaked out. Her grief is over-whelming." Annie paused. She badly wanted to talk to somebody about this whole David mess but she wasn't ex-actly sure that she wanted that person to be Mac. She could be so flip. Annie needed someone to help her think it all through, not just react. She wanted Jim. He'd be so good at analyzing it with her. But that would involve explaining everything she knew, much of it from the baby monitor, and that was impossible. She couldn't share this with Jim and confronting that again made her feel terribly lonely. Mac knew a lot already. Annie took a deep breath. Mac was all she had. She would have to do. Annie just hoped she'd go easy. Mac in a rough and feisty mood was more than she could bear right now.

"Do they know what went wrong?" Mac asked, and shifted her weight under Annie. "You know, I want to be your mama right now, Annie. I want to offer you comfort, but I'm afraid you're just a tad heavier than I'm used to holding in my lap."

Annie managed a small laugh and moved to the couch near Mac's chair.

"Neither Jane nor Walt mentioned David giving them much info. But Lesley told me David said it wasn't a prob-lem that would recur. I mean, it wasn't something like an in-competent cervix or that horrible allergy Lesley has." Mac looked puzzled.

"Didn't I tell you about Lesley?"

Mac shook her head.

"When we were in Mexico she told me Millie is adopted. She had a pregnancy but she miscarried and they discovered that she would always do that, her uterus is allergic to the fetus or her body is allergic to her uterus or something." Annie was too upset and distracted to call up the details, which she hadn't understood well in the first place.

"Jesus," said Mac. "I suppose they didn't have to wait long to adopt what with the good doctor's connections. Probably a nice, quick, clean, *white,* adoption."

Annie hesitated. Did she want to get into her suspicions about David's adoptions-for-pay business? She decided against it for now.

"Anyway, back to Jane," Annie said. "She's really in bad shape. Aside from the normal grief of losing a baby, she's terrified that she'll never conceive again . . ."

"Unh." Mac looked genuinely stricken.

"—And she's blaming herself. You know Jane—'if I had only toughed out'—what she's now calling—'the morning sickness.' She doesn't seem able to acknowledge how sick she was, that she wasn't a normal pregnant person."

"She *had* to go to the hospital," said Mac. "They told her it was the only way to save the baby, didn't they?"

"Yeah, but now she's telling herself that she was exaggerating her symptoms, that a tougher person would have managed to get through it."

"What? You can't fake the weight loss she had. She wasn't eating enough to keep a flea alive. She couldn't have bribed a doctor to let her stay home. Why does she think going to the hospital caused the miscarriage?"

"She says that David came into her room last night and was fiddling with her IV. He didn't turn on the lights so she didn't get a good look at what he was doing."

"So, there must be a notation on her chart that tells what he did. What does she think, that he changed her medication or changed the speed of the drip or something?"

"Well, that's the thing. Walt went and checked with the

nurses and there is no note on the chart. They say he wasn't in last night, that she dreamt it."

"She dreamt it? That doesn't sound like Jane to me. Maybe it was the pain."

"According to her, the pain didn't start until a while after he left. She fell asleep again and woke up with the pain. She thinks David did change her medication. She thinks he's really into research and publishing and that he was testing some new drug on her, some cure for hyperemesis."

"Well," said Mac. "If Jane says he was in her room then I'm sure he was. But, changing her meds? That doesn't make any sense, Annie. If he was experimenting with a new drug in the hopes of beating others to publishing results, it would be futile and he would know that. You can't publish results involving untested drugs unless you're part of a federally sanctioned drug trial. And then he wouldn't have to sneak around in the dark. You can't mess around like that. He'd be drummed right out of the corps."

"But—" Annie hesitated. Was she really ready to voice these wild thoughts? What the hell—she had to do some reality testing, try out the idea that she knew was only partially formed on someone. "What if . . ." How could she say this? "What if David wasn't trying to save Jane's baby? What if he put something in her IV that made her miscarry?"

Mac's eyes widened.

"What if he *made it happen*?" Annie said.

"Well, from what you've told me about our boy wonder, he's just the guy to do something that heinous. But why?"

Annie shrugged her shoulders. She hadn't gotten that far in her thinking. "I have no idea," she admitted. "I just have this feeling, this incredibly uncomfortable feeling. Ever since Jessie called me about the damn list." Annie's eyes filled with tears. Mac came and sat next to her.

"You're under a lot of strain. A lot of bad things have happened in a short time. And you're really still recovering from Rebecca's birth. You didn't even take time off afterwards. I know David Shields is a larger-than-life asshole, but I'm not sure he's making people lose their babies."

Annie sighed. She should have just kept those dark thoughts to herself. She hadn't told Mac about how weird Mexico had been. Mac couldn't understand what Annie was thinking because she didn't have the whole picture.

"You probably think I'm crazy."

"No, hon, of course not. I think you're probably too sane for your own good."

"Jane was really upset, Mac. She seemed certain that David had done something. And I have this horrible feeling of dread hanging over me."

"Well, I'm a great believer in your gut feelings. I think you should trust them."

"Mac," Annie said, "I'm going to find the list, the one Jessie was so upset about."

"How?"

"I'm babysitting for Millie tomorrow."

"You sly fox, you."

"I just have to see it. You should have heard Jessie when she called me. That list had her panicked, and now she's dead. Jane had the same tone in her voice when she described David in her room. I just can't stop. I have to find out whatever I can."

Mac leaned over and kissed her cheek.

"Annie, be careful. You're really caught up in this. Go slow. If David is doing something illegal or whatever, it could be dangerous. Call me as soon as you've seen the list, okay? Promise?"

Annie nodded absently. She was thinking about tomorrow.

Chapter Thirty-two

Annie held the notebook in her hand, flipping pages. The first quarter was completely blank. If someone found the notebook—say, Lesley, for example—they would assume it was empty. Clever David, Annie thought. And then she came to the list. It covered two and a half pages, and the first dates were two years old. The first ten names were all followed by American cities.

Cindy Davis	Chicago
Marilyn Burke	New York
Tanya Gonsales	Houston

In the beginning, Annie thought he must have just been doing adoptions for pay. But she had a feeling something else was going on at the hacienda. Something even more horrible.

She checked the list. Cucharita didn't appear until a year and a half ago.

Joyce DeAngelo	Cucharita
La Teesha Adams	Baltimore
Marty Stein	Cucharita
Fleur Graves	*

Fleur Graves. The name jumped out at her. That was the name of the student Jessie had mentioned. Annie felt her eyes sting and tears spill out of the corners, remembering Jessie's panicked voice. "I think he's evil, Annie. I don't believe Fleur committed suicide. I've got to find out . . ." Why hadn't she waited like Annie had asked her to? Why hadn't Annie forgotten about the stupid dentist and just gone to Jessie? Annie wiped her tears and scanned the rest of the list quickly. She found Jessie's name at the top of the last page, and just as she had assumed, La Cucharita was after her name. She didn't want to look any further, but she forced herself to read the remaining names carefully. Don't be here, don't be . . . But even as she repeated the words she saw it. She'd known it would be there.

Jane Barrows   Cucharita

She threw the notebook to the floor and letting out an anguished cry, she wept, huddled at his desk.

When the racking sobs subsided, she sat replaying events in her head, trying to make some sense out of the horror. She was terrified—of what, she was not yet exactly sure, but underneath the terror was another feeling of dread, a queasy-stomach, guilty-conscience feeling that it seemed she had been familiar with since early childhood. A sense that you have done something very wrong, something that calls for severe punishment because it has affected someone else's life. She had told Jane that David would take good care of her. Guilt tore through her again. Jane had wanted that baby so badly. And it's my fault, Annie told herself. And then Annie sat up, a new fear gripping her gut. Two of the women on this list were dead. Was Jane in danger? How could she possibly know? Annie looked at the list. There must be fifty names at least. They can't all be dead. Fifty women of child-bearing age dying within two and a half years in such a small community, surely that would have been investigated. But two college students? Jessie had said she didn't believe Fleur had committed suicide. It must be the same Fleur, and now Jessie's "accident" wasn't an accident, she was sure. Jessie was frantic that day, she was scared, but she did not drink. Hers was not an accidental drunk driver death. So Jessie had known something—or thought she did. She had seen this list, and as for Fleur . . . What kind of girl was Fleur? Had she known something as well? Something that had gotten her killed?

Pull yourself together, Annie told herself, you've got work to do. She went to the bathroom and wet a face cloth. She peeked out the door at Rebecca, lying in her infant seat, gazing at the toys hanging from Millie's toy bar. Millie sat on the floor near her, brightly colored blocks strewn all around her. She held the damp face cloth over her face for several seconds and then went to the phone book, found the university's number, and pushed the buttons on David's desk phone.

"Dean of students, please." Annie was surprised at how steady her voice sounded.

"Yes, my name is Grace Brown, and I'm a grad student in the psych department. I'm writing a paper on undergraduate suicides, and I wanted just a few minutes of the dean's time. . . .

"Yes, I'm sure she's very busy, but I really only need ten minutes, just a brief questionnaire. It would help so much. Otherwise the administration's expertise and views will be left out, and I will have to comment on that in the paper." As Annie had thought, a few minutes were pulled out of the dean's tight schedule.

"Thanks so much. I'll be there at two." Annie glanced at the wall clock. 1:00. Lesley was due back any minute. If she hurried, she could check a few things in the library, meet with the dean, and be back by three for Alex's bus and Rebecca's return. Thank God for first-time moms like Jeannette who thought three-month-olds needed friends and loved to take Rebecca to "play" with her son, Isaiah.

Annie hastily scribbled down the contents of the list on a piece of paper torn from the back of the notebook. She opened the drawer and then heard Lesley's car pull into the drive. She lifted a pile of folders and other papers and shoved the notebook back into place. When Lesley walked through the kitchen door, Annie was already lying lazily propped up on one elbow on the floor next to the girls. To anyone walking in, it would look like they'd been playing like that all morning.

In record time, Annie was pulling into the parking lot of the university library. A few minutes later, seated at a microfiche carrel, Annie looked over her shoulder before removing the list from her bag. Fleur Graves' date was September, 1996, and Annie reasoned Fleur's baby must have been a pay adoption. She began looking through *University Herald*s beginning in November 1992. Finally, in the January 1997 issue she found a front page story and picture. Having a face, no longer just a name, made Annie feel dangerously close to tears again. Not now, not here. She willed herself to gain control. STUDENT'S SUICIDE LEAVES CAMPUS MOURNING was the headline.

Pregraduation jitters and typical grousing about finals were disrupted by the news that one of our respected and beloved peers is no longer among us.

Few students knew until returning to campus that shortly before she was scheduled to catch a plane for her California home, Fleur Graves, a senior premed student, apparently committed suicide. The shock waves on campus were palpable. Fleur was a resident assistant in Bryant Hall. Among her duties was peer counseling,

which included helping students cope with and overcome
suicidal feelings.

"It makes absolutely no sense," said her suite mate,
Jill Eckenberg. "Fleur was a contented person. She had recently gone through a difficult period, but she had come
through it. She was stronger, and I believe had found an
inner peace."

Eckenberg was referring to Graves' pregnancy. The
baby was given up for adoption at birth last August,
shortly before the fall term began.

Graves' other suite mate, Ellen Brady, was too grief-
stricken to issue a comment.

Dean English said Graves was "a lovely, warm human
being. She gave to this campus and to life a unique gusto.
Fleur expected the best from her fellow students and
from herself. Perhaps she was too self-critical. We will
never know, but we must go on; it is what Fleur would
want." The dean also stated that a memorial service will
be held tomorrow, at 2:00 P.M. in Whitley Chapel.
Graves' family will be present and after the service will
announce the establishment of a medical scholarship in
Graves' name.

Annie went back to the suite mates' names and wrote
them down:

> Jill Eckenberg—"makes no sense."
> Ellen Brady—"too grief-stricken to comment."

Annie wanted to talk to this Ellen Brady.

She glanced at her watch: 1:30. The dean's office was
just across the quad. She unfolded the piece of paper with
the list on it again. Cucharita. Immaculata had miscarried.
Jessie and Jane had miscarried. What were Jaime and David
doing in that clinic? She felt certain that the Arab was not a
heart patient. An idea began to take shape, still rough and
barely formed. She remembered a conversation with Jim.
She began typing on the microfiche computer, F-E-T-A-L

T-I-S-S-U-E. She was overwhelmed by the computer's response. In all, twenty-eight titles scrolled by on the screen. She went to the microfiche reader and instructed the machine to print out copies of all twenty-eight articles, many of them from right-wing, religious periodicals, she noted with distaste. She waited impatiently for the machine to spit out the paper and stuffing them in her bag, just had time to run across the quad.

Dean English was a pleasant, tall, sixtyish woman with a Brahman accent and a warm smile.

"Now, you are in our psychology program, my dear?"

"Yes, and I'm enjoying it immensely," Annie lied.

"Where were you undergrad?"

Annie made a lucky guess. "Bryn Mawr."

"Oh, my, I'm a Vassar girl myself, but my mother was Bryn Mawr '24. We went with her to all her reunions. Lovely, lovely campus."

"Yes," said Annie, although she had never seen it, and feeling nervous about getting a question she might be unable to answer, she moved on quickly.

"Dean English, I'm working on student suicides, particularly female students. We are exploring a theory regarding possible physiological predilections toward suicide." Annie was surprising herself with how believable she was. The dean was nodding attentively. "We're looking at two areas, one involving genetics and undivided chemistry, and the other, hormones. I am particularly interested in the hormonal theory; are there hormonal surges or hormonal inadequacies that may push a female student to plummet into such a severe depression that suicide results? That kind of thing."

"Yes, I see," said the dean. "I believe the effects of hormones are being looked at regarding women who commit violent crimes as well," she continued. "Lizzie Borden, for

instance. And I also think I read an article suggesting hormones may have influenced Jean Harris's actions."

Annie smiled politely. She had to move this along. She
needed to be home at three. "I'm looking at specific cases
here on campus."

The dean interrupted. "You understand, of course, that
most student information is confidential and unavailable for
research purposes?"

"Of course." Annie smiled again. "But I only want to ask
questions about information that is already a matter of public record, information that I obtained from the *University
Herald.*"

"Yes," said the dean.

"I'm particularly interested in a case from two years ago.
Fleur Graves was the student's name. It appears that she was
a stable personality, well respected among—"

The dean interrupted again. "Yes, I remember Fleur well,
and I can see why on the surface she would seem an appropriate choice—"

Annie jumped in. "Yes, I read about her pregnancy. She
seems a good candidate for inclusion in the hormone-related
study."

"I'm afraid I don't know enough about the current science to comment; however, it would seem to me that five
months after a birth, without the child present, that the hormones would have resolved themselves into some sort of
state of equilibrium."

"Not necessarily. If she had unresolved anxiety about her
decision to give up the child, hormones could have remained
active, out of sync. They could have inhibited clear, rational
thought." Annie felt herself venturing onto shaky ground,
but she wanted to find out as much as she could. "What do
you know about Fleur's decision to give up the child? Was
she counseled here on campus?"

"She most probably had an initial consult with somebody

in Health Services, either a nurse practitioner or a social worker. But that, too, would be confidential information."

"Would she have received her prenatal care here, on campus?"

"No, no. It's only been recently, ten years or so, that we've allowed pregnant students to remain on campus. They used to be required to take a leave. Now, although they may retain their student status, and even their residency, they must seek their prenatal care elsewhere."

"Why is that?"

The dean bristled visibly. "It is not the responsibility of the college—" Then, perhaps sensing her defensive posture, she softened a bit. "Our health clinic offers basic gynecological care. We do not have an obstetrician on our staff. The insurance cost for that would be staggering."

"Oh, of course, I see. Do you refer the students to any particular practice?"

"You must understand, Ms. *Brown—?*" The dean faltered, and Annie had a moment of panic. The dean was expecting verification that she had remembered the correct name. Had Annie used Brown when she made the appointment? She nodded at the dean, hoping they were both right.

"We rarely have a pregnant student," the dean continued, "or at least rarely one that we know about. It is impossible to know how many students arrange abortions without going through Health Services. But when we do have one, we refer her to Crawford Maternity Hospital. It is affiliated with our medical school, so we know the quality of care will be excellent."

This wasn't getting anywhere. Annie decided to jump right in, and hoped the dean wouldn't notice the question straying from the supposed research topic.

"What about adoptions? Does the college help a student with that?"

"Oh, gracious me, absolutely not. The university is not an

adoption agency. As I've already said, Fleur Graves was an unusual case. Pregnancy is not commonplace on our campus. I am not an ostrich, Ms. Brown. I am very aware that we have a sexually active student body. Health Services does a brisk birth control business, and because of that, pregnancy is not frequently dealt with."

Annie had a flash of optimism. The dean was excited now, really rolling along; maybe something helpful would pop out.

"Fleur Graves chose to see her pregnancy through and to offer her baby for adoption. I assume, through an agency recommended by the hospital. I imagine her decision and the entire ordeal just became too much for her to live with. Fleur was a perfectionist. She expected the best from people and she could be especially hard on herself."

The dean rubbed her hand across her forehead. Whether she was disturbed by the memory of Fleur or by having said more than she meant to, Annie couldn't tell, but it was clearly time to leave.

"Thank you, Dean English."

"You're welcome, my dear. I don't envy you your choice of research topic."

Annie glanced at the clock over the secretary's desk on her way through the outer office: 2:50. She'd have to rush to be home for the children.

Pulling into her driveway, she was thinking that she had gained very little from her meeting with the dean, only a confirmation that Fleur must have made her adoption plans at the hospital and very probably, through David. With a few minutes left till Alex's bus, she reached for the thick stack of xeroxed articles. The top heading caught her eye. FETAL TISSUE GIVES PARKINSON'S VICTIMS HOPE.

Rifling through them, she saw that they all seemed to be talking about a possible cure for Parkinson's, with an occasional mention of possible benefits to Alzheimer's patients.

Parkinson's disease, she thought, Mother's friend Ellen Downing died of it. She picked up an article from *Science News* and scanned it for more details.

> ". . . animal studies in monkeys indicate that transplanted fetal brain cells can reverse the symptoms of Parkinson's disease. . . . Fetal cell transplants into the brains of human Parkinson's patients have been performed in a handful of countries, with preliminary results recently reported in Sweden and Mexico."

Mexico. The word jumped out at her. She continued reading.

> "The ethics of research on human fetal tissue transplants is not inextricably tied to approval of abortion, any more than recovering organs from accident victims is equivalent to approving of auto accidents. . . ."

That's what Jim's new case was about, wasn't it?

> ". . . One major biotech firm estimates that the potential market in treating diabetes and Parkinson's disease through the use of fetal tissue from induced abortions exceeds six billion dollars. . . . Thus a vast new and lucrative market would be created for fetal tissue from induced abortion—a market whose gross revenue would exceed that of abortion clinics by 30 times."

Jesus, thought Annie. This was bigger than she thought. She grabbed her highlighter and began marking passages to show Mac.

> ". . . Parkinson's disease, which affects about 500,000 Americans, destroys cells in the brain that manufacture dopamine, the chemical that allows smooth walking and lucid speaking. Thus, shaking of the hands, head and feet and general body rigidity characterize the disease. In No-

vember 1988 in the first operation of its kind in the
United States, surgeons at the University of Colorado
drilled a quarter-sized hole into the skull of fifty-two-
year-old Parkinson's victim, Don Nelson, and implanted
fetal brain cells deep into his brain. . . . To date, there
have been nine implants performed in the United States
for Parkinson's."

She tried to remember what mother had told her about
going to visit Ellen Downing shortly before she died. "She
couldn't even drink her tea, Annie. I had to hold the cup for
her—the poor thing kept on spilling and when I took it and
held it to her lips, tears just ran down her cheeks. I think she
was embarrassed, but I couldn't understand what she was
trying to say. It's criminal what that disease does to people,
Annie . . ."

Criminal.

The Arab man in Jaime's clinic flashed into Annie's
memory, the water glass hitting his teeth, the liquid dribbling down his chin, his hand shaking uncontrollably. And
the boy, her last morning in Mexico, so feeble in the arms of
the Indian, his arm trembling as he reached up to push the
hair out of his eyes.

She'd found it. Oh, God, she'd found it. She read on.

"Citing ethical concerns, the National Institutes of
Health, in the last days of the Reagan administration, de-
clared a halt to the use of federal funds in fetal research.
This ban effectively stopped research. . . . It is also illegal under current federal law to buy or sell fetal tissue.
. . . an NIH panel made the following recommenda-
tions regarding research requirements: a woman must
give her informed consent to any use of fetal tissue taken
from her abortion, and that consent may be asked only
after a final decision to abort has been made.
The woman should not receive any sort of compensa-

tion for the tissue donation and may not direct the tissue
to a specific recipient."

Annie thought of Jessica, Immaculata, Jane—what kind
of "consent" had they given? And how about their "com-
pensation"? Grief, shame—death? With each word she read,
she hated David more intensely.

> ". . . Payments and other forms of remuneration and
> compensation associated with the procurement of fetal
> tissue should be prohibited, except for reasonable ex-
> penses occasioned by the actual retrieval, storage, prepa-
> ration and transportation of the tissues."
> —*Christianity Today*

Annie hardly thought fifty thousand dollars and first-
class air travel were what the NIH panel would call "rea-
sonable expenses." An article from *Vogue* caught her eye.

> ". . . people in medicine bend over backward to do the
> right thing . . . but somebody's going to try to corrupt the
> system.
> . . . one danger of having the federal government duck
> this question is that research will move into the private
> sector. It may be done without supervision or ethical
> scrutiny.
> . . . one company now in the development stages
> plans to begin marketing cells grown from fetal tissue
> within a few years. While it says it uses tissue strictly
> from "third- party, nonprofit procuring agencies," that
> could change as more and more tissue is needed to sup-
> ply the expected demand . . ."—*The Progressive*

There was a knock on the car window and Annie jumped,
scattering pages onto the floor and into the backseat.

"What are you doing in the car, Mom?" Alex called
through the closed window. She'd totally forgotten about the

bus. And Jeanette would be dropping off Rebecca any
minute. She had to get a grip. She had to figure out how to
put David away, so she could get back to her life! It was all
there in the articles, the how, the why . . . But it still wasn't
enough to go to the police. She wondered how much time
she had before David helped another woman to "miscarry."

Walking Alex to the back door, Annie glanced at the
house across the street and felt a cold dread settle in her
stomach.

Chapter Thirty-three

Rebecca nursed briefly and went right to sleep. Feeling guilty, but knowing she was too agitated to entertain him, Annie put a video in for Alex.

Then she called Mac. The damn machine. "Mac, it's Annie. I'm home. I've got that thing we talked about—and a lot more. It looks bad. Call me, or I'll see you at the track at six."

Annie cleared her desk of everything but a pad, pen, the telephone, and her Rolodex. She needed to feel that she was in a real office. If she was going to pull this off she needed a staged set and props to buoy her up and make her believe she was not just a nosy neighbor, but a Blue Cross investigator. Efficient, but a little beaten down by the system.

So, okay, thought Annie, I'm a woman who's unhappy at work and puts up with a lot from the people around me, so I don't take much from the clients. I'm officious and impatient. That'll work, she told herself and began punching phone buttons with a vengeance.

"Crawford Maternity Hospital."

"Medical records, please," Annie snapped, and then thought to herself, let just a touch of boredom creep in. She glanced again at her clock as she listened to the phone line ring. 12:45. Please be at lunch, please be at lunch.

After ten rings the line connected. "Records."

"Yes, this is Blue Cross calling. Who is currently in charge of your department?"

"Donna Petrarca."

"Uh huh. Spell that, please." Annie shuffled papers noisily. "Yes, I've got it. Is she in now?"

"No, I'm sorry, she's at lunch."

"When do you expect her back?"

"Around one-thirty."

"That won't work. I'll be off-site all afternoon. When will she be in tomorrow morning?"

"Eight-thirty."

"And will she be in all morning? What about lunch? I've got a hell of a day tomorrow. I can't be trying to track her down."

"Well, let me check her book." Blue Cross must really put the screws to the hospital, Annie thought. They certainly were willing to accommodate her pushy investigator.

"She does have an afternoon meeting but it looks like she'll be in in the morning. She lunches from twelve-thirty to one-thirty."

"Thank you." Annie hung up. Blue Cross doesn't say good-bye, she thought.

She picked up the receiver again and dialed Tricia's number from the babysitting coop list. She hated to use the coop when she was too busy to pay it back right away, but this was definitely an emergency.

"Hello." Tricia sounded sleepy.

"Hi, it's Annie. Did I wake you?"

"No." Trish laughed. "I was just sitting here imagining what a nap would feel like. I guess I was completely into my fantasy. What's up?"

"Well, I need a short-notice favor. Could you possibly take Rebecca for about an hour and a half tomorrow at lunchtime?"

"Just a sec, let me check the calendar. Okay, yup, it's fine. Molly will love it, she's so into babies these days."

"Oh, great. I thought you said you wanted points. I'm glad it works out."

"Me, too. I'm trying to sock points away for when the baby comes, then I'm sure I'll need to cash them in."

"Well, you can call me then and don't worry about the points—use them on someone else. I'll be glad to help. I really appreciate you doing this for me."

"Thanks, Annie. I'll see you tomorrow, around twelve?"

"Yeah, that's great. Go back to your fantasy nap. Bye-bye."

"Bye."

Annie picked the sample clothes up off the floor and put them back on her desk. She retrieved her folder of copy from the couch. Her desk was hers again.

Now for the hard part, she told herself and headed up to her closet to find an outfit appropriate for a Blue Cross investigator.

Her maternity dresses and jumpsuits were still hanging in the front. She pushed past them to several dresses that she liked but they didn't seem right either. She didn't think office workers wore drop waist jersey dresses that came to well below the knee. "Annie sacks," Jim affectionately called them. She came to a jumper that she wore early in her pregnancy. It was short, above the knee, but it was cut big and loose and was definitely too funky for Blue Cross. Then she remembered a suit she'd bought for a wedding last spring, someone from Jim's office, before she was pregnant with Rebecca, another lifetime ago. She stepped into the closet to reach way to the back and pulled it out. Great, navy blue linen jacket with matching pleated skirt. She had worn nothing under it to the wedding, just pearls at her neck. That would be too dressy for work. She began opening drawers: just T-shirts. No good. She checked her lingerie drawer and down toward the bottom she found a silk tank top—one she's bought with Lesley before Mexico. A soft violet tone, it would break up the harsh navy nicely. Shoes. Annie loved shoes but she had a great collection of casual shoes and very few dress shoes. She got down on her hands and knees to examine them more closely. What had she worn to the wedding? Oh, yeah. The heel had snapped off one of them the last time she wore them. . . .

Lesley. Lesley would have dressy navy blue. She knew from shopping together that they had the same size foot.

She sat on the bed and pushed Lesley's speed dial button.

"Hi, Les. It's Annie. I have a just-called meeting tomorrow. They've got some last minute catalog additions. This always happens. Anyway, I want to wear a navy suit and I don't have any shoes that are right with it. Do you possibly have something I could use? It's just for a couple of—"

Lesley cut her off.

"Of course I do. No problem, really. Do you want flats or heels? What's the suit like?"

"Navy, pleated skirt, short, classic."

"Above the knee?"

"Yup."

"Heels. You need heels. Annie, you've got the best legs, show them off."

"It's just business, Lesley."

"Exactly, Annie. Wow them. Maybe they'll give you a raise."

"I want one for my writing, Les, not my legs."

"I know, I know, I'm politically incorrect, but those creeps don't recognize talent. From what you've told me you're way overdue for—"

Annie interrupted her. "Lesley, you're sweet, but you sound like my mother."

"Okay, okay, when do you want the shoes? Come over now if you want."

"Great. See you in a couple of minutes."

Chapter Thirty-four

He had to do it. Now. No other way.

He resented being put in this position, but Pam had gotten to be like a goddamn addict. She was getting so fucking demanding, even directing him in bed. He hated that. And now she was threatening to tell Lesley everything. Jesus, he should have been concentrating on holding on to Lesley instead of wasting time with this . . . liability. Lesley was what he needed, so sweet, so pliant. Lesley, who would do whatever he asked, in bed or out. Sole heir to the fabulous fortune amassed by her father: the Canadian gentleman who had, thank you very much, built an empire from paper towels. And from her mother, Lesley had inherited taste. She had an edge over the bitchy doctors' wives who went in for glass and chrome and whatever the new hot decorator brought them. Lesley stuck with William Morris in the living room and Liberty in the bedroom and the effect was Money—always been here and always will be. That was the kind of woman a man in his position needed behind him. Lesley was the jewel in his crown and this Pam with her big glorious tits and her hot desire had almost made him blow the whole thing out of the water. Jesus, he had acted like he was fifteen, thinking with his prick.

But he was back on track now. He'd have to do it. It

couldn't be helped. It was the only way. Pick up the phone. Make the arrangement.

Second ring—as always—she wouldn't miss a call from him. Keep it light, he told himself.

Across the street Annie switched on the monitor.

"Ms. P., it's me."

"Hi. I'm just getting ready."

"I need to change plans, a bit."

"What do you mean?" Her tone was demanding.

"The baby's sick, so they're not going out."

"David—" Annie sensed her disappointment, edged with anger.

"Can I please come to you instead?"

A relieved rush. *"Yes, please, hurry. I've been thinking about you all morning. I'm so ready for you."*

"I've been thinking about you, too, babe. See you soon."

He hung up and went to his gym bag at the back of the closet. "No more demands, Pammy," he said out loud through clenched teeth. Inside the bag was the zippered pocket with the small black case. Quickly and easily he filled the syringe, put the plastic tip on, and slipped it inside his jacket's inner breast pocket. His heart was pounding with a combination of nerves and excitement. Christ, he was getting a hard-on.

Inside the Jag he pushed the A/C and slipped *Die Valkerye* into the CD player. The music was so powerful. He was so powerful. He changed people's lives. Keeping young girls from destroying their futures. Bringing the greatest gift of all to childless couples. And even curing the incurable. A fucking miracle worker.

He parked a block away from Pam's building. He had insisted she take this apartment. A friend at the club had been talking about it. The entire second floor, ten apartments, were occupied by very high-class call girls. The neighbors were used to seeing men in business suits coming and going all day. It was a bigger turn-on to use his house but today he was glad he wouldn't stand out in anyone's memory. In fact, two men were just entering the building as he came up the walk. He bent to tie his shoe outside the door. When they were in the elevator he entered the building. Pam was on the third floor. He opened the door to the fire stairs.

Pam hung up the phone and clapped with delight. She had been so sure that he was going to cancel, and if he had canceled, she had promised herself that would mean he wanted to end it. She was glad now about the letter she had mailed to Lesley. She had done the right thing after all. David did love her, he just needed a little push. She knew he wasn't happy in that marriage and why shouldn't he have another chance? Why shouldn't she be happy, too? Once everything was out in the open and they were married, she would devote her entire life to pleasing him. She wouldn't need to work anymore. David needed a full-time wife, one undistracted by babies. *He* would be her baby. She had been silly to have those doubts. *He* was coming to *her.* He was really getting dependent on her now. He was hers. All hers.

She hurried into the bedroom, slipped out of her bathrobe, and adjusted the pink push-up bra and matching garter belt with white stockings. No panties—David was going to love this. Should she unlock the door and wait for him on the bed? No, she'd hide behind the door and surprise him right there in the front hall.

She heard him coming down the corridor now and she quickly eased the door open an inch and stepped behind it. As he came in the door she slammed it shut and watched his startled expression turn to desire as she leaned back against the wall.

"Why, Dr. Shields, you made a house call. I told you I was ready for you." She took two steps forward and slowly began undoing the buttons on his shirt. She could see how much he wanted her. He took her hand and led her into the bedroom.

"Lie down, Ms. Perfect," he instructed her. "You look like you need to be examined."

She lay down on her back with her knees up. He'd like that. But then it would be her turn.

"Okay, Doctor. You can examine me but then I'm in charge. I'll tell you how to make me feel better." What was that look on his face? Had she done something to make him angry? She looked up at him questioningly.

"Roll over on your side." It was an order. So the angry look was just part of the game. She complied.

When he saw her leaning against the wall, he was instantly ready for her. But that was impossible. He couldn't leave anything to trace. He took her to the bedroom and told her to lie down for her exam. God this was hard to pass up. The whole thing was harder than he thought. She was so hot. Then she blew it. Telling him what to do. Suddenly it wasn't so difficult. He rolled her over. The needle was in and out of her right buttock before she registered the prick. He dropped the needle back into his jacket pocket.

"Ow." She was facing him looking like an angry little girl. "What did you do?" At the sight of him her eyes widened in fear, then rolled up, fluttered and closed. Okay, he told himself, it'll be easier now. He took off his necktie and wrapped it once around her neck then pulled the ends. He watched her breasts until they weren't rising anymore. He couldn't watch her face. He slid the tie off without looking at her.

He pulled on a pair of black kid gloves and began to ransack the apartment. This had to appear to be an attack, a robbery. He couldn't risk any gossip at the hospital. People had seen them together. Who knew what they might assume if he made it look like a suicide.

Before leaving, he wrapped the brick he had brought in his briefcase in the bedsheet, climbed out the bedroom window to the fire escape, and broke the window. Then he unwrapped the sheet, threw the brick through the hole in the window, climbed back in and put the sheet back on the bed. He took one last look around the bedroom and noticed the watch on her right wrist. It was a bitch undoing it with gloves on but he didn't dare leave it. In the front hall he stopped to reknot his tie in the mirror there. Perfect.

On his way to the car he passed a deli, ordered a hot pastrami. Outside again he took two bites out of the sandwich, opened it up, put the watch inside and closed the Styrofoam package. Then he drove a few miles in the opposite direction from his home and threw the lot into a dumpster behind a Burger King.

Back in the Jag again, his chariot. In control. A blonde in a Mercedes sports car pulled up next to him at the light and stared until he looked up. She smiled approvingly. He was at his peak, physically, mentally. On top in his career, money, looks. He slid a disk into the CD player and accelerated to Aretha belting out R-E-S-P-E-C-T. Beautiful wife, perfect kid, plenty of money, good music. On top of the world now and back in control.

Chapter Thirty-five

Annie got to the track just as the bell tower outside the stadium was ringing six o'clock. Mac's car wasn't in the lot. A couple of students were stretching on the grass and a gray head or two were walking briskly around the track. Mac had been right. This was a great time to run. They usually had the track to themselves, or almost. And it was great to be out of the house at the witching hour. Jim fixed Alex a light supper and snacked himself. When she got home she showered and nursed Rebecca. With Beccs down she and Jim could have a pleasant meal. Alex sometimes used the quiet time to talk with them and sometimes drew intricate superhero cartoons inspired by his comic books. Jessie had introduced him to the joy of comics. Oh, Jessie. Annie opened the glove compartment. Good, the list was nestled among the road maps.

The beep of Mac's horn startled Annie. Mac came around to the passenger door and climbed in next to Annie.

"Look, doll, I can't stay. Nick has to work late. I know—" Mac held up her hand. "I told him he owes us both big time. I'm really sorry. I sent Sam next door but I'm pushing it good-will wise. They run a tight ship and I'm messing up their dinnertime. So I can't stay to run but I had to come see The List."

Annie pulled it from the glove compartment and carefully unfolded the well-worn page. "See." She ran her finger down the first column. "I think these are adoption-for-pay notes. And look at this." Annie turned the page over. "These all say La Cucharita."

She pointed to Fleur's name. "This is another student. Jessie knew of her, knew she went to David, that she gave her baby up for adoption. She supposedly committed suicide. The day Jessie died she told me she wasn't sure Fleur's death was a suicide. One of Fleur's roommates isn't so sure either."

"How do you know?"

"I did some research at the university this afternoon."

"Busy beaver—"

Annie held up her hand for Mac to be quiet.

"Here's Jessie's name." She ran her finger under the name and "La Cucharita" and the $50,000 figure.

Mac whistled softly. "Big bucks," she said, awed.

"Wait," Annie said, and turned the page. There were tears in her eyes when she pointed to Jane's entry.

There was a sharp intake of breath from Mac.

"Goddamn dirty bastard. I feel like I could vomit. Annie, this is serious."

"I know." Annie bowed her head and a tear dripped onto her bare thigh. She felt cold in her running shorts and tank top. "There's more, Mac. Look at these articles I got out of the microfiche. They explain how you can use fetal tissue to cure Parkinson's disease. Mac, I think I saw something in Mexico—a man who may have had Parkinson's, in the clinic. I wasn't supposed to be there, it was at night . . ." She handed the highlighted pages to Mac, who read silently for several minutes.

Finally she lifted her head. "So you think Jane was right? You think David made her miscarry so he could do this Frankenstein thing to some man in Mexico?"

"Well, not him, because she hadn't miscarried yet when I

was there. But"—she looked down, and a tear fell on the list—"Jessie had."

"Sweetie." Mac put her hand under Annie's chin and turned her head so she could look into her eyes. "They're playing hard ball, Annie. What are you going to do? Who are you going to tell?"

"There's nothing I *can* do yet. I need to find out more. I can't go to the police with some crumpled-up piece of paper and a story about stuff I heard over my baby monitor. They'd lock me up. Jim would divorce me."

"Oh, right. Mr. Constitutional Rights doesn't know about Annie's Addiction, does he?"

"Thanks, Mac. You make me sound like a junky. I did tell Jim about it in the beginning and he freaked out completely. I can't tell him I kept on doing it."

"Oh, darlin', I'm sorry. I'm just following my mama's advice—laugh in the face of adversity. You need a plan, Annie."

"I know. I think I've got one."

"I'm all ears."

"I need to get a look at some hospital records. I need to see how David's miscarriage rate stacks up to some of the other doctors'."

"Good idea. Even factoring in an expected higher rate because of his high risk practice, it seems like you're gonna find he's off the charts. This is a long list."

"Right. So do you think I can pass myself off as a Blue Cross investigator?"

"Yeah, if you completely change your personality. When have you ever dealt with a nice Blue Cross employee? Go in there with an attitude, darlin'. 'I'm Blue Cross and I want those records *now.*'" Mac paused. "It could work. Yup, Annie, I think it could work."

"Great. So I get the records and then I can decide whether

to go to the police or hospital administration or get Jane to a lawyer or something."

"Right. But, Annie, you better move fast and be careful. You're playing in the majors now. These are big stakes."

"I know." Annie's tone was fierce now. "But I've got to find out what's going on. I sent Jane to him, Mac."

Mac hugged Annie hard. "I know, sweetie, I know. I want to catch the bastard, too. Just be careful."

Annie pulled away and unlatched the car door. "I'm sorry you can't run."

"So am I, damn Nick. You look like you could use some pavement pounding. Pretend you're coming down hard on Shields' head—no, his balls." Annie managed a small laugh. "I'll call you tomorrow, okay? Have a good run." Mac blew her a kiss.

Annie stretched next to the car and watched Mac pull out of the lot and turn right toward home. She put her right foot up on the rear bumper and bending her knee, bounced toward it several times. She did the same thing on the left side. With her back turned she didn't see the Jaguar turning into the lot.

She jogged slowly to the stadium gate and up the incline to the track. Annie didn't like running alone, it seemed so tedious. She and Mac talked and distracted each other from the pain they felt. Alone, she was all too aware of each lap and she never ran as much. Mac kept count, so Annie didn't have to. She was often pleasantly surprised at how many laps they'd done. Mac was obsessive about doing three miles and Annie found her competitive streak surfacing. She didn't want to appear to be a wimp. Alone she often quit at two and a half, sometimes only two. She concentrated on her breathing now. She couldn't let it get ragged.

A strand of tall pines lined one curved end of the track. The sun hung just at the top and then, as Annie banked for the corner on her third lap, it dropped and was gone and the

darkness had arrived. The timer on the lights must have mal-
functioned again, Annie realized, annoyed.

One minute it had seemed pleasant and dusk and the next
it was night and sinister. On the other side of the track, she
could just barely make out a figure beginning to run. He was
tall and somehow familiar. She scanned the parking lot and
saw the Jaguar.

Annie felt her pulse race, her breathing which had been
even and smooth was ragged and short. She looked back
over her shoulder and saw that he was already gaining on
her. She couldn't get enough air and she knew if she had to
make a break and run for her life she couldn't. She could see
the parking lot at the other side of the track. She would not
get there. She could hear his footsteps now, his even running
stride coming closer, and then she could hear his deep
breathing. The hair on her neck bristled. She could almost
feel his breath. Any second now, his hand would reach out
and clutch her neck. She closed her eyes and braced herself
for the attack but she kept moving. And then she felt his
hand on her back. She jumped. His hand moved up her spine
and settled in a firm grip on her shoulder as he matched his
stride with hers. "Be careful, Annie," he said. His tone was
not one of concern. She thought he sounded cold, menacing.
"It's not safe out here all by yourself." Then he slapped her
behind and ran off.

Annie realized she was trembling violently. She was humiliated by the slap, and at the same time felt furious and
scared. Am I going crazy? she asked herself. Thinking my
neighbor is going to murder me on the track? Am I completely wrong? God, get a grip, she told herself. The man
was always bragging about his mileage on the track. He had
just come out to run, like her.

Or, was he warning her to stay away, stay out of his affairs? Now she wondered again if it had been David behind
the incident with the cat in Mexico. Was he really that sick?

Annie felt panicky. What had she gotten herself into? All she wanted to do was get into her car and lock the doors. Go home to her family and forget about David.

But she couldn't stop now. She had to find out what he was up to, for Jessie and Jane's sakes at least. Annie eased off the track and jogged to her car. When she looked over her shoulder, David was still going around the track. She got in the car and locked the doors, without stretching first. She knew she'd be stiff in the morning but she couldn't bear to stay at the stadium another minute.

She got control of her breathing again. She put the key in the ignition and turned over the engine. In the almost total darkness she could just make him out, coming around the far end. As she drove away, she asked herself, was David Shields dangerous?

Chapter Thirty-six

Annie nursed Rebecca at five-thirty and then was unable to go back to sleep. What if the head of records didn't go to lunch? What if she called Blue Cross to check on Annie? What if someone asked her a question she couldn't answer? Could you be arrested for impersonating a Blue Cross official? She looked over at Jim sleeping peacefully, ignorant of her duplicitous ways, her invasion of the Shields' privacy, her plan to copy confidential records. If she was caught . . . it was too horrible to contemplate. She had violated everything Jim stood for, everything he worked so hard to protect. How embarrassed he would be. Would he forgive her? Would he divorce her? Would he take her children? Her chest tightened, she had trouble catching her breath, getting enough air, her lips tingled. Was this an anxiety attack? If so, she had only herself to blame. You've brought all this on yourself. *You* listened, *you* stole the list. *You're* continuing to snoop.

But, her other side argued, I'm doing this for Jessie, for Fleur, for Jane. What about their rights? What about how they had been violated? Sweet, young Jessie's face appeared before her, saying she was glad she had miscarried but then weeping. Jane holding up the beginnings of her first knitting, a baby sweater, and now Jane wouldn't leave her house, couldn't shed the pain that encased her like a cocoon.

Dammit, she would find out what happened. She would nail David Shields. Still, a tiny part of her whispered, what if you're wrong? What if he hasn't done anything illegal? But he has, you know it, you just have to prove it. You're the one who sent Jane to him and you have to make sure he doesn't hurt anyone else.

And so she argued with herself back and forth, panicking and letting her anger quell her panic until Jim woke up at seven and the day began and there was no more time to think. But in the midst of checking homework, finding knapsacks, fixing breakfasts, packing lunches, and sticking Alex's favorite dungarees in the dryer again because her ancient dryer never seemed to do the job completely the first time, she would glance at Jim and feel a stab of guilt so intense she felt she wanted to confess everything. Only his hectic morning demeanor and Alex's constant demands kept her quiet.

And then, somehow, she had Alex and Jim off to school and work. Rebecca napped, she showered and dressed and having just dropped Rebecca at the sitter's, was on her way to the hospital, no longer Annie Morgan, but now Catherine Moore, a Blue Cross investigator with an attitude. They better just hand over the requested records, if they knew what was good for them. Annie jockeyed for position on the highway, cutting people off at every opportunity. By the time she parked the car she was ready to do battle with Medical Records. She was tired of going to parties and having people whine at her about the high cost of their medical insurance once they found out where she worked. Did they really think in their wildest imaginings that she could possibly affect rate hikes? Annie chuckled, pleased at how easily she could slip into character.

Medical Records was in the basement. Annie squeezed into a crowded elevator. She wondered why the basement was such a popular destination until the doors opened and she saw an arrow pointing out the direction to Medical Records, Medical Imaging, and—the Cafeteria.

She hoped the close proximity of the cafeteria wouldn't interfere with her plan. She didn't want a clerk running down the hall to check her request with the supervisor. Hopefully the supervisor was bitchy and nobody would be anxious to interrupt her lunch break.

Medical Records was busy. Several doctors and nurses were examining files at a side counter. An elderly man and a woman in her late twenties or early thirties were waiting at the front counter. Annie couldn't tell if they were together or not.

She stepped up next to them. Nice pushy touch, she told herself. Behind the long front counter were rows of desks five or six deep, each with a computer terminal. Behind the desks was a wall completely covered floor to ceiling with built-in horizontal filing cabinets. Annie could see a good-sized room off to the left also lined with the same filing system. All the clerks were busy at their computers or searching through back-wall drawers. Annie turned away. A couple of very young doctors entered the room—residents. They looked about seventeen. I must be getting old, she thought. The wall next to the entrance was tile halfway up and then glass. Annie watched a steady stream of people going by, headed for lunch. A clerk had finished her computer task and headed for the counter. She was pretty in a brassy way, Annie thought. Platinum hair done up in a high pony tail, a cotton lycra sheath and spike heels. She had great legs, Annie noticed.

"Hey, boys," she said to the residents. She had a soft southern accent like honey, Annie thought, smooth and sweet. "How many have you good ol' boys killed today?" She laughed a deep throaty chuckle. The residents blushed. The elderly man looked up briefly from a chart he had been given. Annie thought he was going to say something but he only glared at the blonde and, shaking his head, turned back to his papers.

"What can I do for you, sugar?" She smiled at Annie.

"I'm Catherine Moore from Blue Cross. I called yesterday, I do hope everything's ready." She paused.

The blonde looked puzzled, not a clue.

Annie sighed, in what she hoped passed for exasperation. "We need to check some miscarriage stats. I need to see records on procedures by three or four doctors." Annie snapped open her briefcase, rifled through some papers and pretending to read from a list, said, "Let's see. Shields, Casey, Martin, and Sorenson. There seems to be a rise in spontaneous abortion rates at this institution. My office wants it checked out before the big boys start panicking and screaming false claims." Annie paused again. "Not a pretty picture for any of us. Once they're involved it's worse than an IRS audit."

The clerk's sexy looks and southern charm had disarmed Annie and she was having trouble staying in character. She thought now that the ally approach—we're all victims together—might work better. She held her breath, hoping she was right.

The blonde was shaking her head. Strands of the platinum mane had fallen loose around her neck. She was quite gorgeous.

"Tsk, tsk, tsk," she said. "You Blue Cross gals are always forgetting about one little bitty thing—'patient confidentiality' ring a bell? I'm not about to hang my nice pink butt out in the breeze just because your boss is heavy breathing down your neck."

"Look," Annie sighed again, hoping to emphasize a growing impatience, "I talked to Ms. Petrarca yesterday. She assured me there'd be no problem. We share information frequently. I am aware of patient confidentiality statutes. I don't need any patient names. I just need records of procedures—number of, type, date, doctor, let's say for the past two years, May through May—that will get us current."

The blonde glanced at the wall clock. Annie looked out the glass wall at the people heading to and from the cafeteria. What did Donna Petrarca look like? What if she came back? Then suddenly, behind a group of nurses, was David Shields. She whipped around to face the counter. Had he seen her? The blonde smiled and waved—at David? Would she tell him about Annie's visit? But of course, if she did, she'd be telling him about a Blue Cross investigator, not about Annie. And if he saw her, so what? She could need a record, her kids were born here.

"Fill out this form." The blonde slid a paper in her direction.

Yes, Annie thought, she's going to do it.

"It's gonna take a while for me to call this all up, so I'll get started. I'm not supposed to do it until you've signed the form, so fill it out fast, okay?"

Annie began filling out the requisition slip. Jail, she thought, I'll go to jail, forging a form. Obtaining medical records illegally. This must be a crime.

The form completed, Annie stared at the lithograph equivalent of muzak on the office walls and occasionally glanced at the parade from the cafeteria. What would she do if the supervisor came back before she'd gotten what she needed? What if the blonde said something to Ms. Petrarca about her? Finally the clerk approached her from the back room. She had a sheaf of papers in her hand and a receipt.

"That's forty-five dollars," she said. "A dollar a sheet."

"Charge it to the office," said Annie, and taking the papers, she turned to the door, then stopped and turned back. "Thanks a lot," she said. "Believe me, you've saved us both a lot of grief."

"It's all right," said the blonde, dismissing Annie with a

wave of her hand. "I'm always happy to head off trouble, especially from you all."

Annie's hand shook as she pressed the elevator button. She was dying to look at the records but she had promised herself she'd wait until she had them safe at home. Maybe she'd take them to Mac's. She was good at making sense of statistics.

By the time she got to the parking lot she couldn't wait any longer. She stood on the sidewalk, waiting to cross to her car and began reading the first sheet. She was just checking for how often David's name appeared. She walked slowly across the lot and was so engrossed that she didn't see Lesley get out of her car and stand by it, staring at Annie before heading off in the direction of the wing that Annie had just left.

Lesley spotted David right away. Her heart still quickened at the sight of his handsome face. God, she quickly prayed, he can't be having an affair. I love him too much.

He stood up and kissed her cheek.

"Hello, I got you a BLT, one of the more palatable menu offerings."

"Thanks. Guess who I just saw in the parking lot— Annie!" She watched his face intently for some sign of, what—guilt? Anxiety? Love? She saw nothing.

"Oh, really?" said David.

"It's so strange," said Lesley. "She told me she had a work meeting this morning. She even borrowed a pair of my shoes."

"You're too nice, Lesley," David interrupted. "I'd never let anybody else put their feet in my shoes."

Lesley laughed. "I'm glad she could use them. It makes me feel better. I looked in my closet the other day—it's pretty disgusting. I have an Imelda Marcos thing going on. I must own fifty pairs of shoes. I'm happy to lend them."

"Poor little rich girl," David said. "You've got to stop feeling guilty. You're a wonderful person, Lesley. You can't help it if your husband is brilliant and rich." He beamed at her. "Stop beating yourself up, Les. Lola's the one with the Imelda thing going on. I've never seen that woman wear the same thing twice."

David began talking about a meeting he had had with Morris Bigler about establishing a high risk unit within the hospital as a mini hospital that David would run completely.

Lesley listened with half her brain while the other half chased the picture of Annie with a missing earring and Annie in some sort of preoccupied daze crossing the parking lot. Why was Annie lying to her about her meeting, if she wasn't the one? Had David replaced the earring for her? That was something he would do, especially if—oh, God— he was the one who had given them to her in the first place. Could it possibly be Annie after all? Now she didn't know what to think.

She picked up her sandwich and took a bite, but the anger building inside her made her mouth dry. She looked at David, so handsome and self-assured, digging into his sandwich. Anyone looking at them would have seen a happy couple. Lesley wanted to slap him. Why did you do this to me? she wanted to scream. She wanted to tell him she knew, wanted to make him choose. He looked up then, and with a puzzled look said, "Are you okay? Is it the sandwich?"

"Yes, it's the sandwich," Lesley said. "How can you eat this food?" All her anger went into attacking his taste.

"Whoa, Les. I'm sorry you don't like it. It's all I had time for. You suggested lunch today, remember? I said I didn't have time to go out."

Lesley took a deep breath and looked down at her plate. She could compose herself better if she wasn't looking at him. This wasn't the time or place to unleash her anger, she knew that. She thought coming here would help somehow, that she might discover his lover by the way he looked or spoke to someone. That was silly, this wasn't a soap opera. It was "real, true life," as Annie's Alex said.

"Sorry," Lesley managed. "I didn't sleep well last night. I'm just tense."

"Okay, it's okay," David said. "Why don't you go home and rest. Maybe your friend Annie will take Millie in exchange for the shoe loan."

"Maybe," Lesley said, and again wondered why Annie had lied about her plans for the day.

"I'm sorry, sweetheart," David said, "but my time's up."

"Fine. I'm ready."

David gave her a chaste kiss by the elevator and then disappeared into the crowded tunnel heading toward the wards.

Lesley waited for the elevator, feeling furious with David and confused by Annie. I need answers from both of them, she thought.

Chapter Thirty-seven

She had her back to him, standing at the stove. Something smelled wonderful. His nose tried to decipher the exact herb—tarragon? She was so intent on whatever she was stirring that she hadn't heard him come in.

He moved closer to her. Caught up in a clip, her thick, lush, blond hair was escaping. Wisps clung to her neck, damp from the steam escaping from the pot.

"Hi," he said, and kissed the side of her neck below the ear. The spoon clattered on the tile floor.

"Jesus, David, don't sneak up on me like that." Why was he torturing her like this? Kissing her as if she were the only woman in his life.

"Sweetheart, I'm sorry. I didn't mean to." David looked down into her eyes and smoothed her hair back with both hands. He concentrated on sounding patient and loving. He really ought to be satisfied with what he had here at home from now on. He had found her completely satisfying before he married her. He could do it again. She avoided his gaze. He pulled her close and gave her a long, deep kiss, which he couldn't savor because she jumped away.

"God, my sauce," and she was back at the stove in the cooking mode. "Set the table, will you?"

He felt his mood drop down to his shoes. She could make him feel like a ten-year-old. He hated domestic chores.

"After I clean up," he said, walking toward the back stairs. He'd wash his hands and change and by that time she'd have the table set. Why wouldn't she just hire a fucking cook. They had the money. They'd been around that one many times. Lesley had had enough of domestic help growing up. There was never any family privacy, she said. Rosaria was the most she would agree to and she only worked part-time. Lesley wanted Millie to grow up in a normal, everyday household. Oh, well, in a couple of years Millie could set the table, he told himself. Good to instill the work ethic early. He slid his long legs into a pair of lightly starched khakis and caught a satisfying glimpse of his flat gut in the mirror.

At the foot of the stairs he peeked in the dining room: still not set. He walked to the kitchen and poked his head in. She was jabbing at something under the broiler.

"Honey, I've just got to make a quick call to the hospital." She looked up and sighed, just the way a mother would at an exasperating child. "Hurry," she called after him, and began pulling silver from the drawer. He closed his study door and sank into his chair. It creaked and groaned, emitting a comforting leather smell. He pulled out the bottom drawer. Might as well check on the list. He lifted the manila files: no notebook. His heart skipped a beat. Jesus, he told himself. Get a grip. Everything made him jumpy. He needed a break. Chill out, he thought. Go easy.

Under the manila files were some reprints from medical journals he'd brought home to read. He began lifting these up and under the first couple he found it.

Jesus, what was it doing there? Another man might have slipped it in between the reprints by mistake if he were in a hurry. But not him. This was too important. Especially since Jessie. Now he always made sure he replaced it in exactly the same position: under the manila files but on top of the reprints, and pushed precisely into the upper left-hand corner of the drawer. He sat for several minutes breathing deeply, trying to regain an equilibrium and calm his frantic mind. Lesley would be calling him to dinner. The role this evening was Charming Husband, with no hint of any unusual stress during the day. He shook his head to prevent Pam's image from appearing. Shit. What was going on? Everything had been rolling along fine. Pretty little wife, cute kid, big house, the right cars, respect of colleagues, adoration from patients.

Then—*wham*. First Pam acts up, now someone else has found the notebook? Someone had to move it—did they read it as well? He could feel paranoia, tangible as a hand, grip his head and spin his brain. Someone at the hospital? Did someone know something? But how? He hardly ever made calls to Bernie or Jaime from work, almost always from home, and not ever when Lesley or the sitter was around.

"David? *Da*-vid!" Lesley's head appeared in his doorway. "Dinner."

David smiled.

"Honey," he said, "have you been in here? Did you need anything from my desk?"

"No," she said shortly. "This is your space. I never use it for anything. Why?"

"Oh, no big deal. I just can't find some papers I thought I had. They must be at the hospital or the office."

"Sorry." She turned toward the dining room. "I'm sure they'll turn up. Now come on—everything's ready." She started to walk away. "Oh, could you grab the wine please, it's in the fridge. I'll get Millie."

Great, he thought, as he headed for the kitchen. Just what I need—dinner with a one-year-old. And Lesley with an attitude. It must be that time of the month. Again. Why couldn't Lesley feed the kid first? He'd have to speak to her about it again. He liked his baby clean and smelling good, to tickle or even to carry upstairs, her little head finding a place in the soft skin against his neck; that was fatherhood. Her soft little sighs, her big eyes gazing into his . . . *not* watching her smear peas in her hair or up her nose, and throw milk onto the oriental. He was losing his appetite already.

He carried the wine to the table.

"Look, Millie," Lesley singsonged. "It's Daddy. Oh boy, he's home in time for dinner." For once, she thought. She clapped her hands. She felt split in half, one half acting like everything was fine, the other half alternately burning with rage and immobile with sadness. She knew she couldn't go on much longer without confronting him, but she just couldn't bear to, not yet.

The baby clapped, too, and beamed at David. He ran his hand over her head, while it's still clean, he thought, and bent down to kiss it.

He lowered himself into his chair, suddenly feeling very tired.

"So, darling"—he flashed a smile at Lesley—"how's everything working out with the new sitter?"

"Karen?" asked Lesley and looked sad. "You never remember their names."

Right, thought David. It was more convenient for Lesley to think he never remembered the names of sitters, so he wouldn't know this one's name, either.

"Oh, yeah. Does Millie like her? Did they have fun today?"

"Oh, she's great, David. Millie loves her, I love her, she's lots of fun."

He smiled and feigned interest but his brain was impatiently rejecting all this useless information. It urgently needed its pressing questions answered and it screamed at him: was she in the study today and did *she* move the notebook?

"That's wonderful that you like her so much. And you,

Millie?" he gave his biggest Daddy grin. "What did you and Karen do today?" Lesley loved to answer for the little girl. Normally it annoyed him no end, how was the child ever to learn to enunciate if Lesley did all the work for her? But tonight it was unimportant.

"Um, I think they went to that playground around the corner . . . and looked at books . . ." Suddenly remembering something, she became animated. "And you have a new trick, Millie, don't you?" She leaned over to stroke the baby's sticky cheek. "Annie came and played with you while Mommy went to the dentist yesterday, and she said you read her *Pat the Bunny!* Did you say Buh-buh? You did, didn't you, you little smarty pants?" Lesley was lost in the baby.

David tuned out her goochie-goo-honeyed voice. His eyes narrowed. His heart was pounding again. Annie? His mind flipped back to the Indian in Jaime's garden.

". . . the dark-haired Americana. She was in the kitchen, very late . . ."

"She must have been hungry."

"I do not think so . . . She was coming from the direction of the laboratory and the medical wing."

He had all but convinced himself that it was just a harmless attempt at extortion on Ricardo's part, but had he been foolish? Had Annie seen something? But even if she had, how would she know about the list and where he kept it? It was too complicated. It didn't make sense.

Lesley put a key lime pie in front of him, not, she thought, for him, but because she felt like making one.

"That looks great. You're my sweet girl. Have I been a grouch? I've got a lot on my mind, sorry. Hospital politics, the usual bullshit."

"I'm sorry you have to deal with that, Davey. They should just leave you alone to do what you do best."

"And what is that, my darling?" He smiled at her and felt a wave of desire.

"That's not what I was thinking about," she said, then uttered a small dismayed "Oh!" and rushed to the baby who, while her parents were not focused on her, had upended the bowl of applesauce on her head.

She lifted the baby out of the high chair, in the process getting applesauce on both her bare arms. "Millie and I will be in the shower."

As soon as they had left the room, David headed for his study and closed the door. He stood examining the room for any signs that someone had been there. The walls were lined with books floor to ceiling, broken only by large windows with navy velvet window seats. The massive oriental looked just vacuumed, as if no one had walked on it for days. His desktop with phone, a PDR, several prescription pads, his Mont Blanc, and a recent journal of *OB-GYN* looked pristine, as usual. He sat in his chair and slipped off his Belgian tassel loafers. He rubbed his toes along the carpet, and stretched his left foot out. It touched something distinctly unruglike. There, lying on the floor next to his bottom desk drawer, was one of Millie's little books. *Pat the Bunny.*

Annie, he thought. She had been there with Millie. He pulled himself up and back into the chair. "Fuck, fuck, fuck!" he said, pounding his fist on the glass desktop.

What did this mean? Did that bitch, Annie, know something? How? How could she possibly follow his well-concealed twists and turns? How could she know about the notebook? His head hurt. He walked to the front window and looked out at the Morgans' house. Their living room was wide open for viewing, no curtains. There was Annie, talking to her kid, hair in that scraggly ponytail. But a nice body, firm legs—even in his anger he admired the way her

T-shirt pulled across her chest. Jesus, how could he figure this out? His back hurt. He lay down with his feet flat, knees up on the window seat, the way Larry Metcalf in Orthopedics had told him. He closed his eyes. "What a mess. What a fucking mess."

Chapter Thirty-eight

David bit into his corned beef on pumpernickel, the only sandwich they did really well in the cafeteria. Jesus, what a morning. They were having babies younger and younger. He needed the clinic exposure for what he thought of as his "extracurriculars," but recently his clinic on-call time had lost its thrill. He just couldn't divide up his attention like this anymore. He felt as though his brain were being chopped up in little pieces and he was losing a grip on things. He no longer felt like he was driving the machine, just running around putting out fires. There was always something; this morning it had been a fourteen-year-old with a posterior oxy. He hated to just cut the kid, seemed a shame to leave a cesarean scar on that cute little bod. And besides, he had this baby placed already and it was always easier to have a vaginal delivery. He had put on mid forceps and tried to turn the head but it wouldn't budge so they'd gone ahead and done the C-section and only OR 6, the tiny one, had been available. Hotter than hell, with all those bodies, OB and Pediatric residents all wanting to see the master at work. Mother and baby were both fine, of course, and he could finally eat now and then what? He was tense. Eyeing everyone suspiciously.

Hell, he had to relax. He had the afternoon off and no Pammy to play with. He already missed those steamy trysts.

Don't think about it. He could go home to Lesley. No, she'd never been the afternoon type. Besides, this wasn't physical tension; he was anxious about something in particular.

"Hey, David." Gloria, the Memphis belle from records, was at his table with another, uninteresting secretary—he didn't know her name.

"Hi, sugar plum." David winked.

"Oh, Dr. Shields, you don't have enough sugar for this old gal." She flashed him a wicked smile.

"Hmmm." David found himself wondering. She had always given him anything he wanted from records. Maybe he should give her a spin.

"Have you been up to no good, blue eyes?"

David started—what the hell kind of a question was that? Just keep up the banter, he told himself.

"Wouldn't you like to know?" he parried.

"No, really, David. A sweet little Blue Cross investigator was in yesterday asking questions about you and Roger Thomas and a few others. Wanted your stats, miscarriages mostly."

David could feel his blood pressure rising. Was this what he had been anxious about?

"Who—?" he started to ask, but Gloria went right on smiling and teasing.

"You haven't been double billing those nice folks at Blue Cross, have you? Don't want to get caught with your pants down, Dr. Shields." She flashed him a last smile and started to move on. David caught her arm.

"Who was it from Blue Cross?"

"Oh, gosh, I don't remember her name, but she was cute. You probably saw her. She was standing by me when you walked by and waved yesterday. Ummm . . ." Gloria frowned now. "Well, come to think of it, I guess she had her back to you."

Damn. That's why he'd been so tense. He knew he'd seen

something yesterday, something that didn't fit, but he'd been too hyped up over the Pam thing to pay attention to it. Even when Lesley had given him the answer. Sloppy.

David had what he wanted.

"Never mind, Gloria. I guess if they want me for something bad enough they'll come to me. Thanks, though."

"Well, you're welcome. I sure hope it's nothin'."

"You know me, sweetheart, pure as the driven snow. Nothing to hide."

He stood up and without bussing his dishes headed for the parking lot. He was outraged. That bitch. She wasn't going to get the best of him.

He gunned the Jag out of the parking garage. Didn't even wave to Tommy. Annie! That fucking bitch. She was everywhere. He no longer wondered what she knew, she must know it all. Mexico, the notebook, Pam? Well, two could play at this game. Thank God it wasn't really Blue Cross snooping around, only Annie—she'd be easy. He slammed a hand down on the horn as some wimp made a feeble attempt to pass him and almost ran the guy into a parked taxicab.

He'd have to cool the Mexico deals for a while. Maybe he'd slow down all operations. Bernie and Jaime would be pissed but what the hell. He was in charge and it was getting too fucking hot. Who the fuck needed this?

He'd just take a vacation. He and Lesley—a cruise. Her parents could take Millie. They were always whining about that anyway. "Let us have the baby." Hell, her old man would probably pick up the tab as well. They could do one of those twenty-one-day Greece and the Mediterranean jobs. Perfect. He looked at his watch: 2:30. Where would Lesley be now? Why didn't he listen when she nattered on about what she did all day? Didn't she take some aerobics class or shit like that in the afternoon? Maybe she was shopping. She sure knew how to spend his money. He slammed on the breaks for some geriatric idiot crossing on a red light, then got caught up in Country Day's afternoon pickup traffic. "Just get your fucking kid into the car," he muttered at the woman stopped in the middle of the street ahead of him. Come on, come on. He honked. She moved. He swerved to pass her on the right, whipped the car around the corner, sped up the hill and, spraying gravel in all directions, pulled into his driveway. The Range Rover was in the garage but Lesley's Saab was gone. Lucky boy, he told himself, lucky boy.

Chapter Thirty-nine

Lesley could feel a familiar throb beginning at her left temple. Damn, why hadn't she grabbed something at the mall? A cup of fruit salad, a cookie and milk? This traffic wasn't helping. She sighed and pushed the window button. The breeze helped a bit. She reached to turn on the radio and thought better of it. Quiet was best. She groped in her pocketbook for the pill bottle, got it open and swallowed two, dry. Yuck. She winced.

She glanced down at the gas gauge. Oh, goddammit. Well, there was a station up ahead. Please be full-serve, she thought. She hated to pump it herself, especially when she didn't feel well. No good. It was self-serve. She stared at the gauge; there was a hair left in the reserve tank. You can do it, she told the car. One more exit.

Easing off the highway, the car jerked but recovered and she sailed down Western Avenue toward home. Five blocks from the house the car bucked again. She put her foot down harder on the accelerator and felt no response. Shit, she hissed, and coasted to the curb.

She took her bulging Gap Kids bag and her pocketbook, carefully locked the car, and walked the rest of the way home. She'd have to send the garage for it later and David would make her feel bad about her pump-your-own phobia.

"Millie was a perfect angel," the girl said. "She had about

half a grilled cheese cut up the way you told me and almost a whole yogurt. She just went down for her nap about fifteen minutes ago."

"Thanks. That's great. I'll see you tomorrow, same time?"

"Great. Bye-bye."

She hoped the sitter didn't feel like she'd given her the bum's rush, but her head was killing her and she just wanted to grab some peace and quiet while Millie was napping.

Lesley took a bottle of peach Clearly Canadian and an apple out of the refrigerator, stopped at the hall table to pick up her mail, and headed upstairs to lie down. She thumbed through the envelopes, sorting them by how interesting they were, David's mail and bills at the bottom of the pile, magazines and personal letters on top. She tossed the newspaper aside—she didn't feel like reading that now. Ah, she thought, as she came to a pink envelope, a letter, addressed to her. Good, something fun to read. It was puzzling, though, because there was no return address. She sat on the edge of the bed and kicked off her shoes. A college friend? But the envelope was lightweight, cheap paper. Her friends mostly used heavy stock, and she didn't know anyone with pink stationery. She lay back on the bed. The postmark was local. Hmm. She ripped it open and unfolded the page. What she read made her stomach lurch.

"*. . . he loves me. I love him . . . You are living a lie . . . Did you find my earring? I left it for you to find . . .*" Lesley was sitting up now, clutching her stomach and rocking back and forth. "David, David." She sobbed, but made herself read on.

"*I know him better than you ever could. I respect his genius, his drive. I am his partner. His helpmate. He confides in me. . . .*

"*Let him go. Give him his freedom. He needed you and*

your money. But not now; he has made his own and he has me . . ."

"Damn you!" She ran across the room and swept their wedding photograph off her bureau, along with everything else, the baby monitor, her loose change, a hairbrush. How could he do this to her? How could she have been so stupid? She skipped to the signature. Oh, God, *her*—one of his nurses. Lesley had met her at last year's auxiliary. How typical, how humiliating.

Lesley stiffened. She hadn't heard the door but now she could hear David whistling downstairs in the hall, heading toward the stairs. She grabbed the letter and jumped off the bed. She couldn't let him see her like this, makeup smeared, crying over *him*. She wasn't going to give the bastard the satisfaction. Her eyes darted around the room. The closet. The entire side wall was composed of louvered doors opening to a vast shared closet. She opened one of the doors at her end and pushed her way to the dark back wall. She squatted there clutching the letter, trying to calm her breathing. The cracks in the louvered doors were just wide enough for her to follow his legs as he moved around the room. She heard him walking on the bathroom's marble floor, heard him urinate and flush. Oh, God. She held her breath as she watched his legs coming straight for the closet.

Annie paced the living room agitatedly. "Just go to sleep, Beccs, please? Mommy has to work." Work? she chided herself, was that what she was doing? More like Invading the Privacy of Others, to the point of criminal activity. But if what she was thinking about David were true, it was he who was the criminal, not she. She began rubbing Rebecca's back in a circular motion, slowly forcing herself to seem calm for the baby. Rebecca finally burped and then rested her tiny head on Annie's shoulder and slept.

Annie tucked in the baby and ran down the stairs to her

desk. She was dying to compare the stats from the hospital
with David's list. She reached in the bottom drawer and
pulled the hospital computer sheets out from under some old
Cotton Tales catalogs. Then she went over to the bookshelf
and pulled out the drawer at the top of the massive Oxford
English Dictionary case. The magnifying glass was supposed to be kept in the drawer but she and Jim had never
bothered with that; they always laid it on top of the case. The
drawer was the perfect hiding place for the well-worn piece
of notebook paper. Her hand shook as she unfolded it and
went back to her desk. From the hospital she'd gotten list-
ings for ten OBs. A careful counting showed David to have
twice as many miscarriages as the doctor with the least.
Next she compared his rate to the two other high risk OBs.
David was still one-third higher than the next highest. Annie
began to feel sick. What she had once thought of as an exciting game was becoming a horrible reality. She lay
David's list next to the spreadsheet. Her eyes darted back
and forth between the two.

Miscarriage	Oct. 3	*La Cucharita (Oct. 3)*
Miscarriage	Dec. 12	*La Cucharita (Dec. 12)*
Miscarriage	Jan. 26	*La Cucharita (Jan. 26)*

The lists coincided every time. A full-blown wave of nausea hit Annie. She went to the bathroom and hung her head
over the sink. She heard Jessie's terrified voice, *"He's evil,
Annie."* She saw Jane's tear-streaked face. *"I think Dr.
Shields came into my room in the night. I think he put something in my IV."* Immaculata's moans rang in her ears. She
sank to the floor and buried her face in her hands. She
wanted to sob and sleep and wake up and discover it was
just a nightmare. Instead she splashed cold water on her face
and went to her briefcase. She got out the stack of articles on
fetal tissue and piled them next to the other papers. Part of

her had felt that in the end she would, of course, discover that David wasn't doing anything wrong. Well, of course, being with Pam was wrong, but nothing *medically* wrong. The miscarriages would turn out to be as Jim had said, coincidental.

"God knows I don't like the man, Annie. He's an arrogant shit, but causing women to lose their babies? Someone would know about it."

"Jim, he's *chief of obstetrics*. He's God over there. Nobody's going to question him." She hadn't gone any further though, hadn't shared her suspicions about David selling babies to adoptive parents because that would have involved fessing up to her listening-in habit. Jim, with his sense of right and wrong, all black and white, no gray areas.

But now—she looked at the stack of evidence and then finally said it out loud.

"David Shields is causing women to miscarry their babies. He is selling the fetal tissue to some Mexican quack so that he can deceive anybody rich enough to pay for it into thinking that he can cure them of Parkinson's disease. That 'heart patient' in La Cucharita had all the symptoms, the shaking, the rigidity. I saw it, I know. And I saw poor Immaculata lose her baby, in terrible pain, and all alone." She paused and took a deep breath. "Okay, Annie, you've said it. Now figure out what to do about it."

She could go to the police. With stolen evidence? She could call Jim. She could confront David. Talk to Lesley?

She had to clear her head. Now that she had it finally figured out she wanted to do the right thing, not just react impulsively. Would he go to jail? What about Lesley and Millie? Don't get carried away, she told herself. Think. Think clearly.

Maybe a soak in a hot tub would help her sort things out. She had a little time before Alex's bus. She went up to the bedroom and pulled the small portable TV out of her closet, carried it into the bathroom and positioned it on the shelf so she'd be able to see it while she was in the bath. She had to rummage around in her closet, pushing shoes and bags of tooth fairy gifts and odd rewards out of the way before she found the thick orange extension cord and the multiple plug outlet. Taking a bath was so complicated in this house, Annie thought. As she fiddled with the plugs she looked out the window at Lesley's house. She whispered, "I'm sorry, Les." Sorry that she would be the one to expose David, sorry for all the times she'd listened in. "I didn't turn out to be a very good friend after all, did I?"

She removed the plastic dinosaurs and Power Ranger figures and the yellow duck from the tub and turned the water on, hot. She poured in some Vitabath gel and watched the greenish white bubbles rise for a second then turned to get the monitor.

At last she lowered herself gingerly into the tub. Leaning back against the inflatable pillow, she reached for the newspaper. Finally beginning to relax in the mountain of bubbles and steam, Annie wasn't prepared for the small item hidden in the metro section of the paper. When she saw the black-and-white photo of Pam Fowler above a small headline she had to grab on to the side of the tub to keep from sliding under. She read quickly,

> The body of Pamela Fowler, age 25, was discovered yesterday in her apartment. The victim had apparently been strangled. The police believe Ms. Fowler had been dead for approximately four hours before her body was discovered. She was due at work at the Crawford Maternity hospital at one o'clock and when she hadn't shown up by two another nurse began to call her home.
>
> Although the body was found partially clad there were no visible signs of sexual assault. The state Medical Examiner said they would not know definitely until after all test results were returned. The apartment had been

ransacked and police are considering the possibility that
Ms. Fowler surprised the robber.

Annie let go of the paper and it sank into the bubbles.
David's words rang in her ears. "No more demands,
Pammy." He had sounded so angry. He had lied to Pam
about Millie, too—she wasn't sick. And he could have been
at her apartment four hours before the police found her. The
realization hit her and she was momentarily immobilized.
Then she began to shake uncontrollably.

"Oh God." She sobbed. "Oh God, I'm scared." She
jumped out of the tub and grabbing her robe off the hook,
ran, dripping, for the phone. "Please be there, please be
there."

It seemed a long time before Jim came on the line.

"Annie." Jim's voice was calm, concerned. She loved his
gentle, deep voice, and now it felt like a lifeline.

"Oh, honey"—she could feel her eyes watering—"I'm
scared," she stammered. "I—" She couldn't hold off the
tears.

"Annie, what's wrong?" Jim tried to push thoughts of
Sudden Infant Death Syndrome and overturned school buses
out of his mind. "Is something wrong with one of the kids?"

"It's David." The words spilled out now, all in a rush.
"We've got to stop him, he made Jane lose her baby, he
killed Pam . . ." Annie was sobbing so hard she couldn't
speak anymore.

"David? Shields? Annie, what are you saying? Sweetheart, I can barely understand you." Annie tried again.

"Jim, it's awful. I found out things. I know, I said I'd
stop, but I didn't and now I know . . . Oh, God, maybe if I
had . . . Pam would still be alive—" She was weeping again.
Jim tried to wait but Annie just kept on crying into the
phone.

"Pam? Annie, who is Pam?"

"The nurse, the one I told you about, the one David was having an affair with. He killed her." She remembered something. "Is stolen evidence proof, to police?"

She was going too fast for him. It made no sense. What was this? Annie calling in the middle of the day, hysterical about stolen evidence and murder and that incredible jerk, Shields. Could she be having a breakdown? His beautiful, strong Annie?

"Annie, sweetie, where's Rebecca?"

"Rebecca? What do you mean?" Why was Jim being so thick? Why wasn't he responding to this? She needed help quickly. What if David did think she knew something. She shuddered. Were the doors locked? She started to put the phone down when Jim's voice came out of the receiver and she jerked it back up to her ear.

"Annie." Jim sounded worried. "Where is Rebecca?"

"She's here with me, of course," she snapped. "She's in her room." She glanced around the room automatically for the monitor's receiver, then frowned when she saw the transmitter instead. Oh God, she'd never switched it back to Rebecca's room from when she'd fallen asleep in here this morning. Irrational panic at not being able to hear her baby clawed at her. She had to get a grip. She realized now she sounded like she was out of her mind.

"Look, Jim, I need your help. I want to go to the police. I want you to go with me."

"Okay, Annie, of course. But, I need to know more—"

She cut him off.

"I have lots of stuff, records and a list with names and—"

"Sweetheart. Look, whatever you've done, whatever you think David's done, please, don't call the police until I get home. We'll talk everything over and decide what to do together."

Annie sniffed. "Okay, but hurry, please, I'm really

scared. I don't think he knows that I know, but if they tell him at the hospital . . . *He killed Pam.* I'm—" She was crying hard again. "I'm sure he did."

"Okay, Annie, look, lock all the doors and try to calm down. I'll get home as fast as I can. I have to tie up some stuff here but I'll come fast, honey."

"I love you, Jim. Hurry, okay?"

He started to answer but she had already hung up. He didn't know what to think. She hadn't stopped—what? Listening in? Jesus Christ. He'd really just told her to lock the doors so she'd know he was taking her seriously. But if she *was* in danger—then he remembered. He was the guy who always insisted on riding his bike to work, for the environment. He'd never find a cab at this time of day.

"Christ!" he yelled and slammed his fist down hard on the desk. Did he always have to be so goddamn politically correct?

Okay, okay, she had to get a hold of herself. Jim was coming. He was on the way. And David *didn't* know what she'd been doing—the snooping in Mexico, the trip to the hospital, oh, God, all that listening in. Or did he? But he couldn't. Annie groaned. She was just going around in circles. She took some deep breaths and went to put the monitor in Rebecca's room. Then she tightened the belt on her robe and went back downstairs to check the doors. The back one was locked and she added the chain. She pushed the button on the front door's locking mechanism and walked back up to the bedroom. She checked her watch.

Oh, God, Alex's bus! It was due at the corner any minute now—and she was still in her robe. The driver had been running about ten minutes behind lately—she could just make it if she moved fast. She grabbed a T-shirt, underwear, and a pair of jeans and took them into the bathroom. She passed the blow-dryer over her head a few times and then bent for-

ward, throwing her hair up over her head to dry the underneath. As her chin hit her chest she saw Pam's face staring
up at her from under the water on the bottom of the tub and
the panic began to take hold again. Without even turning it
off, she returned the blow-dryer to the shelf and reached
down to bring the bleeding newsprint up to the surface. She
felt cut off, in shock. She was living across the street from a
murderer. She couldn't sleep another night in this house,
knowing he was right there.

She had to go to the police, as soon as Jim got back, as
soon as Alex—Alex! Oh, God. She fumbled with the knot of
her bathrobe sash. "I'm coming," she whispered, "I'm coming."

David lurched across the floor to the bedroom closet and
threw aside the door. He reached toward the shelf at the back
and then stopped. What the—? It was coming from the baby
monitor—a very familiar and unpleasant voice.

"*. . . causing women to miscarry their babies. He is selling the fetal tissue to some Mexican quack so that he can deceive anybody rich enough to pay for it into thinking that he
can cure them of Parkinson's disease. That 'heart patient' in
La Cucharita had all the symptoms; the shaking, the rigidity. I saw it, I know. And I saw poor Immaculata lose her
baby, in terrible pain, and all alone.*"

What? David was reeling. That bitch! Who's she talking
to? She can't be doing this to me. Had she beat him to it?
Had the bitch beat him to it? It was all over, everything. He
was a dead man. Could he get out of the country? Then the
voice started again.

"*Okay, Annie, you've said it. Now figure out what to do
about it.*"

He had to laugh. The bitch was talking to *herself*! She
hadn't spilled it yet. The little mouse was practicing. Ha! He

was still on top. Okay, okay, let's get this done. Soon you'll be soaking up the rays in sunny Greece. He turned back to the closet and reached for the hidden syringe.

The cramp in Lesley's left leg was bringing tears to her eyes, but she didn't dare move. David was standing at his end of the closet now. She could see only his feet and legs, not even to the knee, under her hanging dresses. He squatted and reached back to his gym bag. His head was still above her line of vision. She tried not to breathe. She heard a faint buzzing, like a radio turned down, but she couldn't identify the sound.

Suddenly she heard him laughing. The way he laughed sent a chill up her spine. She was already furious with him, her heart torn in pieces by him, but now, for the first time in her life, she was *afraid* of her husband. The way he laughed, he sounded like something out of a slasher movie.

She watched as he pulled a small black case from his end of the closet. He unzipped it, held it open, and slipped a syringe into the case. Next he grabbed a bottle of medicine, the small kind that the pediatrician used to fill the syringe for DPT boosters. He put the medicine bottle in his outer jacket pocket and, standing up, left the closet. By leaning back she could see his upper body and face through the upper door cracks. He was slipping the black case into his jacket's inner breast pocket. She watched him go to the mirror and check his hair.

"Goddamn bitch," he said out loud. "It's my life and she'll stay the hell out of it." He turned away from the mirror.

Lesley could see his eyes and with the light from the window behind him they seemed to glow. He was furious. She had never seen him like this. Did he know about the letter? Was this Pam person the one he was so furious with? Lesley felt her heart leap. Maybe she was just a crazy patient. Some woman who had fallen in love with her doctor. Maybe it was all a delusion. She wanted to run from the closet and hug David, tell him she understood. She knew he loved her. But then she remembered the earring. The letter was not the ravings of a crazy patient, it was from a woman who had made love to her husband in this room, *their* room. From a distance Lesley heard the front door close and she was free to release the sob that was building in her throat.

"I hate you," she sobbed. "I love you. Oh why? Why, David?" She waited for the sound of his car. It didn't come. She walked across the room to the front window. David was standing on the sidewalk in front of the Morgans' house across the street, waving to Alex, who was coming up the sidewalk with his schoolbag. When the boy reached him, David squatted down and put his hand on Alex's shoulder. Lesley watched David talking. Alex had an earnest expression. Suddenly he broke into a big smile and, producing a key from a pocket of his backpack, opened the Morgans' front door. Then David followed the small boy into the house.

Once inside, David walked to the foot of the stairs and cocked his head, listening for Annie. She hadn't appeared at the sound of the front door opening. He could hear some kind of a motor running upstairs—it sounded like a hair-dryer.

"I think your mom's upstairs, Alex. I don't want to disturb her. What do you usually do after school?"

"I watch TV if Mom says it's okay."

"Well, since she's busy with the baby, why don't I say okay? I don't think she'll mind."

"Great. Thanks, Dr. Shields."

David watched the boy turn on the set and settle into the

couch. It only took a minute for his eyes to glaze over and his mouth to hang open. David was amazed. It was as if someone had given the kid some Demerol.

He turned and walked to the bottom of the stairs. The noise was louder. Keeping to the center of the stairs, he discovered he could stop the old wood from creaking and he made it silently into the first room he came to, the baby's. He stood for a minute, getting his bearings, listening. Judging by the sound, the master bedroom was next door and the bathroom beyond that, forming a straight line with the baby's room across the front of the house. He crossed to the adjoining door and put his ear to it—nothing. Just the whirring of the hair dryer beyond. He walked to the window and taking the black case from his pocket, withdrew the needle. He then pulled the medicine bottle out of his jacket and leaning against the window casing to catch all of the natural light, began to fill the syringe.

Lesley had seen Alex sit down in front of the living room TV and seen David walk out of the room—toward the back of the house?—and then she lost him. What was he doing at Annie's? She scanned all the first floor windows, straining for a glimpse of David—just Alex and the TV set. Maybe David was in the kitchen with Annie. Maybe he was confessing to Annie, asking her to look after Lesley once he left. How humiliating.

But where was Annie? And why hadn't she greeted Alex yet? Lesley had been there before when Alex came home from school. Annie always made a big deal about his being home. Her eyes went up to the second floor, where she thought she'd detected a flashing light, some movement maybe. Sure enough, in the bathroom window, there was Annie. She was blow-drying her hair in her bathrobe, clearly just out of the tub. She watched as Annie bent over, then straightened up, put the hair dryer down, and then bent over again. What's she doing now, Lesley wondered. Doesn't she know Alex and David are downstairs? She tried to wave to Annie, thought she could point at her watch, remind Annie that it was time for Alex to be home. But although Annie appeared to be looking in Lesley's direction she didn't acknowledge the wave. The sun must be in her eyes, Lesley thought. And then she stopped waving and stood there thinking. Annie must be very distracted to forget about Alex. And why hadn't David let his presence be known?

David. She began to scan the windows again, no one in Annie and Jim's room, or Rebecca's room—but then he appeared at the window, filling a syringe. What on earth? Lesley asked herself and then a cold chill ran up her spine and the hairs stood up on the back of her neck. She remembered his words: "It's my life and she'll stay the fuck out of it," and that terrible laughter. Across the street she saw him tap the syringe. And then his voice was suddenly, eerily in the room with her.

"Curiosity killed the cat, Annie. Curiosity killed the fucking cat."

Lesley sucked in her breath and stared, horrified at the monitor lying on the floor. The anger and hatred in his voice came through loud and clear. Terror and disbelief made Lesley's abdomen tighten. David was opening the door into Annie and Jim's bedroom. Quickly, she looked over at Annie, who was just untying her robe, but then looked at the window. She must have remembered the blinds, thought Lesley, because her hand reached out for the Levelor cord. Without knowing she was going to, Lesley began waving frantically and yelling.

"No, Annie! Annie, wait!"

The blind shot down. Lesley grabbed her head and moaned. She could see David creeping across Annie and Jim's bedroom toward their bath. And then the shade shot back up again. Annie must have seen her. Lesley waved both arms across her face. Annie looked puzzled. Lesley motioned hysterically, thrusting her arms out at Annie.

There was no time to waver. Lesley had to make a choice she would live with for the rest of her life. She grabbed the phone and punched clumsily on the buttons, finally managing to dial 911. As it rang interminably, Lesley screamed as loud as she could, "Annie, run! Run, Annie!"

Across the street Annie heard the sound of the bathroom door opening. She gasped and turned away from the window. There, over her shoulder was David, syringe in hand, a terrible smile on his face. Annie's hand dropped the cord, and the shade shot down again.

Annie was too shocked to react physically. Her mouth snapped open and shut, idiotically. "What?" she managed to get out.

David chuckled. "What?" he mimicked. "Come on, Annie, I know you're smarter than that. You wanted to play in the big leagues. But you don't even know the rules of the game."

"David . . ." Annie's mind raced. He knew. The hatred in his eyes was terrifying. Stall him, she thought. Lesley must have been trying to warn her. Would she help her? But Lesley worshipped David.

David took a step toward Annie.

"I—I don't know what you mean," she stammered.

"Oh, Annie." David's voice rose. "Don't fuck with me. You know it all." And then he lunged. She darted by him but he grabbed her robe and spun her around. She was fighting for her life. She reached out, grabbing blindly for his crotch and instead got his belt.

"You bastard!" she screamed and bit down hard on his arm. It was like fighting a robot. He had on so many layers and his arm was so big. It couldn't have hurt much but he dropped the syringe. He reached up and his arm went back. Annie's body tensed for the blow but then he let the arm fall. No marks, his angry brain reminded him, no hitting. He made a dive for the syringe and Annie tried the doorknob. Her hands were so sweaty she couldn't turn it. She clawed wildly at the door and looked over her shoulder, cringing. David had straightened up and was backing away from the toilet fast. Where was Lesley, where was Jim? She screamed as loud as she could, but she had no words left. It came out as a guttural, primitive cry.

David whipped his head around.

"There's nobody to help you, you stupid bitch." He took another step backward, and his legs caught on the taut extension cord. Jim's electric razor came crashing off the shelf. David threw his arms up to steady himself, and hovered for a second. Annie ran, butting his stomach with her head. He lost his balance and sat down hard in the tub, his legs straight up. "Shit!" he yelled and tried to pull himself out. The tub was small; he was wedged in. He hooked an elbow over the side of the tub for leverage and slipped back full force on the extension cord. The baby monitor tottered on the shelf above, about to fall into the tub. David saw the shaking wire out of the corner of his eye and, twisting around, thrust an arm out to deflect the monitor. His hand banged against the cords and both the monitor and the old TV hurtled toward the bath.

David only just managed to grasp the horror of what was happening before the electrical current met the water. His face froze in a terrible stonelike grimace, but his body twisted and jerked uncontrollably. Annie, sickened, fell to the floor.

On hands and knees, wailing like an animal, she half crawled, half ran through her room to the hall. At the top of the stairs she collapsed again, sobbing. The front door opened but she didn't hear it. She only knew her sobs and the distant police siren and then Jim's arms and Alex's small voice.

"It's okay, Mommy, it's okay."

Epilogue

The sound of hammering brought Annie out of her daydream with a jolt. She went to stand by the living room window and looked across the street. The big red maple at the edge of the yard was starting to turn, and the huge pots of geraniums that Lesley had planted on either side of the front door seemed to be thriving in the crisp October air. The lawn in front of the old Victorian was littered here and there with the first brightly colored windfall of autumn leaves. A man wearing a Century 21 blazer was nailing a FOR RENT sign into the ground.

Good luck renting that place, she thought to herself. The usually staid neighborhood was abuzz with rumor and speculation. Annie went out lately only when she felt she wouldn't be pounced upon by a neighbor. Thank God the reporters had finally given up on her. But of course Lesley would have to try to rent out the house; she wouldn't be able to sell the place, not with an investigation underway, and all of David's assets frozen.

Annie watched as the man from Century 21 tested the sign with his weight, and satisfied with the job, returned to his car and drove off. Annie shivered. The weather was changing, it was really starting to feel like fall. She tugged on the window, swollen from yesterday's rain until it finally gave and slammed down with a loud thud.

She stood for a while gazing at the house until the phone's ring startled her. Few people called these days, since their number was now unlisted. Still, each time it rang she was afraid some talk show producer or reporter had somehow gotten the number. She picked it up on the fourth ring, annoyed with herself for her pounding heart, which made her sound out of breath.

"Hello?"

"Hello, Mrs. Morgan?" Annie tried to get her breathing under control, but the unfamiliar voice didn't help slow her rapid heartbeat.

"Yes," Annie said, hesitantly.

"This is Gloria Wells." The name meant nothing to Annie but the southern drawl was familiar and Annie felt her stomach turn. "I'm sorry to bother you, Mrs. Morgan. And I know y'all probably don't know who I am." The "I am" sounded to Annie like "Ah em." I know this voice, she thought, and the knowledge didn't comfort her.

The voice continued, "But we have met. I work at Crawford Maternity." There was a pause. Annie sat down hard on the desk chair. "In Medical Records." Annie had to cover her mouth to keep from crying out. This is it, she thought, I'm going to jail for fraud.

Then the voice continued in a rush. "I'm sorry, I'm so sorry to disturb you, but Mrs. Morgan, I just had to call. I just had to call and thank you."

Annie had been prepared for a blow and was still waiting for the impact. She couldn't register the actual words yet.

"I just had to tell you how much what you did meant to me and, well, to a lot of us here. I played along with Dr. Shields—you know, gave him plenty of sweetness and light because that's what he demanded, and one thing I've learned in this life is to watch my butt. A lot of us feel that way here and let me tell you, it doesn't matter what the Supreme Court says, there isn't a girl working in a hospital who's gonna cry sexual harassment against a doc, 'specially not one as high up as Dr. Shields was. Anyway, Mrs. Morgan, I just had to call and say thanks. That old boy got all he deserved. Imagine, we all knew he was up to no good, but— we had no idea. You're a brave woman, Mrs. Morgan, real brave." She finally stopped for a breath.

Annie managed, "Umm. Thank you, uh, how did you get my number?"

"Oh, I was afraid you'd ask that. I've got a friend at the phone company. Please don't complain about it, she'd—"

"No, no, of course not, I won't. Thank you, uh—"

"Gloria. Thank *you,* Mrs. Morgan. I'll let you go now. I just wanted you to know, nobody's going to hear anything from me or anyone else in the department about—you know, the last time we saw each other—okay? I'll let you go now. Bye."

Annie walked numbly away from the phone and wandered back to the window. The thing that had been nagging her that day at the hospital, impersonating an insurance worker, forging a signature on those forms, apparently now she could relax about all that. Gloria's call had upset her, though, because she didn't want to be thanked. She had killed David Shields. Yes, it had been in self-defense, and yes, he was committing all sorts of crimes himself, but still, she didn't like bearing the responsibility for anyone's death. And "brave"—calling her brave was the worst part. A really brave person would have spoken up that morning in the emergency room with Jane.

Still, Jane had been wonderful about that. Annie had finally talked to Jane about it just last week. She hadn't wanted to bring it up until she was sure that Jane's pregnancy was secure. Annie smiled to herself. It was wonderful how quickly Jane had managed to conceive again. "It had to be the underwear," Mac had said. With Jane safely fourteen weeks along, Annie had gone for tea one afternoon and told

Jane how badly she felt about not speaking up when they said David would be her doctor.

"Annie, Annie, haven't you been through enough? Hush now. It wasn't your fault. What that man did, he did alone. And, Annie, thanks to you, no more women will go through the hell that I went through. Do you have any idea how I felt, with everyone telling me I'd dreamed it? You showed everyone, most importantly me, that I was not insane. Come here now and let me give you a hug—and stop feeling guilty!"

And then, after Annie'd gone back to her tea and heard about Jane and Walt's trip downtown to look at cribs, Jane had asked her, "What about Jim?"

Annie leaned her forehead against the cool glass of the windowpane now and closed her eyes. Well, she thought to herself, what *about* Jim?

In the months since David's death, she and Jim had tried to put their lives and their marriage back together. Jim's initial response had been only relief that she was safe, but as more of her story came out, his relief turned to anger. He felt, he told her, that they had reached an understanding regarding her listening in. He had thought she knew how abhorrent it was to him. And for her part, she had gone through hell and had a man's death on her hands. Despite all the horrible things David had done, and more was coming to light every day, she still felt guilty about and responsible for his death. She also felt Jim should be more supportive about what she had been through. And then there was Alex.

When everything had first happened, the reporters had thrown their life into turmoil. Annie couldn't open the door to take the kids to the park without reporters shoving mikes in her face and flashbulbs popping. *People* magazine had called on the phone and offered an unbelievable sum for her exclusive story. She and Jim had actually thought about it for a day. It would have paid for Alex's college tuition, with a big chunk left over for Rebecca's. But once they thought about Lesley reading it, or Millie finding it years later, they knew they had to say no.

The media had made life impossible. When they began firing questions at Alex, Annie told her therapist she just couldn't cope with fending them off anymore. So that weekend in the middle of the night Jim had snuck Annie and the children out the back door where Mac's husband, Nick, was waiting in his car. He had driven them the four hours to Annie's mother's. Annie had felt like a fugitive. Alex had seemed to enjoy it, said they were like the family in the *Sound of Music*.

But once at her mother's, Alex behaved horribly, refusing to eat dinner and then whining for ice cream. He acted angry all the time—slammed doors and kicked toys—and when he began having nightmares, Annie decided it was time to go home. She had been relieved to see that the reporters had given up, but Alex's behavior did not improve. Friends recommended child psychiatrists, but Annie and Jim felt uncomfortable putting Alex in therapy.

One day Jim came home and announced that he had made plans through some old college friends to visit them in Nova Scotia and take Alex camping—just the two of them, he explained. Annie didn't like thinking about being away from Alex but Jim seemed so sure about the plan, and her relationship with him was so tenuous at that point that she reluctantly agreed. On the trip Alex had talked and Jim had listened. Alex had told Jim how he felt guilty about letting Dr. Shields in the house that day. "He was a bad man and he tried to hurt Mommy."

The week had been good for both of them. Alex had come home happier, and more his old self every day, and Jim was more relaxed, too. He told her he thought they should get away, too, so now that Alex was settled in school her mother was coming to take care of the children and she and Jim were going on a cruise.

She had taken a six-month leave from Cotton Tales and they had promised to save her job for her, so getting away was no problem for Annie. Time for just the two of them could work wonders. They were still too careful with each other. She was hopeful that a week alone would bring them back to where they once were. Jim seemed to want it, too.

There were still trouble spots; days when she had a hard time dragging herself out of bed. Little things would remind her, like when she called Mac's and her Hispanic cleaning lady answered the phone. One word of Spanish and she was back in La Cucharita.

Jaime's clinic had made it onto *20/20*. Mac had called all excited and made Annie turn it on. The camera crew had only been allowed to film the entrance to the drive, and after medical experts testifying regarding the procedure Jaime and David had performed, the anchor explained that because of the acrimony between the American Drug Enforcement Agency and Mexican drug officials the United States had not been allowed to interfere or prosecute Jaime. As far as anyone knew, Dr. Ruiz was still taking huge sums of money for a procedure that according to American medical experts was far from a guarantee.

In spite of all this, Annie thought, life was *beginning* to feel good again. But there was still one unresolved piece to it all. She opened her eyes and gazed at the house across the street. The one person that she desperately needed to hear from hadn't contacted her.

She had hoped Lesley would be in touch with her but now, perhaps buoyed by Gloria's phone call, she made a decision. She sat at her desk and fished through a group of cards she had collected from trips to the art museum. She settled on a lovely Carl Larsson of two women talking in a garden, with children playing all around them.

"Dear Lesley," she began.